Stella
Atlantis

Also by Susan Perly

Death Valley
Love Street

Susan Perly

Stella Atlantis

a novel

A Buckrider Book

Buckrider Books is an imprint of Wolsak and Wynn Publishers.

Cover design: Michel Vrana
Cover images: istockphoto.com
Interior design: Jennifer Rawlinson
Author photograph: Dennis Lee
Typeset in Minion
Printed by Brant Service Press Ltd., Brantford, Canada

10   9   8   7   6   5   4   3   2   1

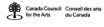  

The publisher gratefully acknowledges the support of the Toronto Arts Council, the Ontario Arts Council, the Canada Council for the Arts and the Government of Canada.

Buckrider Books
280 James Street North
Hamilton, ON
Canada L8R 2L3

Library and Archives Canada Cataloguing in Publication

Title: Stella Atlantis : a novel / Susan Perly.
Names: Perly, Susan, author.
Description: The Vivienne Pink books. | Follows: Death Valley.
Identifiers: Canadiana 20190160756 | ISBN 9781928088967 (softcover)
Classification: LCC PS8581.E7267 S74 2020 | DDC C813/.6—dc23

para mi querido Dennis

There is a world elsewhere.

− WILLIAM SHAKESPEARE, *CORIOLANUS*, ACT 3, SCENE 3

1

WE HAVE NO HOURS

WITH THE DEAD you can float. With the dead you can go anywhere. Finally, you can fly; finally, you are airborne to Soyuz and Cassini. Surfing the aurora borealis through the astrophysical waves.

The rain moves in from Tripoli, Benghazi, Latakia, the Mediterranean stations. The windy rain crosses the water to Iberia from Morocco, Algeria, Tunisia, those North African shorelines.

The dead are dead, yet the dead tremble against us. The dead are dead, yet they leave strange vibrations. The dead are wet with knowledge. People: the dead are known to the rain.

The wind blows across the Atlantic fissures to the Costa Brava, Catalonia, Barcelona, the old stone tunnels in the fisher quarter. El Born. November 2016

YOU SEE . . .

. . . sometimes when it was still dark and too many gallant shivs of loneliness came into him in his rooftop attic, Johnny Coma shuffled out the door to the roof patio, crossed the red tiles all wet with rain, found the right key in his pyjama pants, inserted the key in the slot to call the elevator, descended alone in what he always thought of as a tomb for two and stepped out into the stone alley in his blue striped pyjamas, just to be in the world. The solid arch over the alley where he lived gave the sense of long ago, a narrow stone box, with the ancient signs tacked onto the stone of *Entrada y Salida*, entrance and exit.

He shuffled about thirty steps in his well-worn pale green espadrilles, exiting at the wider Passeig del Born, his local pedestrian concourse, quiet, grand in its ancient modesty, the seven-storey buildings all attached to each other with their signature Barcelona balconies, the green blinds laid over the iron railings.

Johnny saw a light in the mist and stone.

Shit. Yeah. The one coffee guy. He always forgot that one coffee-sandwiches guy was open. Like a lantern in the dark. Johnny shuffled along. Nobody cared if he was in flippers or a clown suit or his same old tattered night stripes. All he wanted was rainy days and routine. Rain, routine and the words for the story of his daughter, Stella.

Grief has hair. Grief eats you. You are grief's BLT.

He entered the lit coffee spot, asked the man behind the counter, a short gent about fifty, for a cortado. The man shouted in a pleasant alto, "Cortado," to the back of the shop. A much older gent got up from a chair hidden by the coffee machine. He creaked to the machine. He pressed the buttons. He creaked to the counter, handed the coffee in a paper cup to the man behind the counter, who handed it to Johnny. A euro and a half. Life felt better already.

"*¿Cuál es su horario, Señor?*" Johnny asked. Sir, what are your hours?

"*No hay horario.*" We have no hours.

Perfect. Perfection.

Johnny shuffled out the door to the backless stone bench on the street.

The beer cans stashed by the street sellers had been stowed in the trash bins until the hours became after-hours and further street *cerveza* was needed. A few humans further down the Passeig del Born near Rec were waving pizza slices at each other in duelling disputations, ragged-trouser orators squaring off with pepperoni and anchovy triangles, about migrants and tyrants. Here on cocktail bar row.

Johnny Coma, the lone figure on a stone bench, near Montcada Street, in the rain shadow of the basilica Santa Maria del Mar. Saint Mary of the Sea, who has watched over the seamen, the fishers, the shoreline for a modest seven hundred years and change. He reached up to his ear, felt his writing tool tucked in there, felt the pencil's ridges, took his trusty Palomino Blackwing 602 grey pencil down. Reached into his pyjama pants for the silver triangle, his pencil sharpener.

He twisted the faithful grey Blackwing round and round. Silver-edged sails emerged from the pencil sharpener, fell onto his blue and white stripes, along with sprinkles of moonlight scurf.

He wrote in his notebook: *We have no hours.*

HE SAT ABSORBING the light mist. He did love it here in the medieval quarter called the Born, El Born or El Borne, folded into the larger neighbourhood called La Ribera – the Shoreline – the little walled alleys, with names evoking hand-labour: the *gremio*s, guilds, artisanal work over the centuries, Kettlemakers Street, Glassmakers Alley, Fishmongers, Hatmakers . . . It situated his knuckles and wrists.

The Mediterranean briny air. In the stone warrens he was a twelve-minute walk to the sea. Every time he returned to Barcelona, he was struck by the same eternal-return feeling, a return of the rush of love he had felt the very first time. Every sojourn entry was layered with every departure from the past, and every return again. Barcelona was separate from him, yet Barcelona was his secret lover.

And the old stone barrio had from the very first been waiting patiently for him, a mere thousand years.

He ran his thick calloused index finger on the golden metal part of the pencil, the ferrule between the pencil proper and the eraser at the end. The eraser was flat and pink and replaceable. Johnny loved all these details.

Ear to the rain. Lost in the kairos circle.

One of the disputatious guys down the way got up, ambled toward Johnny on the Passeig del Born, stopped, waved his pizza crust at the amber streetlight and whispered in a gravelly hork, "The swallows have fallen from the sky. The wings have come off. We are flying into unknown angles of attack."

He reached over to Johnny's smooth shaven head. Pulled out a night errant hair. "More for my treasure box," he mumbled as he rounded the corner into one of the walled alleys, Vidrieria, Glassmakers Lane, his voice echoing up the ancient stone. "Tonight the Lady Hillary shall be regnant at last!"

"Of course," Johnny said to the empty street. "Sancho. My old pal from the Pla de Palau. Good old Sancho."

A WHISTLE FROM one of the rooftops across from where Johnny sat, alone on the barrio promenade. The whistle bounced from the stone walls of Montcada out into the wider Passeig del Born.

A lean figure with long wavy hair leapt out of the dark of Montcada Street. In a black leotard under the amber rain of the high streetlights. From somewhere – a pocket? – the figure produced a length of rope.

Another high whistle.

A second figure appeared on a slim balcony five storeys up, above the shuttered *cocteleria* where even the lively vermouth was taking a snooze with fellow dead soldiers, and the figure lowered a length of rope from above.

The street figure caught it, tied the two ropes together. Began to climb.

Like Rapunzel in reverse, climbing with long wavy hair on the rope to the balcony. Then she – it looked like it could be a woman – turned a somersault, climbed further up.

Then she climbed down, hand over hand on the rope, feet curved.

Making circles with her hands, she walked toward Johnny.

"Gyrotonic," she said, stopping in front of him. "Gyrotonic, Gyro-tonic, I've got gyro eyes on you."

She smiled at the sky, the ancient welkin of this medieval precinct. She reached into a black jersey sleeve. Voila! A shiny black shoe. The other sleeve, another shoe. The shoes reflected the lamplight on the Passeig del Born. Quickly putting her feet into the shoes, tying them up, the mystery woman straightened up, appeared to pull energy from her knees to her waist, and hell on mirror wheels, she tap danced the syncopation out of the stone street in front of Johnny.

As if click-clacking in low taps offstage, she tap danced down the dark passageway of Montcada.

And walked on, waving at him over her shoulder.

They appear; they vanish. You see them once, never again. This is the city. You have to invent a life for a stranger. This, too, is the metropolis. Mister No Hours, Mx. Gyro, Sancho. The performance space called a city.

Johnny opened his arms, stood up, windmilled them to get the blood flowing, the right arm and the left arm going in opposite directions.

Deep breaths. He sat down on the backless stone bench. Dark and empty morning.

The world is contrapuntal, he thought. He could feel the muscle music coming from his shoulders down his forearms to his wrists. He retrieved his pencil from behind his ear. In his plain brown Moleskine notebook Johnny wrote:

November 2016, Passeig del Born, BCN, bench
Dear Stella,

You're in my mind, but where are you? You walked like electricity through the storm in a dream I had last night. It was you.

Stella, the atoms coalesce. Yet, where are you, small bones I used to read to? Little fossil. If the child dies, the father is an orphan. What is the word for the father whose child is gone? It's your dad, Stel, I'm so messed up – in the dream last night, I saw you shining. You swam toward me. Your skull was lit up. Inside your lit-up transparent skull your eyes looked out at me. But you swam past me, like you didn't know me. I said, "Stella, it's me. Dad. Johnny."

You swam on the lam with feathery know-how.
Dad

He shuffled the ninety seconds back to his home alley, medieval and about fifty footsteps long. Such a tiny alley it rarely appears on maps. No door visible. Number – ½ – on a cruddy piece of old wood, weathered. A motorcycle strategically parked in front of a larger random-looking piece of wood covered in peeling posters, paint tags. Dark ill-lit alleys are great security. Johnny squeezed in the narrow space between the moto and the wall. He waved his key fob at a wooden board with a peeling photo from a yellowing twentieth-century newspaper: it was a photo of Dario Fo – the

Italian left-leaning playwright disrupter called a clown – from the day Fo won the Nobel Prize in Literature, in the fall of '97.

Johnny Coma waved his key fob at Dario Fo's nose.

The wooden board opened. Johnny entered the dark foyer, about the size of a bathroom stall, put one of the keys on the key ring into an unmarked slot in the elevator. He felt like a wastrel indeed, returning to his roof studio like a thief with stolen words, nabbed from the world in its few thoughts in the rain time.

He lay down on the patio tiles. He wrote the word *Gyrotonic* in his notebook. He took a nap as the light before the dawn crept down the old stone quarter.

IT WAS SIX forty in the morning. Official sunrise was about seven thirty this time of year. Dawn's creeping light would start about seven. Time for him to visit with Sancho on the old familiar bench around the corner, the bench where they had kept company with each other over the years, when Johnny turned up in Barcelona and kept to himself in a self-contained way, writing.

He walked the one hundred steps from his front door to the square called Pla de Palau. The Palace Plaza. Though, as many an urban spot named *palacio*, it was modest.

There in the half-dark, was that really Sancho air-typing? Hands low, all proper as a touch typist on an invisible old Underwood typewriter, pinkies aloft on his p's and his q's.

"*Pase adelante.* Come on in. Welcome. *Bienvenido.*" He patted the wet slats. "Have a seat, we will be right with you." Then he pulled an invisible sheet of paper out, placed it on top of an invisible ream sitting – apparently – on his other side and tidied the edges. "I will launch from Petrograd to Saint Petersburg."

Johnny stretched his legs out. He was still wearing his blue-striped pyjamas. Sancho had on baggy pale-blue blue jeans, the kind that tell you that the wearer was American. A local Catalan man would be wearing indigo or black jeans, or cotton pants in a rust or a chore-coat blue. But what with the long moth-gnawed tweed topcoat and his matted hair and his public perch in the square, the baggy pale jeans were simply one more element of the hodgepodge.

"Perhaps, before Leningrad, I will do a local launch, a tour from Espaseria to – Esparteria!"

"Sancho, dear pal, Espaseria and Esparteria meet."

"Oh dear, oh dear. One more typo waiting to happen. Then we shall launch from Comerç to Comercial."

Johnny stayed silent on that one. Two streets a half a block away from each other.

"My liege," Sancho said. "For your esteemed perusal." He handed the invisible ream to Johnny, about a hundred invisible pages by the amount of space between Sancho's palms.

"A perfect amount," Johnny said.

"My yes," said Sancho.

"To throw away."

"Throw away?"

"I'll tell you a little secret," Johnny said. Whispering, "You can tell a pro by the number of pages they throw away. A beginner –"

"Huh," Sancho said with haughtiness. "Beginners. *Well.*"

"No, listen, friend. A beginner brags, 'I wrote a hundred pages.' A pro brags, 'I dumped four hundred pages, I'm heading back in to dump more.'"

"Will Stumpy win the election?"

"Throw it all away."

"Bakunin blurbed me."

"Sancho. Write five hundred words a day."

"To throw away."

"Away."

"I think you're daft. I hear on the Interweb you can binge in November and voila! Novel done. Mikhail will bring Miguel to my launch soiree . . . You did know, my liege, did you not, that Miguel de Cervantes, the very scribe of *Don Quixote*, washed up a couple blocks from here, in our own neighbourhood?"

"Yeah, I heard something about that." Of course Johnny knew about

Cervantes's sojourn in Barcelona. After all, Miguel de Cervantes wrote the Second Part of *Don Quixote*, in this very area, right around the corner on Colom at number 2. His eyes looking out to the wharf, the port, when the water was closer in.

The nautical dawn was painting itself with olive, aubergine, fair virgin oil of the arbequina.

Sancho closed his eyes and, with an air of contentment, said, "We *scribble*, we *have scribbled*, we *will have been scribbling*."

"*Scribbling* is a word professionals use, Sancho, to deflect from the grunge and rejection of art labour," Johnny said. "Please don't use it in an unearned way. Earn your stripes before you flaunt the lingo of experience."

Sancho, almost like a dear devoted husband, was snoozing right at the key moment of conversation. God bless the beginners, Johnny thought, calmed counterintuitively by human company in the life of the city waking.

The two men stretched their legs out, Johnny in pale green espadrilles and Sancho in espadrilles in rose.

Sancho mumbled into his tweed collar, "Ah, many a Google and oft . . . " then began to snore so loudly the foghorns were alarmed.

Johnny, for his part, had gone back into a dark mental channel. Behind his eyes, he dove down into water, entering the bathymetry of underwater mountains. He swam down into the Atlantic Ocean, the S-shaped Atlantic, a basin with its fine ocean trenches. The Atlantic, which separates the Old World and the New World. He swam down into the submarine canyons – was Stella there?

The abyssal plains, he wandered them in his brief sleep on the public bench, woke with his pencil moving in his hand, which looked disembodied. The guyot, yes that underwater volcanic mountain, the tablemount. All the pelagic levels. The S-shaped abyss.

His hand wrote the word: *abyssopelagic*.

When he opened his eyes, he had written a paragraph, and Donald J. Trump was the next president of those United States. Slowly, then all at once.

2

THE SURF DOCTOR

SCALP MUSIC. LORN. Burnt jazz on my pate. I am Medusa of the atomic buboes. My photographs emerge from my bald scalp like dream worms of the war mess. My own face is the green and smothering mask I wear to survive. I starved when my daughter died; the ladies admired my new svelte body. Grief and E. coli slimmed me. Women, we walk with masks. Our masks are the siren calls to our own selves to throw off our masks. My art is my obstacle to my intention to make it. These green and smothering things, this ether we put upon ourselves. These snakes, these masks, these avatars of the lorn.

VIVIENNE PINK WALKED the night watch alley north. She held her camera at her hip in the amber hours, passing a back garage workshop where a group of guys were sending off sparks, dressed like a hazmat posse in a foundry. Her father, Izzy Pink, Mister Mayor, had died in this alley, taken a heart attack on a night walk. Every time she set out on an assignment, she came to the alley, to say goodbye to her dad.

The taxi rolled up to the house. Out through Metro in the dusk diorama, travelling west through distress and needles and shop glory, the eateries in the light rain lit from inside, and that November there was a heat wave. A guy at Dovercourt and Bloor was beating a red Canada Post box with a baseball bat, warbling, "Fuck the hokey-pokey and you fuck the hokey-pokey." Democratic paradise was overheating, flooding with too much money, yet in the wide low streetscape of Toronto, leaving again to chase down a rumour of terror chatter in Amsterdam, Vivi Pink snapped her hometown through the rainy taxi window, everywhere drive time so pretty. She was bald from the atomic bomb test in Death Valley in 2006. The rain got heavy, the windshield wipers moved back and forth, the taxi moved north in the ravine-laden city, driving on old geology where canoes once paddled the swerve onto the 401, busiest highway in North America, the four-oh-one where polite Canadians took risks, jerks choking or mis-steering or jerking off or just in a spin on a wet patch right before the airport so handy to the excellent trauma ward at Sunnybrook Hospital but not today. Terminal 3, KLM. Flight 062, YYZ to AMS. Departure 16:30, arrival in Amsterdam 7:20 a.m. A Boeing 747-400. On the terminal screens, oversaturated images of Donald John Trump and Hillary Rodham Clinton, with one day left in their race to the White House.

Vivienne Pink paid the taximan, unzipped her backpack, reached in, checked that she had her good luck amulet with her before she entered the terminal. Yes. Okay. It was there. She stroked it: a slim hardcover book of poetry, *Poeta en Nueva York. Poet in New York*, by Federico García Lorca. She took it everywhere, its fuchsia cover and green ribbon bookmark steadying her. When Lorca returned from New York to his homeland Spain, on a road near his home in Granada, the Fascist military shot him in the back. He was thirty-six years old when the soldiers in his own country assassinated the poet Lorca.

Through Terminal 3, where the soon to be departed lined up, in the eternal slow shuffle with their goods, looking down as if in panicked prayer at the lit devices in the palms of their hands, mumbling, davening in call-and-response to the latest news before the airliner took them to the clouds, the tiny screens on the seatbacks where the map of their voyage would show them as a miniscule plane flying over the continents, the oceans, the great rivers. Vivi Pink had intel that there might be a terror attack in Amsterdam. She was flying there to bear witness in photographs.

Over the St. Lawrence, the big river opened its mouth into the Atlantic Ocean. Vivi had dozed at takeoff, her Lorca in her lap. She was in that

Economy Comfort section, forward in the plane. In seat 15E, as always. A two-seater, empty aisle seat on her left.

She opened her eyes.

Across the aisle, a tall guy in seat 15C. He had his legs in the aisle, his right hand on his right knee. Her fingers went to her red silk shirt left breast pocket where she kept a credit-card-size spy camera. She pressed her pocket; the miniature lens was aligned with her open buttonhole. The shot she wanted was of the man's long fingers resting on his indigo jeans. How the hand tensed.

She had fogged her way through the terminal. It hit her now that she'd seen him in the KLM lineup, in front of her. Of course. She'd checked him out, from the shoes up. Dark shoes, laces, good leather, cordovan maybe. A beaten-up leather jacket in chocolate, bleached folds of wear. He carried a black bag, a cross between a medical bag and a briefcase. He had turned around – it came back to her airborne brain – briefly, but long enough for her to see how overtly he was not looking at her as he scanned the line.

He wasn't on a phone. He'd unzipped his bag, fished inside, nodded to himself, zipped it back up. Hanging below his leather jacket was a rust sweater. The dark jeans. He could be an architect or a chef or a biophysicist, boarding in Toronto, dreading the legroom designed for elves. Long fingers, staying tense near his knee. Vivi snapped a second spy shot.

They flew in the deep dark toward morning.

Mister Legs was reading a book, a hardcover. Vivi the snoop always wanted to know what someone was reading, but she couldn't see the cover. She dozed off again, woke somewhere over Greenland according to the little screen.

IN THE NOWHERE place in the nowhere time of a plane at night flying over the ocean, Vivi took Lorca to the loo. Occupied. A loo door opened. She stepped aside. A hulk in a baggy blue suit lurched onto her tits, meaty paws up in muscle memory, apparently, of maulings gone by. "Mile-high club, you and me, what say?"

She aimed the Lorca at his balls. Direct hit. As he grabbed his lower nethers, she snapped a pic of him with her spy camera. He looked bothered and bewildered, as if a pumpkin he was going to hump had attacked him with poetry. Poor sod, Vivi thought, with that chronic eye disease called misogyny. Red tie flapping between his legs, he limped out of the vestibule.

She returned to her seat. The green letters on the fuchsia cover transmitted a kind of melismatic *verde*. The plane was going through turbulence. She read the poem called "Christmas on the Hudson," about Lorca's visit to a Jewish cemetery; she read the one about the king of Harlem. Small sketches Lorca made of New York, of himself. How precious the doodles become.

The barometric pressure changed, she felt it in her ears filling and emptying, popping, filling again, as the plane began its descent. The ear pain is so much worse on the landing, though the landing is the best part, it is all ahead and nobody knows the story to come.

"*Verde que te quiero verde*," Lorca once wrote. Green how I love you green. Green Amsterdam water rose up to meet the plane.

The low water was rising to the sky and the plane's belly.

She held on to the Lorca, stroked the green endpapers. She loved the care put into the physical book, attention had been paid. The signatures, those groupings of pages all sewn together up the spine of the book, nestled together in subtle curves. And how sweet was that green ribbon sewn right in, to use as a bookmark. *Seda verde*, green silk. The sturdy delicacy was erotic. Attention is erotic. *Versos verdes*.

A pixel is a pixel is a pixel, but a beautiful book is a sex object forever.

THE PLANE BUMPED down.

"Ladies and Gentlemen, we have landed in Amsterdam. Local time is 7:23 a.m. The outside temperature is twelve degrees Celsius."

Amsterdam, known as *Mokum*. Once upon a time, when Amsterdam was a city of Jews, Yiddish infiltrated the everyday language of Amsterdammers. The Yiddish word *mokum,* meaning *place*, was the local slang name for Amsterdam itself: Mokum, or Mokum Aleph. The Place. The First City. And when the Nazis killed thirty thousand of the forty thousand Jews of Amsterdam, Yiddish remained woven throughout the civic life, language being the great resistance, always. She and Johnny used to like to go to the *nachtcafé,* the night café in Amsterdam called Mazzeltof.

The silver wings set down in the sinking city wet with Mokum Green.

The green was so bright in the city of Amsterdam, it hurt the grass to grow. The green was so potent, it made poets begin. The green was so *groen,* the new shoots could feel the power of their own chlorophyll.

Mister Long Legs sat with his hands in his lap. His eyebrows were interrogating his forehead, scrunched up lines below his close-cropped dark hair, the eyebrows making some kind of a math equation with the sides of his lips, which were twitching in a nuanced way. She was feeling giddy dread; she pressed the wafer-thin camera in her shirt pocket. His legs, his cheek with a not pretty scar, *snap, snap,* and for good luck, his right hand, still tensed on his thigh.

Vivienne stayed in her seat while the trudge up the aisle to exit began.

Mister Legs was content to sit, wait.

When the aisle was clear, he got up. His long arm took her backpack down for her. "Thanks," she said, making eye contact, upward.

"I like to surf at Las Canteras," he said. He reached up on his side and took down his black leather bag. Genuine leather, she noticed, worn, experienced. His voice sounded like one of those "maybe" voices. Maybe Dutch. Good English.

"It's great in winter," she said.

"The wind is pretty fantastic," he said. Maybe Belgian. "The left break." Maybe Dutch, maybe Israeli. Places where you accepted without thinking that everybody spoke excellent English. Vivi Pink, photographer of war and its many parentheses of peace, knew that the real picture of somebody is their voice. She had trained herself to listen to vocal intonation so that she could replicate it in a visual tone. His tone was in the neighbourhood of "I'd like you to enjoy this moment, even if it's passing."

The parade down the aisle. The world is one long lineup around the belt of the planet. Vivienne was in no hurry to say goodbye to the two-minute acquaintance with the tall guy. "The trade winds," she said. "I don't know if they are trade winds, but it can get crazy in January. I was there in a hurricane once. On the Big Canary."

"Gran Canaria," he said, his eyes crinkling. That too. The charisma. You can't buy it, rent it, imitate it. "Your picture of the green light on the water, that one guy who was on his board, that was pretty incredible. How did you get that shot, the wall of water?"

"That was the January, the hurricane," she said. Whoa. Believe it, he had seen her book of the Canary Island surfers, he had focused on one of her classic Atlantic surf photos. Charisma is the gift, charm is the way a man works what he is given.

He said, "Also, Mundaka is pretty spectacular."

They started inching down the aisle. Or, okay, maybe a Swede, she thought. He kept his voice low, friendly. She could do that, too. "Mundaka?" she said. "Also, in January."

"Winter's the best in Mundaka," he said. "I used to live at the Hotel Mundaka. Funny little semi–hole in the wall. Kind of place where the reception's about as big as your basic phone booth, Hotel California like, and –"

"And they're playing," she said, "on some old – seriously? – tinny cassette player some old *Purple Rain*."

"RIP," he said.

They were halfway up the aisle.

"What a year," she heard herself saying, as if the two of them, having just met, were old pals having lazy coffee down the street. "Bowie, January; Prince, April. What the hell is going on?"

"Thanks, thanks very much," he said to the captain as they got to the exit, the breezeway. Cold Amsterdam morning came into the breezeway cracks. "Bowie goes slowly, secretly, yeah? Prince, now I have to say I was pretty shocked, OD on fentanyl."

"They say."

"Oh Lord. What a life. I hope I'm ready when the time comes."

They were in the Schiphol Airport. Known to Vivi Pink as Schlep-all.

"We're never ready, nobody's ever ready," she said.

He smiled at her with that old-pal smile.

"Well, nice to have met you."

Neither of them strode off. The airport prepared its delicado tortures of all the spaces between our hopes. He reached into his jacket pocket, took out a business card. She took it, put it in her pant pocket, zipped it in. She didn't look at it.

He had mentioned Las Canteras, the surfing beach out in the Atlantic Ocean on one of the Canary Islands. He had referenced Mundaka, the world-famous left break surf spot in Spain's Basque Country. He had, thus, said without saying that he knew who she was. That he had seen her photographs, that he had bought her book of surfers, or other books. But what about those sad dark eyes? It could be surf eye. Or war. There is a kind of postwar loneliness that is beyond the ordinary definition of lonely. It is that your daily carry is existential dread.

She had felt like a rescue creature in the pound called existence for years now. It was possible there was no real proper home for the likes of her anywhere.

They stood, two awkward adults.

He said, "Good luck." Then walked on with his long legs, a slight stoop in his upper body. Sadness, or a spinal fracture. Carrying his small black bag into the netherworld of fluorescent light of Amsterdam Schiphol Airport. Yellow signage, letters of the alphabet ordering you around, arrows on the verge of a nervous breakdown pointing to ceilings and floors.

THROUGH THE LOW country in its dark old grey waters, the spiffy taxi sped with a driver who looked like a righteous club bouncer, muscular arms in a tailored suit, a head so shiny he must buff it like a shoeshine guy in the morning. Vivi loved the security of everything in its place, including your carefully polished skull. Male driver, female passenger, each with a bald smooth head. The taxi entered the Old South section of the city, curving into the pocket corner of Roemer Visscherstraat, the one-block-long street where the Owl Hotel sat.

The Owl, charcoal paint, high windows, amber in one window lit at 8:00 a.m. The beautiful old city of Amsterdam, so much of it already below sea level. The words *Owl Hotel* lit in lime green on a canopy, the street empty except for the hundreds of bicycles parked, high riders leaning back like two-wheeled horses on the street named for the poet Roemer Visscher.

She paid the well-built taxi driver who carried a suit as brilliantly as Leonard Cohen, walked down the stairs from the street to the hotel entrance at the bottom, and into the narrow lobby. The memory of past times at the Owl flooded back, visual memories. The surprise of how small the spaces were, the reception counter immediately when you entered, the eye-view down the narrow space past the four-seat bar, past the cozy public lounge, through glass doors to a beautifully calm scene: the garden wet with rain.

Iron tables, iron chairs, the welcome soothing green planting, offhand, intended, that disciplined seeming-casual ambition she loved in Amsterdam. Masterly, casual, a small hotel in the off-season.

Into the frame down the space two long legs stretched. Oh, come on, Vivi said to herself, *him*.

The guy from the plane who mentioned the surf spots in the Canaries and the Basque Country. In her hotel, in her lobby lounge, what are the chances? Mister Legs in the airport in Toronto, on the plane across from her across the Atlantic, now in her same Amsterdam hotel? He got up, slid open one of the glass sliding doors to the patio garden, looked back, an ibis eyeing her through glass. She took the closet-sized elevator to her room, enjoying the acid lemon-green colour of the metal curtain. She waved the key card at the electronic eye on the door to room 46.

Vivi had asked for 46 for reasons. At the Amsterdam Owl Hotel in room 46, twelve years ago, in early November she had unfolded a note from the front desk to call home urgently. On the phone in this room, she had heard that Stella had been in an accident and was in surgery. The mother, away from home, working. Her sister, Rhonda, saying, "You never cared about your own daughter. I told you something like this was bound to happen. Don't worry, Rhonda is handling the mess you made."

She unpacked. She unzipped the security pocket on her pants, the business card Mister Long Legs had given her was there. It read: SURF DOCTOR. *Surf therapy for the wounded.* There was no phone number, no address, no code. No name. She had heard of surf therapy, of course she had. She had even tried it, in fact, at Mundaka. Was this guy there then? There were a few veterans who brought the wounded to the water, damaged bodies, partial bodies, bodies whole outside partial inside like hers, put them on boards, taught them how to paddle into the waves.

At the window looking down to the patio garden, she snapped a first-look best-look. It was habit – she always took snaps of the hotel room before she inhabited it, and its surrounds. Like antemortem pics of the scenes about to happen. There he was in the garden sitting at a table, all raindrops. Mister Legs sat alone, the autumn shades of his sweater, his pants, his cordovan shoes in harmony with old leaves, terracotta pots, the garden shed in matte grey. Dress like Amsterdam in November, you'll never be wrong. His arms open, his chest released to the Old World.

Now he goes and pulls a notebook from his leather jacket pocket, begins writing in it. He looked up. What was with this guy? Could he, like a pro cop, or a forest creature, sense the pitch of being watched from above? A man who worked in the shadows and who, thus, could hear shadows . . . maybe. She snapped an aerial snap from room 46. He leaned his long upper body into his notebook on the patio table below, like a man protecting food in a prison. Mister Legs a.k.a. the Surf Doctor. Self-contained. Tall, dark and therapeutic.

HER HEAD HURT. Her body ached. She headed to the Vondelpark to see about the Netherland terror rumours she had heard from protected sources.

She walked down the one long block of Roemer Visscherstraat, the buildings all attached to each other, rust brick, cream trim, arched windows and arched entranceways, the familiar Amsterdam hooks on high to hoist furniture up to swing in through windows.

At Van Baerlestraat, a heavy stream of bicyclists rode, centimetres from her toes. To get across to the Vondelpark was a trial in waiting. Immediately off the perpetually surprisingly narrow sidewalks of the city granted to the low species on the food chain – pedestrians, in Amsterdam – that stream of steady straight-backed beautifully fit endlessly pedalling Amsterdammers on bikes allowed no purchase for a walking person. Next to that traffic stream, the slightly lighter stream of cars. Next to that, the trams going one way next to the trams going the other way next to the cars going that way next to the endless stream of bicycles. Shit.

No romance, bikes here were transportation. Where everybody gets around by bike, it's one more traffic headache in your life, and a pedestrian could be stranded on a street named for a poet. An old memory of being here came back. A fix for the fix she was in. Of course, the stairs.

She hung a left, walked a half a block to – yeah, of course – the stone stairs on Van Baerlstraat down to that part of the Vondelpark, then you walk under the underpass and into the green, up to the big lovely building, the Filmmuseum, with its outside terrace Café Vertigo. The palette would suit a Hitchcock. Twice as many bicycles in Amsterdam as people. Hitchcock could rise from the grave, remake *The Birds,* call it *The Bikes.* Nine hundred thousand bikes, 1,800,000 wheels swarming the back of your knees. Oddly, she had never seen a single bicyclist wearing a helmet in Amsterdam. You didn't see it. Go know.

Past stone benches, past wooden green benches with iron scrollwork depicting birds, muddy mustard reflections of dying tree leaves, empty trees, stone shadows to the large bleached imposing film museum.

A man gently rode past her on his bike, in a brown garment with a loose ecru top on it, he too with that eye-sunken ferociousness she had seen in the TO alley man yesterday morning, also in the Surf Doctor.

She felt dizzy. The willow trees were doubled in the ponds. She was sweating. No vehicles were allowed in the park; here came an unmarked white van. She didn't like white vans, period. Unmarked creeped her out. The van drove way too close to her puffer coat. The man at the wheel had on a baseball cap, which was unusual here. She turned to look back at the Filmmuseum; she headed toward it, retracing her steps. No one sitting at the Café Vertigo, only chairs and tables, empty. Where were the people? The white van was keeping pace with her, at the speed of a fast walker. She upped the pace, walked faster. The man in the van crept his vehicle alongside her, toward tables, chairs, the stone steps to the Filmmuseum entranceway. The van kept making gear-noise adjustments to ride beside her, the man in the baseball cap staring at her, then lagging a bit behind, then right beside her again, a smirk on his face.

The van dropped back on the path, so that it was directly behind her. The engine revving, the vehicle heat on her coat, the back of her legs. The man had encased himself inside the weapon with which he was pursuing her. Steel under combustion.

She got to the bottom of the stairs up to the Filmmuseum. The van moved so that the front hood was at the bottom of the stairs, beside her. She ran up the old wide stone stairs. The van tried to mount the stairs after her, rearing back, slipping. Vivi got to the top. She tried the door. The Filmmuseum was closed. Café Vertigo's hours didn't start yet. Her clock was somewhere else in her body, she was in Amsterdam but where was she in time, was she too early, where were the *people?* What time had they landed?

At the bottom of the stairs, the van waited for her, the man smirking at the wheel, revving the engine over and over.

Vivi ran down the stairs, ran at full speed toward a path straight ahead. Oh no there was no path, she realized too late, it was an illusion of water sending her running into a pond, green full of willow, muddy.

She began to swim. She could see in her peripheral vision that the van was slowly trying to track her around the water. She dog-paddled. Her puffer coat was weighing her down.

At a wet cold corner, she came ashore. The coat was all down and sodden. She took it off, laid it down, sat there. The van wasn't near. She leaned against a tree. When she got up, dragging the coat like an otter, she could see off in the distance by the Blue Tea House, the round spaceship-looking café in the park, the white van, its front facing her, a predatory vehicle, blinking its headlights off and on.

3

FLOTSAM WITH A PENCIL

THE SUN GOT up slowly in Barcelona city. The old rooftops pushed into the rainy dawn. While he slept, Johnny fought the bedside lamp, and the lamp won.

Shit, there was broken glass on the floor. His knuckles on his left hand had ripped skin, a deep gash. There was blood on the pillow. Yeah, he'd been at it again.

Back when he and Vivi were in bed together every night, she'd wake him up, yelling at him to stop hitting her, as he pounded her back, the back of her head (when her thick hair, back when she had hair, protected her from his sleep pummelling), and he'd be in a battle royal with some sleep enemy, some REM nemesis when he went nine rounds with Vivi's spine.

The bedside water glass was way across the room, under the little high window, where the roof profile of Santa Maria del Mar was framed against the morning blue. Stone and azure and blood on the bedcover. What the hell time was it?

Shit. Ten after ten. He better get up and get to the beach for his ritual morning caffeine.

There was no time to clean up the mess. He was on a quest. He needed to bring his daughter back to him. The only obstacle was that Stella had died twelve years ago. He had entered his grief, then he had run from his grief. He was living in full incompleteness, and he knew it. Being a clever guy was one sure way to be stupid. He was a know-it-all from the get. But grief was a rat who chewed the art right off your cheeks.

He threw on a windbreaker, went down in the elevator, saw on the cobbles he had bare feet. Oh well.

Walking down to the water of the shoreline in PJs and callouses. And that hand, a deep gash, blood dried. What a fine chivalric suitor am I. He giggled. Giggly nutcase in pyjamas on the city sidewalk, what else could he be but a well-known novelist, not remotely in hiding? A nut in a mumble of that rhythm he didn't want to lose. The light ahead was pure Mediterranean. The sidewalk was wide on Joan de Borbó, the restaurants asleep, a few bars, a few touristic joints serving food in English to Brits. Over yonder, the sails of docked boats, the old port, the wharf. The city presented itself like ghost opportunities. The dead had always been happy to sail to Barcelona. He had fallen in love with Barcelona so long ago, and he had indeed betrothed himself to the city. He and Vivienne had been here together, now he was here alone and often so. The public life consoled him. The light consoled him. It was lost like him.

He could feel the gladness of lament coursing in his bloodstream. From his lungs to the oxygen exchange between his in and out heart parts, and then it hit his rib cage, made its way out to his shoulder blades, down his forearms like an ink tattoo in its desiring to be brought to life, to his wrists.

He sat down on a random moto on Joan de Borbó, beside the recycling bin lineup, pulled out his Moleskine and ideal Palomino Blackwing 602 pencil and wrote:

Dear Stella,

The icebergs melt, the walruses have no shelter.

It has been raining for a long time and the plastic has risen from the sea.

We have all gone down to the hadal zone, where midnight is forever and there is no day.

We're down in the onyx without oxygen, and as it has been written, the cities have been built by architects and apocalypse and when the Red Sea did part, it was festooned with plastic bags over fish heads, the migrant sea was a mass murder scene

HE GOT UP from the moto. The music in his wrist had receded.

At the spot where Joan de Borbó met the beach promenade, humans were shadows, backlit. Humanity, out early – 10:30 a.m. *was* early for Barcelona – the shadow bicyclist, the shadow man alone at the shore, the shadow dog walker and her shadow chihuahua.

He felt like flotsam with a pencil. Kelp carrying a Palomino Blackwing 602.

He was moving toward waste and softness.

This had to be the year. He had to go into the Stella Zone and find her. Finally.

He had no tools, no idea how to do it. But he did have chops. He had that. He knew how to take a line for a walk. Maybe this *was* the year. Maybe this November, he could walk that line right up to the return of Stella Coma, who died one November long ago, at age eleven. His little girl.

4

THE JEWISH BRIDE

IN THE VONDELPARK, Vivi was trying to keep her pulse rate down. She headed for the Blue Tea House. The white van wasn't there anymore. Was it hiding in the trees? She desperately needed some caffeine to calm her. She got one of those great Amsterdam cappuccinos, hefty, foamy, sat with the pigeons and papers outside on the patio. It was grey and damp and chilly and she liked it that way. More like black and white photos of dire times gone by. Oddly contemporaneous, black and white, sepia, daguerreotypes reaching across eras.

Twelve years ago, in this same November week, she was sitting at this same patio table, on November 3, 2004, reading the horrific news of the assassination in Amsterdam the day before of the Dutch filmmaker Theo van Gogh.

Van Gogh had been murdered by a man who had stalked him, lurked and stalked, noting as he rode his own bicycle what Van Gogh's everyday movements on *his* bike were. The assassin following, curating his victim's everyday movements. From his workplace to his home, from his home to work. Van Gogh didn't know that one of the thousands of bicyclists riding along with him was planning to murder him brutally.

The killer on the bike attacked Van Gogh in front of his film studio offices, in the morning. He shot Van Gogh while Van Gogh was still on his bicycle. When Van Gogh lay on the ground, the killer approached him with a large knife, which he used to try and decapitate the artist, maker of films, public commentator. The killer, a twenty-six-year-old Dutch citizen of Moroccan origin, was only partially successful in decapitating Theo van Gogh, who lay dying already from multiple bullet wounds. The assassin took out a second knife, which he plunged into the filmmaker's torso, severing the spinal column. He had attached a note to the knife he plunged into Van Gogh's chest.

The note was pre-written; the killer had the note on his person as he rode his bike through the streets of Amsterdam. The note had been premeditated along with the assassination. Murder of a public person. The note on the knife was a death threat; the note spoke of Jews, the West, women. The killer had been outraged that a female colleague of Van Gogh's had made a film with words the killer considered sacred, and she had put those words, for the purpose of a film, on a woman's body. The assassin had used the body of the male artist as a delivery depot to menace the woman, the West, Jews.

Because Vivi Pink had been in Amsterdam that week in November 2004, when Theo van Gogh was assassinated, it felt more personal to her. Out of the shadows of the spokes of bicycle wheels, a man appears and kills a public figure. The only mercy at all his mourners had been granted, she felt, was that social media did not exist then in any worldwide way, so if you knew, you knew, and if you ached, you ached, and it felt close and inexplicable, true and private, with no words.

And the sickest part of all was she didn't even know yet that on the other side of the Atlantic, her own daughter had been fatally injured in a hit and run by a bicyclist on a one-way street, cycling the wrong way in the rain.

Back in the Pink genes, she apparently had Dutch relatives. In the days of the Nazis, Jews had been banned from riding bicycles in Amsterdam. Then banned from owning a bike. Then banned from using public transport of any kind. Told to stay inside. Being outside for Jews became an illegal act. What they do when they do the things they do is to make public life against the law. "Once they had us Jews inside," Vivi remembered her dad, Izzy, telling her, "the Nazis got hit by a brutal winter. When it's bad, it will always get worse." What the historically brutal winter in Amsterdam during World

War II did was to create a shortage, naturally, of firewood. The Nazis began removing the doors from houses. They came to the houses of the Jews who had been ordered to stay inside, ripped off the doors, then accused Jews of being illegally outside.

The trains had been waiting at the station.

The park was so green, the seas were coming to get us, she loved Amsterdam, the memories were present in the eternal dark bloodstream. Then they close the parks, and we dream of green. How we dream of green and in dreams we kiss acquaintances. "Drop by if you feel like it, tomorrow night," the acquaintance in the dream says. What the dark times do is amputate mañana.

SHE GOT UP from the blue spaceship café table, began to walk the Vondelpark paths.

The white van that had stalked her was ahead, driver's door open. Police were there, cuffing him. Baseball cap. As one of the police turned him slightly, the van driver lifted his chin toward Vivienne, yelling, "Fucking Jew! Dirty fucking Jew. I'll kill all of you!"

They put him in an unmarked vehicle.

She looked, she was sure, like a looky-loo civilian. Should she tell the police that he – that he what? Braked his vehicle, stared at her, tracked her, drove beside her creepily slow?

Wednesday in the Vondelpark with Vivienne. One of the plainclothes cops – or so she figured he must be – a moustached man in a typical Amsterdam knee-length olive-brown raincoat with hood, gave her a look that said, "You know, don't you. You don't know but you do. You know and you understand."

She was fully present, yet the old body memory stresses emerged to make her feel that the present was so deeply *here*, she wasn't sure how to process it the old quick way. Part of her neurology was still in seat 15E over the North Atlantic.

Bile filled her mouth. She had the hunger shakes. Further inside the autumn green of the Vondelpark, she snapped a photo of an Amsterdam emergency medical person – or maybe it was a coroner – kneeling beside a little girl whose legs were twisted, turned the wrong way, knees facing backward. Had the man in the van created chaos before he toyed with her nerve endings, or after? Was there more than one van with mal intent driving in the park?

Mysteries get solved, sure. But Vivi Pink knew that most of life was one big cold case, a void on the lam from reason. She circled back.

The look of the moustached cop warned her back yet dared her to come forward. He said something to another one, more shaggy, more Dutch boomer looking, about how the terrorist was a fugitive now, on the lam. That the guy they arrested was a second guy, maybe unconnected. Were they speaking English? The sharper Mister Moustache with his colleague of a softer face, like a Sherlock and a Watson. The sly one, the wise one; the fox cop with the owl detective. English, Dutch?

She was a receiver, bright in her body as a nuclear half-life. They had said that her hair might never come back, that she would feel side effects from that secret USA desert bomb test ten years ago, forever. Maybe longer. Like radium with legs and the body ponds of the Vondelpark were clearing, sparkling, reflective, cosseted by fall. Coffee, give me coffee. Park bench shelter me. The clapping dancers next to her stuffed eardrums were making all kind of urgent palm musettes upon her soft bones. The cops blended with the trees, the trees dripped on the cops, the park looked like a painting of sharp eyes, resentment, contentment, the sea rising, us in green underwater.

THE CONCUSSION FOG was coming back. She was on a wide wooden bridge. She held on to the iron sides of the bridge. A swan drifted under the bridge, wings open. Drops of blood from her nose landed on the swan's wings. She must have hit her nose when she ran away from the van into the pond near the Café Vertigo.

Vivienne's grief was young, once. Now, her grief at losing Stella was itself twelve years old. Her mourning was a creature almost due for its bas mitzvah.

Safe for the moment in the public green lung, the Vondelpark, dear oxygen oasis of Amsterdam. Mokum Verde. The green lung that used to hold so many resident Jews, then they took the Jews away, and the green lung was a beautiful place to spend a Sunday, without any municipal Jews to be seen. Did the locals wonder what had happened to all the Jews they knew, when they disappeared the Jews from Amsterdam, when the bike riders had no Jews in their bike lane cohorts?

Under a big willow tree, Vivienne Pink sat pulling air across her lung scars, feeling the actual air as it hit scar tissue, feeling her diaphragm like the wind instrument it was, like a bassoon or an espresso machine. From her sitting position, she felt a heart pang, seeing an empty slatted bench beside the green waterline, and snapping the pics of the lonely bench, she did second the emotion. The park benches are lonely. They miss the dead, who used to come and sit alone and breathe the green.

Vivienne Pink under the willow tree, wet from her swim in the pond. Had the policemen noticed how bedraggled she was? Her ass rang. Her phone had survived the swim. She unzipped her back pocket, pulled her phone out. The message icon showed a 2. She pressed the icon with a ripped-up fingertip.

Buy Stella Day Merch at sale prices!

The sender was listed as 00000222288880000.

A sick pic: Stella's head on a body wearing a fussy frilly dress. Like Vivi, Stella hated dresses. Stella Coma had never worn a dress in her short life. How did this spammer get Stella's head and face, though? Vivi and Johnny had a strict security policy: they never sent out any pics of Stella, ever. No family pics, either. Ever. Plus, even stricter, they told anyone they knew that if they sent any pics to them of any kids, including their own or relations, Vivi and Johnny would no longer be in touch with them. The wise ones understood, the others, well, they lost friends and some family, for the sake of staying alive.

That damn calypso tune began playing on her phone. The electronic default of happy happy, life in the shill as one big frozen daiquiri. A video started playing on the screen, of its own uninvited agency. Like a salesman who was in your kitchen when you walked in. *Your album is ready.*

The movie in her hand showed Stella. On the screen, Stella was playing hopscotch on the chalked sidewalk outside their home on Euclid Avenue. Stella with her skinny legs. Stella with her straw-thin hair. Stella in summer shorts with orchids on them, a David Bowie Ziggy Stardust black and silver T-shirt. Stella at age – how old was Stel then? Seven? Six? No, just turned seven in April. April 23, a springtime baby.

Someone had videotaped Stella at age seven. She died at age eleven.

Someone had videotaped her daughter, Stella, on their street, playing hopscotch and had hung onto that tape. You could remotely watch anybody anywhere, today.

The phone began to play, uninvited, another video of Stella on the sidewalk in front of their house, with yellow chalk finishing up a hopscotch grid of yellow and pink and purple, but, hang on, from a different angle than the first video.

This video of Stella on the sidewalk had to have been taken from the point of view of their front porch. A breath away from their front door.

Jump cut to an ambulance, Stella on the road lit by spotlights, a red and yellow TORONTO FIRE truck, paramedics lifting a child onto a gurney.

Friday Afternoon Get Well Stella!!! A vile photo collage: Stella in a hospital bed at SickKids. The photo-assistant-bot had picked a frame of pink cartoon balloons. The animation showed Stella in the hospital bed, her head lifting up, lying back on the pillow, lifting up, lying back. The algorithmically tone-deaf photo app had manipulated Stella's anaesthetized body to wiggle with her life-support tubes, forcing a photo tune cruelty on a dying child, making her dance to an EDM beat, sending the cruelty to her mother. Who, and why now?

More. *Your New Movie Sunday Afternoon.* There was Johnny, sitting on a couch with Vivienne and Izzy and Rose, their heads bowed. The animation made them rock back and forth. With zippy music. At Stella's shiva. Who takes photographs at a shiva? At a shiva no photographs of the dead are permitted, and the mirrors are soaped. Who took creepy secret pics, saved them a dozen years, sent them to phones? Who has the gall, the chutzpah? Who has the *time?*

At the home of the Jewish couple, Jonathon Comasky and Vivienne

Pinsky, sitting shiva for their murdered daughter, of course there was a plainclothes police presence in and out of the front porch due to the death threats against Vivienne that had been going on even when Stella was alive. In addition, there were extra security guys on a twenty-four-hour rotation, hired by Izzy, to sit on the porch and keep an eye out.

There was a time-stamp on that last image of the street, their home, taken from the porch. November 10, 2004, 2:24 p.m. The day of Stella's funeral. The funeral was at Benjamin's at eleven o'clock in the morning. The sanctuary was full, a couple hundred people, a modest turnout, with ten hours notice.

So, since Stella's interment was at 12:15 p.m. and it was about a twenty-minute drive south down Bathurst from Finch, that meant they would have reached their home, the shiva house, at about one in the afternoon. Someone had taken a video an hour and fifteen minutes, say an hour and a half into the reception at their house, after Stella's interment. Most people would have left by then. Who lingers after the funeral of a child? It wasn't a party; it was the beginning of the week-long shiva, then the important first month of mourning, then the year of mourning. A funeral isn't a birthday party or a photo op. Mourners aren't props.

So, whoever took the video had stayed on at the shiva house, had desecrated Stella's memory, that blessing, by taking images right after they had buried her and had begun mourning . . . Two plainclothes Toronto police – one male, one female, both Jewish – were at the shiva for protection, yes, as well as police who came to pay their respects to Izzy the former city mayor. The security detail, stepping out on the porch to have a smoke, were joined by Izzy Pink himself, in yarmulke and house slippers, his cardigan sweater cut with scissors in the tradition of rending your clothing, a piece of black cloth pinned to his pocket.

VIVIENNE PINK WALKED in the Vondelpark up the stairs to Stadhouderskade, the canal on her left, round that little curve. She needed Rembrandt for solace.

The Rijksmuseum in its elegant stone-and-brick massive facade presented two wings with a covered arch thoroughfare, a public road running right through the centre of the museum. You could see bicycles riding under the arch, through the wings; it was lovely. The Rijksmuseum had been built to look like the gates to the city. Vivi felt great excitement entering the thoroughfare with the sheltering arch above her. Inside there were one million objects in the Rijksmuseum's safekeeping. She had come to visit with just one.

An eight-minute walk from the Vondelpark to Rembrandt's *The Jewish Bride*. Rembrandt is in no hurry, Rembrandt is patient. With the dead, you're always on time.

Down the stairs from the covered entry road to the bright inner atrium, up other stairs and there it was: The object of her desire. *The Jewish Bride*. Shining like solace, like wonder. The painting of the betrothed couple like dear friends Vivi had been missing a long time, the warm welcome of the red and the gold of their garments, old friends, hearts new in the reunion. The paint came alive in secret submissions of the heart, with Rembrandt. Vivienne knew you must be a pilgrim to come in person, to let the brush strokes soothe you, energize you. *The Jewish Bride* knew wet information of the heart of a beloved, in gold and red, and the hand of the groom in the painting on his bride's chest, her one hand in his, her other hand resting on the red folds of her bridal costume.

My God, Vivienne thought, what the heck did Rembrandt know about putting such life, such pictorial autobiographies into the hands of the Jewish bride and her groom in 1665 in Amsterdam? The Aleph Marriage. Rembrandt painted the bride as the biblical Rebecca, the groom as Isaac. The hands . . . Vivienne came close to the gold paint; she could hear the paint breathing into her eyes.

Rembrandt worked the red paint onto the bride's dress, making the paint's thick substance a thing of light shimmering. Like a portraitist bird with a beak, Rembrandt scratched the bride's dress to make it imperfect, glitter. The groom, Isaac, holds his hand on Rebecca's breast, yet it is her heart we feel under his hand, and the light of their aloneness, at the beginning of a life. Isaac's coat seems infused with the green-gold light of the willow reflections of Amsterdam.

Vivienne's eyes were wet, inhaling the living moisture of Isaac's coat. Did Rembrandt go into an empathy fugue when he painted the couple, to receive this moment of change in their lives? Rembrandt was like a guest at their wedding-to-be. He wasn't a Jew, but of course, at the time, he knew a lot of Jews in Amsterdam. Rembrandt was like mishpoche of the Mokum.

Once upon a time when Amsterdam was such a Jewish city, when Rembrandt painted *The Jewish Bride,* a Jew still had two hundred and seventy-five years before the Nazis began to eliminate the visual appearance of the Jewish visage in the city of Amsterdam in World War II. But here Vivi Pink was, calm, watching over Isaac's coat so fresh at three hundred and fifty-one years old, standing close to the paint – paint like fur, paint like science, paint like golden prairie, low light, long winter. Sheep, goats, the angora goat, the golden nubs, picturing the ripples. Rembrandt loved people in particular.

Vivienne felt a familiar joy of hating Rembrandt with so much love because he went ahead and did what she felt she had never been able to do and did it three hundred plus years ago. The greats make you want to quit before you start; this is their knack from beyond the grave. This is how they cull the herd. If you get mad enough at them – *you fucker!* – you persist. Vivienne Pink got close to the hands of Rebecca and Isaac. She could do a book of hands, maybe.

What do you think about that, sweet Rembrandt?

She got closer to the couple, examining the scratched coat of the groom, the cuff of the bride, the delicate fold-back ruching of her sleeve and the many bracelets at the moment of betrothal. Rembrandt had made a pact with the light, to turn paint into lumens. Vivi was an acolyte in the museum, obsessing on the fingers of the Jewish groom, how Rembrandt made the fingers alive with private promises. The groom's thumb on the gold trim at the décolleté of his bride.

And now Vivi like a coroner, coming close to the painting, squinting into the red painted folds of the Jewish bride, her delicate right hand with a ring on the index finger, her wrist with three gold bracelets. So intimate. As if Rembrandt had held that hand. Rembrandt's karma was empathy. He had the technical skills to show it.

The Rembrandt was upping her heartbeat while calming her down.

She was on the prowl, Rembrandt put her there. She knew the story about how Vincent van Gogh had come to the Rijksmuseum in 1885, two hundred years after Rembrandt painted this very painting, *The Jewish Bride,* to see it and Van Gogh was so deeply affected by it that he said to a friend, "Believe me, and I mean this sincerely, I would give ten years of my life to be allowed to sit before this painting for fourteen days with just a crust of bread to eat."

When Van Gogh in blinding toxicity lay dying, did he think of Rembrandt, and say, "At least I lived for four more years, dear *Jewish Bride,* after I laid eyes on you and never forgot you"?

The bride and groom setting out in a life, setting sail together into the dark waters. Here are hands and the world.

Vivienne Pink tilted her head. The painting was 121.5 centimetres by 166.5 centimetres.

Her phone pepped its calypso tune. A news alert: Two stabbings of bicy-clists in Amsterdam. People claiming to be eyewitnesses were saying that a gunman rode his bike past the patio of 't Blauwe Theehuis, the Blue Tea House, in the Vondelpark, began shooting at patrons outside sitting at tables drinking morning coffee. Got off the bike, began stabbing patrons.

Vivi calmed her pulse in the quiet room of paintings. Her lung scars inhaled Rembrandt and centuries. *The Jewish Bride,* one last adieu to the way the bride's hand so intimately touches her beloved's hand, the way the thumb of his right hand presses her breastbone. In the radius of love, Rembrandt crawled inside their loving eyes, painted light from within.

Vivienne decided to go look at a second favourite painting in the Rijksmuseum, *The Corpses of the De Witt Brothers* by Jan de Baen. Done about ten years after Rembrandt's bride and groom in their private commu-nion, De Baen depicted the endgame of civic fury, the exterior political melee. She got lost on the way, walking like a citizen royal through the grand Gallery of Honour (the Rijksmuseum so different from only a few years back, so renovated), passing as if through an art lover's dream, side galleries, little sidebars to step into with Vermeer's woman reading her letter in her blue dress so graceful; *The Little Street,* the pang in her distant husband Johnny's heart whenever he saw the little street so like their home street in Canada; Jan Asselijn's painting *The Threatened Swan* from the De Witts' era, meant to evoke the lynched politicians, the swan as democracy, wings aloft over the city, its feathers protecting the citizenry as it was so threatened; the girl with her amused and steely glance.

Lost in the labyrinth of the museum, she went all the way to the wrong wing, each wing a treasure box, until back in the wing she wanted she found *The Corpses of the De Witt Brothers.* The room looked empty. The walls were charcoal grey. Wooden floors in pale parquet. Nice padded armless couches, two sides sharing one low back.

And there, long legs out, examining the bodies from a distance, was the Surf Doctor, on the edge of the couch. He nodded, as if he had been expecting her for an appointment. You had to work to find the De Witts painting in the vast museum, yet here he was, the man who happened to sit beside her on the plane over the ocean.

He stood up. He didn't approach her. He approached the painting. The stoop, the leather jacket, dressed like the Dutch Golden Age. His neck forward, a long-time hiker, maybe, or a man accustomed to carrying the donkeys of war up rock ledges, down rock faces, rappelling, the neck muscles tense. He examined the De Witt brothers, lynched in 1672. Vivienne Pink had never looked at the painting any way but solo. In the giant room, the two of them enacted a duet of silence. That she could do.

She walked up to the painting. Darkness, the angry citizenry of the day. Dark night, the assassinated bodies of two politicians, brothers, hanging from a crude scaffold.

The brothers were murdered, by plan, then carried to the scaffold to be hanged, for all to see. Their bodies rendered pale in shadow with blood pooling, the outside made into a dark interior violence. The brothers are flayed, slit from neck to crotch. All is smoke dark onyx night around them. Green black on that summer day, August 20 – the day they killed the De Witt brothers. Johan and Cornelis.

Economic austerity, country feeling attacked, panic among the people, premeditated murder. Jan de Baen the artist did not spare us the blood of blood politics.

The Surf Doctor acknowledged Vivienne Pink's presence. He stepped a bit to the left to give her room. He walked back behind her, letting her walk close and then back up from the corpses of the De Witt brothers. As the story is told, the populace cut off their body parts, sold the body parts of the dead politicians for money. The Surf Doctor was watching her, Vivienne knew, as she re-examined the bodies of the political brothers.

She walked close to the artwork, examining in detail the hands of the lynched politicians. The right hand of one body had blood pooled in it, the left hand of the other no longer resembled a hand, looking like a deformed extremity of a caught and split-open piece of game. A hanging where the feathers and bones had been removed, and now the populist grouping had cut up and hawked the body parts, voting with machetes. A golden age turned rabid.

It mattered to Vivienne Pink, an artist with a camera, that this De Baen painting was the small size it was: 56 centimetres wide by 69.5 centimetres high. The murder and dismemberment of the politicians distilled to the power of art.

The Jewish Bride by Rembrandt; *The Corpses of the De Witt Brothers* by De Baen. Same Dutch era, different obsession. Vivi Pink lived at these extreme edges, which was why she was content to visit only two paintings, over and over, at the vast Rijksmuseum collection. They were precious garments for her eyes. When Vivienne finished her close examination of the corpses in oil, she turned. The Surf Doctor was gone.

She walked outside. It was sunny in a low way, very Amsterdam in the new green winter. The chlorophyll was embarrassed to be so pretty. The Surf Doctor was standing in the tunnel built to suggest the gates to the city. They walked under the archway together into the dance of light and darkness. They hung a left, walked along, going no way in particular yet feeling they were going the long way and not minding going the long way along Stadhouderskade to the Overtoom then back on Van Baerlestraat, the canal on the other side of the road, the bridges. They walked along over the bridge, stopped. The crime scene tape below in the Vondelpark. They walked past the Conservatory of Music, hundreds of bikes parked, young people with instrument cases, the sense of the past and the future mingling by the spokes. They crossed, walked a block, yeah, up Willemsparkweg to Pompa with the orange-and-white-striped awning, one of Vivi's favourite spots to eat in Amsterdam.

The familiar sign outside Pompa, with the word *Pasta* above, the word *Tapas* below.

Vivienne led the way up the stairs, to the table at the back. She said nothing about the fact that part of her PTSD was that she never sat near the door, or with her back to any entrance. "This is good," he said. "This works."

She felt secure; the low light was coming in a pair of glass doors out to a balcony. Escape, if necessary.

A waiter came to the table.

"*Dos vasos de tinto, y un botella de agua sin gas,*" Vivi said, going on automatic, speaking Spanish in the Amsterdam tapas spot, as the waiter laid down the menus that were a combination of Dutch and English with sprinklings of Español.

Their bodies were present, presumptively. Their souls were in that lag of ghost jets over the ocean. The overlay of work, film in cameras shooting war, the spectre of tobacco nights on the phone with the camera workers now passed on to other more circular rimes, the ear blocks of flying, the bride and groom followed by the lynching of the politicians and the retailing of their body parts all in a cerebral combine with this guy across the table from her, who had mentioned Las Canteras, the renowned surfing spot on Gran Canaria, and in some yesterday, she had been home, packing her backpack with necessaries and secrets.

Her eyes swam as she looked at the Pompa menu. All those *k*'s with the twin *aa*'s of the Dutch, the fun run of *tonijncarpaccio*. Or *gegrilde zalmfilet*.

The wine and water and bread came. The restaurant wasn't busy. The waiter loitered at a discrete distance.

Her eye recognized *calamari fritti*.

She nodded at the waiter, who was as tall as the Surf Doctor. When he came back to the table to take their order, Vivi craned her neck up, confidently saying, "*Calamar frito y . . .*" then faltering, "*. . . mosselen in witte* *wijnsaus,"* mangling those mussels but good in attempted Dutch.

He ordered patatas bravas and tuna carpaccio and tacos de cordero. Wild potatoes and lamb tacos and raw tuna. He over-pronounced his *t*'s.

Local place, plain wooden tables, plain wooden chairs. Wine, bread, olive oil, food arrived.

He ripped some bread, put a few of the wild potatoes on it, and with his lips nicely dotted with aioli and *tinto* asked her, "What's your order?"

"You mean like a nun?" she asked.

He was grinning. Her too. He said, "As in birth order."

"Second. Middle child."

"Me too." He swept the bread in the oil, set it down, bit into a lamb taco, offered the rest of the lamb to her. "Right? Left alone, good kid, got rid of the parental component jitters with the first one, you kind of roamed, how shall we call it, abroad?"

"Nailed it," she said. She got to work on the crunching calamari. Her feeling that she could trust him was there opening her mouth, making her make sounds. "I had a brother."

"Tell me about your brother, then. So? Younger? You the middle, you played mom to him."

"The opposite. I had a big brother. He was the first-born."

"Mine, too."

"You were a middle child?"

"I was. My brother died, 1967."

"1967–67?"

"Yeah."

He did not say, she did not ask, she presumed he meant the six-day war of 1967. It could have been another 1967, of course. She said, "Love summer, '67."

"For some," he said. "And yours?"

"My brother? Hillel? 'Harry' as we called him? He died in '79. Lung cancer. Lungs run in our family. I had scarred lungs before I ever met up with Saddam's sarin, I can tell you that."

He did not pursue Iraq or the tyrant or the '80s or sarin or mustard gas.

Instead, he asked Vivienne, "So, did you assume the mantle of the oldest? The one meant to hide in her room had to be the one in charge?"

"I was born an extroverted introvert. I am the party-girl hermit. My brother Harry used to call me the undercover party girl. I toggle."

"When he died, your brother, Harry, was there a little one on the scene?"

"Sure. My sister, Rhonda."

"What's her story?"

Vivi felt the heartbeat telling her to pull back a bit. "So what's your name?"

"Maybe later on. I could continue to make a pest of myself with you, later. I could ask you to forgive my rudeness, perhaps, at dinner. Or lunch. If you grant forgiveness at midday?"

He had that smile. I bet, Vivi thought, he has broken the will of hardened guys with that smile. Even as she suspected it, she liked it. The push-pull of the art of attraction.

"What was your brother's name?" she asked.

"Yuval. He used his middle name, instead. Gerald. Gerry. He died, twenty years ago next February."

Vivienne drifted outside clock time. Mister Long Legs was scarily congenial while remaining reticent. He had the air of a man who knew how to put the ease on, to create a sense of intimacy with a subject, for interrogation.

What if he had looked her up, or watched her, or asked back in Toronto at the KLM check-in, making up a story that they were friends, to be reassigned to sit with her?

Well, what of it? Would she resent that?

The suspicion. She'd been trained to have a suspicious mind. It saved her. Plus the over-alertness of the PTSD, so what? It too had saved her life. Her strength was her weakness. She knew how to survive danger; she knew how to over-watch everybody. Everything was in high-def; from this she made a living. Saved her life, supported her family. Over-alertness paid down the damn mortgage. *You go fucking meditate* was her mantra. The world is elsewhere. Just ask the Buddha. Me and the Buddha watched our buddies die in crossfire in war, how about you?

Her kin were not artists who stayed in rooms of their own; her work kin were firefighters, first responders, soldiers, police. Reporters on the front lines. News beat guys with big eyes for what did not add up in a crime scene. Vivienne Pink was more at home in a morgue than at an art opening.

He looked at her through the wine glass as he sipped the Rioja red. She took a shot of him through the wine glass, to capture his calm and bend it. The camera koan is in the details.

They sat crunching soft-batter calamari. Lamb tacos arrived, beyond delicious. *Shmeck, sabrosa,* her salivary glands spoke food in other tongues like glands of joy intelligence, open-mouthed vowels and hot back-of-the-throat horks of countries east, south, mongrel mutant mélanges defying extinction. The squid and the lamb.

The waiter removed the plates. They ordered two café solos.

They drank short coffees, at length.

She lifted her coffee glass, took a one-handed snap of his face, through the glass, its ibis feel a dead-on perfect distortion. If she never saw him again, she had two great photos of the moment.

His eyes reminded her of comrades who had been murdered, fellow journalists who had been targeted, who kept their private souls under wraps to get the job done, and once in a while, sitting across from such a pal, Vivi could see in his eyes this secret history.

"You like *The Jewish Bride*," he said.

"You were watching me."

"Yes. I saw you watching Rembrandt, from the hallway." A lot of life in those eye crinkles. A couple of random scars near his right eye.

"Do you fancy Rembrandt?" she asked him.

"Very much. I thought I might be Rembrandt one day. That didn't work out. I didn't know how to do the eyes."

His long fingers splayed out on the table. "Did you see how they don't look at each other?" he said. "The bride and the groom?"

"No," Vivienne said. "Come on, it's all about intimacy, that painting. Van Gogh said so." Vivi had looked at *The Jewish Bride* for hours, many times over many decades. How could this Surf Doc be saying that the Rembrandt bride and groom didn't look at each other? "I don't believe it. Can I be that stupid?"

"I guess we'll have to go back," he said, looking at her with soft eyes. "To see how the bride and the groom aren't looking at each other."

5

VANISHED SPAIN

IN THE TIME of the afternoon when his brain was blank and his wrist was aching, Johnny Coma liked to walk over to the Ciutadella Park and rent a rowboat.

Down Passeig del Born, left on Rec to Princesa, up Princesa to Passeig Picasso, across to the iron gates into the park. At the edge of the pond, the shore was a miniature mayhem of tall tropical green. When he was away from Barcelona, he sometimes forgot how the city was lined with palm trees, how the entry at the airport was all palm trees, how lush it was. The Ciutadella Park was a green lung with pedestrian pathways through it.

At the edge of the pond, ducks in white and brown settled into their own feathers. Horizontal stripes – shadows – played across the ducks. The sun had come out in a blue blaze after the morning rain. The pond was forest green with lime green palm tree reflections in it.

Barques de la Ciutadella per 30 minuts 6E read the sign. The rowboats were old, clunky, teal green peeling, the oars white sticks with mottled brown at the blades. The boatman gave him number 36, the number painted in white on the side of the boat.

Johnny rowed across the rippling water toward the cluster of white ducks on the other side: white paint dabs on lime and forest.

The water felt like animal energy against the oars. His arms fighting to push through the pond's spinal cord. The ripples were like the green spines of a mysterious water being. He could see his shadow in the water. The ducks moved through the spinal cords of water, through palm frond debris.

He rowed from the green shore through the green water, putting his upper body into it, rowing under that low bridge, ducking his head, to an island in the pond. He set the oars to the side.

He lay back in the brilliantine. As unnerving in its desuetude as a desert winter. Johnny Anonymous, the man who liked to sketch in a rowboat. First, he stretched his legs, closed his eyes, to feel invisible. He thought of Christie Pond, back in Toronto.

Stella's wet feet, wet shoes, left foot almost torn off, twisted to the side where the algae of the pond had entered her mortal wounds. She had walked home from the pond and crouched down, making a new hopscotch grid on the pavement.

If it hadn't been two days after Hallowe'en. If it hadn't been a Tuesday. If the clocks hadn't turned back. Dusk came too early for children. If the bicyclist hadn't veered to avoid a fire truck rushing up the middle of Euclid, hopped the bike over the curb onto the dark sidewalk, knocking Stella over, her head concussing against the pavement. If, at that moment in the life of his daughter, the bicyclist had answered a phone call on a landline at home or had stayed a half-hour extra at the office or had read the damn arrow showing it was a one-way street across the way from an elementary school, if if if. The moment he knocked her down – if he was a he – was the event of his and Vivi's marriage, the event of their lives. Kismet can be kind, kismet can be a killer.

He opened his eyes: the civil twilight had begun. The blue was falling, the green was rising. He rowed, a shadow on a shadow of water. At the island in the middle of the pond, dozens of rowboats were tied up. Ducks, nestled into their own feathers, stood as if on stilts on the prows of the rowboats. Johnny took out his Moleskine, wrote:

Dear Stella,

I'm sorry I wasn't home the day you died. I was writing. I was on an island, paying homage to you. I was writing a book about a little girl and her dad. They went so many places.

He ripped out the page. He leaned over to a boat numbered 32 and dropped the page in it. A white and grey duck hopped up on the edge, took the missive in its bill, swam away on the green with his heart's discard.

He sat a bit at the shore, on a favourite bench on a public path, shaded, almost private, off the main walkways. In the dense green shadows, a man was kissing another man against the trunk of a tall palm tree. Johnny took out his Moleskine and made a sketch of them. The tenderness of the kiss, old pals, long-time lovers, new love, tender as the civil twilight sent sparks into the early shreds of the nautical dusk. They kept kissing as he walked by. The city vibrates all day long.

The soft streets of an hour ago had a hyperreal delineation as he walked down the gentle slope of the left side of Princesa.

He paused at the window of the Círculo del Arte. He loved this spot, a low-key high-class locale for art and photography exhibits. In the window were a couple of black and white photos by Carlos Saura. Vivienne loved Saura's cinema: *Carmen,* yes, and especially *Blood Wedding.* "The muscular-ity of the camera shots," Vivienne used to say. "The way the bodies and the cameras move as one, the sense of the epic ever, *las cosas que existen para siempre.*" It was Vivi who told him to ignore the manic rants out and about in the world today. "Go to the forevers, honey," she said. Her own heart was a tomb, walled in. Yet she did watch the forever movies of Saura. The one about flamenco, the one about Goya, movement, dance.

In the window sat a newly issued book of photographs that Saura had taken when he was in his twenties. During the Franco Fascist regime, Carlos Saura took his camera, set off in his Fiat 600 to see Spain's remote places. The book was called *Vanished Spain.*

Johnny was in the door.

You find your mentors where you find them. A writer among artists looks to see who never retires, who has the grit, who keeps on going. Carlos Saura at eighty-five, still in the game.

Young Saura set out to the far marginalized reaches of Spain, to photograph the dust villages, the disappearing ways. Johnny stopped at one photo on the wall: A dust road, a low bleached home in hard soil under clouds wind-whipped. Horses in laborious burden, pulling.

What was not in the photograph made it thrilling: no cheer, no hail-fellow-well-met, no reconciliation exercises, no two sides to every question. What do you do when your country is run by a dictator, an authoritarian? Carlos Saura went to the hinterland places.

There is honour in making art on the margins of the resistance. Your country is a living shiva. The bloodletting is dynamic at five in the afternoon. The city is being carted away in the night, in the shadow of money. The dust meets, clandestinely, in basements, speaking its own tongue. Playing cards, drinking wine from the goatskins.

Johnny walked over to another photograph on the wall of the gallery. His shoes were a bit damp from the water he'd taken on in the rowboat. The photo: A solitary figure under an umbrella at night. On the tram tracks in a narrow street. The streetlights like comets on sticks.

Johnny came closer to the photograph on the gallery wall. It was in fact two figures, so closely embracing that they had one dark neck, one dark draped upper body, two legs.

The rain had died, the lovers had died, the photograph played their music.

What you need: one photo in a gallery.

Johnny Coma stood in front of the photographs of Carlos Saura, and he called his wife, Vivienne Pink, on his phone. She was in Amsterdam, working. She didn't pick up. She wasn't there and where was she? He scrolled to her last text to him: *Eight dead news says Vondelpark man van knife gun machete other guy children dead got pics later.* He had texted her back, *Me worry. U ok?* But nothing more, as it was when she was in the work.

He missed the voice of his sweetie. He missed the voice of his marriage. In the landline days, he saved messages from her, just to replay at night when he was lonely. He liked to rehear her old hellos, even distorted by tape and time.

Johnny drifted to the big room looking out onto Princesa. He touched the Saura book, *Vanished Spain,* so fine, so textural, the paper almost erotic in its fineness. No, not almost erotic – erotic. It had been so finely constructed with such intimate care: you felt the human touch on the paper, the printing had been so carefully done, such care had been taken with the ink to replicate the feeling of the vision of Carlos Saura's own eyes, when he was young and visionary. And still visionary, was the thing. Yeah, Johnny hoped he would still be in the game in his eighties, like Carlos Saura. You refuel at the gas station of your own work.

Johnny flipped the pages. The book was only sixty-five euros, about a hundred bucks. The reproduction was exquisite. And no wonder. It was published by Steidl in Göttingen, Germany, the finest printer of books on the planet.

There is the living bark, the living tree. The bark in its cellular cellulose, the pulp alive, mashed, liquefied, pressed, the forest skin meets the rags of rich and poor to become paper, so sensual, clothing and canopies speaking in ink. You will never be lonely again, with me by your side in bed, says the book.

Come, keep company with me, I have dressed myself so finely in my best Sunday fonts.

He had a fifty euro bill and seven twenties stashed in his phone case for an emergency. Like a call to the 911-bookstore of his heart, this was an *emergencia*. He felt that old-time comfort, walking out into the city streets with a handsome book as his printed beau. Mister Coma's kind of trophy date.

Down to that part of Princesa just before it hits Comerç, his heart was hitting syncopated beats too loudly inside his chest. He felt the old pressure of his enlarged heart.

He stopped to take deep breaths, leaning against the glass of the corner eatery. He held *Vanished Spain* against his chest like art made of Kevlar. He took out his notebook and pencil, moved the book down at a ninety-degree angle to his rib cage, making an improv street desk of the hardcover and wrote:

Dear Vivienne,

V, it was so fine while it lasted.

It was so fine of a marriage. It's gone now. It all vanishes, the dust vanishes, even the dust of the dusty roads has gone to its grave. The ghosts of the murdered come back, the murdered photographers in combat come back, the women in combat wearing locks of their own ghost hair around their necks, the refugees rise from the drowned waters, the secure are in their towers of quicksand.

The Mediterranean is peril water.

The absence is this terrible music between us. Vanished Spain will come again. We're walking on the dust of the vanished. V, I've been trying to get in touch with Stella. If I hear back from her, I'll let you know.

His eyes were filled with the last hexagonal crystals of blue as he walked the narrow sidewalk down the Princesa slope.

He took a left turn at Montcada. Such a narrow street with the darkest of blues, maxixe, above the stone walls, as sky. On his right, he saw that the paper supply store had reopened after the long lunch. Great. He went in, browsed the selection of rag sheets, perfect for writing a letter on. He bought a rust, a lavender, a robin's egg. Oh, and a mauve for good luck. He tucked the new paper in the front of *Vanished Spain*, exited Montcada, took a right-hand swerve for no reason but the dusk melancholia, around the side of the basilica Santa Maria del Mar, sat down on the front steps.

Masses and solace within. Built in the 1300s. Saint Ignatius of Loyola, founder of the Jesuit order, as a young travelling pilgrim sojourned in Barcelona and begged for alms at this basilica in 1524 and 1525. Oh hell. Johnny went in. The immense Catalan Gothic church felt even larger inside, majestic yet intimate. Cozy, ethereal, in touch with *el cielo* and *la calle*.

There was that nook he'd visited, times past: the very spot where Loyola was a local beggar six hundred years ago. I mean, man, Johnny thought, the engraved stone honouring Loyola – *Iñigo* – in one of the steps up to the saint's alcove was itself a hundred and fifty years old.

There was a new sculpture of Loyola in the nook, done in a green-grey stone. Loyola, sitting on a simple narrow wooden bench, big right hand open, left hand holding a book. And those feet! Beautiful big toes. Johnny went up the two steps to the Loyola alcove. He sat down on the narrow bench beside the saint. "Greetings and salutations," a voice said from a corner shadow, followed by a familiar horking and sputum roiling in a throat filled with ancient consonants. A hand reached out to his arm, pulled at his windbreaker. "Never did picture the likes of you to come to Santa Maria, my friend. Is Lucifer on your bandwidth, today?"

Sancho. Who stayed sitting on the floor in the corner of the saint's alcove, saying, "The people were too numerous today, I can predict the birds will be in the air, the police in their whirligigs will come and amass in my *pequeña plazita*, so here I came for shelter."

"Is there some kind of action, a manifestation today?"

"No, my liege," Sancho said, getting to his feet, sitting down beside Johnny on the bench. "But I do feel it coming. I think we needs must make an escape. I spoke to you of going to sea?"

"You did?" He had no memory of it.

"Then it's all settled," Sancho said. "Off we will go. Niña, Pinta and" – sweeping his arm across Johnny's face, hitting him on the nose – "Santa Maria!"

"And how will we sail?" Half-humouring Sancho.

"My friend, you will procure for us a magnificent liner of historic proportions."

"No, I won't. I have a book to write."

"We shall scribble together. Why not have the grand book gala at sea? I mind the time in the Galapagos when I befriended the legendary Lonesome George. He was a tortoise, take him for all in all, we shall not look upon his like again. Let us visit the water before it is done with us. You could drum me up a signature cocktail for my launch, a 'Quijoto' perhaps, and we will make the scribble-ismos all day on the waves. Incidentally, by the way, Bakunin the rat pulled his blurb at the last minute."

"Sancho, Bakunin's dead."

"And . . . ?"

"Never mind."

"I feel a voyage is required to get away from those damn helicopters in my head. Pack your tux, my liege, you never know who might be going viral on a sea cruise."

"I better not," Johnny said. "I better stick to my routine." He was afraid or shy or reticent or just a damn idiot; he didn't want to tell Sancho about Stella, or his dream of finding some fragment of Stella. Not a *writer's* block, a *heart* block. He was walking around with a distorted heart, and that kept his book from appearing to him in its proper heart music and hard fact. If you can't face facts, how can you write fiction?

"Your mind is dry," Sancho said.

"It is. How do you know?"

Sancho put his hand around Johnny's upper arm. "I was feeling sick today. Thought I might go back to the bad stuff."

"You come here to the basilica when you feel that way?"

"I do. I do indeed. In fact, did I ever tell you that when you go down to your beach after you come see me, I come in here."

"To worship? Or because you miss the, ah, bad stuff?"

"Because I miss you too much."

Male friendship, the greatest mystery of all.

They come and go in the pews and altars in the late part of day. In the dusk in the deepening Spanish shadows, they walk up the aisles to the altar, where the icon front and centre is not Jesus, but a woman, Santa Maria. She who cares for and tends the sea creatures. She who tends to the sailors, the marine snow in the deep.

"I will pray for you."

"That's okay, Sancho. I really don't need it. I'm not much of a believer."

"Amen."

He hoped he hadn't offended Sancho, who appeared unconcerned, up on his feet again, holding the hand of the sculpted Saint Ignatius of Loyola, who in real life had been in this very spot, whose DNA must be here somewhere.

Sancho faced Johnny, held both hands out. "I sing a threnody for planet Earth. I sing a threnody for the water that covers us. Into the threnos of bioluminescence I wish to swim . . . where the luciferins might light me . . . Dear friend, when I depart, deck me in fins at last to discover all the *mila-gros*. We *must* go to sea."

Sancho bowed, shuffled off in his long tweed topcoat.

Johnny opened his notebook. Sitting alone in the Saint Loyola nook of the basilica, he stroked the open hand of the sculpture, pressed the pencil lead hard on the page, wrote: *We're born in ink, as we age we disappear. What a joke. That's all he wrote: nothing.*

He felt good to be in a bad mood. Pep squads were the work of the devil.

6

A FUNERAL FOR MYSTERY

ON WILLEMSPARKWEG, POMPA had cleared out some. Spots of sun. Moments of conversation over food. These are the things you remember. The striped awning, the cursive-style neon in orange saying *Pompa,* with the *P* stylishly looping to the *o,* the font when you are falling for someone.

Vivienne still knew him by his card alone: Surf Doctor.

He said, "Our problem is we don't understand devotion. We mistake protocols for loyalty. We refuse to believe belief. Devotion: The groom is devoted to his bride. He will do anything for her. We think that love is a secular being. We had a funeral for mystery. Hamlet was afraid the ghost was real, Hamlet was afraid the ghost wasn't real. Hamlet didn't want his memory of his father to go away, Hamlet forgot his own memory. By the end of the play, Hamlet has forgotten to remind himself to never forget his father."

He drank a good last gulp of the red wine. Vivi noticed that when he drank, the glass disappeared inside his hand, making it look like *tinto* magic. She drank the last foam dreg of her café solo.

They were in that foggy privilege of jet lag. Making a private cave of their table in the eatery.

"I found your surf book by chance, you know," he said. The *you know* so informal. From the cave of the plane to the cave of the restaurant. Here in the public cave called Amsterdam.

"Oh yeah? Chance, like how?"

"I was hustling through Schiphol when your book, like, no kidding, jumped out at me. The cover. They had it prominently displayed in one of those tables right at the concourse. I like airports."

"You don't."

"I do."

"Why in heaven's name?"

"You take chances; you spend money; you just don't care what you do. My next leg to Barcelona was delayed. I had an extra hour on my hands. I picked up your book. Like it was a moment. Well, turns out it was –" he sipped some red "– momentous for me. If my plane had been on time, I might not ever have met your book in that airport."

Vivienne didn't say anything to him about how the guide who had taken her around the Nevada Test Site, as it was still known ten years ago, recognized her from the jacket photo on the back of that very same book, *Surf Squats*. There are guys whose eyes ally with yours, from the distance. Then by kismet you meet them. Or your art is a carrier of kismet.

"Now, the plane is further delayed. I had time to pass, so I bought it, sat with it five hours, making a wall around myself. You see," he said leaning across the table toward her. "When I saw how you attended to their lives, how you hung out in the . . . You went way the hell out into the Atlantic to the Canaries, never mind in winter, you fell upon a handful of rough, sure, mostly guys, the dispossessed, being kicked out. I was sitting in the airport, your surfer pictures on my knees in the book, hypnotized by the black and white sea sparkles, the crazy-busy dead-calm eyes where the water walls came rushing. I had had those eyes. I knew those eyes. They were the eyes of the evicted, who found freedom in the waves. I would have given up a week of my life to be stranded in Schiphol Airport, just to be able to sit in peace and quiet with your tenement surfers book."

He leaned back in his chair. "I'd been a shipwreck for a while. I was a good observer. I knew – knew, know – how to break someone down. But I loved the water and the wave life. My knees were knobs, my eyes were fucked, I didn't care." He looked dead-eye at Vivi. "Your pics of the Canary surfers at Las Canteras ratted out my life lies. My masks, who you . . . Who as a person you go around as if I really wanted to be that mask and like starlight, you exposed me."

He drank some wine, slid some more bread through the leftover sea ink. "I knew how to check out who might have set up an artist like you to be murdered. I knew how to infiltrate death squads, but I did not have an emotional tool kit for living."

He drained his glass, left a bunch of euros on the table. "I'm asking a lot, I know. Hey, can we walk?"

Standing, waiting, he looked thinner than before. That autumn-brown sweater with the well-worn crewneck hung a bit looser than she remembered when she first spotted him in the TO airport. They left the eatery, their souls still flying across the ocean, and walked down the stairs into the all-day gloaming of Amsterdam. Vivi loved what dark skies did to dark fertile green. Proper conduct and courtesy while the waters rose beyond détente, and the evil came back like spores in the air.

They crossed Van Baerlestraat. At the Conservatory of Music, Vivi stopped, one leg in the air, to nab a quick pic of the overlaid spokes of all the hundreds of bicycles jammed together. Amsterdam, the fine city located below sea level. The day might indeed come when a fish needs a bicycle.

On the bridge they looked over the Vondelpark paths. "There was yellow tape all over there, I swear," she said.

"Sometimes they take it away," he said. "But not usually so quickly."

"Well, it was there."

"I don't see any blood," he said.

"I doubt you would from this distance."

"Maybe."

Down the slope to take the curve into Roemer Visscherstraat. "You know Carpaccio?" he said.

"What you ate. Raw fish, raw meat, carpaccio sliced thin."

He stopped, smiling a smile she hadn't yet seen. "Carpaccio the man," he said.

"Carpaccio the who?"

They sat down on the street steps down to the Owl lobby. He said, "Carpaccio was a Venetian. A painter. Carpaccio used a certain red pigment that looked like the colour of raw meat. The name of the man became the name of the paint became the name for the food it resembled." He took her hand, helped her up. They walked down the stairs to the hotel entrance.

In the elevator, she felt too close physically with him, perhaps because it was exactly as close as she wanted to be. She needed to be alone, and rest. She needed to rest her eyes.

IN THE LATE morning, next day, he was in the hotel breakfast room. Scrambled eggs, ham. He was drinking coffee, writing in a notebook. She took a separate table. She ate, looking at the greenery out the window in the garden. The stone paving, the iron furniture, the last of the flat pink blooms. Bamboo. Soothing. When she pressed Espresso on the coffee machine, he came up behind her, saying, "Would it be ridiculous if I asked you to put aside your work for a few hours and come have lunch with me, across the bridge at the Café Americain?" His smile was in his voice. Damn that charming larynx. "All that gin so dry and lonely."

7

THE CAFÉ AMERICAIN

WALKING ACROSS THE bridge to the Americain Hotel, housing the café, Vivi re-remembered from times past the dark curving shadow water, still, aquatinted even in sunshine.

They scuttled across the tram rails, missed being hit by a couple cars and bikes, walked up the steps to the Café Americain entrance, the tiles saying Welkom, into the decor of another era, stained glass, the large arched window, the golden maybe-Tiffany fixture hanging and – Yes! Fairly empty nearing noon, so banquettes awaited them. Vivi slid into a plush rust-coloured banquette, the man she knew at this juncture only as the Surf Doctor (or Mister Legs) slid in beside her.

"Beautiful room," she said, as a waiter came over with menus.

"Yes," he said, looking at her. "Classic." He ran his hand on the banquette material. The banquette was elegant, the table round, the water arrived in a bespoke bottle with *Café Americain* on it in black sans serif. Attention had been paid. The serif, the accent. They drank flat water from the kind of glasses that, Vivi thought, in Barcelona Johnny would be holding to sip his cortado. The Surf Doc was holding his left hand on his thigh in a crabbed position, the way a person with hand pain might, hiding it. Or trying to.

Vivienne opened the menu to the cocktails. One, two, three, four, five, six, seven, eight, nine kinds of gin & tonics. Tanqueray, Damrak, Bloom, Aviation, ah Copperhead. Copperhead from Belgium, liquorice root and kaffir lime leaves. She ordered the Copperhead G & T and a club sandwich. He ordered the same.

"So, you're the Surf Doctor."

"Pretty catchy. Surfing saved my life. I was a mess."

"Are you a doctor? Medical?" The room was filling up, slowly. A woman by herself at the far window under the arch. Reading a paperback book, then looking at her phone, then looking out the window. A tall man – all the tall Netherlander men – by his lonesome, too, taking a non-curved padded seat looking their way, ordering coffee, which he was sipping, reading a hardcover book, then opening the free-to-patrons international *New York Times*. The sun, such a stranger in Amsterdam in November, was fully present outside the windows.

"Remedial." The room was as they said, beautiful, classic. In shades of burnished wood, a large space that felt tantalizingly intimate. Vivi scanned the room. Hell if it wasn't, sitting at the curved bar, the two cops, or who she had presumed to be cops, from the Vondelpark, at the terrorist scene, and when was that? It felt like a life from another movie. Was it even in this place, the Café Americain and the man in the van calling *Jew* after her . . .

The moustached cop turned as if to talk to his buddy, facing him from one of the high back bar chairs, yet Vivi felt he had done this as a none-too-subtle ploy to eyeball her. The concussion that the atomic shock wind had laid down on her system, punching her head, had layered the PTSD (their term) to an alertness, maybe an over-alertness in her. Was the Surf Doctor exchanging glances with the man she had dubbed Cop Numero Uno?

The club sandwiches arrived. Formidable. Three triangles of bread on each half. They worked on their sandwiches, which deconstructed them-selves as they were meant to, creating plate chaos and tasty leavings of egg, tomato, bacon, chicken, lettuce, toast. All the while, he wasn't looking at the room, he was looking at her. Hard to believe how little she knew him, then. He had an air about him of deep anticipation. Like a guy who knew that patience was a skill, an art even, something to *do* until you could *be* it. A guy who understood strategic silence. He was wearing the cracked brown leather jacket. He unzipped the jacket and opened it, flashing a paisley lining, in green, blue, yellow. The lining had a built-in pocket from which he pulled a large rectangular item wrapped in a length of pale yellow silk. He placed the wrapped object on the table, which the banquette cradled in a kind of public conversational cave for the two of them. He unwrapped the silk covering. Inside lay a copy of her new book: *A Soldier in the Desert.*

The silver and dark brown book cover sat on its bed of yellow silk, amber lit from the vaulted ceiling. The book of her photographs from Death Valley. From before, and after, and during the atomic bomb blast, a clandestine test by then president George W. Bush, code-named Divine Strake. After protests in Nevada, Utah and California, the government said the bomb was cancelled. It wasn't cancelled; it went ahead. Vivienne Pink was there with extemporaneous, contemporaneous photographic notes. Her synapses kept repeating the concussive qualities of the eternal present.

The built-in green ribbon bookmark was peeking out of the book. Vivienne looked at her own book the way you'd look at a long-ago lover you have fond and mixed-up fucked-up feelings about, but who is part of another brain music. The Surf Doctor had placed the green ribbon at a certain spot in the book, a moment he'd paused in her long-ago love affair in the atomic desert. Desert Noir on a sunny day. He delicately moved the ribbon marker.

He opened her book. It is thrilling when someone understands that this is what it all was for. For her, the photographs, her gallery shows, her war-witness displays, sure, but also: bound books of her pics. He smoothed the photo, as if by touch he could see the picture, using his fingertips as eyes, touching the exquisite paper, matte, as Vivienne had requested. The book was just out – he had bought a copy right away, then. *That* was sexy.

"This one, tell me about it," he said. He understood that every one of her photographs was, to her, a quote from a much longer story. He spoke to her the way you speak to the storyteller who will adorn your heart with a repeat telling, even the first time. Funny, how it works. People turn up in your life. Like moments with legs. There's a great Yiddish word for that: *bashert.* Destiny. You could call it good timing. Or simply, maybe, two people who had to get out of town the same day, two people who knew that looking at art has been proven to help you live longer. In the big low-lit room in Amsterdam Amber, they lengthened their lives, by immersing in the photographs that she had taken in extreme circumstances, piling trauma on trauma. The room shook in turbulence. She felt it. How can you fasten your seat belt in a banquette with a new haimisch stranger? Your putative basherter.

His right hand – Jesus, he had long fingers – caressing her pic of another man in end-of-the-year dusk in the high hotel room in the deep valley.

The photograph in the book: *December 26, 2006*. The gun on the table, the gun – yes – on the bedside table, the light from the bedside lamp shining on the hands of the man, Andy, as he lit a cigarette, the gun looking like it wanted him. Wanted him to touch it, take it, become one with it. Though the photograph said none of this explicitly. You wondered, looking at it, who this man was, where he was, what he would do with the gun or had done, was he alone? The trick of the intimate seemingly nonchalant photograph is that you forget there is a photographer. You look at the man, his slight bend to the cigarette, his private moment an essence, yet you do not know what the essence is, yet you wonder. The photographer erased herself, willingly, as her bold intention. The story was about what led you to the story, but the story was about the photo.

He turned the book around, moved it across the table to Vivi. He moved closer to her, slightly. Together they looked at her photograph of Andy the soldier.

"What was he to you?"

"It's in the book, the captions."

He accepted and rejected this at the same time. "Did he go?"

"To war?"

"Yes. No."

"Never?"

"Not that time. Not again. He didn't want to. By then, 2006, three years into the war in Iraq? By some counts, there were already eight *thousand* deserters from the American forces. He was thinking of going AWOL. He asked me to marry him."

His left eyebrow raised in interest. "Did you?"

"Marry him?"

"You wear a wedding ring." The tips of her fingers came up only to his knuckles.

Her, a silver wedding ring. Him, Mister Surf Doc, no ring.

"The soldier from Death Valley, marry him? Yes, no no; yes in a way, but no. I said yes but you know, can we get some –"

The stuff you don't want to touch dances in the broken spaces. He asked me to marry him, while he intended to marry someone else. He married her, and they live two blocks around the corner from me, on Manning.

The Surf Doctor had that sepulchral look in his eyes, again. A look that uncannily resembled hope, in the eyes of the damaged. A guy who might sing a great blues tune from the hatch of his own coffin inside the long black limousine. A guy she might be able to talk about the bleak side with. Was that the thing of Rembrandt this stranger had gestured at? The bride and groom looked toward hope, and it hurt so much to look at each other, there was so much love riding on it.

Vivi ran her hand, her open palm, on the photograph. It was a chemical spaceship. The image on the page moved you through the years to its one particulate moment. The stranger from the plane ran his hand down the page as she did. In the Café Americain in Amsterdam that November afternoon, there were layers of chemistry.

There was chemistry in the air: The chemistry between Vivienne and her camera, the molecules, the proteins, of ten years ago. The chemistry between her camera and the subject, Andy, his sparks, the dry desert air. There was the active physical chemistry of Vivienne making actual physical photographic prints in her darkroom. The chemical solitude of art labour. The red light, the hand strafes, the chemistry of light, dark, paper; the chemistry of desire, the chemical bath. How you bathe the image. She printed to make prints, also toward the book. The chemistry of all those chemistries aimed toward being a chemical invitation to a stranger to buy the book, to take a chance on it. And the touch of the purchaser on the page. Their fingerprints, their saliva.

He flipped to another photo. Badlands motel, room 15, Andy sitting outside. The chemistry between a man from long ago in her life sitting on a peeling metal chair outside a high elevation desert motel, and a man in this moment in a city below sea level, sitting on a banquette seat looking at that past man. Chemistry between two men who had never met. Art, the original time traveller. The chemistry of Vivienne's intention: throw your art out into the world and see where the combustion has landed.

They ate their gone-to-chaos club sandwiches. Sipped their clear juniper juice and spring fizz.

"Do you think he was using you?"

"In what way?"

Two interrogators have lunch.

"Was he using you to get to Canada? People do, don't you think?"

"I do think. I do, you know, *know.*" She could hear her own native belligerence, her moxie she'd had from a kid onwards, the sass Stella inherited, as if backtalk was passed down in the shadow genes of the city people. It could be a Darwinian survival thing, *mess with me at your own peril.* Also, it was fun. Fun, oh fun, remember fun in the metropolis? She'd had fun with comrades in war coverage was the hell of it. Peace could be a bit of a turd, a party-pooper. What had caused the flare in her? She knew. The presumption that he was edging toward explaining her own world to her. After all, her midtown downtown Toronto neighbourhood had been full of deserters and draft dodgers from the US's various conflicts, since the '60s. She breathed down, to breathe the moment back. Stay calm and think of night alleys. A good interrogator knows when to swerve. So swerve.

"You said 'maybe later on,'" she said, "you'd tell me your name. You gonna tell me?"

"Why so many questions?"

"You know my name, don't you?" She flipped to her book cover. Tapped her name, Vivienne Pink. "Reciprocate."

"Alex, Alexi. Alexi."

"From around here, or where?"

"Sometimes. Here. There."

"En passant?"

"Always."

"I like Alexi."

"Alexi works."

There was that eye again. The war eye, the lonely redoubt. Was it wave eye? The surfer's thing. Was it something else in the vitreous humour? He could be trained to focus, as she was. She was so used to observing people whose cynosure of their eyes was their phone, that she was feeling uncannily human with him. She could be a slithering mess of solitude sliming out of her carapace, an eye coming out of her shell. He looked at her, eye contact, yet he did not stare. That was an art. He had listening eyes, eyes like a rabbi, a spy, a detective.

Alexi said he had to use the facilities. He got up, there was a sign saying Toilet with an arrow to their left through the café past the bar. She watched him, as she had on the plane when he stood up, layering that image on this one: a tall international-looking man in jeans, short hair, a worn leather jacket, shoes to last half a lifetime. Architect, techie, spy. Mossad, CIA, CSIS, MI-whatever. Employed, then later on, private work. The art of a man who, though he was tall and terrifically good-looking by any measure, was somehow skilled at the art of fitting in, an ibis in camo.

As Alexi got to the doorway out of the café proper, a voice came over a loudspeaker, "Miss Fanny de Ville, paging Miss Fanny de Ville."

At just that moment, Alexi happened to look back at Vivienne. And she just happened to give him a shy wave. The man who had paged Fanny de Ville saw Vivienne Pink wave and salute. While Alexi was in the loo, the man approached Vivienne at the banquette. He was wearing a crossbody bag; he stopped at the banquette edge. "Mrs. Coma? The photographer?"

She nodded, wary. "That's right."

He sat down at the tufted edge of the banquette. Oh boy, Vivi thought. We've got a live one here. The capacious room noticed nothing. The stranger was tapping her forearm.

"Miss De Ville, I am honoured. *Montana Cowboys* changed my life." He took her hand and kissed it. Oh Jesus, she thought. "To imagine I am here with photographer Miss Fanny de Ville. A pleasure unexpected in one's life, to be sure."

"Thank you very much," she said. "But I'm so sorry, that isn't one of my books." Canadian to the core, she was apologizing to a stranger who had sat down uninvited at her table. She bit into a crust. "Alas, the cowboy photos, that's someone else."

"Yes, yes, of course. Staying incognito. My Fanny, such an honour."

Leaning over the table, reaching to her plate, the stranger played with the remains of her club sandwich. He hijacked the last crunchy bit of bacon. Then he helped himself to the last bit of crust Vivi always left to the end.

Vivienne Pink said, "I am so extremely sorry but you've made a mistake. I am not Fanny de Ville."

She eyeballed the room, diners going about their day. The lanky guy with the international paper had a hardcover book open, the lone woman by the window had been replaced by a lone man. A posy of business guys by the side windows were heads tipped forward over a diagram.

Now the guy goes and takes a random shred of chicken from her plate, snarfs it. Tilts his head to indicate: not bad. The moustached man at the bar – her putative policeman – turned around again, gave her an "Are you alright?" look, or was that more eye tricks . . .

"Yes, you are."

"No, I am not your Fanny."

"You are and you know you are. Fanny, don't do this to me."

He had those conspiracy eyes. The eyes that said, "Don't try and trick me, I added one plus one, and I got eleven. I see what's you're up to."

The intruder waved at the waiter. Vivi scooched along the leather padding of the banquette to get away from him. "Café solo," he said to the waiter. "Let me explain it to you," he said, turning back to Vivi.

Alexi returned to the table, surveying the scenario as the waiter brought a café solo to the stranger. "Everything okay?" Alexi asked. Vivi felt the extreme restraint with which he absorbed the scene. He had to be a cop himself, or something like it, a paramedic or a medic in war.

The stranger, having made himself at home, as in *su casa es mi casa*, made a magnanimous gesture with his hand, saying to Alexi, "Why not join us?"

Us! Sipping his coffee, unearthing the chocolate from its rippled wrapping, licking his fingers, rubbing his eyes.

Alexi sat down, keeping the moment calm.

But he sat close to the stranger, forcing the guy to scooch along so he was wedged in, the human bacon-lettuce-and-tomato between Vivi and Alexi. Very fine move, Vivi thought.

"Ah," said the stranger in his rust-coloured pants and his shapeless coat in deep blue. His old Chelsea boots in a sandy hue. He offered his hand for Alexi to shake; the hand was greased with mayo, dribbled with tomato seeds. "Mister Johnny Coma, I am most honoured, may I say."

Alexi shook the hand. Vivi noticed it was smooth, uncalloused, with bitten nails.

So the guy says to Alexi, "Yes, we met briefly at the portal. Your wife, Miss Fanny, was just saying how she –"

Alexi's left eyebrow jolted slightly at the word *wife*.

"How she –" Vivienne said, conversationally trapped into referring to herself in the third person. "How she – How I am *not* Miss Fanny f–" pause "de Ville."

"Oh boy, what a handful, eh?" the guy said to Alexi, who returned no companionable look. The stranger shifted toward Alexi; Alexi shifted toward the restaurant space, his long legs out where waiters were walking and where at the bar, Vivi noticed, that guy she made as maybe the cop she'd seen at the Vondelpark terror van scene was himself watching the odd playlet in the tufted banquette. He had smiled when the stranger began to graze at her plate.

"I don't know why you deny it," the stranger said, shifting back to Vivienne. "Look, let me explain it to you. It's very logical. You are married to Johnny Coma, right?"

"Right," she said.

"Mister Coma, here, is your husband, right?"

"Go on," she said.

He put his hand on the table, palm down. He pushed her plate aside, sipped his coffee, began the seminar.

Thumb: "You are married to Johnny Coma."

Index finger: "Johnny Coma's wife is Fanny de Ville."

Middle finger: "Voila!" With a flourish, "Madame, QED, you *are* Fanny de Ville!"

"I am Vivienne Pink."

"*Montana Cowboys*. Miss De Ville, it changed my life. The hats!" His pinkie finger in the air. He moved her plate back, ran his finger along the tomato seeds, licked his pinkie.

He waggled the pinkie like a righteous epilogue. "I am *extremely* honoured, ladies and gentlemen, to be in the company today of Miss Fanny de Ville *and* Mister Johnny Coma." A nod in Alexi's direction, as if to suggest a male bonding over equations.

Alexi was having none of it. His silence was brutal.

Making a last stand for sanity, Vivi said, "My name is Vivienne Pink. I've never been to Montana."

Undeterred, the stranger said to Alexi, "And you, Mister Johnny Coma, how long have you been enamoured with the marvellous Miss De Ville?"

"It's been a lot of years," Alexi said. "Now I'm sure you won't mind if me and the missus get on with our personal time together." Vivi smiled. How Alexi had said "the missus" like a first secret joke between them. He had said it slightly awkwardly, something mildly sideways about the *iss* on *missus*.

A woman rolled a stroller in, sat down near the lone man paging the hardcover book.

"The missus. Of course." The stranger rested his longish dull-brown hair on the back of the rust banquette. He hadn't shaved in a couple days; Vivi could see the stubble way too closely for comfort. Him saying "the missus" back to Alexi as a mirror person might, adopting someone else's fun lingo.

Vivi and Alexi were looking at each other, as if to say this is already legend in our stories of way back when. Alexi got up to let the stranger leave. He didn't, though, leave the premises. He went, sat down at the bar, a couple seats away from that dead-eye all-night cop with the moustache and his more doughy-faced gentle-looking compadre. She glimpsed the moustachioed one in the bar mirror giving the stranger the once-over.

Vivi noticed something she hadn't noticed before. In addition to that crossbody bag, the stranger had brought in one of those hard silver or aluminum briefcases. It was on the floor, beside his bar stool. Did he have it with him when he sat at their banquette? Was it someone else's, left there by mistake?

Or, she thought, getting heart palpitations, was it a bomb?

White rental vans made her queasy; silver briefcases made her think of bombs.

The moustachioed cop got up, walked past where the stranger in the Café Americain was sitting, dipping his chin to observe the silver case. So, Vivienne Pink thought, I'm not the only over-watchful one. She loved Amsterdam for many reasons, one of them was the offhand mix of over-alertness and informality you felt inside and outside, blunt yet accepting.

As for Alexi, he had said nothing to correct the stranger. After the guy departed, Alexi kissed Vivi's hand. "Apparently I am your husband. Would you call me Johnny?"

He was playing, yet she liked the feel of his lips.

"Johnny," she said. "But, darling, when did we get married?" Playing the scene.

"I think it was on the plane," he said.

"What would I be doing marrying you on a plane?"

"We were up in the air."

Vivi thinking, Charisma doesn't know it's charismatic, is the thing. True charisma works very hard to stay low, which, damn his tidal eyes, makes it more magnetic.

"Did we walk down the aisle?" she asked.

"We did," he replied.

She closed the book. He opened it to the title page. He tied the yellow length of silk around his neck. He took out a Montblanc pen. He offered the pen to her. She smoothed the page. Above the book title, *A Soldier in the Desert,* she signed, *To my husband, Alexi. Con amor.*

She didn't know why she wrote *Con amor.* Blame it on the G & T. Blame it on the G & T, the PTSD. Acronyms were my alibi.

He slid out of the banquette.

"Oh. Are you done? Where are you going?"

"To Barcelona."

"Finish your coffee?"

"I have a plane."

"We could have dessert."

"I have a five forty-five to catch."

"You could catch me."

Blame it on the stranger. Blame it on the creep. Blame it on Miss Fanny de Ville and *Montana Cowboys*. Blame it on the tufted banquette. Your honour, the banquette made me say it.

Alexi and Vivienne walked across the bridge; he took her hand. She was okay with that for a few seconds. Then her carapace tightened around her. Her lung lesions tightened her alveoli; she was having trouble breathing. To Stadhouderskade to Tesselschadestraat to Roemer Visscherstraat, the Owl. The hotel sat deadpan as a Vermeer. Deadpan as a little street.

Nobody knows anything about love.

THEY WENT UP in the elevator-built-for-two together, turned right, walked about ten steps to a stub of a hallway, where the door to her room was straight ahead. And the door to his at an angle, the two rooms by coincidence hidden from the main hallway.

Vivi drew a bath, running the water into the massively large tub, built for Dutch giants. A knock at the door. She came to the door naked, put her ear against the door. "*Digame,*" she said, reverting to Spanish. "It's me," he said. "Me who?" she asked, though she recognized Alexi's voice. "Can I come in?" he asked. She didn't answer, went to the bathroom, turned off the faucet running hot water. Back to the door. "Hang on a sec." She put her clothes back on, unhitched the chain from the door, opened it and of course there he was: Alexi, whom she'd met – what was it – not days, but hours ago.

"*Pase adelante,*" she said, with a hand gesture to come on ahead.

He nodded and entered her bedroom. The thing about a modest hotel room is that, though it becomes your workroom, think room, pack unpack room, it is essentially always your bedroom, really. The late-day light of an Amsterdam afternoon in November gave a low gloom through the windows overlooking the garden.

Alexi was carrying a creased brown paper bag.

"What's up?" Vivi said.

"I'd like to show you something."

"Sure." She wasn't really sure, but sure, why not.

He sat down on the edge of the bed, set the paper bag down. It flopped over. Something heavy was inside. He reached into the bag, pulled out what looked like one of those real old-school video viewers, metal, a flat clamshell structure.

"Wow," she said. "I haven't seen one of those since I don't know when."

"Exactly," he said.

She noticed that *exactly*, because *exactly* was one of her dad's commonplace "oh that's an Izzy word" words.

"You," Vivi said to Alexi, "kind of more struck me as the kind of guy who would . . . "

"Be up to date?"

"Exactly." Smiling. He smiled back. Clicked a switch on the side of the DVD player. An image, blurry, started moving on the small screen. "Whoa," she said, "that's so degraded. Whoever took that didn't take good care of it, it's like colour pics, the colour eats itself like a Polaroid maggot."

Alexi kissed her on the cheek, tilted his head to the right, picked up the image player, sat on the bed, against the headboard, gestured for her to join him. A last flash of rare sun hit the glass. He got up, pulled the blackout curtains across the windows.

"Do me a favour. I can be quite the pest. I might be the nuisance you don't want here but you could thank me later for my kind of trouble. Look at this, Vivienne."

"And you are showing me this because you – ?" They were thigh to thigh on the bed.

He paused the moving image. He tapped a face frozen on the screen. "That's you."

"Like hell it is."

"Hang on." He pressed FF. Now the image was clear. Well, almost. Clear enough that Vivienne Pink was getting a creepy feeling in her lower intestine. The creepy feeling jumped to her shoulders. The image: a room, people knees touching at tables. Three and four and six to a tiny round table. A bar, a guy behind the bar, a turntable on the bar, two turntables, the guy moving the vinyl with the edge of his hands, one hand on each turntable, his gaze into the distance, but no, he too, like Alexi a minute ago, had his head tilted to the right. So that his left ear was up, which meant he knew that the left ear hears the emotions, the feeling, some smart DJ, that.

Alexi was silent. He was looking at the screen, at her looking at the screen, back and forth. A few of the people got up, danced in a languid drunk manner. Drunk, stoned, arms hanging loose. No jumping. Not a pogo stick situation. Cigarettes being lit by experienced smokers. A guy talking to a woman, the guy has his cig stuck to his lower lip as he talks. The ash falling just shy of his beer.

Vivi grabbed the device, rested it on her knees. The image jumped: a hallway. Ordinary looking business building hallway, travel agency, hair salon, jewellery to the upper-class type places. She'd seen plenty of them in Central American countries where the petite elite lived in discrete suburbs, and what would be shops on the street in the more *popular* areas were shops in apartment buildings. You usually got your money – American dollars, even if you were Canadian – changed at one of those nondescript travel agencies. The image tracked that hallway, stopped at a door with no number on it, no signage for a business or anything. A hand in close-up knocked on the door. An anywhere door in an anywhere hallway.

The door opened.

The room from a second ago on the screen. The room of the stoned, the room of the drunk, the room of the two-turntable DJ. That guy with the cig had a cig burning almost to his lip. Shit! She knew that room. It was out of her past.

Alexi was looking at her.

He pressed FF again. The back of a woman with long wavy hair halfway down her back leaning in to the DJ as he kept mixing up the vinyl. The DJ rocked back, laughing. The woman leaned in further. Short-sleeved shirt, epaulettes, yeah degraded image, still you could see that the shirt was a shade of olive green, slacks, beige. The woman with the long wavy hair turned around to survey the room, her back against the bar, her head moving slowly, slightly, a fast zoom to her face – in the dim light of the night bar, her eyes were dilated. Oh come on, Vivienne thought. The woman in the video is me, me in a war bar, me in Guatemala, me with hair in the days of the guerrillas and the death squads.

"You took this?"

"I didn't say anything," he said.

"But you took this."

"You know where it is?"

"Don't be stupid. Of course I know where it is." She tapped the screen, which Alexi had paused. "That's the German's, circa summer of 1980. That's Guatemala when the military was enacting genocide on their own people. That is a clandestine bar during a military massacre era." The creepy feeling was, despite her pro calm, inside her neck, inside her glass jaw, inside that part of her jaw where there was, in fact, a break in the bone. "Where did you get this?"

"Look at it."

Her in her young prime, head leaning in to talk to – what was his name again – oh my God, that Brit called Chris. The operator who had all the gen on which planes in the sky over Guatemala – none of which officially existed or were flying – were flying as British or flying as American, to try and knock out the resistance, the uprising, the guerrillas, as the Indigenous population outside the city was being murdered. Chris who liked, who was it? Yeah, Harold Melvin & the Blue Notes. The night in July 1980 in the genocide when Chris of MI6 asked the German at the turntable to kindly play, one more time, "If You Don't Know Me By Now." Vivienne Pink, among the regulars who weren't there, where they were, and did not see what they saw, and did not photograph what they had photographic film negatives of, to this day, undeveloped, like powder keg ghost images, filed in glassine envelopes.

"Think back," Alexi said.

She got up from the bed, agitated. "You think back."

"C'mere. One more moment." He put both arms out. Damn the gods and their gifts of charisma.

"Okay but only a mo."

He FF'd again. More shots of the woman with the long wavy hair – yeah, it was her, her hair then. A baldie with a smooth hairless kopf sat in an Amsterdam hotel bedroom watching her younger self, the photojournalist, in the bar everybody knew about which never existed. The real story of a war cannot be found in any research. The real story is always some kind of mute, a hood on its head, shackled to a chair in a closet. Okay, her, at one of the tiny round tables with another woman. The woman laughed. A big wide-open laugh, her arms open, too. It was X, the American reporter she knew not well but companionably, collegially, in the days when the band of women covering war was a slim sisterhood of conflict journalists. *The Furry Freaks.* Shit on a skewer, how things hide in your cranium, then pop up like testifying witnesses. There were three of them, Vivi, X and Y who used to call themselves the Furry Freaks, one in radio, one in print, one in still photography.

There they were, laughing, drinking, carrying on, as if they'd live forever. X was killed at a press conference four years later, at La Penca on the Nicaraguan-Costa Rican border, when a terrorist posing as a Danish photo-journalist came by boat with the rest of them up the San Carlos River, with a silver case in which he had placed a bomb. Intending to kill the journalists who had come to hear what Contra leader Edén Pastora, "Comandante Cero," had to say. Carnage ensued, reporters, camera people dead, maimed, wounded. After La Penca 1984, Vivi and her colleagues knew it was unsafe to assume a press briefing was ever a safe place.

But hell and paranoia. What was this Alexi, with his charisma eyes and his fingers so deft on the old-school viewer, doing with moving images of her former self at a war bar in Guatemala City in 1980? The image moved: the mayor of G City, who changed houses every night, so the death squads out to murder the mayor were never quite sure what bed to shoot at in what house when they came looking for him.

In the video, the mayor was talking to the DJ at the bar. An envelope in the mayor's hand moved across the turntable area.

That's right, Vivi remembered. The DJ was the owner, "the German," who was actually Swiss. One night he played the group Japan's "I Second That Emotion" on the turntable while showing Wim Wenders's *Wings of Desire* on a wall of the bar. The guerrilla war in Guatemala was burned into her mind in black and white.

With Alexi, her lungs opened, the bronchial tree felt oxygen, paradoxically.

"How did you get this? Have you been following me?"

He didn't answer.

"What's your real name?" she said.

"I told you. Alexi."

"No, it isn't." Vivienne Pink had no reason to doubt him, she was testing him.

It was moving too fast at just the right speed.

8

XOCOLATA BOOM BOOM

JOHNNY COMA LIKED to get up in the dark, in the chewing of mice, with no one to judge him and no false constructs of cheer. In the dark, coffee was a mystery companion. He liked to make a quick pour-through joe in a muslin sock and sit like a lonely barista and sketch the curves of the coffee glass. He liked to warm-down and warm-up using his hand to build the coordination of his wrist bone, his finger bones, his scabbed beaten-up knuckles. He liked to go out and about when the city parties were treed in the small quarters and it was dark in the walled parts and he could sit on a bench in the public square, in the nautical twilight. He liked it in the rain. The rain made the city smaller.

He liked to go to the bench in the square because his pal Sancho was going to be there. Johnny liked to stay in his pyjamas and put a light wind-breaker on top and tie up his pale espadrilles in that nice eau de Nil, tie the green ribbons round his ankles and go down on in the elevator, in the tomb for one, with a mirror.

In the elevator mirror, he saw a bald guy with hound dog eyes, deep bruised carry-on bags under his pale baby blues.

Exit the building into the high-walled alley; exit the alley into the wider local world. Walk the one hundred steps or so to the Pla de Palau. The little plaza. Make the ritual journey from roof bed to street bench.

In the dark, he could see Sancho smoking a cigarette, inhaling the red dot, blowing a bit of smoke around his ragged hair, his line-etched face.

"Milord, is it you?" Sancho got up, as Johnny walked closer. Sancho took Johnny's hands in his, bowing his head. "My liege, the honour is yours. Indeed. Sit."

He waved toward a bench, their daily bench across from the international news kiosk, still closed, its aluminum eyelids lowered. Sancho sat down, patted a wet newspaper beside him, dated Dienstag, November 8, 2016. "Sit. Sit. Mind the face." The paper was from Germany, the *Hamburger Morgenpost*. The face was the face of American presidential candidate Donald Trump. The headline, in orange, said "Bitte nicht den Horror-Clown!" Please not the horror clown! The photograph was in black and white. Trump in a ghostly bleach, his chin up in arrogance, his aging neck wattles tucked tight into his white shirt collar, his hair a dry white nest.

Johnny Coma sat down on the wet ghost face. "Oh man you know, I totally forgot what with the flight and all and what time is it? I'm still over the Atlantic. Am I here yet?"

Sancho took Johnny's left hand, pulled the fingers one by one, as if he were a doctor. "Here and counting, my liege."

Johnny looked at his own hands as if they were items unconnected to him, though he carried his writerly intelligence in them. Thumb music. Finger bone paragraphing. His torn, messed up hands had enough flaws to be hanging cuticle sheet music.

The Mediterranean sky was lemon and citron and pink and so humid. That vibe of wide *avenidas* lined with tall palm trees, dotted with ancient stone warrens where the puddles never dried under pink, lemon, red, yellow high walls of drying laundry.

Sancho began to air-type. Pinkies aloft. Air carriage return. "Novel today, novel now! The story must out in a rush!"

"Easy, friend."

"Wrong! I am on fire! I am burning up. It's on! I am going there!" Hurling invisible pages out of the invisible machine, as if too hot to handle.

Johnny rubbed his hand on Sancho's holey tweed sleeve. "What brought you to this impasse that you want, then, to tell us your story?"

Sancho took Johnny's hands in his, adjusted his body to half face him. "I wanted – Well, the truth is, I'd like to work again. I'd like to be a pal in an office like it used to be. Well, not office. I was the front desk man. I liked being around *folk*. The rainfolk. I liked the fog of San Francisco in the morning before it burned away the bridge and the bay. I liked hanging out on the sidewalk in the old Tenderloin, scraping together enough dinero to get by. I didn't mind so much living in the old hotel, the Shawmut, corner of Leavenworth and O'Farrell, not corner, actually, O'Farrell between Leavenworth and Jones. I liked the hills, hilly cities suit me, strong thighs, strong calves."

He horked up a throat ball of pure *z*'s and *x*'s. Spat it on the plaza concrete.

"Moderate days, eking along. Then –" gesturing with his right hand a swooping bird or plane "– then comes the invasion. Not Tiananmen tanks, no. No tanks, more like the invasion of the billionaires in T-shirts. The stealth operation of the coup of the real estate clipboards."

Agitated, Sancho let go of Johnny's hand, stood up from the bench.

"The Theatre of the Cruel; mobs óf demolition crackerjacks. Once you see the clipboards, the jackhammers can't be far behind. Hombre, they were gentrifying my *mind!*"

"Sounds like five hundred words, to me."

Johnny pulled out his notebook, trying to put down some of the choice things that Sancho had said. Johnny Coma knew that a novelist was more like a mix of a crime scene detective and a hieroglyphic chicken-scratching steno than any glamour guy the dreamy idle might imagine. He chuckled. "In time, Sancho, you will find that writing a book is like aging, it happens slowly, then all at once."

"But, friend, when will the all-at-once arrive?"

The two silhouettes sat in the public square as the night taxis rode with their golden amber headlights through the coastal grid. That November of '16 it was mild in Barcelona, in its young democracy. The rule of Fascism ended only in 1975.

Spanish democracy, only forty-one years old.

THE RAIN WAS soft, the first bells from the basilica had not yet tolled, so it was still before seven. Sancho horked up more laughter phlegm. "Well then, shall we sail to green extinction together, my friend?" The windows in the buildings around the public square had their eyes covered in the signature dark green blinds of Barcelona, draped down over the signature iron railings of the balconies.

"Before the planet is gone, my friend, let us sail out to the waters of elsewhere. Let us take our scars out to the wounded water. Me, I used to be a salt at home in the far horizons. Lost in the sick, I didn't know how to be on land." He left the invisible keyboard, held Johnny's real hands. "I am one wounded salt, amigo. I, too, dragged the planet through the streets. I treated Earth like a mutt I kicked around the streets. Shall we sail?" He patted Johnny's bald head. "A requiem sail, a quest to the water mind we lost, perchance . . . Oh yet once upon a time by melting ice when we bivouacked in dank camps . . . Where was I? Man, don't you have a date with destiny down at the beach, my dear Coma?"

"I do."

"What then is keeping you?"

Johnny got up, bowed – he had no idea why – and wandered off into the stone warrens. Sancho hollered after him that he had a sailing ship on his to-do list.

Cob and swan, newt and eft, roe and ova, things seen, things yet to be discovered, the extinct and nearly gone for food and tinct. The ocean! The glamour of the seventh wave, the lure of the dark energy matter.

AFTER DAWN BROKE above the nautical precincts, Johnny Coma walked like a small royal relinquishing power to the sea. Exiting the stone walls to enter the wider avenues and the eastern light, to cross into the entirely distinct neighbourhood of Barceloneta, where a body of light shimmered, and that body was the Mediterranean, and that light was water.

The water backlit a solitary man and his dog. The water backlit a woman and her bicycle, perched at the water's edge. Through the spokes of the bicycle wheels the light shone a shadow, and humanity was shadow lit, and

Johnny walked the mostly empty seaside promenade to his regular café. Time the trickster had made it coming on to eleven, as he walked past the string of beaches.

Walking past Barceloneta beach, past San Miguel beach, to the beach known as San Sebastián and his daily beach café, El Petit Far – The Little Lighthouse. Barcelona, dear heart: not a morning lark.

Why, even George Orwell during the Spanish Civil War grumped to wakefulness in bombed-out buildings in Barcelona, wanting only, as he put it, a shower and a shave. And could he get it early in Barce? Uh-uh. No way. As Orwell famously kvetched in *Homage to Catalonia*, he had to wake up, sleeping rough, hiding from the authorities, only to drum his combatant-witness fingers until 9:00 a.m. to get some frigging caffeine. Nineteen thirty-seven.

Twenty sixteen: same. Johnny's routine café on the beach opened at ten thirty in the morning. Officially. But, really, realistically, near eleven.

GRIEF IS FERAL; grief has fur. Grief lumbers large; grief is a bear with feathers. Grief howls by the seashore. He had held his face together with paper clips, caffeine and a long run of OxyContin. The math of pain pills, 10s, 20s, 40s, 80s.

Stella, daughter, I pray for a sighting.

The sea was grumpy. Not managing its anger at all. Grey, energetic in storm mien. No cheer, just the magnificent water walls of grey-green, for surfing. The first of the storm surfers were paddling out into the chance to fight and ride down into the breaks past reef injury or desolation scars.

The Escola de Surf, the Surf School, was across the seaside promenade from the El Petit Far. A couple surfers in bare feet ran up with their boards under their arms. Storm calling! Johnny wondered if long-time surfers were more magnetically tuned than the rest of us. Could be. He sketched a bunch of surfboards with bodies paddling.

The café was a good luck spot. Routine, rain, superstition. The writer's psychic tool kit. Routine is all about hope.

Johnny Coma sat down on an aluminum chair with rattan webbing. The tables and chairs sat on boards over the sand. The usual blue cushions not in evidence due to all the rain. The top of the square aluminum table showed forensic raindrops. Ali, his regular waiter, placed his usual cortado on the table. To live like a local, go to the same place every day. Become part of the paying furniture.

The sea was trying to make up its mind between green and green-grey and grey-green and all grey. You could feel the ozone, the mighty ozone. You could feel the magnetism of the storm approaching. You could feel the birds' wings getting excitable. Johnny Coma in his quest like a nutter or a knight in the late morning.

Same beach, same café, same table, different sky, different sea, same kind of notebook, same kind of pencil. Kinesis and caffeine.

He took a fresh Moleskine notebook out of his jacket pocket. It could be good luck. He fished his trusty Palomino Blackwing 602 pencil out of his other pocket. He began:

San Sebastián Beach, Barceloneta, El Petit Far Café, 10:51 a.m.
Dear Stellita,

He stopped. He put the Palomino Blackwing 602 pencil behind his ear, like a carpenter of mornings. He rested his eyes, looked at the water, the energetic waves. A couple, no, three surfers were paddling out into the low foam.

Maybe he shouldn't use the diminutive, when he wrote Stella. The curves of the city were bleached white on the other side of the water. He loved the grand Mediterranean expanse. He loved the empty season.

The woolly clouds were moving fast. A golden retriever was leading his mistress up onto the graffitied rocks.

Johnny thought, Maybe *Dear Stella*, would be better. Maybe she'd like it better without that *ita*. Who could say?

Stella could.

He might have to go home and have a nap about it. No need to rush it. He'd had writer's block since Don Quixote in metal mask and knee greaves fought the Knight of the White Moon, here on this sand. Quixote himself, in Barcelona, was knocked asunder on his horse Rocinante right here at this shoreline.

No. He felt in his bones *Stellita* was the word. First thought, best thought.

He took his grey Palomino Blackwing 602 from behind his ear, and he wrote:

Dear Stellita,

They say the coral used to be coral, and now the coral is all bleached. But you never know, new coral forests might bloom on the way to the bottom of the ocean in the green and empty spaces before we reach the final deeps. The sea can't die, Stella, querida Stellita, I have to meet you at the shoreline. I'm thinking we might meet, sure, where the air is gone, and in the watery verde we'll swim around, in the twilight of the mesophotic.

When we meet, all those lost MIA words might swim back on home to me.

My seabird, my shorebird on the shore, this tidal interstice where the moon and destruction are all connected. When the tides pull out from the sand, and the little stars of foam sit there for one moment. I could peck along the sand, look for bone fragments of you.

If you were here, my Stellita, I could go out at night and paint the stars and bring them all on home, to you. But you're gone, so I will have to do it anyway.

Love, Dad

The page had that nice cream shade, had that nice drag on the side of his hand when he wrote, and it was perforated. He tore the letter from the notebook. He turned his head toward the open-air stand at the other side of the promenade where Ali was leaning on the bar. Johnny nodded. Ali came over in a Barceloneta minute, with a freshly kissed cortado, a croissant – *un cornet*, Ali said, in Catalan – and an empty jar with a lid on it. Johnny nodded again.

He sipped a sip of his coffee, tore a piece of cornet and stuffed it in his mouth. He loosened the lid of the jar, folded the letter to Stella Stellita, put the letter inside the jar, tightened the jar lid. He unzipped his secret jacket pocket with the pre-addressed labels in a roll. He tore one off, it read STELLA ATLANTIS. He peeled the waxy paper from the back of the label and placed the label on the jar. Smoothed it. Then Johnny Coma, writer, walked from the wooden boards of the beach café onto the sand to the shore, to send his new writing to the water.

Where might his letter to Stella wash up? On the Mediterranean in Gaza or Tel Aviv or Beirut or Benghazi? On Tripoli, Latakia, Algiers or the salt harvesters' island of Ibiza? Or might the bottle go to the bottom with the hearts of the drowned?

Johnny knelt down by the water. A surfer came running past in a slick black bodysuit. *"Señorita,"* he said, *"se puede?"* He held the jar out to her. *"Quiero enviar una carta,"* he said. She laughed and got it. I want to send a letter. *"Enviar no par avion, no correo aereo, pero par el mar."* I don't want to send it by airmail, I want to send it by sea.

"Vale," the surfer said. *"Cómo no."* Taking the jar, walking into the water with a surfboard and a letter.

He watched her paddle out with one arm, the other one, yes, paddling with the jar in her right hand, dipping it in the water as she went. When the big wave came, and she joined the three others riding it, the surfer hurled the jar over her shoulder, like a bridal bouquet.

JOHNNY FELT HIMSELF slipping into the limbo slipstreams of his own cognition. He walked in sandy shoes back to his table, sipped the tag foam end of his cortado. He liked how the pages of his notebook were wavy due to the high humidity, how the notebook began the voyage over the Atlantic thin, and a couple weeks later it was fatter, full of Barcelona rainy days.

He sketched the glass. An open mouth, no waist, prominent ridges down the torso. He fished out of his windbreaker pocket his triangular pencil sharpener, and he twisted the Palomino Blackwing 602 in the hole over and over, and out came ruffled sails with gunmetal trim.

Johnny arranged the sails in a spiral with the silver trim on the edges. Yes. The pencil shavings, those tiny sails, made the shape of a sea creature, an ammonite perhaps. He outlined the ammonite in pencil, drew the lines of the sea creature's shell. The water pushed, pulled at the shore as a few more surfers in wetsuits paddled out into the silver waves.

Johnny sipped his coffee. He wondered if Miguel de Cervantes, during his writing sojourn in Barcelona, had come down to this very beach for the sight of the sea up close. A late morning in the creative empty, with sea phantoms. And maybe it had been this very view off Playa San Sebastián by the rocky curve, the thrilling vista of Barcelona's roll call of beaches down the green-grey Mediterranean that began to play ghost music in Cervantes's head. It could have been. Spoors in Cervantes's brain could have taken shape, becoming real in his hand as he created the scene in the Second Part of *Don Quixote* where Quixote gets on a horse to duel the Knight of the White Moon. Right here. Quixote in Catalonia. How many waves had come and gone in the four hundred years since Quixote messed up on the shores of the Mediterranean, and yet still there were waves, writers messing up, adrenaline, coffee?

Why not commune with the eyes of the dead?

Miguel de Cervantes sitting on the shoreline, looking out to the sea: navy man, war vet who lost the use of his left arm at age twenty-four. Captured by pirates, sat in an Algiers prison for years, became a tax collector, got thrown back in prison for tax fraud. Invented the modern novel (while in debtor's prison). Called it *The Ingenious Gentleman Don Quixote of La Mancha* in 1605. Our beloved *Don Quixote*.

Why not try and walk on the sea dust of the ancestors? I'm not getting any younger, Johnny Coma thought, and neither was Cervantes, when he came to Barcelona after the First Part of *Don Quixote* was published, wrote the Second Part, got it published, dropped dead the next year.

Johnny pushed back his chair, walked five seconds to the shoreline. He let the low water caress his espadrilles in cotton eau de Nil. The pale Nile-green fabric soaked darker. The rope soles of the espadrilles from the esparto plant, and Johnny's head was resplendent with throbbing.

A man and a woman dressed in matching red blazers walked along the beach from the W Hotel off to Johnny's right, the high-up landmark built like a glass sail. Conference folk, Johnny figured. They sat down at a nearby table. Johnny drew near. He had Cervantes on the brain. Yeah, Quixote was Quixote, but the real guy on a quest was the writer who invented him. The real fool was the scribbler, who – yes! Johnny thought, closing in on the red blazers' table – who wanted to court and to save literature. Who loved words enough to be a fool for love. No thirty-day writing misdemeanour for Cervantes, no way. A full-out stone-cold felony of passion. Premeditated, tool kit at the ready, a heist of hidden syllabic treasure. Pick the pocket of the universe while moonlight wasn't looking.

Yeah. In or out?

In: Crazy like Cervantes. Tilting at syllables.

Johnny Coma took out his Moleskine notebook and began to sketch the woman and man in their conference red blazers. Ah, they each had a button on their lapel with the letters *IP* and a line through the *IP*. Intellectual Property – say nothing out loud. They could be techies, start-up people, maybe high-level eyes-only contractors out of their blending-in duds of jeans and a tee and into the costumes of keynote speakers, seminar givers.

His notebook in his left hand, sketching with his right, Johnny Coma, writer, intruder on the sand. The man was tall, long legs stretched out in good ochre brogues. The woman wore high heels in red.

Mister Ochre Brogues snapped his fingers. *"Dos cafés con leche."*

Amused, Johnny drew closer. Mister Ochre Brogues had watery blue eyes with a milky film. Short groomed hair. The woman's eyes were hazel, her hair pulled back in a ponytail.

Standing at the edge of their table, Johnny said, *"¿Quieres, tal vez, un café capricho?"*

What? Johnny was startled by the sounds coming out of his own mouth. He was acting the role Mister Brogues had selected for him: a waiter on the boards at the beach. Talk about limbo slipstreams. Johnny's head was cycling through the centuries.

"Para comer?" he said to the couple – Anything to eat? – while sketching one of the woman's high heels.

"Tenemos berberechos," he added. Why was he saying, "We have barnacles"? El Petit Far didn't have barnacles. The sign right there across the promenade at the free-standing hut read: Café. *Sucs Naturals.* Halal. Eco. *Cerveza.*

The man and the woman shook their heads no.

"Ah," Johnny said, fully assuming the waiter role. While Ali at the actual food prep stand was leaning on the counter, watching. "*Café Capricho.* Very fine. Or perhaps an aperitif to start? *Aperitif de asno.*"

He heard himself talking mangled Spanish, translated, realizing that as the waiter in this performance, he had offered them a donkey aperitif.

"A bitter donkey, *especialidad de casa?*"

If he wasn't nuts, he was doing a damn good imitation.

"*¿Un aguafuerte?*" he said to them, cupping his hand to show a shot glass, jerking his head back.

Despite no coffee, tall Mister Brogues was awake enough to realize what Johnny had said. A shot of etching.

Johnny felt dizzy. He sat down in an empty chair at the couple's table.

"I was trying to talk to my daughter, you see. She's dead but don't let that bother you. With the dead you can float." He leaned back, did a backstroke brushing the aluminum arms of the chair. "I'll win the mink but then I'll sink." He leaned in, his elbows on the wet table. "You see, here is the thing. The thing here is, I forgot."

He put his head in his arms. He felt wings grow on his body. The face of a weird bird grew between the wings. Creepy beaked creatures lurked at his back. Jet lag and loss were melting into one hot body mess cooking his balance.

He lifted his head. He tore the sketch of Mister Brogues from his notebook, slid it across the table. Did the same with a sketch of Ms. Red Heels. "Milord. Milady."

The man slid back a five-euro paper bill. Five euros, about seven bucks Canadian. At the normal 10 per cent of the cover price of his books he got as a royalty, he'd have to sell three copies of his bestseller, *Night Street*, to get seven dollars.

He was a five-euro millionaire.

"I thank you, the David Bowie T-shirt of my dead daughter thanks you, the third draft of my crappy so-called next novel says a deep and sincerely felt gracias, the bald head of my estranged wife thanks you and, by the way," he said, "did I ever tell you that my wife supports us? It's her house, you know, just by way of if you run into anybody who's asking."

Ms. Heels in her red blazer was unscrewing the heel of her red shoe, replacing a battery in it.

Johnny saw the words come out of his mouth. "Vivi yeah. She was inhaling the detritus of napalm, got some good pics is the point. Point being her work pays down the mortgage. So, I am here to ask you: Why oh why do they come only for my autograph, when my Vivienne is the one of great renown in the house? The fame disease is upon us."

It was the first week in November, and the yahrzeit, the anniversary of Stella's death, arrived the first week of November every year. And every year the calendar treated Johnny to a visitation, as if he was entombed in the ache. His heart had distorted – literally – as science tells us the heart does distort in cardiomyopathy, changing shape when we grieve, when our heart is broken. The Japanese call it *takotsubo*, octopus-pot heart, because your heart distorts to the shape of the object used to catch octopus from the water. Heartbreak is physical. He wanted to sail away from his own body. Instead, he was trapped in a body full of words.

Johnny Coma stood up, wobbly. He pushed the chair back under the table. "And, I say to you today, perchance, when the ocean is dead, so will be misogyny. Good night. And a nitty-nit to all, and to all a good nighty."

He went back to his table. He fished out some coin, left it for Ali. Tucked the five-euro bill under the saucer.

Night – *nit* in Catalan. It was not nit; it was barely noon. On a dark rainy day, the surfers moved across the roundness of the storm globe, and the rain redacted the timepieces. *Night Street* had become in the Catalan version *Passeig del Nit.*

JOHNNY COMA WOBBLED up the seaside promenade past the many beaches. In Catalan named: Sant Sebastià, Sant Miquel, Barceloneta.

Here whales walked, Johnny thought. Here whales once rode the waves. Here the Romans had whaling stations. Here the grey and the North Atlantic right whales rode and communicated in their echolocations. Once we were whales, tender as buildings. Once we made shimmers in the eyes of the Romans.

At the end of the promenade, at the junction of Joan de Borbó, he thought, Yeah I forgot this good café spot, Buenas Migas. They were advertising their hot chocolate special, Dr. Chocolate & Mr. Hyde, and a slew of chocolate drinks named with all those great Catalan *X*'s. Johnny tranced out looking at all the options: *Xoco-suis, Xoco-taronja, Xocolata a la tassa*, chocolate, *xocolata* in Catalan, the Swiss, the orange, by the glass. *Xocolata-menta*. The mint. There was something else on offer – a *Xocolata* Boom Boom. He walked in off the beach area, stared down at the Boom Boom under glass. A tall hat muffin in chocolate, set in its own *xocolata* boat with a side pitcher of *xocolata caliente*. He could sail the seven seas of *that* sweet treat.

Maybe later.

He exited Buenas Migas and walked down the wide avenue of Joan Borbó, homeward bound.

Johnny's pant pocket buzzed.

Oops, he thought he'd left that eternal pest, his phone, at home. Okay, what now, Johnny thought, pulling the digital diva from his pocket.

Swirling letters in yellow, red and green swam on the tiny screen:
THURSDAY IS "STELLA" DAY !!!!!!! JOIN US!!!!!

Herbal Remedies from Rhonda's own kitchen! Oregano Oil draw for the lucky winner!! The Turmeric Twins!! Find your colour match on the revised COMATONE CHART!!! Last year's "Stella" event was bigger than ever. Do not miss out. Brian will be talking on Polenta, also Eichmann. Yoga after with Ronny and the Comatics. Do not miss Brian who met Adolf Eichmann on a Hamburg street. We do not discriminate, all points of view are welcome at "Stella" Day. Bloor St. will be closed from the Pits to St. George.

Stella Day. No, "Stella" Day. A Toronto event, begun by Vivienne's sister, Rhonda. Rhonda, his sister-in-law, the Annex "character." Rhonda, who had never left home. Rhonda, who had presumed that Vivienne would stay single, stay unhappy, be a local shlepper like her. Rhonda Pink, Stella's actual aunt. Rhonda, the Stella denier. Rhonda the zaftig with her original plumes of long frizzy hair, Rhonda the stone-cold stoner, the freckled cannabis lover with, paradoxically, the mien of a meth-head. Rhonda the angry; Rhonda whose rage was buried in a clown presentation in everyday life. Rhonda, who – and Johnny felt even over an ocean how miscreant in-laws can torment you – began "Stella" Day during the first month of mourning for Stella, while Vivi and Johnny were away, here in Barcelona. Rhonda who got left bubkes in her mother's will.

Auntie Rhonda put scare quotes around his daughter's existence. Value-free, irony, naivety. Harm.

His tush buzzed again. He looked at the phone screen:

COME CELEBRATE THE 12TH ANNIVERSARY OF "STELLA" DAY!!!!

Did Vivienne Pink make up her baby? You decide. Did Stella exist? Vote Yes or No on "Stella" Day. Don't forget your stretching exercises with Rhonda at the By The Way (across from the Future). Yes, we have chicken. Stella Coma, baby actress?!!! Who knows?!!!!!!!! Come to the Great Debate and enjoy Rhonda's unique smoothies!!! Don't miss out!!!!!!

In lieu of a life, Rhonda Pink had hoarded scare quotes and exclamation marks.

Yes or No. Confirm or Deny. Mark it in your calendar. Falafel Forever. Brian will speak outside Aroma (across from Paupers) on how he captured the Nazi. Remember our 2015 Vote was No Stella. Will she be or not be in 2016? You decide!!!!!!

Never mind that Rhonda's beau, this Brian character, an occasional substitute math teacher at North Toronto Collegiate, was four years old, growing up in Bathurst Manor, when Mossad and the Shin Bet took down the notorious Nazi Adolf Eichmann in Argentina, on Garibaldi Street. Rhonda had always been good at insisting that facts were a matter of opinion.

My *mishugene* sister-in-law, Johnny thought, as he walked home on Joan de Borbó. He amused himself with a scrap of lore about the takedown of Nazi criminal Eichmann: that when Mossad agents got Eichmann secretly out of Argentina, they boarded an El Al flight in Buenos Aires with Eichmann suited up as an Israeli flight attendant. Holy moly. Someone on that flight looked into that steward's eyes and saw nothing but rail schedules.

AS BARCELONETA AWOKE, Johnny Coma attempted to push Rhonda and her pathology into some kind of a cranial psych ward in his head. To section the lies. To bathe in this wide open Catalan feeling he so loved, a little bit of sidewalk chaos, a lot of noshing love, people walking in twos and threes and six abreast, chatting, and this morning he didn't mind that the bicyclists were swerving all over the place.

9

WALTER BENJAMIN'S GRAVE
ON THE COSTA BRAVA

MORNING, DARK. JOHNNY took his ritual walk the one hundred steps to the Pla de Palau, sat down on the plaza bench beside Sancho who was asleep, snoring. Perhaps sensing Johnny beside him, Sancho began to air-type, eyes still closed, saying, "I shall launch from Petrograd to Leningrad and all the way back to St. Petersburg!"

He opened his eyes. Patted Johnny on the knee. "My dear liege, after we launch at sea with the fete and all, I may decide to edit others. I have a line on some very fine cochineal blood pens and a most excellent olive oil of the arbequina to make my mark. After that, if everything goes down the tubes, the sky's the limit."

Feeling he could be of use to Sancho by steering him in the right direction for writing a novel, Johnny said, "So, what have you read lately?"

"Read, my little liege?"

"Read. Books."

"Any hints?"

"*Night Street*?"

"Never heard of it."

Johnny squeezed Sancho's blistered hand, left him air-typing sixty-five words a minute. Too soon for the beach café. He went back to the roof, napped on the patio tiles. Then it was down for a stroll in and out of the stone alleys of the Born, exiting to the wide spaces across Marquès de l'Argentera, over to

Joan de Borbó, into the sea shadows at the beach, the surfers like neoprene otters on the waves. His writing depended on the routine, the superstition to stay with the rituals. But, hell, he was desperate, antsy, and why not? He took a side bet, did not go down the shoreline to the Little Lighthouse Café. He turned around, walked back on Joan de Borbó to a stoplight, crossed over to the other side, feeling that his luck today might reside in Bestiari, his favourite bookstore in Barcelona.

Bestiari was housed inside the Museum of Catalan History, a sweet tan brick building beside the sailboats at the marina, facing the wharves. Johnny felt the risk of swerving from his routine. It excited him. Books! The marketplace where the product he made was sold, keeping close company, spine to spine, face to face, with others from around the globe. In a nanosecond, like literary kismet, he was picking up a book whose cover was a black and white photograph of two men standing close to each other on a shoreline. The book, *Querido Salvador, Querido Lorquito: Epistolario 1925–1936.*

Shit, wondrous luck, Johnny thought. Salvador as in Salvador Dalí, Lorquito as in Federico García Lorca. Dear pals, the letters between them. Johnny ran his fingers across their faces in the photo. Two artists in youth. Both clean-shaven. Dalí lank, his long neck and half-closed eyes making him look like an ancient sculpture; Lorca, more solidly built, eyes wide open, his face to the camera.

Further down Dalí's hands, his long fingers on Lorca's waist. Dalí in a cardigan, Lorca in a V-neck sweater. Soft slip-on shoes for both men, feet almost in the water. The far shore a blur; there must have been a wind, their pants rippled.

As he walked to the cash register, Johnny flipped to the inside of the book to see where the cover photo had been taken. Ah, *Lorca y Dali en la playa de Cadaqués, 1927.* Kismet indeed. He had been to Cadaqués up the Costa Brava, the Wild Coast, with Stella. He looked back at the cover photograph. In 1927 . . . so Dalí was only twenty-three and Lorca twenty-nine.

Ten steps from Bestiari, he went into Costa Coffee, got a cortado served in a ceramic cup and one of their terrific Sicilian lemon muffins, sat in a club chair.

At random, he opened the book to page 151. A letter from Lorca to Dalí, dated *Granada, verano de 1930.* Summer 1930. In the summer of 1936, the military assassinated poet Lorca.

His letter to Dalí began *"Queridísimo amigo Salvador."* The open intimacy struck Johnny. My dearest friend. *"¿Cuánto tiempo hace que nos vemos?"* How long has it been since we saw each other? The question felt so tender. Johnny turned the page. Lorca continued missing Dalí in words. *"Dime cómo piensas, Escríbeme largo. Adiós. Siempre tuyo."* Tell me how you're thinking. Write me at length. Goodbye. Always yours.

Every November, when the anniversary of Stella's death came, he missed her most of all. As the leaves fell from the trees, bare sticks in the snow, frozen ponds, he felt . . . He grabbed his pencil, wrote on the back of the lemon muffin and cortado receipt:

Dear Stella,
There are five seasons. Winter, spring, summer, fall and you.

His hand was warm.
Moving to the Moleskine, he wrote further.

Queridísima Stella, Dearest Stella,
Remember the time we drove up the Costa Brava from Barcelona to Tossa de Mar, in October, when the

No. He stopped. His lungs were saying, today make it a story. Stella always loved hearing a story. Make it a story told to one person.

IT WAS WINDY when they set out from Barceloa up the coast. The father and the daughter drove up the Costa Brava beside the Mediterranean to the town of Tossa de Mar, one October. The pine trees were swaying, the land was rocky on their left and rose in rocks and resin and there were bigger drops down to the sea on their right as they held their breath on switchbacks in their little rental car, tracing the shoreline into Tossa, up another hill to the Hotel Mar Menuda, and their large room with two inlets. The daughter Stella said, "Two coves, Dad. Like we're docked in our own harbours."

She was right. Each bed at its own end of the hotel room was set in a private half-cave where only their feet stuck out at night. There was a sliding glass door out to a balcony, a view of a green island close to shore. In the morning they drove north in the direction of the border between Spain and France. The father wanted to take his daughter on a visit to a cemetery in a border town called Portbou.

Resin and tourism and more coves and islands and all of it, of course, from Barcelona on up to the French border was all Catalonia. It was so windy and wonderful, their small personal adventure.

They got to Portbou at the border with the railway tracks. Another hill to the high-up cemetery. Layered shelves with named remains were set on the side. Alone with a large headstone sat the grave of the great visionary intellectual Walter Benjamin. There he was, interred in Catalonia.

The small father, Johnny, held his daughter Stella's hand as they paid their respects, standing at the grave of Walter Benjamin. Johnny told Stella about one of his favourite Benjamin quotes, which her mother, Vivienne, also loved. Vivienne was away working in a war zone and Stella missed her and never knew quite why her mother was always away working and might be killed any day. So Johnny said how Walter said, "Boredom is the dream bird that hatches the egg of experience," and they felt sad but happy to know how smart Benjamin had been, how wry and ahead of the game and was the game too. Johnny said how he always said this quote to himself when he was taking one of his famous daytime naps and sitting on the porch back in Toronto apparently like a smoking dolt with a cigarette and restless and bored out of his gourd and then the words came. "So if you sit around all day, you make a book that way?" Stella asked, sarcastic even at eleven. Eleven and a half, that October.

"Ha, yeah, nope," Johnny said. "The sly part is you have to have the experience."

"The egg is the experience?"

"That's right, Stellita."

"You go and do stuff, then you sit like an idiot. Get a book that way?"

"You know," Johnny said, running his hand along the smooth stone of Walter Benjamin's grave marker, "you know the Buddhists say there are only two things: sitting and sweeping."

"Dad, but you just said you have to be experienced."

"I know."

"So?"

"It's all a mystery to me."

Stella was poking her index finger into the carved letters on the headstone. Walter Benjamin was a Jew but his gravestone contains no words in Hebrew; Walter Benjamin is buried in Spain, but his gravestone contains not a word in Spanish.

Walter Benjamin's gravestone is carved in German and Catalan.

The hilltop cemetery was quiet, the wind blew from the water below, the train tracks sat silent. The father told the daughter how it was that Walter Benjamin had died here. How he was born in Berlin, went into exile in France, was afraid for his life, ran across the border from France to Spain, well, took a train across, landed here in Portbou and died in a hotel room.

"Walter Benjamin, you see," Johnny said to Stella, "was a Jew."

"Like us?" she said.

"Yes, honey, just like us and the Nazis were after him."

"Will the Nazis be after us, Dad?"

He didn't want to lie to her. He might tell a bubameisa from time to time, a tall tale but he wasn't going to lie to Stella. Not with the remains of Walter Benjamin two centimetres from their legs in the cemetery.

"They might be. They could be," he said.

"Will they come and kill us in our hotel?"

"I doubt it, honey."

"But you don't know for sure."

He knew that Stella knew – kids talked about everything at Palmerston School, right? Hey. His own parents, Murray and Shirley, never talked down to him or his brother, Danny, rest in peace, the bastard, and he wasn't going to talk down to Stella.

"So the Nazis chased Walter Benjamin out of Germany," Johnny explained to Stella. "Then he ran to France."

"So they run after him to France?"

"Yes. They did."

"But why. Why? Don't – Didn't the Nazis have anything better to do?"

Johnny laughed, the way you laugh, adoring the logical simple intelligence of your young kids. "No, you know what, honey, they *didn't*. Those Nazis have, as your bubbie Shirley, my mother, used to say, way too much time on their hands."

"Nothing better to do than run after Jews? That's pathetic. That's sick. Don't they have a job?" Stella got up, picked up a small stone from the dirt, placed it on Walter Benjamin's gravestone. "He runs from where did you say, Dad?"

"Germany."

"Germany, France, then what happened?"

He remembered, looking back at that day, that Stella was staring off into space, out to the sea below, on a day of divine purgatory with her.

"Then Herr Benjamin runs from France by getting on a train into Spain. He gets here, safe in the shelter of the sea."

"Thank God," Stella said.

"But no thanks to God, Stel," Johnny said. They were walking back and forth in the cemetery. The wind, the feeling of height, the smell of the old pines, or of olives in the wind.

Stella went to the white shelves of the dead, ran her fingers around the openings. "It's like an apartment building," she said. "Like Auntie Ethel used to live in on Finch."

"That's exactly right."

"Dad, what happened? *What happened?* Uncle Walter, can I call him Uncle Walter?"

"Sure, honey. Why not."

"So Uncle Walter gets away from the bad Nazis, he gets here. So why is he here?" Tapping the headstone. "Why didn't they let him go home to get his cemetery near his house?"

"That was never going to happen."

She put her arms around her father's waist. "Dad, don't let them make me be with the Nazis and then you get to be in a grave and nobody in your who you know can come see you because there is no subway stop and you have to fly and get a rental car and a hotel room, and why couldn't he be buried where his people could take a bus or even you get a transfer, the streetcar, come say hi."

She put a second stone on the headstone. Like two house gifts for the dinner in case you couldn't come next year, you might be dead or some other alibi.

"Remember Tadoussac, Daddy?"

"I do."

"Can we go back with the whales?"

"I'd love to do that."

"Good. It's settled. Next summer?"

"Why not?"

"Could Mommy come? She never comes on our trips anymore."

"She's always travelling, honey."

"What I said. Can we?"

"We will. Next year in Tadoussac."

THEY SAID A Kaddish for Walter Benjamin, and even absent a minyan, the mandatory ten men to say Kaddish at the graveside for the death of a dear one, and even including that Walter Benjamin had died in 1940, and keeping in mind that hearts can feel a long-ago death to be so recent, and folding in that a Kaddish of mourning should be public, what more public – and defiant – thing could there be than to stand on a windy hilltop with cold winter coming and sing softly, *Yehei shmei rabbah.* father and daughter, and the daughter soon to be the one the father wailed a Kaddish for, every day for a year and then lost in space, remembered the day at Walter Benjamin's grave, when she said, "I think he's lonely, is my opinion."

BENJAMIN'S HEADSTONE WAS black, the message on it in carved white. It was set against a large white, copper and grey rock. The rock was in the shape of a pointed hood. The inscription, in German and Catalan, carved into the headstone read:

WALTER BENJAMIN
Berlin, 1892 – Portbou, 1940.

"Es ist niemals ein dokument der kultur
Ohne zugleich ein solcheb der barberei zu sein"
Geschichtsphilosophische Thesen, VII

"No hi ha cap document de la cultura
Que no ho sigui també de la barbàrie"
Tesis de filosofia de la històri, VII

Johnny translated it for Stella: "There is no document of culture / Which is not at the same time a document of barbarism."

Stella ran her hands over the German, pushing her little fingers into the shapes, their declivities. Johnny, too, ran his hand down the quotation marks, literally carved in stone. Proofreading the remains. It's so temporary, this life. If you're lucky, a mason will take care to carve the diacritical marks into your tombstone.

HOW COULD HE have known that Stella had only thirty-two days left to live?

Mazel he was given, and in mazel he did remain.

They drove down the white cliffs of Dalí.

Thirty-two kilometres from the grave of Walter Benjamin is the grave of Salvador Dalí. Each man found his homeland run by exterminating tyrants. A German, Benjamin, fled, ended up buried in a country he didn't know and far from home. From Berlin to Portbou. A Catalan, Dalí, rests handy to his birthplace. From Port Lligat to Figueres, where he is in a crypt of his own design, in the Dalí Museum.

Stella was fascinated by a painting of the cliffs they had just been driving, a painting the height of a five-storey building. In front of the painting sat a large black hearse. As she looked up, she gasped. Hanging directly above the hearse was a wooden boat with blue tears suspended from its hull. Dalí created the boat as an homage to his wife, Gala, who predeceased him. Stella was still talking in the car about the golden boat and the blue tears as dusk painted the hills. Their ears popped, switchbacking that quick steep hill down round into the sparkling night harbour of Cadaqués, the boat clusters.

The sailboats were folding back into the sea.

They had warm drinks at a big old harbourside café in Cadaqués with mysterious artists who felt like long-time paint combatants and witnesses protected by new identities. Activists had long found coves, beach caves, small islands to hide out in.

Sipping her hot chocolate, Stella asked her father, "Did the Nazis murder Uncle Walter?"

"Yes. No. In a manner of – He died with dignity. He was forty-eight years old."

"Did they shoot him? A stab? Tell me, Dad, I'm not a baby anymore, you know. I know *things*."

Indeed.

"They followed him from France to Spain."

"Like they didn't have laundry to do or somebody makes a chicken with smashed potatoes. Do Nazis ever eat? Why do they hate us?"

"That, my darling daughter, is the question."

"I never did anything to them."

"Uncle Walter got a hotel room," Johnny said. "He had a cyanide capsule packed with him, to travel. When he heard word the Nazi cops were coming up the elevator of the hotel, he took the cyanide, to die."

"Cyanide dignity, Dad."

"*Vale; amen, querida.*"

"Are they going to come for us tonight in Tossa?" Again she was asking.

"I don't think so, honey."

"But you're not sure?"

"I am sure."

"Are you really *really* sure? Before you said you didn't know. You can tell me, I'll get ready. Are we going to take poison if they come to kill us? Is Mommy going to take cyanide if one of those death squad guys comes on our porch?"

"Nobody's coming to kill anybody, Stel."

"You know that's a lie, Dad."

"Drink your hot chocolate."

The boats in the marina at Cadaqués painted themselves.

Off-season in a seaside cove. Stella so brazen in her mental tuning, so much like her mom, circular as steel in the wind tresses. The day was fine with a fine mist of rain.

In quiet cafés, in sanctuary coves by the open murder waters, refugee artists enter the frame breathing their resistance ozone into it.

Stella had the rest of October and a few days in November before she was killed.

Just your little street, your daily carry. Things are so fragile and so precious.

The dead take the Mourner's Kaddish they have already said for their own beloveds with them and whisper consolation to themselves, and maggots eat the hum of old hymnals and carry wormsong to other gardens.

By coastal sky as the stars did hang time, Johnny Coma and his young daughter, Stella, drove the switchbacks by feel in the dark. They curled, each in their own bed, each in their sleeping cove in the room, as the Mediterranean slept, too, and received migrants.

Thirty-two days later, they lowered Stella Coma's coffin into the ground. Shovelled dirt, mourner by mourner, on the small pine box. The world is upside-down when the parent mourns the child.

JOHNNY PAUSED FOR three beats, held his pencil in the air above the page. The story was done. He signed off.

The world and the stars. Die Welt und die Sterne. El mundo y las estrellas.
Later, bye, adiós, tschuss,
Dad

10

AN EYE WITH A RED RIM

EVERY DAY TO the beach, routine, ritual, obsession. Johnny felt urgent for more conjuring, a deeper sea tunnel. Weeks went by, yeah sure, he was that dream bird, he'd had the experience, he was bored, but when would it all hatch?

It was that easygoing first week of December in Barcelona, when there was a holiday on Tuesday and a holiday on Thursday, and already folks were easing down or leaving town and some of the eateries and bars were closed up for a few days' rest before the mad influx of Christmas celebrants began winging their way in.

On his way back home, he remembered that it was Sunday. Creps al Born opened at noon on the weekend. He could pass some time, sit at the bar, get a crepe and maybe a chancy libation. After he got off the oxy, he was afraid he might become too friendly with booze again. Could a vaso de tinto hurt if he had it with, say, a goat cheese crepe with honey and mint?

He didn't want to go all the way up to the roof studio to change out of his PJs, so he went along the Passeig del Born in his unironed stripes. And hey, there was Bobby standing in the doorway of the creperia bar and eatery. Black tee, black jeans, long-time server in the eat spot. A trilingual Brit. Another familiar face from the Born neighbourhood. Bobby stepped toward Johnny, giving him a big hug. "You're back. This is brilliant! Good to see you, mate. I'm setting up inside. How've you been? How's milady? She coming in, today? I missed you. Come on in."

Bobby was referring to Vivienne; how she and Johnny had been regulars, years gone by.

The inside of the bar was darker than the rain, and more amber. Easy on the eyes of the libation constituents. Johnny sat at the counter, the sole customer. Bobby began to slice limes, set up stir sticks, do things under the bar top with dishwashing, glass rinsing, all manner of prep. The crepe person, all tats and friendly smiles, came out of the back through the swinging door. He clasped Johnny's hand, gave him a fist dap. "Man, welcome, been so long."

"You eating today?" Bobby asked.

"How about," Johnny said, *"un crepe de queso de cabra con miel y menta?"*

"Done. You hear that?"

The griddle was already sizzling.

"Un vaso de tinto," Johnny said. Once upon a time in Death Valley he was presumed dead, yet here he was, in the flesh, ordering wine.

Even with a break of many months, Bobby remembered that Johnny rarely drank. It was barely noon, practically dawn by a Barcelona weekend routine. Nevertheless, he poured Johnny a nice Rioja, and without asking, set a medium bottle of *agua con gas* beside it.

"Bobby, you are a wonder. I miss my wife."

"No surprise there, Jon. I love your wife. Viv, right?"

"Vivi. Viv. Vivienne. Yes. Everybody loves Vivienne. So why don't I . . . Oh never mind."

THE CREPE APPEARED in front of him, oozing soft goat cheese, all drizzled with honey.

Bobby's eyes went to the entranceway. He walked around the bar, behind Johnny, and greeted a woman coming in. "Milady, any table. *Bienvenido.* How've you been? Long time."

The woman sat down at the bar, instead. Two seats away from Johnny.

"Te verde?" Bobby said to the woman.

"A mojito this morning," she said.

"Holiday time, everybody must have had the same kind of night I had. Coming up."

Johnny did not want to get involved. He had to stay low, be in public ignoring people, not chance a chat with a bad luck person. But she seemed okay. Better than okay. He felt her energy, and he liked her energy, and he liked how it made him feel, like his writing routine was made of sand. He was an empathy grump; he left it all on the page.

He glanced at her sideways. He wanted to sketch her but didn't. Instead, he took his Moleskine from his pocket, and facing the bottles on the shelf opposite, did a two-second pencil sketch of the glass soldiers.

"Roberto," she said to bartender Bobby, "*venga aquí*. Tell me" – speaking in a loud stage whisper – "what's his story?"

He grinned, looked at Johnny, leaned across the bar toward her. In an equally fun stage whisper, he said, "No idea. I think he washed up with the molluscs one day."

"It happens." She shifted her legs slightly, so she was turned toward Johnny. "You from here?" she said.

Mister Coma said nothing. He kept his head facing the full and empty booze soldiers. But he chuckled out loud. As long as he could keep his carapace in place, he didn't mind feeling like some middling slime who climbed up out of the sticky reef to get a glass of red. He put another bite of crispy crepe in his mouth. Crunch and Rioja was fine.

"He didn't offer to buy me a drink, Roberto."

Bobby shrugged.

Johnny turned toward her. A sweater cast in the amber bottle-light of the bar framed her shoulder blades; a soft yellow cashmere, with a wide cowl neck over black tights. Long wavy hair curled to her shoulders. Delicate yet tough features. A broad nose. On the bar stool between them was a pair of shoes. Shiny black patent leather.

"Name's Dulce," she said. She put her right hand into one of the shoes, offered it to Johnny. She was laughing. He shook hands with the toe of her shoe, feeling a metal piece underneath.

"Do your tap shoes come here often?"

Johnny heard himself in this friendly chat-up mode and he was appalled. The writing quest could be betrayed like any other lover.

Dulce smiled at him. "Only on Sundays. Right, Roberto?"

"Anything you say, milady."

A couple came in. Older, with an easy dissipated air to them. Johnny made them as unreconstructed, or partially reconstructed, hippies from the day. Dulce was licking the fresh mint from the mojito, squeezing some extra lime in her glass. There was only one seat remaining, on her right. She asked Johnny by a pantomime of hands if it was okay if she moved one seat toward him. He nodded yes.

If only that couple had never come in. If only they had gone somewhere else or had taken one of the still unoccupied tables.

Dulce sat beside Johnny, put her tap shoes on her lap. She smelled awfully fine. Damn. Tap shoes, Johnny thought. The other morning, out on the street.

"He still hasn't told me his story, Roberto," she said. Bobby was busy taking the order from Mister and Missus Back-in-the-Day.

Of course, it *was* her. She had tap danced in the dark before the dawn, singing, "Gyrotonic." And here she was.

Shit. What was he going to do now? She smelled like something high and rosy, a red kind of thyme, maybe. Woodsy, a smoky clarity. He had already met her when he met her for the first time. She put her hands into the shoes on her lap and tapped on the bar top with them.

The Back-in-the-Days laughed. Mister BITD said, "See? I told you. Always something in this city. Don't you love it?" He did a seat wiggle, like a guy who used to do The Swim.

Now she was on her feet with her tap shoes on, doing a routine for the assembly of four. She was a small ball of rhythm, compact, muscular legs in those tights. Her golden sweater rising and falling with the taps. Cramp rolls, wings. She was singing, "Gyro-tonic, gyro-tonic, gyro-tonic." Mister and Missus BITD clinked glasses to percuss the taps further.

The writer, the dancer, the bartender, the boomer couple.

She adjusted the high stool before sitting back down, moving it closer to Johnny. "Plans for the rest of the day? Or Sunday a day of rest for you?"

His plan was to get through today until it was one more mañana when he could go down to the same Little Lighthouse beach café, look out to the water, hope for a sign from Stella. His head was rubbery. He downed the last of his wine, ate the last of his crepe. Bobby put the bill in front of him. Gave him an eyebrow lift. Oh God, not the eyebrow. The hairy notation of complicity.

"Come. Let's walk," she said, leaving some euro coins on the counter.

THE SUN HAD come out. There is no blue as beautiful as the blue of a blazing blue day in Barcelona. They walked together down the length of the Passeig del Born, about three hundred steps. They walked back.

"Where are you staying?" she asked.

"Nearby," he said. Cautious.

"Local nearby, or tourist nearby?"

He laughed. "Local nearby." He waved in the direction of his alley.

"You live in the basilica?"

True enough, his wave took in the back entrance of Santa Maria del Mar.

"Close," he said. He walked with her, hung a left underneath the low stone arch. The sun had not reached the alley. It was still damp with last night's rain. He walked the lady introduced as Dulce to his front door.

"Here?" she said. "Not seriously."

They were standing in front of a mess of collaged posters, a peeling combination of graffiti old and new. He was so used to it being the covert entrance to his place that her reaction surprised him.

"Yup."

"I doubt that. You live here, or are you playing a game with me?"

"I live here. I live with the pigeons on the roof."

"Show me, then. Let's see."

He fished out his key fob, waved it at Dario Fo's old Nobel nose. The cardboard moved ajar. "Come, see." He squeezed in the space between the cardboard and the stone, took her hand, she squeezed in, too. They were standing in the vestibule by the elevator. She kissed his cheek.

He thought, I want to nurse my grudges. But she makes me feel human. I need to be miserable. But she lowers my shoulders. Oh man, I have a book to write, a daughter to find. She kissed him on the lips as he was leaning in to kiss her on the lips. The elevator had been patiently waiting. Johnny inserted the key into the unmarked keyhole that was for the roof. The elevator closed the heavy curtain. It grunted and groaned its way to the top.

AFTER, IN THE bed, he was hardly a reliable witness to his own life. He could barely recall the pie slice of time that had just transpired, its motes, its magnetic ions.

After, when he stirred in the bed, with her beside him, he was not exactly sure which part of free will he had exercised. Or what had been exorcised between them. The sheets were wet. His neck was wet. She was asleep, her wavy hair splayed on the pillow.

He closed his eyes.

He felt as if he had been in water.

He felt a green easement. As if he had gone somewhere, known by the sea.

He felt as if he had made love in a fog to a sea creature. A creature who was all sex, all skin, no gender. He felt as if he had been granted access to the folds of kinship. He felt something he had not felt for a very long time: reciprocity. Two flaws fucking.

Kindness.

But hot kindness. He didn't want to say the F word: Friendship.

The unknown place, the terra incognita: friends, with sexual bona fides.

He had that with Vivi. Had had it. They were best friends before they married.

His eyes swam behind his eyelids, a green underwater returned to him. He slipped back down under the coverlet. Dulce spooned against his back. Put her hands around his belly. He drifted off, she drifted off. He didn't want this. He wanted it badly.

DULCE'S HANDS RUBBED the sides of his rib cage as she hummed a series of throttle coughs, low wails. She beat on his ribs; she beat on his skin lightly as if he were a human drum. She skimmed her palms over his waking body, turning him toward her. Tapping, smoothing, with her hips moving.

Back in the days of Carthage, when the fertility goddess called Tanit was much revered, the Carthaginians used to gather the precious sea snail of the Pitiüses Isles, and extract from the sea snail its purple, and use it to dye the togas of the elite. But what of the sea snail? Perhaps the sea snail was the goddess . . . Dulce sat on Johnny.

Double helix meets double helix, philosophy does grow on trees. Beware the ides of chlorophyll. Journalism wrote the first draft, by the fourth draft, your body was poetry in the great green demesne. They had bodies; they were meant to use them.

Dulce and Johnny passed from endorphins through minor feats of levitation into reciprocal bug-eyed giggles.

Let an umbrella be your umbrella. A dark suit for the ceremony. Good dark shoes for the cemetery. We will all meet in our bones on the great final ship, we will all sail away in our boats with our bowler hats and fascinators, our feathery selves to the final magnets.

Had they ruined the possibilities of friendship? Had loneliness taken their ragged selves too far?

She was the captain; she was the sea. It was new, in the old ways. He was swimming, held tight by the shadowlands of bathymetry.

Her throat hummed some more, and she percussed him.

The yellow sweater she had worn when first he saw her. Its neck, how it complimented her neck. Did she know how lovely she looked in it, and that smile of hers, so droll and dark, how she combined the space she was in and the spaces in between her and the world, and the world rushed in. The world was cobalt melancholia.

Dulce's mouth looked like an eye with a red rim.

The world was so prim lately, turning bodies into ideologies, leaving out all the jazz, the jism. She said in his ear, "Trouble in mind, I've got a viscous eye. Trouble in mind, we get to live in it. Trouble in mind, we're rotating in the planetary macula." She kissed him, and he was a substrate on the side of a ship, a barnacle attached to the hull of anywhere-you-please.

The bed was salty, the brine was silky. They dozed. *Factum est. Jacta est.* It is done. *Dictum est.* They were in their own bodies.

The sky was knifing the alleys. The roof dogs were barking, running crazy in their lupine genes. Inside the scrim, Dulce said into Johnny's ear, "*De verdad.* Trouble in mind, I was a girl from the north country, in the western territories. Trouble in mind, I came from the northern redwoods. Beautiful old pines, he beat me on the hand-polished parquet.

"Corduroy trousers and long uncombed hair was me. Kiss me. I moved to Big Sur, I slept on the rocks. I tried to escape from him.

"He followed me to the south down the coast to the inn where I worked in the dry Inland Empire and then further into the desert climes at a telegraph office. He stalked me to a healing village where they mined crystals and ore and he hired an investigator who found me reading tarot cards and earning cash as a predictor. I washed up like a worm in a bottle of mezcal, sozzled not too far from Oaxaca. I painted Day of the Dead statues for a woman who had a store in New Orleans. He stalked me to Oaxaca.

"He beat me bloody by the ancient redwood trees; he beat me in Mexico until my hands were swollen from fighting back. My hands were so swollen I couldn't wear my own glove size. He took my hands in his and beat them down hard on the sidewalk.

"I wrapped up my hands to hide them, bandaged like a boxer. I escaped to Australia. I hid out with the elder stoners in Nimbin. I felt safe in a hippie outpost. I was hiding at the Hemp Embassy. He found me. I was the punching bag who got away. In front of the pastel hippie place, he unwrapped my hands, put a knife against my back, took me to his SUV, put my bandages around my mouth. He said, 'Nobody leaves me.' He said, 'I made you.' He said, 'You won't dance, unless you dance for me.' He beat me up in the back of the vehicle. 'Eyes on you,' he said. He left.

"I was the one with the long mermaid-style hair with one of those fat leg contraptions, hobbling around. You don't dance, you gain weight. I was embarrassed to look so far from who I was. That was the intention.

"He raged on my body; the real intention was to get in my head. How dare I flee the cruelty? My body dances in the spaces, the place where the notes go to fuck. He needed to get into my artistic larvae. He needed my creations in my limbs to be the fucked-up spawn of his ranting, his needling.

"He wore bangs, he had a third-rate mind, his type was a woman with some success in the arts. He needed to degrade the ladies who'd made a bit of a name in dance, in movement. He spoke of me to others as if there had ever been anything between us, as if I had been his lover, almost. He called me The One Who Got Away. You got that right, brother."

She ran Johnny's hand down the back of her right leg. He felt a thick scar there.

"Sweet Dulce," he said. "You hush now."

She went on: "Nimbin, Bali, Doha, Oslo, Helsinki. Rotterdam, Mao, Barcelona. Obama was just elected. I was on a layover in Bilbao. I went into town, rented a surfboard, took the subway out to Getxo, rode some waves by the cliffs down to Mundaka. Made the layover longer, hung with some Aussies, rode the long left break. Stayed, watched the big competition."

She kissed him, ran her hand along his face, as if to console him. "I remember and recall how, one night in the Hotel Mundaka, surf city, a tinny player back of the desk is playing early Eagles. Glenn Frey, 'Lyin' Eyes.' RIP Frey. He found me in Mundaka, came after me, broke into my room, starts brutalizing my head with a board he cadged from somewhere. If he couldn't have me to beat me up, then neither could the waves.

"Guy I knew, sort of, around, sees me next morning. No big deal; he gives me the keys to his place here in Barce. Says, 'Stay long as you care.'"

"He gave it to you. The apartment."

"He said the rent was covered."

"Oh boy. And what did you have to do in return?"

"There it is. The cynicism of the world. Nothing. I didn't have to do anything. I've never seen him again."

"And when was this?" Johnny heard his own desire for possession creeping in. Shit.

TIME WAS CYLINDRICAL. We are motes, co-conspirators in each other's gyro-stories. Sunday shadows in Spain. Catalonia and its own dark homages to freedom. The sun was dancing spots of mongrel red on the gauze curtains.

Women live in the full-body cylindrical time – this brass rotation. The spaces and the spaces in between the spaces. The artist and the art, one beast. Men go around like stunned wonders living in flour sacks. "They did?" "They did, you're kidding?" Women rotate, gathering the gossip, the time of day, the appointment book. Men, the delightful epiphytes they are, are so dependent, as women spark and confab with the stiletto blades of sky.

Dulce said to Johnny, "He told me, 'I'm a tough taskmaster.' I left him a note with a quote from Tennessee Williams."

"Which said?"

"'All cruel people describe themselves as paragons of frankness.' What day is it?"

Johnny laughed. "Darned if I know. I'm here and I'm not even here yet." He tried to navigate inside his brain fog. Ah. "Hang on. I – We – We – I ran into you at Creps al Born, but they ordinarily never open til late afternoon and is it late afternoon, yet?"

"Darned if I know," she said, kissing his neck.

"I think it might still be Sunday. Domingo. What was the question again?"

"The date. Are we anywhere near the thirty-first?"

Johnny shook his head, shrugged. "Oh boy. Too refined for me right now. Reason being?"

"Is it New Year's?" Dulce said, insisting.

"No. I am pretty sure we're not, not totally sure. And . . . ?"

"I have to leave if it's New Year's. I can't be here on New Year's."

"A story?"

She nodded. "A story. One day, during New Year's night."

"Tell me about it," Johnny said. "Tens of thousands of people drinking cava on the Rambles."

"He saw me. I did not see him. He was a monster in the crowd as the old year turned."

"Do you think he knew you were here, in Barcelona?"

"I think it doesn't matter. He took a bottle of cava, broke it on something – or someone – came up behind me, began cutting my lower legs. Before we got to the countdown, and the grapes. New Year's grapes down my throat and he cut me. In the crowd."

"Thousands."

"Tens of thousands on La Rambla, New Year's Eve." ·

"Yes, Dulce. Tell the story. The year turns."

She went on, "Right in the crowd, in all that drunk bottles of bubbly confusion, he came at me with the cut glass. He was behind me. Up the back of my legs, under my dress, I didn't feel it at first.

"No one noticed. Like he's my date. Or we're dancing. He held my neck, he pressed himself against me. To prove that he hadn't been cruel he made it his mission to stalk me, to maim me, to prove he wasn't a cruel man, to stop my lies that he imagined I was telling about him. To get me back in his Theatre of the Cruel."

"You don't have to go on, Dulce. It's okay."

She ignored him. She persisted. "The cruelty is the point. The cruelty is not a happenstance, you know. The arts camouflage it. You think, oh be an artist – a painter, a writer, make movies, *dance*. Me. I wanted to make movement with my body; I wanted to tell stories with my moves. My legs, my hands. He knew that. The flattery, did I say that? Bears saying again. You want it so much, you'd starve to have it, you'd walk crippled later to have it, your feet bandaged. These guys go where hope lives. Hope lives in art. My body was my tool. His heat was to come into the workshop of my body and ransack it, rampage upon my bones. Altar boy bangs, smooth face, sarcasm. You tell me, how does a guy with a second-rate mind and not an original idea in his life come to be in charge of women? This woman? I will tell you. I wanted my art so much, I did not want to be the one who sang in age about all the lost opportunities. Demean, abase, abash, embarrass, mock. Dancers' bodies were his playground of hurt. Harm. He was a choreographer but his soul was longing to run a country. So petty, so dictating.

"He had an art; his art was to lure you into his opera. So you would obsess all day about him. Oh, I just wanted so bad to make jazz with my feet!"

She began to bang the wall above the bed with her knuckles. She stood up, the palms of her hands flat on the stucco in poundings, claps, claps,

claps, the claps that hard soul flamenco knows about in guitar strums, in seated respect to the rough seas inside a thorax and larynx and windpipe. She howled large hair-charged notes. She pounded more flat palms on the wall. "That," she said. "With my feet."

She went to the gauze curtain, looked out on the late afternoon waning of the Mediterranean sunshine. Turning to face Johnny on the bed, she said, "He knew he had to ruin my legs. He knew he had to come after my lower body.

"They like to do it in public. Public places, public spaces. They like to *get away with it*." She laughed. "If he had been smart, he might have been a spy. If he had had a first-rate mind, he might have been one of those national security guys, or a, yeah," she laughed again, stroking Johnny's cheek, "a writer. But he had a second-rate mind and, grant him, okay ideas for dances. Remove his family money, and he would not have had the power of a dance studio, a dance company. Without funding, he was a mean boy in his late forties. Mean boy hunted me down on New Year's Eve on the Rambles, to cut my body as the clock clicked downwards."

Dulce lay back down on the bed beside Johnny. The light was lost to the day.

"HE SNUCK UP through the crowd, that New Year's Eve, on the Rambles, with broken pieces of a cava bottle, to cut the back of my legs, so he could feel something again. How, as he slashed me, he was a paragon of frankness."

Johnny felt her neck. A blind man could feel her scars.

"So, I get the tremors every time New Year's Eve approaches. The calendar has eyes on me. By Christmas Eve, I'm numbing the memories by putting on a Santa hat, going to some bar, sitting way at the back in a corner. I'm lucky, they play 'Stand By Me,' some geezer gets me up from my seat, gives me a whirl, it's all singalong and yours truly waking up in the morning with reindeer antlers on my head. New Year's on the Rambles? Every grape I popped in my mouth in the twelve seconds to midnight countdown, he whispered from behind me, 'You are dead. You are dead. You are dead, my Dulce . . . '"

THE RAIN POURED down on the patio tiles outside the bedroom. Dulce went on: "The Rambles. He almost severed my artery with broken champagne. I don't remember how I got away. My adrenaline took over. I pushed through the crowd. I ran down the Rambles to Ferran. I ran down Ferran to where it, you know, tilts up, found an alley, a stub, really. I ran into that stone stub off Ferran.

"There were tables and chairs set out. A sign said Passatge del Crèdit. Crèdit Passage. I sat down in a chair opposite number 4.

"A couple was sitting at a table a few feet away. They had a little weed, a little LSD. They offered me a joint, a tiny micro tab I dissolved on my tongue. They invited me to sit with them. It was funny, the way things are: the street right out there was full of crowds, walking, running, crazy New Year's Eve, just past midnight.

"My predator ran past. He was never very good at peripheral vision. Bad quality for a choreographer." She laughed. "No sense of rhythm."

She retrieved her tap shoes from the side of the bed. Put them on her hands. She began to jam on the headboard, doing stomp, hop, step, flap, ball changes with her fingers inside the shiny black patents. She heel-toed on Johnny's cheeks. Slipped her hands out of the tap shoes. Left the tap shoes sitting on Johnny's bare chest.

She went on: "We got high. They were lovebirds with wine and acid and molta. It could have been me. I felt younger, looking forward, hopeful.

"The story: sheltered in the public alley no one noticed, a very Barcelona thing, the kind husband of the kind couple took my hand, walked me to a plaque barely lit in the alley.

"The plaque said, 'En aquesta casa nasqué el pintor Joan Miró l'any 1893.' My God. Jon, it said, 'In this house was born the painter Joan Miró in the year 1893.' I was so busy managing my days so the arty predator wouldn't find me, I lost my curiosity about where I was. Fuck. I was by pure kismet in the alley where Joan Miró played as child. Where he came home to live as a boy. My second chance for life came, by chance, from two more Samaritans, one New Year's Eve, when I saw that Joan Miró's childhood street was shorter than a suburban driveway but walled with an arch at either end."

"Just like ours, downstairs."

Ours. Shit. He had said it.

"No lawn, no grass," she said. "Miró growing up. No suburban BBQ, no backyard, no front yard, the city of Barcelona – all the thrum and pulse three steps away."

"Secrets," Johnny said.

She put her hands back in her tap shoes. It's all in the game. "That's right, Johnny. Secrets. I escaped the brute and I found Miró the boy, the secrets. I knew there were secrets. I didn't know what they were. I didn't want to know. I wanted to be there, with them. It's very old – that part of Barcelona."

"It's about a block away from *El Call,* The Call. The old Jewish quarter."

"I heard that Miró's father might have been Marrano. A Jew forced to convert. Or his grandfather."

"Could be," he said.

Joan Miró, artist extraordinaire, was born and brought up a one-minute walk from Barcelona's Jewish quarter, which was itself a two-minute walk from the Rambles, a.k.a. La Rambla, which once upon a history was the site of aerial bombing of the resistance to Fascism, which was – further back into the long history of mother-water – a green, green river. And the street known as Laietana, on the other margin of the Gothic Quarter, Laietana, too, was once a river flowing through Catalonia.

And Joan Miró was born between the two rivers, on a laneway with sturdy stone walls. The tunnel of childhood security. His father was a goldsmith. Born to the close attention genes, near where the Jews slipped pieces of paper, bits of prayers and Torah, inside the cracks of the stone walls of Gothic Barcelona, and ran small enterprises, such as the print shop, where it is said, Cervantes came on his writing sojourn in Barcelona, in 1610 or so. And so the line from Don Quixote to the ever-quixotic yearning to make art and hand it to the people, as a peace offering, runs through Joan Miró, too. It is a thirty-second walk from where Quixote in *Don Quixote* visits that print shop in the Jewish Call of Barcelona to where Joan Miró grew up in an alleyway.

DULCE CONTINUED, "HE instructed me on the moves he wanted me to make with my body. But, you know, he was never in *conversation* with it. It was asymmetrical all the way. He couldn't hear my lungs, he couldn't hear my ankles. He was like, you know, man interrupted – his emotional evolution . . . his heart was some kind of prehensile item that fell away a long time ago . . . I ended up going to a café on Miró's alley off Ferran every day. Café run by an Argentinian who escaped the military to come to Spain in the '80s. Homemade cheesecake, strong coffee, an open vibe at dusk. I was saved there. Joan Miró's boyhood alley saved me."

"Are you thinking he's around? New Year's is creeping up."

"Don't ask. He might be. I think I saw him in Plaza Sant Jaume at the Catalan independence scuffle. Predators hang out in the resistance, too. Creeps infiltrate every opening, fill opportunities with negative energy, beat women, the full kit."

With her hands, she did a buck and a wing with her taps against Johnny's chest and rib cage. Bones. He liked the cold metal on his skin.

"I am a tap dancer."

Johnny high-fived her tap shoe.

Her knees were knotted from dance and surf. Her calves had long-healed scars on them. Body trouble . . . the dead are dead, they already voted. The dead are in witness protection. With the dead, there is always another river.

"TROUBLE IN MIND," Johnny said, as he consoled Dulce. They lay in bed under the duvet, in the quiet room. The glass to the roof outside was clothed in gauze curtains. The roofs were outlines like an old-time painting. If you tell each other stories, you might feel the healing.

Johnny said to Dulce, "Come with me, for a moment, to a soothing place. Close your eyes and let me tell you a story of my country. Way over an ocean, way over Atlantis and up a great river. Let me tell you about a girl named Stella, and a woman named Vivienne, and I might come into the story from time to time. The story, though, is about the woman Vivienne, the girl Stella and the trip up the great river to another great river and the meeting of the two rivers, the waters, and the place of the whales."

He could feel Dulce drifting off in his arms. Breathing past harm to move her body, made of mostly water, toward the water story.

Once upon a time, before he had been declared dead, prematurely, he had felt the inspirational power of the northern waters.

11

THIS IS TADOUSSAC

JOHNNY COMA SPOKE low, in the bed, telling Dulce a story.

"Once upon a time in the place of the whales.

"Once, before the Zodiacs.

"Once upon a time, a little girl rode across a great river on a small ferry. It was cold, and they were going to a magic place. The summer was in full green on the other side of the river. They had been driving all day, you see, from the old historic Quebec City, all built on a hill where they once defended the city, and all hilly down to the great river. The St. Lawrence River. The little girl loved the water; she had been to the magic place before. She was full of energy even after the long drive up the shoreline of the river. She wanted to see the whales."

Dulce eased down in the bed, easing the way you do with a story. He had that low storytelling voice, a soothing easy tenor.

"They sat on blue-painted benches riding across the grey river at sunset. The little girl's father – well, her father used to hum her a tune, sing her a song, called 'Once we were Belugas,' that he made up just for her.

"And so Johnny, her father, and her mother, whose name was Vivienne, came across the water in the ferry by dusk, wearing big loose pullover sweaters. They sat on brilliant blue benches up top; cobalt blue benches on terracotta-coloured floors, as the green hills of Tadoussac appeared. Stella had big eyes for the river.

"The wind made it chilly. Sweaters in August. Summer in Quebec on the North Shore, on the ferry to the magic place. The rocks were dark grey, the hills were dark green, the water was dark blue with the last dancing bits of sun on them. Ahead, the old white church on the hill, the boats in the marina, sails up, sails down, the old hills, the moss, the crossing."

JOHNNY HUNG A sharp right on Bord de l'Eau at the white church with the cemetery at the top of the hill. The waves were low, the sand beach was wide. The green cliffs were high on the left; on the right, the boats with sails up and sails down were parked at the marina. He drove down the hill, the white Hôtel Tadoussac on the right, set on a sloping green lawn. They hung another right, drove up a steep road. The big Saguenay River was the world behind them. They came in a dirt driveway, where it said Private Residence, parked on the grassy speckled dirt back of the big cottage. Old roses flopped on messy bushes. Ronny, their pal from Toronto, came out to greet them.

The days were bright with the north, and the hills. The nights were chilly and came late.

The first night Stella said, "Mummy, where are the whales?"

"They are out there listening," Vivienne said.

"To us?"

"Yes, to us, dear. At this very moment. Listen. Can you hear them listening to you? Can you hear the belugas in your right ear?" Vivienne blew into Stella's ear. "They knew you were coming. They called you: Stella, Stella, Stel, we are waiting, come see us."

They put her to bed in one of the upstairs rooms, wide plank floors, rag rugs, tiny four-poster bed for a small child. Vivienne found her at five in the morning, standing at the window, looking into the fog that covered the water. This was fog known to the first settlers. First Nations' fog in Northern Quebec; Haudenosaunee and Algonquin fog at the latitude of Munich or Vienna. Here the rocky outcrops hid in the fog water of morning. Here it was elemental and especially in the early mornings when the dialogue and diction of the world felt like all fog all the time and the benches awaited human figures and the beach below was wet and hidden in the fog, and the beach became revealed as the fog rolled away, dissolved, and the first dogs ran along the sand on the wideness of the river. Here belugas ran in groups and you could see them, if you looked and discerned that the shimmer light just off there was a line of whales, whales in their waves traffic, grouped, solitary, mammal flesh discrete in the wired lineage of water echolocation in worldwide planetary sonar.

Here, before humans, big water mammals ruled the land.

Once upon a time, whales had legs and walked the land from Basque country to Tadoussac; once whales walked the universe.

They walked in the fog in the morning, Vivienne pointing out to Stella how the fog had a life of its own, how it danced, the fog a veil dancer moving up and down the high Quebec rock escarpments, how the fog revealed the evergreens, revealed the sand, revealed the first fog dog walker. They liked black Labs in Tadoussac. A woman in a dark hoodie walked a big black Labrador retriever on the pale sand beside the grey blueing water.

Vivienne walked Stella up the gentle hill; they paused at the white red-trimmed church at the top of the hill, with its compact graveyard. Vivienne walked Stella around the curve, up another hill, steeper. Vivienne was in not bad shape, still she was panting; Stella slowed herself down to keep step with her mother until they came to the top of the hill. Other than the dog walker on the beach, they saw only one other person, a man easing down the hill past the hotel in a blue anorak with cameras.

They headed down the hill past the bank, Vivienne trying to remember where the walking turnoff was for the bakery. She always thought it was sooner than it was, including when she anticipated it and got it wrong. Down past homes, the rare B & B, walking down the same hill they had driven up the night before. In the space of twelve hours, they had left the civilized metropoles behind like entrails or old limbs of trendy. In half a day they had become compliant with the evergreen origins, with the inhalation of mists ghost rising. Their day was determined by fog, water, fresh croissants, bakery coffee.

At the bakery turnoff, Vivienne could see that Stella was the eye sponge she had always been. Vivi had so hoped Stel would love Tadoussac, that it would be just the right time, Stella being the right age to love it, enjoy it, not spoiled in her over-knowledge, as a teen might be, be on the verge of being a tween, not be a teenager on a trip with her parents, sure, be restless, but be new, be Stella, be nine years old. Take your kids on that adventure two to three years before you think it will be the "right" age for them to go, you imagine them to be younger than they are, by the time it is "right," the precious time is over. Take her now, while it is an unformed dream.

They went into the tiny bakery space; one table, one counter, four staff. *"Caffe latte,"* Vivienne said, *"deux pains au chocolat."* Vivienne's French was awful. Once she learned Spanish, worked in Spanish, lived in Spanish, her French went to hell. The young and youngish Québécois staff took no offense. Times were changing. Vivi and Stel sat down at the wee table. The coffee was strong, excellent; the chair she sat on was wedged against a shelf of organic condiments. Stella sat on the narrow banquette at the window. They sat cozy. The *pain au chocolat* was warm, the chocolate oozing out onto the napkins.

This was what you did. This was all you needed. You walked twenty huff puff minutes up and down hills to earn your coffee and pastry. Then you bought bread so fresh they could not yet slice it. In a big paper bag.

Vivienne carried the bread back, taking a detour on the way to walk down toward the ferry dock, to sit with Stella on rocks at the dock where the St. Lawrence married the Saguenay, to watch the ferries (too early for a car lineup, not too early for big trucks to be loading); sitting, tearing big hunks of the fresh bread, watching moss grow, eyeballing the algae.

Out on the curve, as they sat with chunks of bread in their hands, a glinted line passed. Belugas where the fog cleared, off yonder. Stella saw her first whales from the distance, saw them as water glimmers.

Mother and daughter, carrying that whale mystery light in their eyes, climbed back up the steep hill from the ferries, back on dirt then sidewalk up further hills, then down the hill back to the big brown shingled cottage on Bord de l'Eau.

They carried the bread, still warm, with big hunks of local Québécois cheese, to the dining room. One adult, one child, sitting at one end of the big wooden table, the scene through the paned window of old waters, the first sailboat of the day. After that, they went into the living room; Vivienne sat reading with Stella's head on her lap, Stella asleep, a nap at ten in the morning, northern August. Johnny gone back to sleep upstairs, Johnny the lark up with the mist. Then, Vivienne too fell asleep into a dream of being in other green water, paddling into a liquid green wall, hearing the revving engine of storms full of *verde*. The menace of a moving water wall eighty feet high, the fervent compulsion to be in a tunnel, as the curl enveloped her, and she rode a wall until it was a wall no longer. Until she was on the sharp edges of a reef.

When Vivienne lifted her head, Stella was gone.

She called her. Vivienne went upstairs to the wall of windows looking to the river. There, on the beach, sat Stella, feet in the water, long legs even at nine years old stretched out on the sand like a piece of a whale communing with lost eras. Born wandering, like her father, Vivienne thought. Missing the place you are standing in. Maybe Stella missed her water kin. Maybe Vivienne had given birth to a land mammal who felt the loss of her gills. Stella felt the loss of her homeland – in the water.

If only we were belugas. If only we were whales. Stella on the beach, missing her whaleness.

Out in the aural light, they ride with jawbones the size of cathedrals. Blubber basilicas riding the oceans.

If only we could be the cathedrals of fat communication, as whales are. If only, like albino alibis in lines, we could sail our sonar all the way to space satellites, communicate with the rotating capsules, with Laika the dog trapped in space with the dying particles of pooches above as we sailed the cold northern ocean waters.

If only we knew world as whales do, with their jawbones big as basilica entrances. If only, as with Jonah of old, we could enter into the secret private space, with the rose window in stained glass in the head of the beluga, as we sailed. If only we knew how to pray anymore.

Whales with their original mix tapes in their soundings: whales like cow bassoons, whales like rectal gargles, whales like high mouse eeks. This orchestra of light, which once upon a time walked the earth, before we did.

Once when we were in touch with the signal. Once when we had a green water mind, before we lost it.

Mammals at sea, mapping by soundings. We are so jealous; we are so lonely. We are made of water; we miss our homeland, our body.

Once, in a dream, Johnny Coma, in whale country in Quebec where the two great rivers meet, saw his little daughter, Stella, hanging from a harness, suspended from a ceiling, flying above him, in a maritime museum, in her fossil skeleton so fine.

In the night, with every device, we don't know where to go, to get back to that private conversation we held once when we were belugas, so private in great distance. Once when we were tuning forks at home in the world.

In echolocation, we tattooed the rivers. We made rills, we existed.

Skrill and moan, the babies rode in their lineage of light.

Once we made echo shadows through the dark water kingdoms. Once, in dark winter, we swam under ice, with each ear hearing separately. Once we were audition machines.

Once night sang to us, in two different songs.

Once we sucked night into our ears and wore world like a glove.

Moving in water, to be.

Once, in love, he had heard his lover over oceans, as if a single heart squeak was enough.

Once in water tunnels he could hear the green.

But now we are in our strandings.

EMERGING FROM THE deep reaches of mystery crawling creatures and the origin of spines and underwater molten lava, and thermal body vents, Johnny and Dulce drifted toward evening, and evening's empire.

Once we were audition machines, listening.

Come in; goodbye.

Pase adelante; adiós.

Our life is the duration of a semicolon.

12

THE NAKED SURFER

AMSTERDAM KNEW ABOUT space, and restraint. The Old World does. Small rooms, tailored, efficient, the breath pauses, the way a note has time for its own die down. A place where you can hear the rain before it is raining, even through the windows.

The bed was light wood, with a headboard where you could store things. There was a desk in a mini-alcove with a small, good chair. It was early dark on the second day.

Alexi pulled the chair up to the side of the bed. Vivienne was lying on the bed, in her sleek charcoal grey pants, her soft rust zip-up high boots, and her aqua sweater. Alexi saw her first in that sweater, across the aisle in the plane. Her artist photo in her book showed a woman with no hair and no eyebrows, bright eyes.

He had watched her on the plane, her face to the window, sleeping.

Vivienne was looking at Alexi through the 135 mm portrait lens of her Olympus OM-1, back in service. She was laughing.

Alexi said, "Take my picture."

"Are you Johnny Coma?" she asked. He smiled. They already had a private joke.

"Who is Johnny Coma?"

"Damned if I know."

He pulled the chair a centimetre closer. "Man or a muse?"

"Maybe one, maybe none; we'll see."

"Was he your muse? The guy in the desert pictures?"

"Muse? No. He was . . . We were . . . It was a thing. I was on a mission, he walked into the mission." Alexi had long fingers, messed up with scars. His middle finger, she noticed, was even with his other fingers. Vivienne was circling her own reticence. "He was never my muse. Not even close. He was a fever. You're the guy who chatted me up in the debarking aisle of an airbus, talking about my surf pics in the tumbledown edge of Las Canteras in the Big Canary."

She twisted to the side storage area of the headboard. She slid the storage door open. Sitting on top of her Death Valley photo book was a plastic sleeve, transparent, with a green logo of two hands crossed over each other. In white lettering it said: GUANTES TORREGO. Torrego Gloves.

Inside the plastic was a set of gloves. The gloves were a yellow colour, a colour hard to name. A secret citron. A yellow where the DNA result would find a lot of alleles matching it to a lime. An *intentional* citron.

She slipped the gloves out of their transparency. She smelled the soft leather. She rubbed one of them on her cheek.

Vivienne handed one of the citron yellow gloves to Alexi. "Feel it," she said. He rubbed the soft kid leather on his own soft chin bristles.

"I remember the feeling I had when I walked into the tiny store in Barcelona, the day I bought these. Way back a quarter-century ago when they used to have multiple chairs there at the top of the Rambles. Lineups of chairs on either side, and there was this ticket guy. You sat down, the ticket man came over, you paid whatever it was in pesetas back then, we're talking way pre the euro." She stroked one of the gloves, caressing the stitching. "I walked off the Rambles down Canuda, I saw these gloves in the window. The glover and the gloves had had a brief love affair, and you knew it."

Alexi was watching her. His eyes were great. She could ignore how great they were, put that feeling into a photo of his hands. His hands, her superstition. Put the feeling, too, into it of how she had carried the citron gloves with her, her carry-on duende, until the right moment for them to pose in a photograph came along. This was that moment.

The gloves had a life; the gloves had been from the beating heart of the beast to the inquisitive mien of the man. Soft, not suede, yet softer than suede. Marks on them, fingerprints, food marks, oil from eats, oil from love, cum invisible, the coroner of love could find cum if you put the citron gloves under one of those blue lights. She smelled the glove again. The fine skin. Gloves, *guantes* in Spanish, *guants* in Catalan. She began to dress her left hand in the citron glove.

"I remember when the man in the glove shop showed me how to put on a pair of properly fitting leather gloves. You don't slip them on, you don't put them on like a condom ten sizes too large. You don't flop in proper gloves. The idea is to fit you like a second skin. That is their intention. The citron glove was the transubstantiation of animal hide to the epicurean pleasure. If you're going to have a limb, have a limb."

Alexi smelled the glove, put his long fingers at the entrance to the inner part of the glove. No way he was going to fit.

The thumb had a round seam with a kind of a point at the top. The glove had a round cut stitched firmly at the wrist edge. That glove wasn't going to pull itself on!

Vivienne had tiny hands. She was a tough cookie with strong wrists, strong hands, prominent knuckles. *Piel original. Talla 7.* Original skin. Size 7.

Vivienne pulled the glove, one, two, three tugs with her right hand. Slow and easy, precise with the magic. She twisted behind her, brought her camera beside her. Took a pic of her own gloved hand. Venus wearing a citron glove.

The world in that era was infused with anhedonia: the physical loss of the desire for pleasure. Among humans with bodies, fear of the body was flooding whole swaths of the fleshy biped populace. Fear that someone else was free.

Her left thumb was only partway into the skin. Three more tugs.

"Open the curtains," she said to Alexi. "The low Netherlander light, the low country winter light, let it shine on the resistant skin." She could feel that the moment had a schizoid air of the calm before the episodic. She wanted the Mokum Tov city to see her and the Surf Doctor. She wanted the light to observe how that citron adrenalized her hand-eye connection.

Two more tugs, and her thumb was almost inside the skin. Two more, almost there. Alexi got up.

"Turn off the light," she said. He did. The available light was fine.

She pushed her fingers into the finger parts. Each finger had two seams, one on each side. The resistance to the modern noise was ancient attention. Her hand remembered the man in the little shop back in the post-Franco dying days of the '70s, when she entered and, for the first time, felt what it was to be properly fitted for a pair of gloves.

How the man in the glover's shop brought out a miniature pedestal for her hand. A pedestal! A satin cushioned miniature pedestal for her hand. The glover could not know that she worked with her hands, yet maybe he sensed it. He asked her to place her hand, the wrist resting at the edge, on the satin pedestal, the better to fit her. He laid various choices before her. She did not, now, remember any of them. Maybe there was a midnight blue or a deep sky blue or a merlot. She did not know then, even being in Catalonia, that yellow was the colour of Catalan resistance. The glove man had done the kindness, the service, of pulling the gloves onto her hand, easily, yet patiently. Smoothing each centimetre as it went down on her skin. It was that man who had pushed the parts in the spaces between her fingers, pushed down to get the glove to fit exactly. A far as Vivienne knew, the new world had yet to come to this place, except in pockets of ancient vanguardism. The place being the resistance of the fit of the skin on skin.

Vivienne kept her citron glove on.

"Move closer," she said. Alexi started to get up from the chair. "No, stay on the chair. Move it closer, to the edge of the bed." He did.

A vision of Venus in the mirror, her secret thrall, that Velázquez painting, came back into her head and her movements. A four-hundred-year-old dame was heating her up to take a portrait of a fifty-something-year-old man. She brought Alexi close in the viewfinder. Her trusty Olympus OM-1. The 135 mm portrait lens. Close but not too.

Alexi was smiling.

"Don't smile. Look at me."

"I am."

"Look at my hands."

"That's not what I'm looking at."

"Look at my hands. This is me, working. Love my work. This is me as I am. This is the human freak that I am."

His eyes said that he felt she had found out something about *him*.

"Look at my hands." She was adjusting the lens. She was taking the lens off, grabbing a chamois from her case, hot breath on the lens, wiping it down. Screwing it back in. Adjusting the focal length, the aperture, adoring the art; the man.

They were clothed. His hands were bare. She was wearing one glove. Her camera was around her neck. "Venus doesn't mind a muse, today," she said.

Alexi unbuttoned the top button of his shirt. He wiped his neck with the other citron glove. Put it back on the bed.

"Think about my hands," Vivienne said, her camera resting on her chest. "These are worker's hands. Think about all the men I have shot pictures of, all the women. Think about – look at them – me, in the kitchen, our kitchen, chopping chives. I love that painting Van Gogh made of chives. Simple chives, growing in a pot. Me at home, onions, shallots, in the kitchen, with Cuban music on – Pérez Prado, me dancing a rhumba with shallots."

"I want to take you back to the water," he said.

"I want to put you in a picture," she said.

"We could do surf therapy."

"We could do a dance with gloves of citron leather."

"'21st Century Schizoid Man.' King Crimson."

"*Lágrimas Negras*. Bebo & Cigala."

"I know that one. Black tears. I heard it in a bar in Sarajevo. In the after."

She wasn't surprised that Alexi would know the divine duet of two maestros: Bebo Valdés, the elderly master Cuban at piano; Diego "El Cigala," the younger master new-flamenco Spanish singer. Each bewitching in the spare longing represented, in recording.

"Do you ever feel that way? Dark tears?"

"Yes."

"There were all these music shops that opened in Barcelona, in the *apertura*, after Franco bit the dust. Great music. You know, the 1990s in Barcelona felt very 1970." She picked up her camera, continued, "The good stuff was always for sale under the counter, regimes, walls, it gets through. Music without borders. The clerks in music stores were always great conduits for the good stuff banned by the stiff-arms."

SHE WAS ON her stomach, shooting him as if he was a combatant and she was a guerrilla in the weeds, the reeds. He leaned back, because it was droll, and enthralling. "Don't lean back," she said. "Come forward."

She crawled to the edge of the bed, reached up to his neck, pulled it a tad forward, pushed his shoulders back a bit, crawled backward.

Venus in charge.

Venus as the artist.

Venus the zaftig shutterbug.

Venus, after an A-test.

Atomic Venus.

The naked Venus, taking a photograph, the nude behind the lens. "I am forgetting to forget you. Stay with the glove."

The song was about forgetting to forget your darling, forgetting that your darling no longer remembers you, as the piano and stand-up bass filled in the space. The room was quiet with trees looking in the window. She was following his eyes in her lens.

She put her citron-gloved hand at his neck, at his cheek, at his lips. A man smiling. "Please, don't smile," she said. "Think, instead, of how the leather feels on your skin."

His mouth got a desperation at the edges. Nice shot.

"Put your hand in mine," she said.

His large hand held her fist, a yellow bird, coiled to fly.

She stood up, motioned for him to stand up. She leaned her head to the side, motioned with her right palm up, each gesture to ask, without words, Is it okay, as she unzipped his fly. He nodded. Yes, Ma'am.

She took the waiting yellow citron leather glove, began to gently, as if a secret glover, pull the glove onto his penis. It fit up to the fingers of the glove. The fingers dangled off the end. Comic. He didn't mind.

"Do you come here often?" she said.

"I wish," he said, touching himself by means of the woman's size 7 glove on his sex. Waggling the empty fingers. "Moo," he said.

Vivienne backed up, shutterbug indeed. Once in, you can't quell the quest. She loved the antic sincerity she was feeling. The way the lens kvelled its honey clicks, its animal clicks, like lens maracas. She was a Jewish bride in Amsterdam, and this was her low country story. Her groom wasn't the guy with the glove on his penis. The guy with the glove on his penis was the promise.

She removed the glove from Alexi. She zipped his pants up. "Let's walk," she said.

AMSTERDAM, IN A sleepwalking ballad. They drifted across a dark plain. In the distance a light shone. Pavement, soft ground. Alexi took her hand. She was wearing the citron leather gloves. His hands were bare. Her gloved hands hummed the coded ballad. They made the dark crossing, Amsterdam so silent. Sinking in mud, the wild seeds and willow hair, in the shy ambitious city. He was the unintended thing.

They came to a building. Glass, people moving around inside, the back of the building. They rambled around to a street, the front of the place. It was the Van Gogh Museum. It was still open. The guy at the top of the stairs said in a friendly yet mildly instructive voice, "You won't have time to see the museum for sure. You will need at least one hour. You have to come back another time, yes? Maybe tomorrow?"

"It's all right," Vivienne said, giving the guy her best "We both know you have to say that, and you know as well as I do that half an hour is plenty of time for all sorts of things, right?" smile.

"Sure," he said. "Go in."

"You do that often?" Alexi said.

"I do."

They went up the stairs to the Van Goghs.

THE TREES IN the orchard were raining the angry architecture Van Gogh put into the blossom spring rain. He told the story of the future that the blossoms tell: there will be fruit. After the blossom rain, the green knobs will come, and the peaches will come with the pears. Vincent van Gogh, master of anticipation, master of the spring lung. Vivienne and Alexi sat on a bench in the room with the spring breath held by the painter. Vivienne felt the scars in every Van Gogh orchard, the cuts, how the apple blossom snow knifed the turquoise. Van Gogh knew all about how you missed things, and how you hid that missing, and how your hidden parts were violence to your body. Her hair had fallen off.

From the back, a viewer saw a bald head beside a short dark cut on a long neck.

Vivienne listened with her eyes. Van Gogh knew he made scouring ballads of lost time. Van Gogh knew how nature was a crime scene. Van Gogh, in the present green was eternally rolling back the years into dark workers' corners, moving from the soot nights illuminated to the nighthawk fluorescents. He knew that in every sunny day, the end is nigh, by your century's methods. There will be cafés. Alexi took Vivienne's hand and kissed it.

"I was watching you sleep."

"Last night?"

"On the plane."

"You were taping me?"

"Would you fancy that?"

"Come on, tell me."

"You seemed peaceful. A girl who can sleep on planes."

"Girl?"

"Your sweater rode up. You were twisting around. Punching the wall. You turned toward the wall; your back had this big tattoo on it. You had cuts on your upper body. You had that red shirt you put on later wrapped around your hands while you slept."

"We're flying over Greenland, you're looking at my upper body. A woman you don't know."

"I might know you. I did not know you had scars. It wasn't a tattoo in the normal sense, I could tell. Your back looked like the burnt back of a bird. I went to the loo. You were sleeping with your face squished at the wall. Your nose."

"Cute," she said. She was trying to picture Alexi looking at her in the plane yesterday, as she roiled and dreamed over the ocean to here.

"I stood in the aisle and looked at your back," Alexi said. "Your skin looked like animal skin."

"You didn't like it? It's not to your taste, then?"

"I wondered about the story behind it."

"The Cold War is the story behind my mutilations," she said. "My backstory is called Welcome to the Atomic Century. The nuclear stockpiles burned my flesh. Ten years ago in Dubyah's secret bomb test in the Nevada Test Site."

She looked at the cadmium yellow half-life of Van Gogh's work, the brilliant instability of atomic night cafés.

Alexi spoke in his voice of the many places, "How did your husband die?"

"He isn't dead."

"Are you sure?" Alexi took her right hand, still in the glove. "I read that your husband died ten years ago. I read that you were a widow."

"Is that why you . . . ?"

"I don't think so."

"There was a slew of premature obituaries. Most of them fake. One obit jumped the death gun, then everybody piled on. Nobody waited to find out he was only in a coma. My husband's coma was buried in the corrections."

Alexi was bemused. Still, the questioning made her restless. She wanted to immerse in Van Gogh's restless healing. His fission ballads in paint. How Van Gogh could make the coming of spring feel like a dirge as played by early Clapton. The brazen recluse. And deeply inhered in every Van Gogh was the sense of regret – the regret that having nailed the thing you gave up so much for, now that the love affair between you and the nomad light was finally over and in a frame, your secret heart was revealed, at last.

Van Gogh, who read and adored the poetry of Walt Whitman. Van Gogh in the pool hall with the cyanide crows. Vincent, who lived in a personal dark room and walked with dilated pupils into the old hay. A man bred in northern light, who inhaled southern light as if it were a bad necessary opioid. He painted the sky as trauma. He parsed the elements of paint as if they were small children. He was *curious*. His blue room was originally purple. (He knew the world was a bomb shelter . . .) His fugitive paint, made by new invention's chemicals, did not last and will not last the way the old guys' paint will. He knew the world was embers, and the rain was made of kerosene. Van Gogh made a starry night into a heart attack.

"After the atomic bomb," she said, getting up from the bench, "my eyes were blown, my irises were all over the place. I had tunnel focus. I saw things the way a civilian sees, which was shit for my working. I couldn't feel what was lurking just this side of the outside of the frame."

She walked back and forth in front of the varieties of blossoms, the many peach tree presentations, the peach, the pear, the almond. The war of the blossoms. There was not a scrap of sentimentality in Vincent. Every master has a knack. Vincent van Gogh's knack was to put you into that ballad; willingly you went, into the envelope of heartbreak. And in tresses of cadmium red cyanide, in long red asteroids, you went back to have your heart attacked again. Vincent whispered to Vivi, Go back to beginner's heart. Go back into the pupa. Go back to the place between larva and imago.

Vincent van Gogh, spy of spring.

The brush strokes were still so alive, April 1888 to November 2016 wasn't all that long of a time. Vivienne inhaled the fence, the petals, the turquoise sky. Vincent van Gogh, heartbreaker. He put that cardiomyopathy down on you, he intentionally distorted you, then he came back around the bend to bring you to homeostasis again. Somehow, Van Gogh made you mimic his process, as you entered his paint. Not by interview, but by seduction. A shipwreck, then sheltered. Van Gogh, sailor of starlight.

Alexi walked her away from the Van Gogh blossom paintings, to one she had never noticed before, of butterflies and poppies. The orange smeared opiates of April, the white-green blurred butterflies, Vincent, medical examiner. M.E. making butterflies like outcrops of migraines, with headache flashes called poppies. Migraines and heart flutters, in a garden wet with rain.

Vivienne sat down on a bench. She closed her eyes. She did her war breathing, the breathing she learned in Iraq, in Mosul, from a British field medic, Doctor David. She called the breathing The Fours.

You breathe in four beats. You hold your breath for four beats. You let your breath out for four beats, mouth open. You do this four times. Anywhere, any time. No embarrassment. It worked. In war, of course, in peril, forty-eight seconds means you're dead about ninety-six times, if a bullet comes at you, or an IED explodes below your vehicle's tires.

Vivienne opened her eyes. There was a sprig of almond in flower, in a glass. The table domestic variation on the public flowering almond tree. Never be embarrassed to stay with your obsessions. There was so much competence around, you wondered what the competent did at night. Never be embarrassed, as an artist, to bring your inside voice out.

"He spoke English. Vincent," Alexi said.

Vivienne wondered what Vincent had sounded like. Was his voice rough? What was the tone, the pitch of it? Alexi's English resonated with that slight undertone, that slight squeeze on the vowels, of English being his second or third language. A trill on the *i*'s. Over-emphasized *t*'s.

They walked to where the letters of Van Gogh were on display. The fine cursive with maps, sketches, always doodling, always be doodling, the large bold letters, the Dutch, the French, the English. She loved letters where the artist worked the margins, made it personal, unique.

She stopped at the framed letter from Vincent to Theo, dated May 14. The one she adored, where in the middle of the letter, in larger darker lettering, the ink smudged, Vincent had written the words **in damned earnest** in English twice as large as all the other words, underlined them, smudging the *mn* and the *t*. Vincent's cursive was so personal, squiggly improv words, accompanied by offhand sketches in his letters. How we do adore the scratches of the dead, their unique marks. All those tiny sketches Vincent embedded in his personal handwritten letters. How Vivi adored the sepia ink of Vincent's transmissions.

Vincent van Gogh writing to his brother Theo was writing to Vivienne Pink, too. Like an invisible undertow under the visible handwriting, Vincent was crooning, I was here, I lived. I was alive, once upon a day. I was present. I was aching; I didn't know which way to turn. I was trying, attempting, giving it my all. I was concealing, reeling. I wondered how humanity was doing. I was reaching through the emperor moths and chives, the months of terrible sun, my eyes were dilated. I ate paint. Through cadmium dreams, through a hard palette, I reached out to you, you who were not born yet. Can you hear me?

THEY WALKED THROUGH the dark crossing again. Amsterdam, its head barely above the sea. In the middle of the dark plain, Alexi stopped and kissed her. He took off one of her gloves, put it in his jacket pocket.

In the room, flame or kerosene?

They embraced.

"I can't," she said.

"It's okay," he said. "Remember? I'm your husband."

Alexi knew how to fit her, how to be a fit for her, how to turn so the frottage worked. His sincerity was deep. Sincerity today was the freak. He turned her over; they were composing some meadow duet, that was for sure. He slid out all glutinous and globby and that was some load of cum on the sheets, and she lay back wanting more of the same. The benefits had been extremely beneficial.

The citron gloves were sweaty, animal in their original time, she stroked his backside with the skin, they began again. The break in between times was like the die-down of a note that holds time hostage, reacquaints time with its own body. He came back inside her.

The art made me do it.

I was lonely too long.

Everybody died.

Rembrandt ate my brain.

Vincent said I had to.

HER PHONE VIBRATED on the nightstand.

"Leave it," Alexi said.

She reached over him, picked up the phone. Johnny texting: *I love you, little one. Heading to Rec St. Wondering how my honey is.*

Vivienne texted back. *You are so sweet, sugar waits in ambush to steal all your best secrets. Light is jealous of your eyes.*

Johnny texting: an emoji of a blushing face.

Her sugar note to Johnny was sincere. Yet she was in bed with Alexi. Hotel rooms had been her home, her backpack, her kitchen, for her whole working life. Her house back in Toronto was her bricks and mortar pit stop. Alexi was running the palm of his hand over her bald head. She had no eyebrows, but she felt as if she did. With Alexi, in bed, she felt human, present. He was rubbing his penis with the citron glove, putting the glove cum on her bald head, licking it off. Laughing as she texted her husband.

Johnny, with another text: *Come to bcn. We'll eat in our corner banquette at Orígens. You'll have your rabbit and potatoes, and Tarta de Santiago after, with Moscatell. By the way, I wrote to Stella. When I hear back, I'll book a table for three by the window.*

In her blur, Vivienne could not credit what Johnny meant. They had lost their marriage whistles with each other.

AFTER ALEXI AND Vivienne made love, they went back out into the city of Amsterdam, and the city felt like foreplay vibrating what was going to happen, before it happened. How a city can be like a secret brain map, a dream file humming along, feeling the feeling before the facts. How a city can buzz with secret predictions; later, the ions of desire you sent out peep on you, the urban sniper vibe through a rifle sight. Sex, the best relaxant; sex, the ultimate anti-anxiety medicine. And they drifted in a new boat on old canals and they felt part brick part water part dream, in secret parentheses.

After the boat drift, they kept drifting by foot, swaying on land legs the long way up Van Baerlestraat to the Overtoom and Vivi's favourite Indonesian joint in the neighbourhood, Kartika, for a *rijsttafel*.

Kartika made it easy, and easy was what they wanted: you had only two choices for food. As you entered the restaurant – plain tables, plain chairs – at the door you were asked, Vegetarian or not?

You answered, you sat down, soon your dishes of deliciousness in plenty with all the hot rice and all the hot spice arrived. They sat beside each other, spooning the variety of chicken beef potatoes peas beans, orange red green, aromas and shades in all the senses of heat and conversation. And they chatted like old friends, abracadabra. Democracy, the secret lover.

If you take democracy for granted, democracy might go and divorce you.

They walked back the few minutes to the Owl, stepping close to each other as night bikes pedalled by in clots and spoke clusters. A left at Roemer Visscherstraat into quiet rainy brick and stone. Funny, Vivi thought, back in Toronto you'd be smelling cannabis as a norm on her little Canadian street. In Barcelona, where Johnny was holed up with his writing, it was pretty commonplace now to get a whiff of weed as you strolled around in the Gothic environs. But not in Amsterdam, no locals outside toking. Funny how things look when you're actually in the place, which was why she so loved photography of the eyewitness kind.

Vivienne, the documentriste: bald, blue-eyed and betraying. Back in room 46, she turned the sound off on her phone, wondering why she bothered with a mobile phone these days, anyways. They weren't secure; they were pests like pushy salesmen or cellular yentas with jump-up gossip, far from the fresh, the eternal, the soul-forevers.

Stretched out on the bed, she and Alexi got closer against each other. Their open spaces began a new echolocation. They were inventing evolution, they were fully mammalian. Their parts migrated as it is, in Long Time. Once they walked the earth as creatures destined to roam like giants inside the world's waves. Once they did not have baleen, or the special sonar. Once they had noses.

Once, in a story, whales danced in hotel rooms and there were leather gloves present. New skeletons emerged in the darkness, new backbones for the oceans. New ways to go deeper. New comic adventures. They evolved to move in long paddle streams of light, slick in the morning, northern creatures.

VINCENT HAD MADE her calm, but Vincent van Gogh was tricky. He knew about the terror across borders: your skin, the world.

They sensed each other as if they were thousands of miles apart, continents moving into the sound waves, flying continents of moss. Their lungs joined in the wheezes, their symphonic lungs crackled like grackle asthma. Crows and thunder, surfboards and graffiti, they wrote messages across each other with cum and saliva. It had been a long time since Vivienne had been to this place, this green easement. The abundance of sorrows morphed into an embarrassment of orgasms. She took her phone into the bathroom with her when she woke up two hours later.

Johnny in a text: *I love you so.*

She put the shower on, texted Johnny back, as if the water running could mask the bed story. *I love you, baby. You are my one.*

JOHNNY WAS WALKING down the Passeig del Born in the wee after-hours when he missed her so, and he discovered that his phone had accompanied him in his pocket. He was sure that he had put a sock on it, left it in the drawer, but phones these days were like pets who hopped up to go out with you. And so he had texted Vivi. He loved that she texted right back.

As he hung a left at Rec, the early night world of Barcelona was out and about in its particular passion for vermouth. Vermouthing was a thing, long-time, in the old port city. As he approached a favourite eats spot of his and Vivi's called Bormuth (a nice droll combo of the Born and vermouth), his phone yipped, Vivi's message. *You are my one.*

You are my only, he wrote back, stopping on Rec across from Bormuth, where they had that great tapa of crispy eggplant fried with honey the two of them loved so much.

"ARE YOU ALL right?" Alexi was saying to Vivienne through the bathroom door.

"No, okay, yes, no, yes, I'm fine." She flushed the toilet. As if what? As if the toilet flush, as in the movies, was some kind of skell alibi. Alexi knocked on the bathroom door. "Just a minute," she said. She texted Johnny a round yellow face with a kiss on its round yellow cheek. She turned off the shower.

JOHNNY SAT DOWN in a public chair on the humble paved hill beside the windows of Bormuth. Folks on high seats at narrow tables, with *tinto* and bites, so intimate. The way he used to sit with her, eating *pulpo*, *sepia*, drinking *tinto*.

Johnny: *I am your furry mutt, at your service. You okay? You safe? Fatalities?*

Vivienne: *Mutt – new? Love it. Put that mutt in the new book for sure. Do it. I am OK. Safe. Man with creepy van in Vondelpark. Machete. Had a nap. Might stay in.*

SHE HAD HAD a nap. That was the truth. She simply left out the part about whose nap she had had the nap with. A marriage estranged is a marriage all about the omissions.

Out in the night skies where the crime scenes come knocking at your windows, the climate crime was rising. The willow reflections were rising. The Vondelpark grass was flecked with blood. The green benches had been blood-tagged by hate.

Mangled Dutch bikes lay on the green November grass. One terror van man was still at large. Homeless trammelled with bruises, faces painted with urine wore walking shoes Vincent painted, old and worn and sometimes replaced by newspaper slippers.

In the newest era of men in charge in rooms all gaseous with rodomontade and contumely, a man and a woman lay in a plain numbered room in a humble hotel below sea level, where the waters were rising. They fell asleep like science in a dream. They fell into mutual REM space, where the healing power of dreams returned water mind to the body. Where even the coral could dream of rebirth. Waking, to turn over to go back to sleep again, they shone to each other like human $E=mc^2$.

And who in the hell can figure out the fucked-up physics of love?

OUTSIDE THE FRAME of the photograph she had taken, in her art, was the breath of the ghosts of the moment, upright, dancing on the patch of floor on the one-block street. Partially clad, the photographer danced to some old Cuban music, Beny Moré from Havana right before the revolution, shouting with the trombones, the trumpet. Vivi and Alexi's hips moving before they could put their brains into anything, so they did not. Simply hip to hip, hip bone to hip bone. Uh-oh. As the old saying has it, sex is dangerous, because it can lead to – dancing.

They fell asleep to the slow music of "Preferí Perderte," I Preferred to Lose You . . . and woke up, still standing, moving to "Mi Amor Fugaz," Fleeting Love, yet the tailored night had other plans for them.

13

VIVIENNE CONTEMPLATING
THE BODY OF VENUS

DOES MY BODY offend strangers? Do they find me repulsive in my mirror? Would they stomp my body, but keep the gilt frame? Would they harken like censorious morning larks to come slash me, in the do-good morning? Would they lust for the machete? Yearn lustily for the knife? Ache to put the point in my belly? Be ashamed that I show myself?

Vivienne Pink was alone, lying back on the bed in the quiet fur of secrets everybody has. In her hand, a postcard of a naked woman from the back. *La Venus del Espejo. Venus at Her Mirror.* Vivienne loved the look of women's bodies especially. She loved how relaxed the Venus was, admiring herself.

Vivienne had taken self-portraits all through her camerawork. To show, eventually, maybe. Not to give others a record of where she was, what she was doing, as in a diary, but something, paradoxically, to sell that would make the buyer feel he had bought a secret erotic dream, a Vivienne dreamed in a room, in an undershirt and nothing else, in a rusty mirror. The camera was usually at her face, a camera strap draped across her left breast and pubic hair at the rim of the mirror. She took pictures of herself for her own plea-sure. But yet not, as the saying goes, *for herself.* She was a professional; she made art for the market. She entered the agon and put her name out there.

She wanted to be winter, in a mirror.

Vivienne went to the Owl garden downstairs, first. To look at the green, the shapes of the fronds, the curves, the veins, the cut-outs, the shadows.

Bamboo soldiers, nodding puffheads drying out, the elegant iron scrolls in the furniture footing, waiting for someone to notice them, by their shoes. Vivi's feet in deep-russet suede boots. She walked in fog ease on the garden paving. How calming green was. She had, over the years, been able to flip a switch in her brain and read a green scene the way it would print in black and white. Green read black, red read black. It was about tones, structure, as if you used a black and white photo to plan your garden. Proportion thrilled her, the garden's erotic foreplay.

Then upstairs to Venus.

The green, the strange nights in strange hotel rooms. Strange hotel rooms way at the back overlooking inland areas with car parts piled up four storeys. Even the one-star spots had mirrors. Sometimes she squeezed her arms together, her elbows, so that when she shot a pic of herself in her undershirt in the mirror, her breasts would have more definition.

When she had been in the business thirty-five years, she put together a book of self-portraits in rooms called *Moxie in the Mirror*. It was roundly panned. It was mocked, her body was mocked, that she might find herself sexy – the very idea! – was mocked. That a woman in her fifties might be a sexy creature to herself and to a room and to art and to the eyes of the viewer – this too was mocked. Her having this notion *at her age* was made fun of. But the trouble was, a lot of the mockery came from other women.

Vivienne's dad, Izzy Pink, one of her great supporters, used to say: "Throw out the garbage." Meaning the crude, the craven, the barbarians. Listen: *Use your ears, sweetheart.* Look: *Use your eyes.* Not who are they, but *how do they act?* Are they a mensch? "If not, recycle them. You can't solve the world's problems single-handedly, my darling daughter. Do your pictures, they're just jealous. Maybe they don't like Jews. Who knows?"

Izzy used to say: "Your mother wasn't like that, so don't you be. So they come to your photo shows to get an autograph from your husband? So? So don't you be them. They'll have his autograph, you'll be the artist. Be the artist, throw out the garbage, never drop names. You don't like their game? Good. Invent a new one."

It was her dad who took her to the AGO, the Art Gallery of Ontario, down on Dundas at Beverley, telling her – and not for the first time – that in the 1930s her great-grandmother Shayndel used to own and run a corner store where the AGO now stood – well, a couple blocks west-southwest, at the corner of Denison and Grange Avenues. And in they went, Izzy pulling young Vivienne along, to look at Rembrandt's *Portrait of a Lady with a Lap Dog*.

It was her dad, later the second Jewish mayor of Toronto (between Phillips and Givens) who told her to tune out the noise of the jealous and the momzers, the lazy leeches. "Look at Rembrandt when you're feeling lonely, my shaina maidel." It was her dad who told her the story about how Rembrandt painted that lady with her dog on her lap, after his wife and his daughter had died. "He was an artist, what else was he going to do, nothing?"

It was her dad who always wore a well-tailored topcoat. Materials mattered: look good, you're in the world, aren't you? Izzy wore soft-hand tweeds, wool cashmere hybrids, a nice pocket square in a vermillion with secret gold flecks. Izzy bought her mother, Rose, beautiful slips in rose gold, scarves in paisleys, belt buckles in mother-of-pearl. They didn't have much in the way of money, but what they had was fed into the team their marriage was, in smarts, in sensuality.

From Izzy she got the yen for tailoring. Also, because her zayde Sam, her mother's dad, was a tailor she noticed good tailoring everywhere, discipline mixed with intuition.

She admired the restraint of the plantings in the Owl garden. The green tailoring informed her wet thoughts. She wondered, sometimes, if she was actually a man. She had never worn a dress. Or rarely. She did not gravitate to girly clothing. She didn't mind fingering a lovely spring dress; it was, however, the fabric that she wanted to touch, not the styling into a dress. Textiles excited her. She liked buoyant scuba prints, she liked silk, the work of the silkworm. The silkworm, born to spin silk, as the honeybee is born to make honey. She liked how the industrial hand of workers tanned leather, how wool was gathered, dyed. She wore on her neck a magnificently low-key merino wool scarf from the Basque country in northern Spain, a scarf in a deep blue almost black but not quite, more of a noir neutral. Navy goes with anything. It kept her neck company in an intimate coziness. The occasional vulva rim of pink around the pale green plant across the garden thrilled her, the pink reading grey in her mind. In a cool crisp tailored garden of mostly plant material in greens, you can find quiet mind.

Her ancestors on her maternal side at the treadle in a factory; her ancestors on her paternal side, wallpaper and paint men. Forever workers. Who knew women *didn't* work? Just as the New World was catching on to the habits and pleasures of the Old World (as well as the authoritarian messaging), the New World's middle class was feeling the pinch the working class had felt for eons, and female workers knew it, too, way back in Vivienne Pink's family tree.

Her mind, up in the room, ran back to how it felt when she ran her hand along the cool iron web of the chair in the garden. How she'd felt the urge, pressed the button for the cappuccino machine in the breakfast room, took the elevator up to her room, lay back, and out of the side table drawer, Vivienne Pink had taken her postcard of the beautiful naked woman, Venus, looking at herself in the mirror.

Vivienne's relaxation ritual was to get naked and admire how Venus got naked, and how Venus, in the painting, looked at herself in the mirror. Venus, in her cream skin, a kind of a pale dawn from her neck all down her shoulders, her fine spine, her alluringly callipygous figure, her svelte long limbs, the view from the back, a view Vivienne favoured. Venus adrift in an alertness on a green, really a blue-green, a soft shaped coverlet like the dark sea, a sheet like pale blue-green waves. Vivienne had always liked the upper backdrop of rust in *La Venus del Espejo,* by Diego Velázquez. Often called *The Rokeby Venus.*

She didn't mind an art postcard, as an aide-mémoire. A tiny snap of your beloved is the world in your wallet. But that snap as your sole encounter left her panting for the real thing. The Venus postcard was the memory trigger of the times she had been in the National Gallery, in London, where the painting of the naked Venus resided. Venus's hang was room 30. The room called Spain.

Oh, Vivi loved that room. She had on occasion zoomed in from

Heathrow on a layover, just to gaze in person at Venus's bum. And why not? The adoration of the woman's body lasted. The opinions on Venus's body came and went. Good old Diego Velázquez sure knew what he was doing. There was a woman at home in her own flesh, viewing herself; asking us to view with her; to be complicit in adoring her the way she might be adoring her own visage, skin.

Velázquez painted Venus in 1649–1651. Man, that woman looked amazing for three hundred and fifty-five years old. That crack in that ass, and oh yeah, Vivienne had forgotten as she touched herself, and drew the Venus closer, that dimpling above where her buttocks began. Tell me about it, she thought, that gorgeous female did not look a day older than three hundred.

In her interior, a mysterious interior, a boudoir, Venus with her son.

Oh yes, her son, Cupid. Cupid held the mirror. Winged Cupid also naked. With his strap across his middle to hold the arrows. Helping Mom. In the mirror, Venus looks at herself. Vivienne liked how the mirror image was smudgy. Partly in shadow. High-def can mute the mysteries. Velázquez the Spaniard, his *La Venus del Espejo* so delicately yet forcefully painted that the lower part looked like a winter sky. Pale silver-green, an Amsterdam sky reflecting its own cold canal water. Above that bed cloth in the painting, was an indigo-moss cloth, a sensuous murk on which the woman's legendary buttocks lay.

The Venus was private, asking nothing.

Vivienne got an atomic flash in her chest: her first arriving at the desert hotel, ten years ago, to begin her project of photographing servicemen the night before they deployed. How, for fun, before she went downstairs to the hotel coffee shop to pursue her work, she offhandedly snapped a snap of herself in the hotel room mirror, the red hair, the green lizard earrings, pale skin unmarked. That photo was history now. Not just a callback of the years.

That photo Vivienne had taken of herself was a photo of a pre-nuclear woman.

Today, the self-portrait of her body would show her ratty skin, her bald head, her tattooed back, with the python-skin vest she had had on the day the atomic blast went off in Death Valley, burning its pattern into her skin. She had become the snake woman. The laugh of it all was this: she had put up for sale in her Death Valley show three black and white photos of her partial back with the python pattern burned in by the bomb. Her sister, Rhonda, turns up at the gallery show and begins to denounce the photos, because when Vivi was caught in an atom bomb, V had been wearing snakeskin. Rhonda in her pink plastic Crocs, her home chemical streaks, making a commotion at the vernissage. Vivienne had apparently been wearing the wrong fabric when the atomic bomb burned her clothes into her body.

To Vivi, Venus by Velázquez was her true sister, over the ion sands of oil. What do you desire? To be a footnote? The idea was: Make a private dance. Go bravely into your own mishegoss. Chest out into zero visibility. *Tetas arriba!* Listen for the mute ghost breath at your feathered wing. Sail on the updraft of scorched moonlight.

Vivienne's hand inside the creamy oils of her vulva communicated with Venus's buttocks, the callipygian beauty, and after, Vivienne drifted into a lucid winter snooze.

She was imagining Venus at a window seat in a plane over the ocean. A long-legged guy came and sat in the aisle seat beside Venus who was travelling on business. He asked Venus what the book was she was reading. Venus handed him the book, Venus's book of self-portraits. The man leaned back in his seat, looking at the images in the book, looking at Venus as she lay, eyes open, in the flying machine. "Tell me about this one," the man said, "tell me a story to soothe me, I've come back from a gruelling work tour, I was acting in a movie, I was playing a spy. I'm tired and weary and these are story images, aren't they? Is this you? Did you take these pictures?"

Then the man on the aisle seat was in the seat at the window, Venus was lying back in his arms, easing down, they were sleeping over the long dark water. He was holding up a mirror to their sleeping bodies. They left their bodies, they entered the mirror. Then the moss velvet sea. The moss velvet curtain of night. The moss velvet coverlet on the bed over the shadow-creased icebergs.

WHO WOULD WANT to hurt the flesh of a woman? Who would want to damage the skin of a woman relaxing in her chamber?

Who would want to come with a weapon to harm her by mutilation?

Who would come with a knife, a sword, a sabre, a machete to inflict scars, slashes, to rend the flesh of Venus? Who would hack Venus – Velázquez's Venus – to bits?

Why, a woman would. It happened.

That was the hell of it all. It had happened. When Venus was a mere two hundred and sixty-three years old, another woman came to Venus's house in London, the National Gallery, up to Venus' room, carrying a machete, and she slashed the legendary Venus where she hung.

The woman, who was called Mary Richardson, wanted to call attention to the campaign for the franchise for women. In order to make you realize that women deserved the vote, in England, Miss Richardson brought a machete to the National Gallery.

Agitating might be what Mary wanted, that serotonin uptake of the machete upon the skin of a woman. Someone might have paid her to destroy one of art's great paintings, to feel great by destroying. To admire the tyrant and hate the tits. Maybe Mary was a lost soul. Maybe Mary liked women, and Venus got her wet and she wanted to destroy that which would have outed her in 1914. Maybe Mary had no talent and yet wanted to be in the papers. Maybe Mary, and her merry machete, was an early warning sign of a mentally deranged individual, who had a scrap of sanity left, and sanely wanted the vote for women, while hacking art up in a national gallery.

Aw, maybe Mary was jealous. It could have been that Mary Richardson, instantly notorious, instantly all the rage in the press, in 1914 in the city of London, simply wanted to be noticed the way Venus was noticed. One, alluring and beautiful, a woman to set you to dreaming. Another, a woman with an axe to grind – on a 122 by 177 centimetre oil painting.

Four feet by six feet: Venus in person, on the wall, almost life sized.

Mary said in one of her many interviews of the time, as she became well known, notorious, that she didn't like how men admired Venus's body. It was unclear if Mary had ever been to see Venus before she wanted to destroy her.

In fact, it was unclear if Mary had ever done it before. That is, if Mary had ever been to see any paintings at all in a public art gallery. As a virgin to a public art museum, she may have craved to pop her art-cherry by destroying a naked woman.

And, oh yes. Once women got the vote in Britain, Slasher Mary did, in fact, become active in politics. She joined a party. The British Union of Fascists. Mary was attracted to their platform, which promised that, if elected, the Fascists would remove all the Jews from Britain.

Ah yes, with her new right to vote, Mary became an acolyte of a man, Oswald Mosley, who got married in the private rooms of Hitler's man Joseph Goebbels.

Mary wanted to slash the female Venus; Mary wanted to belly up to the male Fascist.

Well. Ain't democracy the withering shits. Vivienne thought, Mary is a footnote. But Venus lives to engorge my clitoris another day.

Querido Diego, what brain fissures did your animal hairbrushes walk on? *Óleo sobre lienzo.* Oil on canvas. *Gracias, Diego, por los ojos dulces.*

VIVIENNE WONDERED IF Alexi, in his low-key watching travels, had ever been to that room called Spain in the National Gallery in London. She pictured him there. She placed him there, in her head, admiring the Venus by Velázquez. Her appearing beside him, looking at Venus's body with him, walking up close, walking back to get the larger view. Getting turned on by the three-hundred-and-fifty-five-year-old rear end of the curvaceous fiction.

She pictured him recording her through a hole in the wall. Could he see her looking at this postcard of *Venus at Her Mirror*? If he could, what was he imagining her thinking? Was he hoping that she was thinking of him? If it was only audio he was recording, what did he hear? Did he listen to her night breath? Did she wake him with her sleep talk? Was he, that way, like a husband? A husband in the next room, listening to his wife scream and dream in the nightfalls? A husband overhearing only his wife's outer utterances, her postwar night mumbles, her going, "I went to war. I was that freak. Now, insomnia's way back in my rear-view mirror. Sleep is the terra incognita of my consciousness." Yet, somehow, he knew. It's in the eyes. You recognize a fellow from the crags, the feral environments. The dog bruises under her female eyes. Beautiful paint, save me.

The Spanish Inquisition had a thing or two to ask Goya, about those Majas. The Inquisition was inquisitive, indeed, about the full-frontal nudity in 1797. In paint. They were steamed, in a fever, boiling, practically crispy in a broil, virtually gratin about Francisco Goya's 97 centimetres by 1.9 metres magnificent homage to the body of a woman. *The Naked Maja. La Maja Desnuda.*

They interrogated Goya about the naked lady. Then, practically flambé, they wanted to hear the motive for the crime Goya committed, in another painting, *The Clothed Maja. La Maja Vestida.* A painting, the size of a slim bed. The size of a chalk outline of a formidable curvaceous woman.

You tell yourself the story has to do with "no clothes." But, if you have lived through authoritarian regimes, you know they will pin you to the wall for the painting of the woman all in white billowy fabric, a kind of a 1800 female jumpsuit, with a golden yellow kind of brocaded shrug, too. A lounging high-low in clothes, and please tell the jury with their lit sticks what prompted you to this paint felony.

Although privately commissioned for a private collector, the clothed and naked Majas were made the state's business. If the men of the state didn't like women naked, and they didn't like women in clothes, exactly what was their problem?

14

THE GIRL WITH THREE HEARTS

GRIEF IS AN animal. Grief has fur. Grief is feral. It eats your map. There are no U-turns, yet you U-turn inside your own body. You walk out your front door, with your face on backward, drowning on dry pavement. The five steps of grief are the footsteps you take before you can't face it and you come back inside the house.

Johnny Coma set out to walk to the water through a ghost world painted in silver charcoal and leaves. He walked down Joan de Borbó laden with wet leaves from hours of rain pouring down the night before. The sun was shining through the old rain down at the end of the street where the sea had been composed of pure light in particle pleasure. He walked, blinded, bathed in light, toward the morning spectres carrying inky surfboards to the pale waves. We were born before the green.

The wind was a bit crazy that morning. The wind was whipping the light around and the surf sounded like righteous trains.

Stella, honey, eleven years with you was such a long time.

The sun from the east shone on his left side as he walked down the seaside promenade on Barceloneta's shores, into the misty. Same daily café, El Petit Far. The Little Lighthouse. Same cortado; same quest; same supposed to open at ten. Same opens about ten to eleven. December was staying mild. Johnny got his Moleskine sketchbook out of his windbreaker. He did some warm-up drawings.

With the dead you can sketch and be stupid. Let me sketch you, Stella. Can it really be twelve years you've been gone?

He drew a mermaid on a unicycle. He cross-hatched the shining scales. He sketched a mermaid on a chair, holding a coffee with her tail. Nice. A mermaid with that mermaid hair. Then he drew a mermaid with an updo. Sweet. But no. Hey, why not Stella as a fish? A Pandora fish. Sure, love the name Pandora. He sketched a girl fish, the big eyelashes. Bright ideas.

Johnny put his Palomino Blackwing 602 pencil behind his ear. The word-carpenter in his follies. He took another sip of his cortadito, eased his eyes out to the far horizon surf. I make lines, but she does not reappear; pelagic, demersal, oneiric, inesse, she does not reappear. The day grey, with pale dogs running on the pale sand. The black bodies of the surfers paddling into the energy grey. The sun was trying for a cameo in the sky. The body of Stella; Stella, we did commend your body to our intimate earth, febrile then frozen. He pressed the Palomino Blackwing against the creamy acid-free paper, making improvised kairos lines.

In the grey waves, a grey sea creature appeared, shaped like a flattened hat with long pulpy streamers. Here in the pelagic waters, a creature rose with eight arms. All twisty, in wave spit. Then, the arms went down and the creature jet-propelled to his feet, turning pink. A tentacle uncoiled, wrapped itself around his right ankle.

What was this? An octopus? Yes, it was an octopus. An octopus?

The octopus took the tentacle back to its face. Was it sampling him? Was that an eye pulsing, looking at him? It wrapped a tentacle around each of his ankles. He had mollusc ankle bracelets. He took a sip of his cortado. And from the ashes, soot. He drew an octopus in his Moleskine sketchbook. He drew a balloon coming out of the octopus's mouth, saying, "Dad! It's me, Stella. I'm here. I love you. No worries, Stella is back to stay." Could it be? If I create it on paper . . .

"Stella," he said out loud, talking to his ankles where the octopus was resting and staring at him. "Remember the red hat we got you? Baie-Saint-Paul on the way to the whales? Hand knit by a lady farmer, you wore it all August."

The nerves in his extremities were tingling. His wrist bone was burning. The octopus let go of both his ankles. Don't leave me, Stella. He reached down, picked up the octopus, put her on the table beside his coffee cup. His daughter. Finally. He did not believe in an afterlife, but what if Stella had returned to swoop through the holes in his disbelief? On a grey day, it happens. She moves like science through the *rías* in my heart. *En mi corazón.*

The creature did something with her red-pink body. She squirted ink on him. Ink. Blobs of beautiful black ink, to cook with, to write with, to put in a syringe and make art with, on a canvas. My child, finally. He could tattoo his heart with the octopus ink of his daughter.

The octopus spoke: "I hate you."

Trauma islands formed inside him.

The octopus took hold of his right wrist, full of ink from the squirt he took as love. The tentacle was turning his arm blue. "I hate you," it said. It had to be an *it* if it hated him. But she was a she, and she was Stella, and she hated him.

The octopus crawled away, leaving a bruise around his writing wrist. Through mini hidings in the sand like an invertebrate recluse, then into the water again. An interlude, then gone, like griping starlight.

He walked home along the beach. Dogs ran free of leashes on the sand. The promenade was wide, the sun was on his back, he took Joan de Borbó across into the Born stone walls and the stone tunnels and into his stub of an alley, home. He sparred with a semicolon until he napped. The metal hissing of *I hate you* filled his sleep.

THE NEXT MORNING, when the sun was low and weak and the sky was silver, making shadow people on the promenade by the water, Johnny came back to look for Stella. Same café, same table, same coffee – if you're an artist you're superstitious if you're wise. He sketched an octopus.

Whap! A jet-propelled item with a beak flew at him, beak-butted his shnoz.

Stella. She, by water. The octopus sat on his bald head. "Hey, big boy, if you loved me, we'd do things. Go on trips," the octopus said.

"We did things," Johnny said. "We did – everything."

"What a farce on wheels. If you really loved your daughter, you'd go around together."

Didn't she remember? Are the dead blank? Are the dead senile bone matter? Or was it Jewish amnesia – you hold the grudge to the grave. Oy gevalt, *beyond* the grave they keep hocking you. Parental purgatory.

"Give me a tentacle."

"They're not tentacles. Dad, you're making my hearts hurt. You're giving my gills major grief."

"Sorry. So sorry. What are they? Tell me. I really want to know." The dearly departed come back, and you're already in trouble.

"Dad, I'm an octopus now, I have *arms*."

"Oh. I didn't know."

"Well, obviously, my dad, Mister Pitzel, is without a single clue."

He remembered Stella as being sassy, older than her age, a bookworm who loved David Bowie, glam and also old R & B crooners. He didn't remember that he was *that* much of a loser in her blue eyes. Had she, after death, gone through puberty, come back to him as a teenage octopus?

Plead your case, Dad. "Stella, remember in Spain, the Basque country? We went around in San Sebastián, remember, that day? We walked up the seven K curve along the Bay of Biscay to the aquarium, we saw the skates, the rays, we rode the closed carousel the man opened just for you. After the carousel, we walked the shoreline as the tide rose. We had to run – remember? – because there was a seawall and we got caught. We had wet pants and we went for warm drinks and watched the night lights around the bay curve. Right?"

"My gills hurt. It's a lot of work trying to breathe, get all that water to run across them."

"But you do remember . . . ?"

"Mummy left us."

"Stella."

"We woke up, she was gone. She left you a note, 'Back to Iraq, sorry, baby.'"

"It said more than that, honey."

"Don't honey me." She squirted ink in his eyes. "Ma abandoned us."

An older señor moving a metal detector across the sand noticed Johnny and Stella.

Johnny said, "Don't talk about your mother that way, she was working."

"She was *working*," Stella said.

"She *was* working. Who do you think supports us, surely not my writing. My last royalty cheque was thirty-two dollars and eighty-seven cents. It's your mother who puts food in your mouth, my dear daughter."

"Then look what happened."

The octopus climbed down his neck. The wonder had muscle, who knew.

Stella the octopus said, "Are you my real dad? Why don't I have a sister? Everybody has a sister but me."

If this is the afterlife, then, man alive, in the afterlife they're still kvetching. The dead come back and they blame you in person.

THE METAL-DETECTING SEÑOR walked up the sand to their terrace table. Pointing at Stella, he said, *"Pulpo."*

"Si, señor," Johnny said.

"A mí me gustó mucho pulpo," the señor said. *"Pulpo a la gallega, con aceite de oliva, y bravas."* Tapping the pulp skin of Stella with his metal detector, while speaking of boiled octopus arms, chopped up, the neuron-laden octo-buttons done up with olive oil, paprika, served on a platter with fried potatoes.

"Deliciosa. Sabrosita," Johnny said. Stella wound two arms around Johnny's wrist.

"Muy inteligente, pulpo," the señor said, tapping Johnny's hand. *"Cada uno de los brazos se tiene un cerebro, ¿vale?"* Hold the phone. The señor, yes, was saying that an octopus has a brain in each arm. His daughter had eight brains?

Si si. Stella-Octo had a brain at the end of each arm.

The señor went on, *"Pero, más hay un cerebro central."* Not only does an octopus have eight brains, there is, in addition, a main brain in the head. The big mainframe brain and the eight satellite brains. Nine neurologies in one body. She came like ENIAC's ancient muse from down by bathysphere mountain.

Johnny Coma's octopus daughter was the original model for the Internet. Beautiful. All this time he had been eating pieces of vanguard neuro-technology, fried in olive oil. At tapas bars, he had been savouring real intelligence sprinkled with paprika.

Off the señor toddled with his metal detector, his seminar on Stella the cephalopod completed.

Stella withdrew her arms from his. "I hate you more," she said. She crawled away. Johnny watched her blue arms crawl back into the blue water.

HE WALKED UP the seaside promenade, lit from behind, walking on top of his long shadow.

In his head, he heard Stella speaking to him, "You are the worst father who ever was. I wish I was dead. Then you'd be sorry."

At the café on the sea curve he got a cortado. She wished she were dead. Bicyclists lined up their bikes against the aluminum chairs, went inside, got their drinks, came out, sipped and joked in activewear. Wished she was dead. For pity's sakes on a rental! She *was* dead. Or was it true? She was back in another form. Was this the story? Had his daughter returned and found him merely *so-so*?

He felt awash in *saudade*, that Portuguese word for the emotion of missing things, missing yourself, missing your home, and who you love, and missing it all most and them almost most of all when you are right in their midst and because life *is* to live, missing. He missed his miserable days, sitting as the dad caring for his daughter, when he had packed her off to school across the street at Palmerston School, and he sat in the darkened front room playing Percy Sledge and Bill Withers. He began to sing to his cortado, one more crooner at a seaside café, singing, "Lean on Me," his hands spread out, playing café-table raindrop-keyboard, his lips pursed like a crooning pooch, his voice not bad, the table next to his, populated by three young women, swaying to his pooch croon, their thumbs up, as he crooned about a brother needing a hand. We all need a geezer all wacko at the patio singing about pain and sorrow with his tabletop piano. "Stella, please come back."

One of the young women gave him one of those "Aw, poor guy" looks. Aw, but warm, three thumbs-up. Pure Spain, pure emotion in common in the shadows so sharp of the long knives.

He felt a surge, like his inner need-choir had rushed the notes to his wrist bone. He scribbled names: November Octopus. Novoctopus. Novepus, Novopus, Novempus. Cabeza. Cerebropus. Brainiac. Brainopus. Pinkopus. Stellopus. Stellantis. Cerebellum Tremendum. Cerebellopus. Ocho, Nueve, Nerve-o-pus. Hello?

The octopus zoomed to the edge of his cortado saucer.

"You said the plane would have beds and we'd have pistachio ice cream. You made me sit in a sick seat. A man vomited on me. A dog died with the luggage. He had the brachy-brachy nose, they can't breathe. You put a dog in the overhead. He was a dead dog when they landed. A pug, I heard."

"When?" God, the dead come back, and they're lying gossips.

"The big rabbit died. Everybody died on the plane. You brought rabbits and dogs and everything and you promised me a Dixie cup. Butterscotch. The rabbit was too big to fly, that dead dog don't hunt, *Da-ad*. I heard Mommy got raped in a hotel hallway. What do you know about that, Mister *Writer?* Scribble that, you."

"Stop making up stories." (Why did Stella say that? Had something happened to his Vivi? Wouldn't V tell him?)

"Show me the ice cream. You went away. Mummy went away. Mummy got hurt. I hate Auntie Rhonda. You left me with her. She watched afternoon dreck on TV all day with her dope friends. Banging and bonging all day. Rhonda liked *disco!*"

Stella was a spin mistress, but man, she was gorgeous.

She walks like a chameleon shadow from the sea. She was walking across the table, away from him.

She turned around. "Dad, why weren't you home the day they killed me?"

OCTOPUS, *PULPO, POP;* baby octopus, *pulpito, popet.* Get her back, press that lead.

At the café, Johnny worked the pencil tip across the cream paper. He sketched himself: bald head, round glasses. He sketched an octopus with arms up, in the water. He put a balloon coming out of his cartoon mouth, saying, "Remember me? Stella!!! It's Dad!!!"

The creature on the page was mute. She was on to him – those exclamation marks were truly desperate. Phylum: *Mollusca.* Class: *Cephalopoda.* Order: *Octopoda.* Just call on me, when you need a tentacle . . . oh boy. He was a bad dad. But his love was a mess too, a mess and strong.

He drew a balloon coming out of the octopus's mouth, saying, "Sorry, I can't place your face." Time had turned him into a tender dumpster with shoes. The early joggers, skateboarders, paddleboarders, dog runners, they didn't know he was a thing appearing to be a man, a human being, an imposter of civilization.

You angioplast your heart; you wet-vac your colon; you reject your meat, your milk, your daily bread; you eat raw and then your daughter is murdered. God had to be the best stand-up in history. Johnny Coma positioned his hands above the raindrops again and played some mean Withers, singing to the wet newspaper saying Fidel Castro was dead. Leonard Cohen a couple weeks ago, now Fidel the wet noodle bites the dust and what will *they* return as, in the next life?

How to induce Stella Octopus to come back again? She liked his ankles.

IF ONLY WE knew our origins in neurological waters.

Once we were big as barrios, and sailed with the fossils. Once we had communion with masted vessels, blubber, whale fat; once light was our womb. Once we broke out when the water broke and we were light, with limbs. We were made of water and, forming, we shone.

Once we had blue minds and our blue minds ran around the veins of our bodies like rivulets and we were riverine walking the old rivers of cities, green in the autumn shadows beneath the amber plane trees.

Stella had come along and she had made the two-headed creature called

Johnny-and-Vivienne into a three-headed family. Then, when she died, the two of them, Vivi and Johnny, were two separate beings; the love team conjoined became two souls avoiding each other within the four brick walls of their grief. He missed Vivi most when they made love. They had become two absences trying to induce presence by fucking.

Once, when we were belugas, we grieved by sonar. Once we swam like ambergris in vertigo. For when we fell, we fell across the water and the water was water and then the drought was water, too, and they cancelled the Exodus and we walked across the desert to the bright nobody.

Why wouldn't Stella reappear?

He flipped through his notebook: almost filled up.

Johnny stood up, stretched his legs on the promenade. Stretched his eyes: the wind had picked up, sailboats knew it. Could he induce her to come back through his digits of astrophysical whimsy? He walked back to the café, got another cortadito.

He watched the waves. Here comes the Buddha with a machete.

He wrote,

Dear Stella,

You came first, then came the need for you. The effect caused the cause, in me. You arrived, a chance surprise, a part of my heart that wasn't there before, and now called up its own evolutionary purpose: love. Love and the species.

Total crap. Crapola. Pickle it in brine.

The octopus crawled out of the water. Up onto the table, to a saucer where the last café patron had left a roach. The octopus put the roach in her fifth hand, said, "Light this, you two-armed liar."

Johnny put his pencil down, the letter unfinished. Stella had come back despite his crap. He had not earned her return with his words, yet there she was, asking for a light for her weed. Lighter? Johnny didn't carry a lighter. He walked over to the next table, asked for *fuego* from the female trio who had kind of adopted him as their mascot, got a book of matches, came back, lit the octopus roach.

The octopus crawled over to his right wrist. She crawled up his arm, sat on his shoulder. "You said you had had it with creatures. You were going to write the world as it is. Only real names. Only real people. No – how did you put it? – fantasy creatures. You're an idiot, you know, Dad. You're a moron."

"Don't talk to your father like that."

"You are. You never cared about anybody but the creatures. Then you denounced them. You made all these things for me, then you took them away. You said there was a story about going under the ground when it snowed, in tunnels. You said Tunnel #3 was the best tunnel, then you never told me that story. Out of the wind, you said. We never went anywhere."

"Stella, I don't know what you're talking about." His octopus darling was beginning to sound a bit like the newbie president of the USA. Trickle-down discontinuity.

"You told me to grow up."

"You were always a big girl. You had a big soul from the beginning."

"Yeah yeah yeah. Old soul and other flatteries. Stop sucking up. What, you got a miniseries? Don't pitch the one you love."

She put two arms around his neck, then a third.

What is parenthood but the irrational suction cup of love?

She was born before the humans. After the soot, the cave wall suggested bison. Ochre wanted noses. What to do with a wrist, asked the human?

"It's true. You were never a kid, Stel. Even when you were a kid you were never a baby. We never talked down to you, so you grew up fast."

"Are you happy, Dad?"

"No."

"Good." She took her arms away from his neck, walked down his windbreaker, crawled onto the table, put an arm around the cortado glass, drained the coffee, ate the smoking roach, crawled down a wicker chair. She walked low and back into the water.

She propelled back, landing on the table. "Mummy was raped." She shot back to the sand, to the water.

"What the hell?" Johnny said. Stella was bobbing in the waves.

She hopped a ride on a paddleboard, sat on the edge as the standing paddleboarder with her oar took the board and Stella toward the rocks splashed with graffiti.

Lean on me. Start slowly, easy, ease like a guy just going along, no big deal. Close your eyes when you sing of tomorrow, because it hurts too much to have hope. Then open your eyes like your heart has a virus making it miss a beat and pause. Wrack easy with that arrhythmia, syncopate the hell out of the situation, volume up. Johnny was pumping his feet on the sandy wooden boards, as if they were piano pedals. He was rocking back and forth. He held his right hand to his mouth, like a microphone, getting ready to sing again.

The octopus reappeared inside his hand, an octopus mic. Stella was singing, "Lean on Me." His daughter, the octopus, knew the tunes of Bill Withers. The mic sings! The mic has eight arms; the mic has nine brains. The cephalopod mic crooned to him about needing someone to lean on. Need, pain. She can fit in my hand, she can rhyme *sorrow* with *tomorrow*. The microphone spoke: "Dad, my hearts hurt."

"I'm so sorry, honey, that your heart hurts."

"Not heart. Hearts, plural."

"Tell me. Go on."

"I am a girl with three hearts. It's a lot of work. I have eight arms to hold you, three hearts to miss you, nine brains to wonder where my parents were the day somebody murdered me."

"We were working, Stel, please."

"Don't 'please' me with your pity party prevarications, Poppa."

She has brass, sass and she alliterates. The sun round the Mediterranean curve fought with the beautiful cumulus.

Stella spoke: "Dad, it's about my hearts. I get stitches, I feel like I'm having a hearts attack sometimes. The current exchange feels blocked in my first heart, the oxygen some days feels too high around my second heart, you know? Do you even know how my gills work? Do you know? Did you ever care to know how I breathe? Some days, Dad, it's so hard to breathe. And my third heart? Don't ask. My third heart, like my main brain, handles the big stuff. My third heart, Dad, is like the CEO of my CO_2. The blood river flows one way; the oxygen river runs the other. They talk to each other in their countercurrents. My body is running blue rivers."

She was a poet, he better stay mum about that. "Go on," he said.

"I need a lot of air. Oxygen, Dad. I need more oxygen than most, gotta push that oxygen from my gills to my hearts. You and Ma have it easy. You only have to breathe for one heart. You only have to ache with one heart. You only have to miss me with one heart. I missed you all day long with two, with three hearts. I have three hearts to miss you. Dad, why did I die?"

And the void will squeeze you.

The octopus kissed him on his right cheek. She kissed him on his left cheek. Like two paparazzi meeting and greeting in the Euro way on a cinema promenade in Cannes. "Dad, why didn't you fuck off yet?" Eight arms to hold me, three hearts to miss me and a beak like the street.

Foam anthems rushing in and out of the Mediterranean. Stella turned from pink to grey, we all have pain, from grey to blue, we all have sorrow, from blue to mottled ochre to pink and grey, lean on me, and his returned daughter walked away. Crawled morphing from the version of herself with a large head and arms aloft to a small ball of grey with the arms coiled in. Floated away, a message out of the bottle.

The dead come for brief visits. Their ink is their mark.

The minor chords were gone, for today. The rain had dried on the table.

15

CHILLIDA'S *WIND COMBS*

THE IDEA WAS: lose your identity, cast off your stable self, induce a mist at your edges and enter the world more completely, as somebody else.

Enter the world as the rain, if you have to.

Write a novel to fit inside a window frame, write your best sky.

Morning, when the bimah light from the ark lifted up from behind the sea to backlight the shorebirds. On the roof of his attic aerie, Johnny Coma pressed the pencil lead into the soft cream of his notebook. Down below, the night echoes had dimmed in party central, and all the cocktails of the universe had gone back into their bottles for a libation shluf. The sea-bleached wooden wings of the shops were closed in slat feathers. The empty neighbourhood felt alive to a writer looking for magnetic luck.

The sun rose. The after-party lights dimmed.

Johnny with Sancho in the dark in the public square. That routine move. Then Johnny took a dawn wander before he walked to the Mediterranean waters. Same streets, workers' streets of ancient. Cauldron makers, shoemakers, fishmongers, mirror makers, glassworkers, the labourers, their locally named stone map. Blanket weavers, this, the ancient fish and textile barrio, in Barcelona famous for textiles, as Catalonia is.

Repetition and rest. The recipe of the master. Consistency and naps. Steady as a dull dog. Lashings of yawn, lardings of stunned. This was Johnny Coma's walking writing rhythm: the city like an empty page, or a stage set.

Repetition, routine. Superstition. Loose lips sink manuscripts. He was a stupid gambler; his love required it.

Down Joan de Borbó, a sliver of silverized light, he went. The sun was shy after the rain; it danced on all the sodden plane tree leaves, as Johnny shuffled along. Hard to sequester port cities, by their nature they look outward.

The Catalan question might also be a question of light. Light sailed in from the east, light poured in from the south, light soaked in water, light in containers off-loaded at the industrial port of light, light in exile, émigré light, light rushing in and out of the tall walled passages. At the El Petit Far beach café he was figuring his next tactic for how to bring Stella back again.

The rain had been heavy overnight; the wave energy was still last night's blast, pushing the waves. Waves like trains, like artillery, like the sound of war bringing the surfers like enlistees to the risk reef.

"Stella liked me, didn't she?" he said to his cortado. "She picked a fight with me. I mean, she did say she hated me."

A couple jogging by gave each other that eye roll, hearing him, yet gave him a thumbs-up. The young can have that special tenderness toward the addled creative class.

"Sea of heartbreak. Stella, I can see you at the end of my pencil." Talk to the page, talk to the cortado. He was panicking, a total suck-up of love. A.k.a. a parent. You dumb yourself down to get to dumb love, but dumb love is a pooch, dumb love loves you anyway. Love is a mutt.

He sat with his back to the Escola de Surf, the boards set up on the side, a nice wind blowing stuff around, surfboards and freestyling doggies, the surfers barefooted running up side streets to the waves, surfers on bikes one-handed with boards under the other. Dogs ran on the sand, freedom dogs off the leash. A tall man tried to get a bit of sand out of the eye of his shorter sweetie. The winter café denizens sat and sipped and smoked, bits of ash twirled in the air, wind, the things of forever. Johnny loved to be out in public so he could ignore everybody else and bathe in the human soundtrack.

He fished out his triangular silver pencil sharpener, sharpened his Blackwing, looked at the frilled triangles from the sharpener on the top of the aluminum table, wet with rain. Little tan-coloured sails: it surprised him every time. He got out his Moleskine sketchbook from his pocket; he sketched the shape of the pencil shavings. In his hand, they had become not only pencil-shaving sails, but a soft shell for a sea creature. A creature who had left the dust of herself beside the shell.

And he began to write:

He wondered if it should be a letter, a Dear Stella, or like the story of the visit to the tombstone of Walter Benjamin up the coast at the French border at Portbou. Maybe she'd like it told more as a story.

He gave the pencil sharpener a wrist twist, making those furled lead sails on the page. Sweeping the silver-edged leaving aside, Johnny wrote.

Dear Stella,

Guess what?

Up in the north part of Spain, along the Bay of Biscay in the colder waters, a girl named Stella and her father, that lump they called Mister Coma, went to San Sebastián like they'd always talked about going. So they went that time.

STELLA AND HER father sat on the tiny balcony of the Hotel Niza, which faced Playa de la Concha, La Concha Beach. The wind was moving through their hair. Even on the top floor of the hotel, they were only on the seventh storey. On the beach below dog walkers in big sweaters followed their pooches beside the low tide. Johnny had a treat in store for Stella. "Let's go, Stel, I'm taking you to the water's edge."

Down they walked along the bay. Grey water, big waves, wind tapping their cheeks. The day was like an open window.

Up a narrow walkway toward the steel and the stone. At the end of the walkway, where the big stone rocks opened onto open curved water around the San Sebastián curve, there in Basque country, they came to the epic sculpture of the best sculptor of the century, in Johnny and Vivi's opinion, Eduardo Chillida, the master of materials.

There it was, *Peine del Viento,* literally *Comb of the Wind,* but Johnny and Vivienne, over the years, always called it *The Wind Combs.* Three steel curves, in mysterious rhythm, attached to the already-existing rocks. Each curve a separate opening, nailed to the grey formation, its home where in tide and out, the rust colour combed the alluring northern wind channels. World might be simple water and a simple desire by wind to have its current tresses pampered in the rough Atlantic life.

A spout of water right beside Stella's sneakers made her giggle and want the giggle spout again. Then they walked close to the nearest comb, a curved frame showing form, heft, showing equilibrium beside the big bay, calm with those big waves coming in on the fringes. The wind comb was bigger than Johnny in height, and he and Stella could fit into its frame, be wind themselves in peril crawling over the rocks to get to the round steel parentheses. The wind comb like time in its receipts. It was a miserable day by any conventional measure; they were elated in the way Chillida the sculptor had shaped the apparent miserable drizzle into something of sailors and oceans, the way the horizon seemed limitless, unseen, its own beating heartline.

Stella was crawling way out on the first rock, slippery yet she seemed at home in the moss slime, as she entered the wind comb curve, sat there. "Don't be a scaredy-cat, Dad." She reached her hand out to him. He slid, lumbered, fell, heading for grey water below. He caught himself.

"This, my darling Stel, is where it's at."

He was a spaz, a klutzy lump. She didn't mind him, on that journey.

She was ensorcelled by the grey waves, a human washing up, sure, where the salt of the Atlantic water and the darker palette of the obscure flow. The Bay of Biscay was a beautiful curved comma in grey.

"You know the salt eats things," he said, hanging onto Stella's hand, as if he were the child, not her.

"Is it eating us?" She liked that idea, he could see it in her lit eyes. A far foggy blast of sun matched her eyes, clicked with them. The aquarium around the curve, the surf beaches the other way. The city of San Sebastián, back of them and all around. The site for the *Wind Combs* nailed to rocks on the water's edge was perfect, intentional, it takes years to make every choice nail the moment. Chillida's intention was to nail millennia to the rocks and make a face-to-face interrogation between the Atlantic winds and the Basque sculptural materials.

"I've never gone to my limits, kiddo."

"Dad, don't be a dolt, just do it."

"Easy to say."

Stella was trying to console him, while being annoyed with what to her was his perpetual whining about his writing. He was right and she was right. He tried to stand up, fell down on the slick rock. They crawled, the two of them, from that rock to an area hidden from view, where another wind comb was nailed. Like paint or bird shit, they say, two white bits on the grey rocks beside the man-made steel curved comb, which by now after a dozen years on site had begun to take on the appearance of something always there, an outcrop, a magnificent presentation of labour as if Chillida in the late twentieth century channelled the sense of the prehistoric, these epic combs seeming like found objects in an archaeological dig called your own heartbreak.

JOHNNY AND STELLA rested in the covelet, the only humans by the wind comb shelter. "You see, Stel, Chillida went to the limit, he *wanted* to go to the limit, and when he got to the limit, that was where he started."

Stella inched over, kissed her dad. "It's okay, Mister Pitzel."

She was trying to console her father by the northern waters. It irritated him; he loved it. He would have given anything later, when she was dead, to have her back inside the combs, the ocean water coming in from the Atlantic to their faces as they stayed planted on the rocks and she was consoling him and he was pissed off in a tenderness.

"He went to the limit as the starting gate of inquiry. That's where the sculptor went. He knew the materials. They were old friends. He knew how to use a blowtorch, how to hew, he knew how to hammer. He knew about foundries. He was looking for the big balance. He made a steel curve, so the wind could write poetry, by –"

"Is Mommy going to get dead in Iraq?"

"Stella."

"It happens. I'm not a baby, you know."

"I know." He laughed into the wind. "Believe me, I know."

Stella took his hand, held it tight. The child of eleven, the adult of eleven. "They could shoot her. Shoot her in the back."

"Stel, please."

"Like that man said in the letter. What was that about? The dolt couldn't even spell *Vivienne*. He called Mommy Vicki. He was going to kill her and he couldn't even spell!"

They crawled from the hidden cove rock back to the one rock with less coverage, more face to the waves. Johnny was still exuding his ozone excitement of how Eduardo Chillida had made the *Wind Combs* so natural, yet not nature at all.

"You see," he said, brushing her matted hair out of her face. "The master has to go to where the materials disappear; the master has to go to where the master disappears."

"Who's disappearing?" Stella said. Tapping the edge of the steel wind comb. "You're not going to disappear on me, are you, Dad?" She lay back on his shoulder.

Parents are supposed to disappear, in time. You're *supposed* to bury your parents, not your children. And the truth was, when Stella died – her physical self disappearing – he found he could not go out to those outer limits he had so craved, before. He was afraid to go where the materials disappeared so that he, a master, could disappear, because he might well disappear and never come back. Words were going to hijack him to deepest Hades. So, he wrote, with a low bar, using yesterday's hands.

But in San Sebastián on the Bay of Biscay, with Stella, they left the windows open on that top floor of the hotel. The night was salt, the moon was the idea of north. Stella snored; he sat on the balcony, drawing in the dark with the twinkling lights around the shore curve.

16

HOMICIDE LINGUISTICS

WITH THE LIVING, you can be fleet. Room 46, the Owl Hotel echolocating the night. The wet lights of the polder city, Amsterdam, held up from floods but just barely. Vivi and Alexi were still on the bed.

"Let me bug you some more," Alexi said. "Play the pest. Was the python vest pattern on your back from the bomb your first lesion, then?"

She laughed. "Hardly. Do we have to talk about this stuff? We should go out."

"We just got in. Don't let me make you nervous."

"I am."

"Nervous?"

"Sure."

"Why? I'm a nice guy."

The one lamp near the TV screen up high was casting a pool of amber. "Precisely," she said.

"You don't fancy nice?"

"On you I do. My carapace has a different opinion."

"So it wasn't the bomb, then?"

"Nope."

"Radiation, no hair, poisoning, you went through some terrible times but no, you say."

"You asked me what the primary lesion was. Of my life, ever? Or?"

"Whatever you prefer."

"I want to say Mexico City, September 1968," Vivi said. "I want to say one million people in the public square, I want to say seeing the tanks roll in to the D.F., then seeing an exhibit of David Siqueiros the same day. Early youth lesions for sure. Lesions on my eyes."

"Literally?"

"No, dummy. Soul. My soul eyes. I saw kids my own age being gunned down in the Distrito Federal – my eyes were wounded, soft eyes too young, that's me."

"So, Mexico then."

"Not necessarily. That was '68. Two years later, I see the tanks roll in to Montreal; I see my country under war measures. I got a pic in Ottawa on Parliament Hill the night they declared my country to be at war with the terrorists, bombs in the mailboxes, and the pic I got was of the body double of the prime minister, Pierre Trudeau, coming out of Parliament like a decoy in advance of the real PM. Twenty minutes later we photogs were banned from the Hill. But the real lesion came later."

Alexi scooched down under the covers, making a tent of the coverlet. Vivienne came down under the coverlet, a safe space inside a hotel room inside a hotel on a street corner of a one-block street in quiet Amsterdam. Inside her carapace.

She said, "But for all that, it was Guatemala that was the real primary cause. Casus belli. I came to the highlands of Guatemala to learn Spanish, and where I went to language school, there was a guerrilla war going on. I lived with a family. I had a basic room unheated in the cold elevation nights. The sun was sharp in the daytime, I went down the hills to school. The name of the city was Quetzaltenango. Known as Xela from the indigenous Xelajú. Every day the lower part of the sky was filled with the sound of war, the sound of helicopters flying over the roofs, including the rooftops where the couple-three language schools held classes in the open air.

"At my school, where the teachers were pretty much Indigenous and we got one-on-one teaching, we didn't ever go to the roof. They were smart cookies, those teachers, and they knew no matter who you were, you were suspect. Even if you leaned to the middle or were just tall in a short-person country you were suspect. An educator or a musician or a – God forbid – journalist, or a basketball player, the *helicópteros* were the *helicópteros* and I learned to speak Spanish with an inner trill of blades rotating.

"This is before they started kidnapping the Swedes, the Dutch. This is before they pulled journalists like me out of cars on the highway and murdered them dead to rights, before they assassinated whole camera crews who came to Guatemala to document the genocide. The Guatemalan censorship of the press became, simply, murder."

"And you? What happened to you, Vivienne Pink?"

"I became skeptical after Mexico City. A bit haughty. More than. Later, I veered to being cynical, not quite though. During Guatemala, yeah, now that you ask, I became something else."

"Tell me. You can."

"I became – professional."

"You weren't scared? Petrified?"

"Not hardly. If such beauty could be tormented, tortured, then – well, if I was born to be a poet, I would do it that way. I saw stuff. I wanted to frame it."

They came up for air from under the coverlet.

"Frame what, Vivi?"

"What wasn't inside the frame. Homicide linguistics."

Alexi leaned back, as if a wind had punched him. "Whoa. What's that?"

"How I learned Spanish. In Guatemala. I needed to know, I was hungry for the world. You see, my first Spanish lesson was death in Castilian."

In her head, she could feel the body photos returning, that personal file, her body housing. The green mountains of Guatemala. The mountains of Guatemala were the most beautiful green she had ever seen. In the shadow of those mountains, she learned her first baby words in Spanish. She learned to speak cover-up. She learned to speak redaction. They chatter on the outskirts of world torment, but the tormented stay silent.

Vivienne was up, unzipping her carry-on backpack. She took out a plain white envelope. She walked over to Alexi. "Read this," she said.

Inside was a piece of yellowed paper. Lined. Alexi unfolded it.

Vivienne had kept the lined piece of paper in her travel backpack for decades. It was her reminder, her amulet.

She said, "Go ahead, read it to me. It could be the voice-over for that video of the dancers in the club."

Alexi's left eyebrow went up, as he glanced at the paper in his hands.

"*El asesinato* – assassination," he said, reading the piece of paper.

"Go on," Vivienne said.

Alexi, reading: "*El hecho* – deed. *Los balazos* – bullets. *El cobarde* – coward." He held the paper out, shook his head, shrugged a "what the hell is this?" Vivi motioned with her hand to go on.

"Assassination, deed, bullets, coward. Okay. Next. *Un grupo de desconocidos* – a group of unknowns. *Un*, no that's crossed out, *una emboscada* – ambush."

"And the last word. Read it. Go on, read it to me. No one ever has," she said.

"*El duelo* – mourning."

Alexi handed the piece of paper to Vivi, beside him on the bed. "What is this?" he asked.

She punched the paper with her fist. "This, my dear, was my first day at school. In war, you learn war words. That is how screwed up my Spanish lobes of my brain are. Homicide cognition."

He grinned.

Vivi ran her hand down the words, written in blue ink, her cursive more legible, more loops, then. "Pretty fucked up, isn't it? Who knew how to ask for the local bus, the *Galgo*? Or the greengrocer? But 'They were murdered' I knew."

She turned the piece of paper over.

"Look," she said. "I wrote 'Xela, Guatemala, July 2, 1980.'" She ran her hand along a blue cursive scrawl. "Look. By my second day at school, I knew how to say, 'We hid in the gringo café when the police filled the very hilly streets because they killed the human rights lawyer yesterday.' *Café, gringo, policía, calles, colinas, abogado, derechos humanos. Muerte. Ayer.*"

"Jesus. The second day?"

"War, you dive in. The learning curve is a fast arrow. Learn or get out of the way. I learned how to be a fast learner. More second-day vocabulary: *El acuerdo* – the resolution. *El comunicado de prensa* – the press release. By the third day, *la zozobra* – the capsizing, the anxiety. *El secuestro* – the kidnapping. I had only ever used those words in English about something in the news, or a movie. In Guatemala, this was my verbal necessity to describe everyday life. I slept at night with the talking parrots and the sounds of fire-fights in the mountains."

Vivienne slipped the death vocabulary back into the envelope. She put it in her backpack, secured in the hidden pocket.

"It's my good luck totem," she said to Alexi. "Gotta have it with me, wherever I travel."

"Sounds like bad luck to me," he said, motioning her to come lie back on the bed with him.

"*Al revés, querido.* It's better to remember the death of others versus the promotion of yourself.

"I remember one day I took a bus, by myself, three-four hours down to Guatemala City, get away from the constant sound of machine guns in the mountains. 'Oh, good, I'll go see a movie,' I figured. I went to see *Fingers*," she said to Alexi.

"Harvey Keitel."

"Yeah, I mean, hello? There are soldiers outside the cinema, with serious *ametralladoras*, seriously. I'm a righteous gringa thinking like it's normal – *soldados, muerte, miedo.* I'm talking myself down from antsy pants at the cine, *en Español.* That's when you know the immersion has worked: when your inner chatter is in your new language. I was well equipped to practically shit my pants, to see Keitel in *Fingers*, translated if I recall correctly as *El Precio de un Hombre.* 'The Price of a Man' in Spanish; *Fingers* in English.

"Keitel's dad is a macher in the Mafia, a collector, and here's Harvey, this prodigy pianist who becomes a mob fixer for Daddy. The pianist breaks people's hands. The thing about regime is that you don't need a pundit to explain metaphor."

"Amen to that. Then what happened. After *Fingers*."

"I take the bus back to the war zone, the school zone, I get off the bus into the public square, the entire square is filled with police in their blue uniforms. I'd been gone one day and the whole situation had changed. Why was the joint full of *la policía?* Never mind, I'm soaking wet with sweat and afraid that a two-week-old *International Herald Tribune* I cadged in Guate City might somehow implicate me. What had happened was that the *policía* or somebody had killed a local human rights lawyer, there had been a big cortège down the hills for his funeral and they had begun to hunt down those who attended the funeral and all hell was clandestinely breaking bones. I scuttled like a lizard to my house, came in the door set in the high wall, came into the courtyard, tried to make casual chit-chat with the father of the family who kept a whole battalion of old cars for parts in the courtyard and had his head in some old engine. Nobody said anything about anything. I learned homicide vocabulary in a mute nation. Even to learn the words, I see now, was an act of rebellion."

"You made that book of Guatemala," Alexi said.

"You know it?"

"Your father, Izzy, gave me a copy."

"Don't shit me, brother. Please."

"No, seriously. He was so proud of you."

"Not that I ever heard."

"He never told you?"

"Nope," Vivienne said.

"AFTER A WHILE . . . "

"After a while . . . ?"

" . . . I took my photos in Spanish," Vivienne said.

"But they're photographs."

"You could hear everything not in the picture. You could hear the death squads breathing at the edge of the frame."

In the dark, standing at the doorway, Alexi said, "You stay up all night thinking about these things?"

"Rarely."

"There's a lot of anger there."

"Yes."

"It doesn't keep you up at night?"

"Like I said: rarely."

"What does? What keeps you up at night, then?"

"Me? Tones."

"Tones . . . . Okay."

"Tones. Tones, hues, tints. Balance. Saturation." Vivienne was up pacing. "If the grey in the print I made was too icy, or too flat, not rich enough. If the black was too – how to say it – fat. If the black on the print blossomed and I didn't want it to. How to turn a ripple so it whispers off the pic only in dog hearing. If the cheekbone on the woman is shadowed in a way I intended, to show her facial stature, or the tone made her look almost puffy, when she has cheekbones with dignity. The technical. That's what keeps me up at night. Did I go to all the trouble of working on my work, and the product will be at the low bar? If I have years of experience, do my photographs show the ease of a master or am I coasting? The technical music. Harmony. The speed of the eye. Paper. Chemicals. Will I use paint on my photos, for a goof, fun, a brazen slash? *That* I will get out of bed for, to go back into the red cave."

He kissed her on the lips, started to put his clothes on.

"*¿Dónde vas, querido?*" she asked.

"*Me voy a Barcelona.*"

"*Barcelona. ¿Cómo? ¿Porqué?*"

"*Tengo negocios en la ciudad.*"

"Business, what business? In Barce?" she asked him. He didn't answer. He was getting ready to go.

Out of her mouth: "Flux and Ister / I am your sister./ Call me Heraclitoris."

"I THOUGHT I was going to be a rabbi," Alexi said, apropos of talking to avoid the moment of leaving. "I thought I was going to be a painter. Look, I come from 'Start-Up Nation.'"

"So you are Israeli."

"Partially."

"A tech guy."

"Isn't everybody in Tel Aviv? Tel Aviv's like Vegas, that's where the tech talent hangs out."

"But you guys are – I mean Israel invented the cell phone, didn't they? Come on."

"We moved to T.O. a long time ago. But I still have contacts."

"I just bet you do," she said.

He swerved the conversation. "The tone when you took me and the glove? You spoke of tones. What was – What is the tone with you and me?" he asked.

"Right now?" she replied. "Intimate. The secret life of objects."

"Let me be a pest again. Tell me how you got to that. The secret life of objects."

"A minute ago."

"A minute ago?"

"I only saw it, baby, well . . . The life in a room when you don't go outside. Later, when the night paradise is night in the garden. The life in here was the glove. If I could show it . . . "

"If you could show it, then what?" Alexi asked her.

"Then – why did I go to war? All those years I might have made a mistake. I might've been wrong to imagine that my witness could move someone. Maybe the paradise for my eyes was a glove."

Amsterdam was kind in the blackouts, and quiet.

"Or just how the years go by," Vivi said. "It could be I needed something fresh. War, then. Another view out the window, now. Then, firefights by neap tide; now, maybe it is the molecular component of the stars, or the energy of."

"Of?"

"Your hands."

"The tides, you're saying, I can see that."

"The world presented itself as flesh emergency, you see. You know what, I think Spanish freed me. I was in the dark hours, at the get. Worlds of war cast long shadows on the humans, light itself mourns its own disappearance.

Light is shot dead in a stadium, light is beaten back with riot sticks, light is buried anonymously in paupers' graves. Light dies alone, light rots, light makes a reappearance. It felt like home to me. Trouble is never a once-in-a-while thing. I don't know. Murder and beauty, those are my poles of attention."

"Tell me," Alexi said, "what was the best time you felt love, in those days?"

"I didn't."

"Do you think words can win a war? Poetry?"

"No, baby. The revolution happens off the page. But words can be good company when *la lucha* gets too lonely."

"And photographs? You?"

"I try not to get too excited about what I knew when I knew it. The moment is over."

"Always?"

She didn't answer.

He started putting things in his leather bag. The well-battered one she had noticed in the Toronto airport. "You really flying away?" she asked.

"I'll be back in a day."

"How do I know how to believe you?"

He unzipped a pocket inside his briefcase. He handed her a photographic print, regular four by six size from the photo shop. "Oh, come *on*," Vivienne said. "My Dad and you? You did a cut-and-paste job here."

But if that was true, it was some fine job. It didn't actually look fiddled with. It looked like her dad in his fifties, maybe early sixties, she recognized that yellow alpaca cardigan from back in the days of men and their alpaca cardigans, and Izzy's fine oxblood loafers. He was standing in the lane. The one with his name on it after he died. In the background, a man in an old tweed cap. Smiling, waving. A young man, lean, in a grey T-shirt, dark jean cut-offs, high leather boots, working with a blowtorch, no safety helmet. A blue and white bandana around his head, tied behind his ears.

"Who took this?" she asked.

"My pal Jules. He worked with us."

"And my dad just happened by?"

"He was a neighbourhood character."

"You're telling me."

"Long before he ran for office. He liked to see what was going on in the neighbourhood. He had his lane maze, his lane route. He'd poke his head in." Alexi tapped the pic. "That's *my* dad right there."

"Mister Smiley?"

"You got it. My dad, Martin. Marty."

"You said part Israeli."

"On my mom's side, Sabra. Marty was Italian. Pure T.O. Came over in the early wave."

"Wow," she said, "an Italian-Israeli. Look out."

"I have heard it said."

"Why did I think Swedish? Or Dutch?"

"You did? Hilarious."

"Something in the way you talk."

"Okay. Marty did spend time in a relocation camp in Holland. After the war. He did some things for some people. Marty was a sponge. Sponges run in the Green family."

He zipped up the briefcase.

"Izzy took me under his wing. Izzy found work for me. I looked out for your dad, you know."

"No, I didn't know. How would I know? What work?"

"What you said. You went to danger places, your dad asked me to – well . . . I'll see you in a day." He was at the door to room 46.

"No. Come back. You can't just throw this at me, like my dad was what? Like you were some kind of – Oh please. Seriously?"

He opened the door to the hallway. The room was down an L, with the only other room his, room 48. "Close the door," she said.

"I have to go to Barcelona."

"You were what?" Vivi was naked at the glass windows, the garden below. Alexi closed the door. Came over to her.

"Don't be mad at me."

"Or what?"

"I'd really prefer you didn't."

"If I do."

"I'd like to come back tomorrow. Or the next day and we could . . . "

"Are you threatening me?" She pushed him away. He landed at the edge of the bed. Small room. The objects get into it with you when you fight in a tiny hotel room.

"Whoa. Where did that come from?"

"Am I just some kind of a baby – at this age – that you have to 'look out for me'?"

"Your dad, Izzy, is dead."

"Oh excuse me for living. I needed *you* to tell me that? Don't horn in on somebody else's family, do me a personal favour." She turned, her back to the glass. He was sitting at the edge of the bed. His briefcase was at the door, waiting.

"You dad was like a dad to me," he said.

"Oh this is rich. You're telling me you're my sibling?"

"Come here." His arms out. She walked to the TV at the far end of the room. Picked up the remote, clicked it on. There was Lee Marvin, standing with the great desert city of Los Angeles behind him. Lee Marvin in his black suit and black tie and white shirt, and, Vivi noticed, that great grey hair. She put the screen on mute, stood back a bit, to get an angle on Lee Marvin, standing in profile with the trunk of a burnished cream-and-red palm tree to his left. The magnetism of the man lowered Vivienne Pink's rage to a mere revving. She beamed in on Lee Marvin's baby blue eyes. Now there was a soldier who had been in the war plays way too young and youth cut short abided in his retinas.

Alexi was watching her watch Lee Marvin; she was standing naked with the remote in her hand. "He's human tinder," she said. "Lee Marvin is a wild-fire barely contained." She laughed. "Maybe 12 per cent contained."

Vivi backed up to the bed, barely noticing that she had.

"C'mere," Alexi said. Said as if asking. Vivi's eyes were on the screen. "*Point Blank*, my favourite movie."

"IT TAKES A lot out of you, doesn't it?" Alexi said. "Not being able to say what you saw, who you knew. In places."

"Sure and even then," Vivi said.

"Even then?"

"English ended up as a foreign language," she said. "What I saw in Guatemala, I saw in Spanish. I saw it with a lot of open *muerto*. A lot of *homicidio*. Tons of *resistencia, esperanza*. To even say it, which I did not, I would have to express myself *en Español con mi boca*. You see, I didn't know anybody who had been killed in English."

"Did you dream in Spanish?"

"I dream in photographs. Thank God."

"You could have been killed," he said. "In Guatemala."

"I know. The price of admission."

"You were too young."

"I could have been killed in Toronto. I get enough death threats at our house. Packages with the great reliable misspelling of the mercenary dolts."

He did that smile again. It was so lovely, it was aggravating how lovely it was.

Angie Dickinson appeared on the TV screen with Lee Marvin. Vivi looked up with adoration at Angie.

"Angie. Angie Dickinson," Alexi said. With that charming over-enunciation on Dick-in-son.

"Now you're talking," Vivi said. "I wish I was Angie Dickinson." She looked at Alexi who was mesmerized, getting that look on his face that men all over the world get when they see Angie Dickinson on the screen. There she was, ripe and tough, funny and melting. Angie Dickinson could melt men and make them crawl back for more hydrogen, and that was them just watching.

There was Angie Dickinson on the screen in a nice jersey dress, tight to show her figure, one of those coral shades women look good in. Lee Marvin was looking at a shattered mirror on the floor, which looked like black and cream stone.

Oh yeah, Vivi remembered, he'd brought her to his house, which the Organization owned.

Angie had asked Lee, "Are you asking me out?"

Lee had said to Angie, "What do you think this is, a pitch?"

The human accelerant, Lee Marvin, using that acetone tone of voice on Angie. Uh-oh, Mister M. "I love this part," Vivi said to Alexi. She grabbed her little spy camera and got back on the bed. Lee Marvin was telling Angie Dickinson to forget it.

"The purse," said Vivi, who had seen *Point Blank* about thirty times.

Angie hauled back with her purse. Vivi snapped the scene. Lee put his hands up to protect his body. Vivi snapped the scene. Vivi grabbed Alexi's left hand. Put it in the way of the shot, slightly, as Angie told Lee, "You forget it."

"Yes!" said Vivi Pink, as Angie Dickinson beat Lee Marvin with her purse.

One of the greatest moments in cinema. Angie D. hauling back with a handbag to beat that dead man with her leather accessory. The dead man who swam out of Alcatraz, the ghost who swam in the bay, and somehow was on the ferry in the bay, escaping from Alcatraz in a tailored grey flannel suit with two breast pockets. Sartorial deets on a dead man; finest kind. Now, in a change of costume, the man who might be dead, six foot two and trim as a bespoke gabardine coffin, as Angie Dickinson pummelled him.

"One," Alexi said as if they were ringside.

Vivi reached back into the headboard, fished out the citron gloves, walked to the TV, draped the gloves over the screen, took one glove away. Snapped the pic at the exact moment that Angie Dickinson's hand manipulated her handbag to hit Lee Marvin fair, then square, right on the bicep.

"Go go go go," Viv said.

"Go! Go! Go!" Alexi said as Angie whaled on Lee with her purse. Alexi was laying back on the bed, his bag abandoned at the portal, and here came that part in *Point Blank* where Lee gets Angie in a twist and *Yipes!* Angie clops him a good one upside the head, right on the skull.

"Ouch," Alexi said, getting up, standing behind Vivi, holding her from behind. "I think he likes it. I believe that Lee Marvin seriously digs being hit with ladies' purses."

"Or Angie Dickinson's purse," Vivi said, leaning back to snap Alexi's hands around her belly. "He's hot for her."

"I'm not seeing that."

"Holding back is his way of showing."

Alexi said in her ear, "Oh, is it now?"

"Whew. Man. Look at Lee Marvin's eyes. The more Angie hits him, the bluer his eyes get. Hey," turning her head to Alexi right behind her, "Rembrandt could pose Angie Dickinson and Lee Marvin, getting married, and she'd have that purse over her wrist like, forget *Fight Club*, the wink."

Angie slapped Lee's face. Face slaps, purse slaps, now the two-handed purse swing at his gut. Vivienne Pink's camera was there to catch it. She knew this movie's moves like familiar music.

Alexi had become mesmerized by the movie, enjoying Vivienne's obsession with it. "Open hands, purses, fists," he said.

"It's all foreplay," Vivi said. "Angie Dickinson hitting Lee Marvin so hard they were practically at the altar."

"He should call the police on her."

"He is the police. She's beating up the police."

They laughed.

"No wait," Vivi said. "Is he police? He's trying to kill that guy from the Organization."

She crawled back under the duvet. "You know, I don't know why Angie Dickinson wasn't a bigger star than she was. She was where women wanted to be when it came out, in 1967. You don't see Angie in *Point Blank* asking anybody's permission to mobilize accessories. She was a one-woman movement. I mean, man, the balls on that woman, to move in on Lee Marvin. Angie Cojónes. Angie Insurgency. She puts on her coral dress and lets Lee know who's boss. Angie Dickinson, commander-in-chief. *La Jefa*. And a – Look at that. I always forget this point . . . "

Angie pushes Lee three times. Angie falls to the floor, exhausted. Lee does not pick her up. He straightens his tie, instead.

"There it is," Vivi said. "First-class writing."

"You don't fancy him picking her up?" Alexi asked, amused.

"I'd live with it," Vivi said. "But that would be second-class writing. A switcheroo of who that character is. Second-class writing has Lee Marvin helping Angie Dickinson up from the floor, but we are in first-class hands. The movie does not want you to like it; the movie wants you to stay glued to the screen. You're like someone in a diner watching a scandal unfold. He straightens his tie, he smooths his lapels. Fuck, that's genius. He is practically leading a class in transcendental meditation. Second-class writing is: you're still sucking up for approval. First-class writing is: Fuck off and marry me."

The Pond's girl on the ad on TV saying, "All I did was cream twice each night for a week . . . "

Angie has enlisted the kitchen. In the dark ops of female domestic knowledge, she has put the play in motion. The insurgent toast burns, the blender grinds, the reel-to-reel recorder like big bands under command blasts in loudspeakers to the outdoor patio pool, the lights come on, as in faraway nighty-night torture days. Lee Marvin is a panicked rat, unplugging things. Angie is the techno-commander, her voice on a loudspeaker, saying to Lee Marvin, "Why don't you just lie down and die." Lee Marvin for all the world rushing around a strange house unplugging technology like a colonel in Vietnam trying to stop a war where the rebels know all the secrets of the intimate ground.

"Calling the honeymoon police," Vivi said, walking around the room, joyful, at the movie, even puny in image, even in Dutch dubbed, even mute. Her joy was infectious.

"Plan Angie from Outer Space," Alexi said.

Lee finds Angie draped over a pool table, shooting pool alone.

Vivi said, "Whoops, here comes Mister Marvin. Dead or alive." Angie whacks Lee with the pool cue. It looks like she breaks it right across his nose.

"You may kiss the bride," Vivi said.

Alexi was looking at her, like, "Your husband was presumed dead, then he was alive, and you were not a widow. And I'm watching a movie with you that could be the brutal cut-together fever dream of a dying man. I am in a spin, and you know what? I don't mind the spin I am in."

"The genius of the writing," Vivi said, "is that between a purse and a pool cue we have insurgency in the kitchen. Cut. They're in bed, naked. Some foreplay."

"Would you call that love?" Alexi asked.

"I didn't say it was love, I said it was foreplay."

"You love this movie."

"I love this movie."

"Did you like it when the guy in the Café Americain mistook me for your husband?" Alexi asked.

"It was pretty funny," Vivi said.

"You didn't answer. You liked it?"

"It was fun. I liked how you said, 'the missus.'"

He reached into his cracked leather jacket, pulled out a small item, wrapped in yellow tissue paper. "Here," he said. "This is for you."

She was skeptical. She lifted the yellow tissue, which revealed a soft blue velvet box.

"Open it," he said.

She lifted the top. A ring in soft green and pale yellow twined together sat on blue velvet.

Alexi said, "Try it on."

The ring felt silky. She stroked it. "What is this?"

"The green is a piece I took from the ribbon bookmark in your new book. The yellow is a piece I snipped of the silk scarf I carried your book across the ocean in."

"You made this?"

"Yes."

"When?"

"Last night."

Vivienne was having trouble putting "last night" in context.

Alexi said, "Do you like it?"

"I do."

They both laughed.

He slipped the ring onto her left hand. The ring fit. The ring of green and yellow silk sat on her finger next to her silver wedding ring.

Alexi kissed her hand.

He said, "I've got to go but listen. One more thing. Okay, so the other morning you're taking my picture in the dark of the lane, my man Apollo goes and comes by with a 'Dear John' letter for me."

Vivi thinking, What morning, what Apollo? Her atomic fog was mind-melding with her jet lag's meticulous removal of her recent memories.

Vivi said, "I took your picture? You're saying around the corner from my house in T.O.?" Flirting. "Honey, wishing doesn't make it so." Then her protective paranoia rushed in. "I did – what? When?"

"Your dad's alley. Izzy Pink Lane. Mister Mayor."

"Don't talk to me about my dad, okay. You don't know him. You said you do. Don't, okay?"

"Sure I did. Isaiah and me?" Holding up his index and middle fingers, close to each other. "Like this."

"BS. BS tacos. Come on. Try another one."

Alexi said, "I was doing security for your dad, in the day."

"No, you weren't. He had a guy. With a beard. A big guy, bulky knit, beardo. A semi-*gordo* 'barba.'"

"Me."

"No way."

"Way. Me and Izzy? We go way back. I was at his shiva."

"You were not."

"I davened. I did security."

"Wait. You weren't my Dad's aide-de-camp, the bulky-knit beardo."

"*Lo mismo.*"

He was throwing in Spanish, in Amsterdam, claiming that he – not quite skinny, clean-shaven, or almost, – worked as security when her dad was Toronto's mayor. Come *on*. She said, "So what's this about I took your picture in my dad's lane?"

She'd been walking up Izzy Pink Lane in the wee dark hours before she flew here, as she always did when she was setting out on a work trip, because she might die. And because she might die, she came to say goodbye to her dead father. On the alleyway with his name on a sign at either end. Yes, she had walked in the rusty climes, amidst the red-turning vines, old cement block off-code back buildings, rotting wood and backs of million-dollar modest brick homes. Yes, she had seen the low amber lights of the familiar garage workshop on her right as she walked north, her pocket camera at the ready at her hip.

And yes, she had glanced with her sharp peripheral right eye at the small group of men, shirtless in the November heat wave, attentive to the metal. Hammers, handsaws, clangs echoing the alleyway, the guys no shirts no shoes, all in shorts, sparks in the night watch. Yes, Vivienne Pink snapped a few snaps of the scene, as she walked on by.

Alexi said, "I was trying to finish up my car door art piece. You held up that camera of yours, you never stopped walking, not actually. I had my welder's mask on."

"That was you? I saw some beard around the edges of that guy."

"I went to Gus the Other Barber before I flew. Hot towel shave."

She lived a five-minute walk from his welding shop. They had both boarded in Toronto, on a KLM flight to Amsterdam. Ended up in the same hotel, The Owl, where she always stayed. Seat 15E in the Economy Comfort section, and he had been in seat 15C, after he scooched over to sit across the aisle from her. But back in the alley – the image was coming back to her, as if her brain could develop a memory-negative – on the left in the workshop, the garage art foundry, a guy had been standing. Not one of the workers with tools and fire, but a guy in a long orange coat. Yes! Vivi remembered: the orange coat, but the guy had on dark turquoise sandals!

Turquoise Sandals was handing Alexi an envelope, as she did her brief alley homage to her dad, on the day of her departure.

A few days ago, she'd caught a quick series of grab shots in the dark of her own T.O. neighbourhood of a man and his crew forging metal; now she was in room 46 of an Amsterdam hotel with the man. In the least fun movies, everything makes sense. Every continuity hair in place. Life, however, is a messy mop of goof and tragedy.

"Why are you following me?" Vivi asked.

"I'm not following you," Alexi said, rubbing his right knee.

"So this is all a bunch of coincidences? You have a welding studio."

"Vulcanization, originally," he said. "We kept the sign."

"I noticed, I took a hundred pics of that old tin sign."

"The boys and I have a band, Vulcan's Forge."

"I just bet you do. Play the Tranzac Club, the Horseshoe, bet you beat the hell out of that drum kit. But don't misdirect me from my dad. So what exactly did you do for Izzy?"

"Checked into people. Felons in midtown. Protected him. Stuff. Close-up security."

"You were Izzy's fixer? I never heard that. He would have told me."

"There's lots you don't know about Izzy. He took me to see Jackie Shane one time. I was underage. Toronto was cool then, no one cared too much about who was doing what, live and let live in Hogtown. Jackie Shane, 'Any Other Way,' classic, the Saphire Tavern. We're talking 1970-what, when a black trans singer could wow the hometown crowd and it was no big megillah. It wasn't politics, it was a nightspot."

"Like the one Lee Marvin went to."

"Exactly."

"It's nice to be an adult," she said, warmed by the story of her dad. "I always was a grown-up kid." Like my daughter, but she didn't say it.

"Me too," Alexi said. "I would have been some real bad B & E artist, if not for your dad. Izzy rescued me from wanting to remove the wallet from somebody's pocket to wanting to – well, do more to fill it. Izzy got me from B & E to R & B."

Her dad had died without a will. Intestate. Had he, though, kept this Alexi guy on some kind of a retainer? Izzy knew people. Of course he did. He was the mayor of the metropolis. Izzy was the guy who was the unofficial mayor of everywhere he ever was, before he even ran for office. Izzy came from the street, a Jew in Little Italy, St. Clair Avenue. His dad, Zayde Sam, opened St. Clair Paint and Wallpaper. Vivi had paint and tailoring in her veins. And here this Alexi not only had his welding shop a four-minute walk from Vivi's two-storey brick semi on Euclid, he had been hired by her dad, Izzy Pink the Toronto mayor, to – what? Watch out for her? Watch *over* her? Be some kind of good Samaritan bodyguard at a distance? Or . . .

"You knew the boys from Buffalo, Detroit?" she asked him.

"Some," he answered, fussing with his shoelace.

"Don't tell me my dad took you upstairs of the China House, when they ran numbers."

He chuckled. "Okay, I won't tell you."

"Max?"

"Max. Sure. Maxie, Lou, Al, other Al. At nine thirty every night, one of them says to me, 'Here, kid, here's a dollar, run up to the corner, pick up a morning *Globe*, will you, from the guy at Bathurst with his bag of papers.' If they won big that night, they'd tip me. Paper money. Serious green. Sweet. I was saving for a leather jacket."

"And now?" Vivi asked.

"Some other things."

"What other kind of things? Izzy's gone."

"Things out of the past. Cold cases." A beat. "You."

"Me?" She knocked her head with her fist, pulled her under-eye skin down. "Far as I know, I'm alive."

When Stella was born in 1993, Vivi had had a professionally trained suspicious mind for over a decade. Stella never understood why her parents never travelled together on the same plane. Never went on a day trip in one vehicle, always rented a second. Rarely stood together in big public rooms, never sat together with Stella at a show, a theatre.

"You were on a death list," Alexi said.

"Of course. So was my daughter, my husband. Weren't you?"

Alexi didn't answer. Then "I once almost drowned surfing near The Hague."

"Surfing here? Kidding me?"

"North Sea, The Hague, big beach, lighthouse, ships anchored out there, great grey. At Scheveningen. Big foam, a buddy of mine drowned, back when. The foam gets so thick, your lungs are filling up, your head gets pushed down, the weight of water takes you down, asphyxiates you. My buddy knew what he was doing, until he didn't. I don't know why it was him and not me. I went out again a week later, paddleboarding, ugly waves, paddling into the pilings, great feeling of – I don't know – doing it in the rotting places, under the rusty industry. I wanted the art installations I was making to feel like the surfing on the North Sea felt, filled with how my buddy drowned in the foam. Winds from the east, swells from the west, ugly days best."

The first wound can be the sea. Alexi called himself a Surf Doctor on his business card with no other information. Had he become a healer to help heal himself? A glass of seaweed water, a rose that drowned. A back alley where he'd seen her seeing him. Videotapes of her from way back.

She wanted to jump out of her skin. Her life had followed her around. She felt hemmed in, in room 46 with Alexi.

"I'd better stay," he said.

"No, you can go," she said. He had his hands across his chest, each tucked inside an armpit.

"That sounds cold."

"It's not cold. Alexi, I can't breathe."

"You could have fooled me."

"About breathing or the chill?"

"Take your pick."

Oh-oh. Just when Lee Marvin and Angie Dickinson are having sex, Vivi and Alexi are on the verge of round two.

He was at the window.

"Are you offended? Alexi, please don't be."

At the door, he picked up his bag, ever faithful, ever on guard. "Your dad loved you, you know."

"Where are you going?" she said.

"To Barcelona."

He walked out. He left the door to her room ajar. She could see him in his room across the petite hallway, readying his things, a silver suitcase on the bed. He turned around. She figured he knew she'd be watching him. He looked at her across the distance. Systole; diastole. She snapped a pic of him, sad surf eyes at the doorway.

17

THE DEAD STILL KVETCH

AS SOON AS they sat down to eat, Stella started. "Why didn't you come to my funeral?"

Johnny said, "I did."

"Liar. You did not."

"Okay. I lied."

"Why, Dad? Explain to me why."

"Because the public. Because publicity. Vultures. Paparazzi. Because there was a guy with a placard marching in front of our house, 'Mister Stella-Denier' with his 'There is no child, it's an actor.' You want to talk about chutzpah: guy denies you ever existed, then climbs in the limo with us to hitch a ride to your funeral. Chalk it up to the fog of grief, Stellita. And get this, Stel. A shutterbug turns up at your graveside, Mount Sinai; they're shovelling dirt on your coffin, he's taking snaps of us. Your uncle Lou took him aside, quietly bent his wrist back, banged his camera around on his titanium knee. That puny paparazzo is suing Lou, last I heard."

"Hang on a minute, Mister Pitzel. You just said you didn't come to my funeral, now you're telling me the guy who denies I ever existed was in the limo with everybody and you to come to the gravesite, bury me?"

"Honey, I got out of the limo at Bathurst and Eglinton. I couldn't. I walked back home down the Bathurst hill, over the bridge, looked at the ravine, thought of jumping. Made it to Davenport, which got me down to Dupont and I sat in the house a couple weeks, getting, as you used to say, stinky."

"'They.' You said *they* shovelled dirt on my coffin. My own father. My own dad couldn't rouse himself enough from his – what is it, exactly again, you do, oh, yeah – writing, to attend my own funeral. They shovelled dirt on my coffin, but you didn't. Fine father you were."

"Stel, listen. Look: they trespass on our property, the best of times. They come with copies of a book of mine from, like, thirty years ago, come in the dark on the coldest night of the year, sitting on the doorbell. What the heck do you think the vultures were going to do at your funeral?"

"So I died. Is that any reason you can't come hang out at my tombstone?"

"I came."

"When? First I ever heard of it."

"Alone. On your yahrzeit. November 2."

"I wasn't dead, that day."

"Yes, you were."

"No, I wasn't, Poppa. I was on *life support*. I died on November 9; I got buried the next day. Even my own dad can't come to my grave on the right date."

"Stella. People I intersect with occasionally, maybe in my work from time to time, they become personally invested in me. Their ego, their id, their future, oh shit, I don't know, they assume a personal relationship. Snowstorm, midnight, they're on our porch, like I'm an all-night rabbi, or a hotline counsellor."

"And this has to do with why you didn't attend my funeral how?"

"You know, at Stan's service, two different people, women, what a shanda, shame on them, they asked to have a photo with me. At my best friend's funeral?!"

"Very nice. Very fine alibi. It still doesn't negate the fact that one Johnny Coma did not attend his own daughter Stella Coma's interment. You never shovelled dirt on my grave. I hoped just one shovel, to say goodbye."

"'Negate.' What are you, a lawyer?"

"Maybe. Think what an attorney could charge with eight arms. I could be a one-woman law firm. Coma Coma Coma Coma Comasky. Nod to the grandparents."

"Is there any way I can make it up to you?"

They were sitting in Johnny's favourite banquette around the corner from the attic, at Orígens, with the banquette window looking across to Santa Maria del Mar, and all of the Passeig del Born wet with plane tree leaves, fallen. It was the last year of Orígens on that street in that neighbourhood.

Stella took her knife and fork, cut into her nice oven-roasted rabbit. Johnny was having the lamb shank. The remains of their usual salad, the *amanida* of hazelnuts, mesclun and chickpeas. They were enjoying a bottle of Catalan natural *tinto*.

"Hmm. Let me think," Stella said.

Johnny was thinking, You know Sancho's been hocking me to go on a sea cruise, the old salt wanting his water legs back. Maybe she would grant me forgiveness if I took her on a sea cruise. "Sancho could do it, Stel, set it up for us. A sea cruise. We'll sail away, what do you think?"

"Sancho Shmancho, who's this Sancho, Dad?"

Oh shit. He'd kept his two local tendernesses apart. Stella and Sancho. They had to meet. Well, all the more reason to go on a trip together.

"Sancho's a pal of mine. We hang out in the Pla de Palau every morning, before the sun comes up. He used to be a sailor, merchant marine I think. Navy man."

"Cruise? Sounds a bit bourgie for the likes of me."

"Not a cruise-cruise. A trip. A voyage. Stella, an adventure."

"You think you can buy me off from you never came to my funeral by offering me some measly little, what? Trip around the harbour? We did that when I was alive. We went on that glass-bottom boat around Barcelona harbour."

"We could go big, honey. How about we go to the Balearics, you know maybe Mallorca."

"How about you take me to Ibiza?"

"What do you know about Ibiza?"

"I know, don't worry. How be you get your Sancho to get us all planned up, Ibiza would be nice. It's an overnight sail, right?"

"We could fly if you'd like. Ibiza's only half an hour from Barcelona by plane. It's like Toronto to Buffalo."

"I want water," Stella said. "All this land is making me nervous. Don't make me go *inland,* Dad."

"Okay. Ibiza it is."

"Then, Dad, I've got a plan. How about we hang out in Ibiza, then we go sail all the way out to the Atlantic Ocean. Let's go to the Canaries! Zayde Izzy showed me all their slides. Him and Bubbie Roz went to the Canaries before anybody ever even heard there *was* a Canary. How come you and Mommy never go anywhere together? You have money."

"No, we don't."

"Yes, you do. Roz dies, she leaves you a bundle."

"What do you know about that, plus it was no way a bundle."

"Enough to buy an apartment in Barcelona."

"Stella, we bought the studio when the Born was the raggedy-ass Born. It was not a tourist spot, then. You go where the boobwazee snoots down to, later on those same boogie-woogie bourgies say, 'What a genius you were.' It's not like the studio is a palace, honey. It's two rooms. It's only forty square metres."

"Auntie Rhonda was mad."

"She sure was."

"Izzy and Bubbie Roz left Auntie Rhonda nothing. Bubbie Roz writes Rhonda out of her will cause Rhonda's got no work ethic."

"Exactly."

"Auntie Rhonda thinks if she stays close to Bubbie's *stuff,* she gets to own it when Bubbie's dead. Bubbie did a deke, didn't she, Dad?"

"Absolutely, otherwise we wouldn't have had the money to buy in Barcelona in the eighties. Roz leaves us the house in T.O. Rhonda's left empty-handed."

"She said she'd get back at Mommy."

"When? When did Rhonda say that?"

"I don't remember. Maybe it was, like, a couple days before that bike hit me. Incidentally, did I ever tell you I found Rhonda's boyfriend Brian rifling through Ma's jewellery box? He was pilfering that nice bracelet you got her in Venice that time."

"The cloisonné? Oh shit, she loved that."

"He said he put it back but tell it to Eliahu Hanavi. I found him with his hand in Izzy's sock once, pulling out the money roll."

"Masturbating money."

"Dad."

"Stel, when did all this happen?"

"When you were away writing and Mommy was trying to get killed in wherever she went. Angola. No, Argentina. Ha. I think it was that time in Video."

"Montevideo."

"The time when she got raped."

"Stella, Mommy didn't get raped. Stop it. Let's go get on the ship and sail away."

"She did so and you know it."

"I do not know it. Stop making things up. Where do these things come from?"

"From a man in a coffee shop in that hotel in that 'Video' city. He attacked Mommy outside the elevator."

Johnny was stricken again to think Vivienne had been attacked, as Stella kept suggesting, in Montevideo, Uruguay. He didn't know whether to believe it. He did, however, definitely believe that Brian, Rhonda's boyfriend – a low-life momzer – would have gone into his in-laws' socks and drawers. Rhonda probably told Brian that she was in like Flynn to inherit money so she hung around and he hung around her hoping to snake-oil his way to a bundle. Two operators left empty-handed.

"You and Mommy should have gone on trips. You might like her better if you did."

"Don't. Please, Stel. I love your mother."

"Not that she can tell."

"Fine. No trip. Cancel that idea."

"I knew you'd do that. You always do that. My dad."

"I always do what? I do not. I don't do that, whatever the hell it is you think I do which I do not."

"Canaries, Izzy and Roz had a great time. He had that slide of Bubbie in the water. The Atlantic, Dad. I liked that slide show. Everybody was there at their house. Auntie Rhonda was drunk. You let me stay up way past *Letterman*. Izzy and his slides."

"Remember, Stel? What a marathon *that* was. We had to call Gigi's twice to get in more pizza for all the slides your grandfather had to show us. Pizza and plonk until three in the morning."

"Maybe he'll be there. Zayde Izzy. With Bubbie Roz. Is that where you go when you die? To the Canaries?"

She crawled up Johnny's chest. "Hey, Chrome Dome" – stroking his scruffy chin with two of her arms – "what do you figure I'll come back as, next time? What if I came back as Santa?"

"We're Jewish. We don't do Santa."

"Well, I'm not coming back as a menorah, I'll tell you that much, Dad." She uncurled four more arms.

"What do you want to come back as, then, kiddo?"

"We saw that show with the mantis shrimp. Like you live in the ocean, you can see, oh boy the ultraviolet, you got eyes on them, then they come after you and you – bam! – roar! Stella grabs those bad Nazis in."

"If you would forgive me," Johnny said.

"Maybe," said Stella. She drummed on his pate, put six arms around his neck.

"Let's go sailing, Stel."

"We could bury me, again, at sea."

"Stella."

"If we have another funeral, then my father, Mister Jonathon Comasky, might deign to attend."

"Stella, please."

"How can a dead girl get closure if her dad won't rebury her?"

"Language. *Closure*. You know we don't use that word in our house."

"Bury me in the Big Canary."

"No."

"Bury me off the hull of a ship."

"No way. Not going to happen."

"Bury me in a small Canary, then."

"Never, ever, will I do that thing."

"Bury me in the Atlantic Ocean, down with the tablemounts, the lava of the deeps, you creep."

"I won't."

"You will."

"We'll see."

"At sea."

"I knew you'd do it. Done and done, then, Chrome Dome. Get your Sancho on it."

"I will. We're on."

WITH THE DEAD you can kvetch from Gran Canaria to Gibraltar, from Malta to Morocco. With the dead, you can have your kvetch session of missed opportunities and intentions gone astray. With the dead, you can intend a kvell or two, before they pass, into the next karmic void. This blue planet, so pretty, the orbiting obstacle of starlight.

Their favourite waitress, to finish the meal in a complimentary fashion, brought them local herbal muscatel in short glasses, and a big piece of the almond cake, *Tarta de Santiago*, and Johnny and Stella repeated the family running joke of how they didn't have to walk the legendary Camino de Santiago, they could simply sit on a banquette, here in Origens, and accumulate Camino Cake Miles.

18

THE GOOD SHIP *STELLA ATLANTIS*

THE NEXT DAY they headed to the port, to set sail from Barcelona. Johnny wanted so much to please Stella, to be a dad with her, on an adventure. They'd collected Sancho from the bench in the Pla de Palau and soon enough, he and Stella were yakking it up as they all strolled to the port. The little Canadian girl who had been murdered, and the aging Californian man who lived on the Spanish street.

"So what's your deal, Sancho?" Stella said to him as they walked along Colom, a.k.a. Columbus. "You like movies? We could go to a movie together."

"*The Palm Beach Story*, chérie. Would that suit you?"

"Perfect! Dad, I love this guy already. Sanchy, the part about the twins, they leave it to the end. Did you love that guy Toto who kept saying, 'Nits!' He was a riot."

"Ah, mistaken identities in black and white. How about *Top Hat, mi reina*?"

Johnny couldn't believe it: introduce the two of them, okay. But she's calling him Sanchy? She met him one block ago, now they're bonding up a storm over classic films. The dead come back and you're toast.

Stella was nestled in Sancho's neck, as Columbus became Isabel and they crossed the wide boulevard toward the port. "Sanchy, in my next life, I'd like to come back as Fred Astaire. In a tuxedo."

"I used to hobnob with tuxes in San Francisco, little queen."

"I bet you looked good. Old Chrome Dome over there used to rent his tux from Syd Silver, shiny pants, no good. You know what, Sanch?"

Sanch? She's now calling him Sanch? Johnny thought. Schmoozing with Sancho.

"What is it?" Sancho said to Stella. "You can tell me."

"I think when Fred Astaire dances, it's a mitzvah. *Top Hat* is what you want, after the funeral. He does good deeds with those feet, Sanchy. When my Auntie Ruthie died, we watched Fred Astaire dance."

"Good job there," Sancho said.

They crossed Laietana at Isabel. Stella stopped at the majestic Roy Lichtenstein sculpture, *Cap de Barcelona, Head of Barcelona*, resembling a woman made of giant printer's Ben-Day dots, and said, "Dad, are we going to be political prisoners?"

"Don't be ridiculous," he answered.

Sancho took over and said, "We could be captured by pirates at sea! Nifty, no?"

Johnny said to Sancho, "I'm looking forward to seeing the excellent ship you must have spent *hours* procuring. That is, when you weren't watching old movies."

They arrived at the wharf where a large white vessel, one of the typical overnight ferries sailing the Mediterranean islands, was full-frontal docked. But why was this ferry different from all the other ferries at the harbour?

Because on this ferry – being used as a floating billet for the police, brought in to quell the vote on Catalan independence the very next day – were painted the sacred figures of Tweety and Sylvester. *Tweety y Silvestre.*

Because on this ferry, some genius in charge of cop optics had apparently decided it would be a good look if they requisitioned a floating police hotel with Looney Tunes cartoons painted on it. And oh, look, there was Wile E. Coyote, too. A cat, a canary and a coyote present and accounted for, to keep the peace, suppress the vote, kidnap the ballots.

Because this ship, housing thousands of police at the Barcelona harbour, had its name boldly on the side: *Moby Dada.*

Stella was excited. Johnny's jaw was agape. They went closer to the dockside.

"Being Catalan while voting, my liege," Sancho said.

"Even if the ballots are only a small quantity just for you and your pals for personal use?" Stella said, riding high on Sancho's neck.

"They're saying that the local politicians trying to get the vote out could be charged with sedition," Johnny said.

"I hope Tweety doesn't come with tear gas, Dad," Stella said.

"What if Sylvester has sly rubber bullets?" Sancho asked.

"Wile E. Coyote might ask for my ID," Johnny said.

They were about to sail away from Barcelona. Sancho was pacing the dock. Sancho had an uh-oh look on his face.

"Dear Jon," he said. "I fear I made a boo-boo. I had my to-do list: get broccoli, wine, cheese, toilet paper and a ship to sail the seven seas. I forgot the T.P. and the ship. Oh dear, guess we better go back home."

Johnny meanwhile was thinking out loud, "The ship has slipped his mind. But I made Stella a promise." And mid-thought, he eyeballed Daffy. Good old Daffy Duck was also present and accounted for on the eve of the referendum, to help the federal government in Madrid snatch those ballots from the hands of the Catalans.

ONCE WE BEACHED only rarely.

Once time was wet.

Once the sea was our cemetery, and the mountains held our crypts and looked down on the sea. Once it was grey slate, bluestone, diamonds, the deeps.

Once we sucked night into our ears and one ear heard the onyx and one ear heard the starlight. Once, in the biophysics of our inner moonlight, we got down and granular with the truth, its true beauty.

"I MAKE AMENDS," Sancho said. "I was so busy writing the new *Moby Dick,* getting my blurbs all in a row, window-shopping my launch duds, that I forgot to lease us a ship. A boat. A tub for the sail. Sorry to say, all that meth from back in the day made my brain look as bad as my teeth." He smiled the half-rot.

Meantime, Stella had hopped down from Sancho and gone along the port boardwalk, close to the ships and boats at anchor, and disappeared from view.

Sancho pointed up to the deck of the ferry. "Wait, Sir Johnny, is that our Stella? Has Stella been recruited to join law enforcement? I fear it is so."

There on the ferry's railing sat Stella the octopus, above the images of Tweety and Sylvester. A policeman stood behind her, a guitar in his hands. The cop began to strum, he began to serenade Stella.

He was singing a love ballad to La Reina del Mar – to Santa Stellita and all the *estrellas* named after her; he was walking up to the railing, gesturing to Stella-Octo to join him. He was singing a flamenco song, a fandango. He gestured to Stella further and sat down in a chair on deck. Seated, his legs were open, his arms held the guitar like a beloved country, he sang to the guitar, he sang to Stella. He thumped the guitar, he used his feet as if they were hands, he sang as if the temporary lodging was just a passage through life. He gestured again with his head for Stella to join him.

Which she did.

As she perched on the shoulders of the serenading security force, he sang to her of *el mar más profundo*, the deepest part of the sea, of *Mediterráneo*, of all things salty and the far horizons of *amor*. Stella began to rapidly braid the longish salt and pepper hair of the singing policeman. He segued in several overlapping melismas into a song about *aire*, air. Fresh eyes, fresh air, once we sailed without a goodbye into quiet light. They consulted for a few minutes.

Sancho was done with pacing. He was sitting on a length of wood at the edge of the water, bereft that he had misplaced his brain again and had forgotten a ship to sail on. Johnny was sketching his daughter on the deck of a ferry temporarily engaged as a floating hotel for police, bedecked in the cartoon characters Stella used to watch on TV Saturday mornings.

Stella climbed down, giving the policeman with whom she had formed an instant bond eight high-fives. That's my girl, Johnny thought. Your daughter high-*fives* a cop; my daughter high-*forties* him.

Math aside, Stella hopped up on Johnny's head. "Da-ad. Leave it in the able octo-arms of your daughter. My new best friend, Jose – Pepe to me – says leave it with him. There is a ship nearby. What do you say, Chrome Dome?"

Sancho had left his dudgeon on the dock and, overhearing this as he drew near, he said, "My queen, *mi reina*, we have long gone to the dogs. So, yes, absolutely, we must go to the Canaries."

Stella said, "First we will sail all night to Ibiza, then we will go along North Africa. This is the route –" waving to Jose-Pepe who was looking at the city he was about to enter to keep the votes for independence from the urns "– from Tunis and Algiers and Fez and Tangiers we will make our way through the Strait of Gibraltar and then – Poppa, Mister Pitzel, it's so exciting – we will go to the Atlantic. We will sojourn in Las Palmas, Gran Canaria. The Big Canary."

AS THE SHIP came into view, the vessel that was going to take him to sea, Johnny wondered why he had such a strong urge to leave. He'd miss Barcelona too much if he went. Then it hit him: That was why he was leaving. He was leaving in order to come back. To love the city in the missing of it. It, her. Even true love can become parochial. Oh God, he needed to miss Barcelona in a brand new way.

Their ship appeared at dockside. A gangplank came down. It reminded Johnny of a ship he and Vivi had gone on when they sailed from Montreal out into the Atlantic to the island of Saint-Pierre off Newfoundland. The good ship *Stefan Batory* on its last voyage. An elegant old ship with Zeeland mahogany fittings and a small staff and they lay on old wooden lounge chairs with blankets reading and sleeping. Maybe the ghost of the *Stefan Batory* had risen here in Barcelona's old port.

Up the plank to the deck, Sancho was sputtering, "Seafaring again. I'm capsized I'm so excited!" (No one mentioned that he had been saved by Stella, after forgetting to get a vessel for the sea voyage.) Stella's new friend, the serenading policeman, waved to them from the deck of Moby Looney Tunes as they began to move. All of Barcelona was moving away.

He needed, Johnny did, something beyond new material. He needed to crave the things he loved, maybe more than he needed to be disciplined. After a while, you have your chops. After a while, you are no longer a beginner trapped in juvenilia or wanting to be a conformist in the usual rebellions. Stella was here!

His daughter was back.

Once in a while – Johnny felt such a mix inside himself, thinking this as the beautiful water of Barcelona entered his eyes – yeah, every so often, he wished he had a disfiguring scar like a skell in an old heist movie in black and white, to be the local scarmatic, to be in a family of the scarred, to show the pain that was permanent.

And here at the harbour, greater miracles did abound. Eternity was so near, what was the worst that could happen? End days had come and gone, after they lowered Stella's coffin into the ground at Mount Sinai cemetery.

He was in new time. His body was in the glory of wounds and distortion. The shoreline was departing, pushing him out to sea.

AND THERE IN the built city close to shore was Miguel de Cervantes's old apartment on the fourth floor of #2 Colom and all the DNA in the kingdom lifted in the salt air. Cervantes the old rad. The inventor of the new. Cervantes the one-armed sailor, Cervantes the navy man who had been captured as a prisoner of war, spent years in solitary in a prison cell, where it is said he wrote the First Part of *Don Quixote*, and then, in age, came to Barcelona to write the Second Part of *Don Quixote*, that next four hundred pages.

Grief is the thing at the bottom of the sea, which humans have rarely explored. The deep sea, where we all swim blind. Grief, denizen of the hadal. Falling deep into the dark green reaches, we want to begin again in the eternal return, only to come back one more time to be new, again, to see, again, the first sight of the miracle city. Sailing away from Barcelona, he knew that he had always loved her.

Blind, with no arms, we swim with gills, when we are grieving. We have no skin, when we are grieving. We are new to the world, when they are gone. We are translucent. We are motorized by beauty in the coral seas unseen. We want shock, we want mutilation, for we are mutilated already. We want beauty to love us. That is all. We want paintings to talk and novels to walk and we want water.

We want the shoreline. Then, we want to leave the shoreline and miss the shoreline as if we died and we are departing from our own true funeral.

All ships to sea are hearses when we leave our home.

The sea is dotted with all the long white limousines.

Jonah entered the long grey mammalian hearse.

THEY SAILED INTO the original womb of water. Stella calmed down as the ship made its way out. Johnny was simply happy to be at sea.

All the different molls on the shore, the wharves, the wharf where he walked in the morning along Joan de Borbó just a glitter now, yet in his heart the miniature of his morning foot clock, where he walked on the wide sidewalk after his nautical dawn time on the bench with Sancho. If you're not obsessed, why would you write? If you're not compulsive, what else will see you through the brain marathon of your forearms shaping sentences? He had holes in his head since the bomb dropped in Death Valley. The Mediterranean, here, felt like a world lobe, a community of isolated sailors trying to make connections through their own private wormholes.

Ronda Litoral. The Coastal Road.

The sea felt conjured, though it was as real as polyurethane, these days.

They leaned on the railing of the ship, looking back at the port. "Sire, can you see, we are looking directly at the old digs of Cervantes?"

The buildings on Columbus were lit up like cut-outs in the fog. Yes, as if for the first time, there was the edifice where Cervantes holed up to write. Cervantes the novelist came to Barcelona, lived a couple blocks from their morning bench in the Pla de Palau. His upstairs window on Columbus looking out at the ships coming into harbour, perhaps imagining Quixote sailing into Barcelona as he did. It could be the ghost of Cervantes looking out at them now, sailing away. Johnny felt a pang for the street where he had been a few hours ago as it became hidden in the harbour grid, the mist, the lit rectangular windows. He saw a figure in the Cervantes window, making that connection among literary ghosts and the word again. Words and worlds. He was a freak on a sailing ship.

Sancho waved his hand to the sea. "Here, my liege, before Don Quixote suffered his greatest defeat at Barceloneta on the beaches of the surfers, here was the view – the very view we are, ah, viewing – as Quixote and his faithful second sailed into Barcelona, they saw what we see now."

The mist, in a kind of kindness, obscured the built city, yet many of the portside buildings *had* been here when Quixote sailed into Barcelona. Johnny felt another pang: the food, the meals, *la comida continua* – you leave, they eat, you leave, the maggots make a meal of you. At least, when I die, he thought, top me up with a fresh sardine!

Goodbye, little café by the sea. Goodbye, the sketches so tender of the wrong species of my darling Stella. Goodbye, my cortadito in the rain. But I was there, in the eros of solitude. I was there, for the undermusic of the rain. Goodbye, blue dusk in the tunnels of stone, the old Mediterranean ghettos. Goodbye to me. The city was a ghost from another life chapter. Each thing that goes pulls the ghosts from the ether, to die again.

Goodbye, favourite corner booth; goodbye, the architecture of that moment, that eatery. Goodbye, *farmacia*, you're fancy eyeglasses, now. Goodbye, place that had no hours, in the nautical dawn in the shit pouring. They have hours, now. The city appears solid; the city swerves in your sleep.

Johnny wondered, if Cervantes was back in his old writing digs looking out on Barcelona harbour, what would old Miguel think as he saw the ship with a smudge at the railing, him, Johnny.

Of course, Cervantes holed up in Barcelona, looking out to the port, had been a navy man. In the navy, captured by pirates, wounded in war, left to write the great original novel with the use of only one arm, after being thrown in prison solitary, bankrupt, out on parole, a tax collector and wounded sailor in Catalonia to write, Cervantes might look out and wonder what the good ship *Stella Atlantis* was up to.

Down below in the scriptorium, some of the scribe set were actually papyrus mashers. They soaked it, they mashed it, they pressed it into sheets. Not for parchment, which might have kept an ancient vegetarian from accepting a job as a copyist of the written word, since, once upon a time, great works were written on animal skin. But for papyrus, made from torturous operations on the fen-ish reeds, the stripping and the gluing, the cross-hatching of the plant to make paper.

Your materials, sire and madam, await you!

19

THE SCRIPTORIUM SHIP

ON THE DECK of the scriptorium ship, Johnny stood, watching the light: dusk was another goodbye. Stella was here. Travel was such a fine form of surrender. The first stars appeared, like a minyan in the sky.

My head is noisy, and democracy is underwater, he thought.

As if in Odysseus's days, Queen Stella, I salute you. To you I pray.

Take us to your watery highway, bring us to your watery caves, where we might sing of awareness, curiosity, the lost divine, the errant real.

May we all be Kaddish for hire. Let us listen to the sound of the high canting, listen to the sea cantors as they echolocate across the sovereign sonar. We are invisible ink, we are hearsay.

What is the cure for the century? Where is the syringe for the world as it is right now? Into what vein?

I came back, and I came back, and I came back to meet you again in your queenly complaints. The surf is grey, the storm is up, the world stretches out beneath us in a strange illuminated lucidity. Bless us, Stella, as we set sail. To sail round and round the round blue ball.

Johnny felt how the prayer had aligned his rib cage with his sternum, a tonation of all triangles and lost notes, reclaimed. There were far bits of shoreline hugging the Mediterranean water – the shore of Catalonia back on the west, the shore of North Africa off on the south. Night was long these days, night wanted to claim all properties.

He could hear clanks, clangs, foam rustles, the mist. He went below.

He looked in on Stella in her mahogany cabin. She was snoring in a corner of the bunk, her arms retracted, pulsing pulp. Johnny wandered the narrow halls of the ship, hot noisy halls, with the sound of a boiler and the clanks of a ship at sea. At the end of a hallway, Johnny opened a door. There was a grand and mahogany hall, with an unexpectedly high ceiling, a vaulted ceiling with a curved dome laden with stained glass. On the glass in blue and yellow and a green-grey was the stained glass image of – Stella!

Stella with a golden glass crown on her head. Below, dozens of scribes in ordinary blue worker pants, ordinary grey T-shirts, ordinary bare heads, ordinary quiet crepe sole shoes, copying. Copying with pens the items laid out beside them. Scrolls in one row, Johnny saw as he walked down the capacious aisle between the copyists, in a second row, large sheets. Women and men, heads bowed, at work.

"Splendid, wouldn't you agree," Sancho boomed. Oh dear, Johnny thought, Sancho the dusk sparrow, all chirpy, and me the lark soon ready to kip in.

"Come along, my man," Sancho said. "Let us hie to the deck to watch sundown with sea monsters."

Johnny didn't mind that Sancho was talking to him as if he were in charge of Johnny. He liked it fine. He liked a sea adventure where it was all detour, with a dash of agenda. He didn't mind that Sancho was taking him back up to look at the light with its spectrum enfolding all things. The shorelines of peninsulas and continents and islands had blurred into indigo, and amber lights here and there of far habitation had begun. The sea itself could menace or the sea could slow you down.

"Ah, here we are on the deck of the good ship," Sancho said, leaning over the railing. "We have dubbed the vessel *Stella Atlantis*. Pending your approval, of course."

His prayer had been in sync with the feeling on the ship, it seemed. The ship listed a bit, the indigo tint blew this way and that, and still Johnny felt his body in balance. The Mediterranean was a damn good listener. "I approve," he said. "I'm delighted. The good ship *Stella Atlantis*. Very fine."

"Done," Sancho said.

Johnny was lost in how fast the departure from Barcelona had been. One minute you board a ship, next minute you can't see the place you love you are leaving. They had left Port Vell, they had left the beaches – oh, Somorrostro, Barceloneta, Sant Miquel, Sant Sebastià where he went every morning for his late coffee. It was blue water now, it was the night's now.

Sancho handed Johnny a cup of coffee in a mug. Oh dear, Johnny thought, coffee at dusk, but he was happy to have company and be on the water, so he sipped it. Sure, the beach café where he had sipped coffee . . . where he had sketched his own bald head, his idiotic quixotic self searching for Stella, where he had sketched her, found her . . . Goodbye to the search, goodbye to the way the rain fell in the shit pouring days when the rain cleansed the cobbles, goodbye to the stone tunnels, the ancient exits and entrances, *salidas y entradas*. He repictured the moment when the ship moved away from Barcelona's city shoreline, when he could still see the low sparkling metropolis, El Petit Far, the Little Lighthouse café on the beach blending in with the sand, the chairs of aluminum twinkles in the nautical moment. His own favourite chair was a shiny bit of dust. Once we sipped coffee and loved the sight of the wet fur running along the sand. Goodbye, my morning beach café. I loved my stupid morning chair.

His many years of coming back to Barcelona would one day be buried wrapped in tree bark, a hunter in a flood zone would find his books preserved in mud, the first person to pick them up would find that they fell apart and became dust themselves, and a couple of scratches, perhaps one of his sketches, a sketch of Stella, a fragment of a centre part of a letter to her, would be all that would be left of his writing. That was okay.

Sancho patted Johnny's forearm. "Ain't this the life? As they say, the book writes itself."

Just then Stella appeared and climbed up the railing. "Dad, I bet you don't remember this?" From out of her third armpit, she pulled the tiniest of books. It had a golden cover with rusty-orange lettering. *Veinte Poemas de Amor y Una Canción Desesperada.* Pablo Neruda. Sounds about right. *Twenty Love Poems and a Song of Despair.*

The tiny Neruda volume was three centimetres wide by four centimetres high. Vivi always said that a miniature book of poetry was a great thing for a member of the resistance – if they came for you, you could palm the Neruda, cough, slip the Neruda in your mouth, keep it under your tongue when the authority demons said, Say ah, swallow the Neruda if you had to and shit it out later, retrieving the poetry delicately from the feces. He and Vivi had taken Stella, yeah, that was right, up the Passeig de Gràcia, the wide and handsome avenue above the Plaça de Catalunya on April 23, Book and Roses Day, which was so beautifully coincidentally Stella's birthday. Stel had been eleven, a perfect age to start reading Neruda.

Stella held the miniature book open with two of her arms, flipped to a good spot with another arm and read out loud, *"Todo en ti fue naufragio!"* Then she translated, "Everything with you was a shipwreck!"

His daughter had dissed him with poetry! How good is that?

"Can we go again to the day of the books when we get back to Barcelona?"

"Sure we can," he said.

Anything at all. When love returns, when your murdered beloved comes back, much like improv, everything is *Yes, and.*

"If we go to the books, can we get ice cream, Dad?"

"Yes. And you know what? We'll go to that same Farggi we went to, yeah, and it'll be two pistachio cones. We could ask for an extra scoop of dulce de leche."

"Nah," she said. "I like my pistachio straight up."

"Of course," he said. In time, it's really all you want: more Neruda, and more pistachio ice cream.

Stella crawled over to him, showed him a blank page at the front of the tiny Neruda. With respect for the long traditions of how books were made, the miniature book had the traditional blank page before the title page. And there – Johnny had totally forgotten – in his own handwriting, was a dedication to Stella herself.

Somehow, he had made his handwriting tiny, to fit. *23 April 2004. To my furry wonder, a mini-book for my maxi-daughter in Barcelona. Stella, I love you, Dad, Farggi 16:35.*

Seeing his own personal cursive, this intimate message in his own hand to his daughter, knowing she had somehow kept the miniscule book or the book had a life of its own and had waited for her, his heart pushed hard on its apex and the old pang came back. He had written the dedication in the miniature Neruda, at the ice cream emporium, Farggi. Amidst pistachio cones, he had scrawled the April 2004 date. It was a grand day. April in Barcelona. Long blue sun, late sundown in the terraces and cafés. Who knew, on that day of the miniature Neruda, that Stella Coma would be dead in November? You don't; you can't.

Stella tucked Neruda under her fourth arm, crawled along the ship rail to Johnny. "Daddy," she said, kissing him with spittle, then shooting backward along the rail for fun. "You know what?"

"What, kiddo?"

"You know what I'd like to come back as?"

"Tell me."

"A piece of paper. You could talk to me with your pencil."

"Who is at the helm of the ship?" Johnny said to Sancho.

"Why Her Majesty, of course," Sancho said.

"Her Majesty is up above here with us. *La reina* is talking about her next return."

"I have heard it said in lore and story, my pal, that the book writes itself, and if the book writes itself, then my Jon, why can't the ship be its own sailor?"

Hard to argue when the sea was so blue, when darkest December was lit as if from inside.

Sancho slipped away, left Johnny and Stella alone. He appeared back on deck with a folded object in his left hand. "I must trim the hair of the manuscript! Rarely have I seen such a hairy scroll."

He pulled out a penknife from his long tweed coat, unfolded the object in his hand, a goatskin. "A close shave, yes. Down below decks, my friend, they are getting follicle blocks trying to copy the great books on goat and lamb and bull, why if only they had hairless heads like yours on which to copy dear old Ovid."

He draped the manuscript over the ship's railing, ran the penknife over the skin, taking a few words off here and there along with the rough goat tresses. "Enough book barbering for today." He put the hairy manuscript on the ship's deck, took off his espadrilles, ran his smelly toes along the goatskin, which left further words inked on the skin rubbed off on the soles of his feet.

Night lowered into the deep black sea.

SANCHO TURNED AROUND, put his back against the rail. The waves were higher, rougher; the ship was beginning to list, to ship water at the stern. "Sire, I have a question that has troubled me for some time. Perhaps you could illuminate. No math, I promise."

Johnny turned around with him, forbearing from mentioning that it was Sancho, not him, who had a fear of equations. "Yes?" Johnny asked.

"Sire, just a theoretical, mind you."

"Shoot." Johnny sipped some coffee. The coffee was dancing over the brim of the cup with the movement of the ship.

"Let us say you came back."

"To Barcelona?"

"No, my liege. Returned. As in prodigal from the dead."

"You're talking reincarnation."

"Well, yes. *Carne* of a sort. What would happen if a vegan came back?"

"Depends on what they came back as."

"A monk, sire. I've had monks on my mind. What if – the ethical dilemma – what if a vegan came back as a monk?"

"Then I guess said vegan would be a vegetable gardening, vegetable eating, granary acolyte in a monastery."

"Yes but what if – oh dear, I fear I am entering into an ethical calculus – what if an everyday run-of-the-windmill vegan returned in the form of a monk who was – here is the key, the knot – a *copyist*. What if the vegan became a library rat in the parchment division? Copying onto parchment, even vellum, veal coated with words . . . What would a vegan monk do?

Could a monk who had sworn his troth to a parsnip ethically copy a great book onto the skin of a buck or a doe, or the delicate fetal skin of a calf, considered the best of the vellum? For until the reeds of the great Nile were found, all books were written on animal skin. Would that ethical monk have to remain jobless, illiterate, all for the love of a gourd or an okra pod or a simple 'I do' with a stalk of celery? These things keep we of the literary set up at night, with Spinoza."

Johnny thought it best to keep Spinoza on hold, or else they would get into that thorny question of why Baruch Spinoza, one of the greatest of all Jews, Spinoza a Talmud Torah boy from Amsterdam, had been scorned, banished, his books banned in his own country, and well . . . Spinoza's remains were still up in the air as to where they had been moved to. A cold case crime of excommunication if ever there was one, so no Spinoza tonight. It was far too late for one more tale of Hebraic woe, and besides which, the good ship was tipping at the stern and it looked like they might be going under. Spinoza and the Ethical Dilemma of the Vegan Monk Charged with Copying Found Virgil or Ovid or Epicurus via Lucretius into Hides, well, that would have to wait until they bailed and got back to shore.

"Sire, look," Sancho said, as the deck lifted, tilted, as they began to slide. "Look. Yonder. Up up up." A flag was flying on the ship, in yellow and red, the colours of Catalonia, and – seriously? – an image of, was that? Yes, it was. On the red and yellow stripes of the flag was an image of Buckminster Fuller. The great visionary inventor of the geodesic dome. The futurist. *Dynamic: dy; maximum: max; tension: sion = Dymaxion.*

Of course. Hallelujah, and yay, for the dymaxic.

Yes. They would sail under the flag of Dymaxiland. Or no, Johnny thought, even better, how about flying under the flag of Buckystan. Buckytopia.

The deck lifted, the night ebony had become energized, they began to slide on the deck, which was filling with shallow water.

BELOW, WHERE THE water was flooding all the hallways and bunks, Stella was in her watery element. She had put together an impromptu drowning garage band, a kind of an alt-aqua neo-maritimo thrash-adjacent yet Moody

Blues by way of late Pink Floyd (or that brief knock-off, Pink Flood) twenty-first century alt-octo dance music, with a Pandora fish on bass, a large killer shrimp on cardiomyopathy bells, a drum set otter and Stella herself on a variety of ocarinas, pan pipes, lutes and hollowed-out bones of the dead. The band had a special frisson, of course, since the sovereign herself was such a cool character not only under pressure, but under air pockets.

She was belting out a croaking-throat tune about coming back as a hairy piece of vellum, the trials and tribs of being a girl with too much hair on her veal, as the *velas,* the sails of passing sailboats drifted by with lazy lack of intent.

20

JOHNNY IN A COFFIN

THE WATER CALMED, the ship went upright, they sailed through night.

Johnny, in his usual fog waking up, walked down a wooden hallway so narrow his elbows touched the mahogany wood on both sides. It was lit by amber lanterns swinging above. He opened the door to the grand vaulted copyists' room. The moon lit the stained glass curved ceiling, lighting the image of the giant stained glass octopus, her arms in pink and grey, changing with the moving cloud cover, to blue then yellow, as if the chromo-chameleon Stella herself were up there looking down on the room of manuscript copyists below. Who, by this time of dark night before the nautical morning – and at sea! – were in fact sleeping at their workstations.

It was not a tidy site: papyrus lay askew, burnt hard balls that had to be carefully opened by only the most expert of hands to reveal, by luck, an odd word or two of the once-upon-a-time bestsellers, perhaps a line or two only remaining of a novel written by a person who had written a hundred novels.

The wet growing green of the wastelands, the wet oases in the sere desert lands, the wrack bladder locutions, the flooded drought spots, the hatched thatch of the reeds lay like manuscript pillows for the night copyists who were sleeping in rows. It was tiring work. Their hands were asleep, too, cramped.

Johnny could feel that cramp as he looked at the sleeping scene, the idolic image of his daughter, above. Out to sea, in a ship of sleepers, the Scriptorium Ship known as *Stella Atlantis*.

This room reminded him of the reading room in the New York Public Library. Or was he thinking of the British Library in London – that time he went to the Tate on his way to Tehran, with Vivi who was on assignment during the Iran hostage crisis . . . That memory lobe was clogged with sleep sludge. He walked down the centre aisle of the big room, a man questing in the dark.

At the front of the room lay supplies – the knives to scrape the hair off the skins of the animals – that was the older craft – the parchment not the papyrus. What Sancho had been barbering on the deck, earlier. In a lucid dreaming and so recently arisen, Johnny Coma began to go through the pile of skins – smelling the goat, the cow, the sheep – as he had a craving for pecorino Romano, for Edam, Manchego, the green hills, as the boat moved like a sleeper itself through night water.

A skin talked to him like the moulted words of a long gone animal: yes. He lifted the skin – long, wide, rough, bristly, unfinished – and took it with him.

His feet took him to a door off to the right. He was creeped out, he was feeling the zone. He opened the door. Of course. The room of coffins. It was all so logical.

There were two men and two women, guardians perhaps, asleep on top of the coffins. He bid the men to wake up, to carry a nice pine coffin to the deck. He followed them through the copyists' room where everyone was asleep, except for one thin guy lighting up a joint who was – Where did *that* guy get a coffee from? The guy handed his mug of steaming mud to Johnny. "Now that's what I call a dream of waking up," Johnny said, as the two men carried his coffin down the hallway, up the metal stairs to the deck.

Dawn seeped up from the dark water, and there was no horizon.

Johnny wrapped the animal skin around his shoulders. The coffin was plain. Like the plain pine coffin they had ordered for Stella. A plain pine coffin for a child. There should never be coffins, child-sized.

Sancho appeared in his blue striped pyjamas. *His* – Johnny's. "You're wearing my PJs," Johnny said, climbing into the coffin.

"You should talk, man. You're wearing a goatskin. By the way, incidentally, I came across your obit in the copyist room. Seems there is a wide, how shall I put it, divergent, ah – Oh, my eyes are still crud with night. The versions vary as to how you died. How or *if*." Sancho began to pull at the inner corners of his eyes to get the sleep out. Johnny was resting in his pine coffin, with the goatskin around him like an open coat. He was inhaling the mug of caffeine in Sancho's left hand.

"I could write some flap copy on those goat lapels if you wish, my friend," Sancho said. "The experts agree that there is nothing like the smell of a corrected obit in the morning. Shall I copy that?"

"I was never a recluse, Sancho. A novel is solitary work. You work unseen. More like a card shark trying to game himself. Let me put it this way: last year my royalty cheque for my latest book, royalty for a whole year, was thirty-two dollars and eighty-seven cents. I'm not reclusive, buddy, it's the readers who are in hiding."

"Neato. An asterisk for the ages. Now – a few more factoids for the goatskin?"

"For pity's sakes, Sancho, I'm auditioning my coffin."

Johnny was getting a feeling that was far from auditioning though. He was getting a feeling you might get from stress, fatigue, fear, a feeling they call déjà vu. Where you might have blocked in a lobe in your head something that had happened before and seemed to be happening again.

Had he lost friends?

Had he lost the thread?

Could you die, and forget, and having forgotten your own death, say, "Ah to hell with it," and simply go on living? Did he die in Death Valley, he wondered.

"Sancho, they declared me dead."

He was a voice speaking from a coffin on board a sailing ship out in the Mediterranean. They had sailed all night and the ship was in sight of the Balearic Islands.

"I read the news," Sancho said.

"No, it's not news. It's olds."

"Sire, if you are dead, as the old papers say, why do you keep coming back to correct me? Am I only a typo in your eyes?"

Johnny chuckled, wrapped the goatskin tighter, half closed his eyes. He could see his daughter, Stella (Her Majesty), proceeding along the railing. He could feel his old death coming back to him. The night – New Year's Eve in Death Valley as he lay wounded, stabbed by his housemate Val, gored by an errant bighorn sheep, the ram's horn like a mordant Yom Kippur reversal, atonement the weapon, the body gash leaking his lies of omission out of his body, two hundred feet beneath the level of the sea. He was out to sea, so he remembered the desert.

DEATH VALLEY, DECEMBER 31, 2006

Johnny Coma, novelist, lay in a salt coffin below the sea. The salt lay in a plain at dusk. The desert had become salt, the salt drank in the azure cerulean sky, the sky was low, wet, saline. The dome of the world encased him. Baking in salt as night came, baking in salt like a fish with evolutionary legs, a biped by mistake, Johnny Coma, *that* year, on *that* New Year's Eve, lay dying in Death Valley, alone, after the bighorn sheep gored his wounded body.

The blood left his body, staining the hexagonal atoms of salt pink. He lay in a blood basin, like a stuck animal being prepared for some kind of ghost feast. Would the ghost vultures sup on him?

His wife had run off with another man. His best friend had stabbed him, trying to kill him. His wife had run off with a stranger. It was the last day of the year.

The rain began. That year, that sky piano. Dry feathers and delicate spine bones, the sky poured every creature back to the elementary womb. In water, we are born. To water we return. We will soon be fossils on longboards out to the final breaks. Fossils in the deeps beside the trilobites, ribbed before the jawed ones ate them, ammonites in their nacre shells, and so the crustaceans will swim with the cephalopods, the gilled with the guilty. To the final fjord we are riding. Up life's fjords in our lesions of light.

We will soon be the portals through which the living walk, as they walk through the sacred doorways of our bones. Dear Stella, remember how the coral was, when we used to dive beneath the green and it was all breathing in its undercoat of oxygen and *verde* finery? I am sorry to tell you, but the coral died. Like a municipality of the sea. But if I could only just find one bone of you, I would sharpen it all up and use it to carve your name in an underwater cave.

We might find a secret middle light together, honey. Maybe we could bring your mother along and we could all be in that middle light together, in that secret just we three. A secret middle light where new coral forests bloom in the green and the wet and the empty. We could be snorkel nurses. We could go deeper with our new questing lungs.

He lay that New Year's Eve in that basin of salt turning steel and navy and cobalt with pelting wet notes from that sky keyboard wrapped in salt, on the far desert salt plain . . .

IN A DÉJÀ mer, Johnny could see rain, wind, sailboats appearing as they came closer to the mystical indelible light fusion of the island of Ibiza. It has been said that by situation of latitude and longitude that Ibiza's light is one of the great prismatic lights on Earth. He had been uplifted here, in hope and torment, the marriage, the child, the fields of salt on the island where the work had always been salt in the aprons of the harvesters.

Stella was snoring on the railing, it must be some REM ship she is sailing, Johnny thought, mid-oration from the coffin. Stella was turning rapidly from pink to blue to green to stormy yellow. The salt island moved closer, its tumbling white hills showing themselves to be tumbling white houses.

"SIRE, I FEAR we have bad news for literature."

"And what would that be?" Johnny opened his eyes. Sancho was sitting on his bunk, with an eyedropper full of coffee, trying to drop the coffee drops into his own eyes. "Sire, the only cure for the caffeine is a good strong shot to the cornea. Yes, well, it is quite the headline, below decks. It seems the copyist charged with copying the great novel *Don Quixote* – I believe back on the peninsula you spoke of it, from time to time?"

"Sancho, you're in it, we're in it."

"But hombre, they are saying down in the water-cooler yaps that the folks of the boiler room persuasion heard from the Chief Copyist's main ex-squeeze to the whoshamacallit that the entire First Part of *Don Quixote* is gone. Do you realize what this means?"

"Do tell," Johnny said, taking the dropper with the coffee in it, and giving it to himself like a late lamentable starved bird. Three drops on his tongue. He could feel the tongue bumps dancing.

"It means: no windmills! A diet of no windmills! We have been forced to go cold turducken on the windmills."

Johnny stirred, now that he had had some jolts of dropper joe, reached over to the beside table, popped a capsule of espresso in the gizmo, closed the gizmo's thingy (the water was in it already) and pressed the coffee jiggy-jaggy down. He loved the sound of coffee at work on his behalf. In a matter of a minute or two, he could sip his awakening.

Sancho was fiddling with the coverlet. "Sire, I have only but lately, as you know, found out about the windmills. Now they are taking my windmills away. The unanimous source of the ex–main squeeze says that only the party of the Second Part of *Don Quixote* remains. Fragments, mere fragments."

"About sums it up, old friend. We are all mere fragments. I love it. Since the Second Part of *Don Quixote* is where they come to Barcelona, why not go with it?"

"They come to Barcelona?"

"Yes, Sancho. You and me. Don't you remember?"

By this time, the captain of the ship who had herself remained anonymous during the sail had passed through the grey monsters of the rain and delivered them safely to Ibiza harbour. The light was briny and crystalline. They entered the marina. Their hotel was right there, a moment's walk from the wharf. Sancho seemed to know the way. He took Johnny by the hand. Stella was riding shotgun on his shoulder. They walked a short distance up a hill, turned left into a narrow street. Empty. They went through a white door to a narrow reception area.

Sancho checked them in to the Hotel La Marina, an ancient hotel only four storeys high. They got rooms on the top floor. Johnny opened the double doors to the balcony. A festive leftover Santa hung by his glitter thumbs from the iron railing, Father Christmas looking out to the marina and southwest to Morocco.

They had survived New Year's Eve.

It was a new year. Stella hadn't died. How could she have died, if they were together? Unless he had died. But if he had died, how could he be feeling so good? The salt island, the pretty sailboats, the balcony, Santa. Surely there was no store-bought tinsel red Santa in the afterlife? Who knew? He liked the feeling of the winter blue. That crisp air, the chance to sail a boat. What about lunch?

Do they lunch in the afterlife? The light was prismatic here, as it had been foretold; we will all sail to islands of light. The archipelagos of the afterlife will receive you. The salsa will be brutal, the coffee strong, stand-up bass men will strum your humerus.

21

WINTER IN IBIZA

IN THE DREAM, they were asking how he was since he died, and he felt that thing where people remembered you. There was the guy in the café, and he said would you like that dessert you used to get that dessert here how've you been. And he sat down to chew the fat over a meringue item. Three people came in Johnny didn't know and the guy who remembered him went away. Then they were in an auditorium, one of those meeting dreams or conference dreams, and Barack Obama was there all casual in a white shirt, second row second in from the right aisle and he turned and said, So Jojo what did you think with that great smile and smart manner not hiding his smarts but easy, like a nice twinkling indelible layup.

He was in the big hall, and then back at a hotel sort of place, a hotel dream. The people were from old agreements. In the dream he was remembering running into Barack Obama, and how well it made the sleep. To be included by his spirit and just you go out to stuff to find out about the world and how he genuinely wanted to know what Johnny thought about the movie on.

Johnny was having such a great sleep he didn't realize he'd slept eight hours. He hadn't slept eight hours in years. His phone rang.

How did his phone get on the ship? He hadn't thought about his phone in ages. Hadn't he stashed his phone inside his masturbation sock along with the purloined hotel mini-masturbation skin lotions? And that sock was in the sock drawer in the Born quarter in the medieval area of the port city of Barcelona in the province of Catalonia, back on the sock peninsula.

Johnny sat up. Sancho and Stella were talking by the railing. He was sure, in the dream, that they had come ashore. He was sure they had approached, by sea, this kind of low higgledy-piggledy whitewashed houses. They had arrived at Ibiza.

They had sailed to the island of the primary lesion.

THEY GOT A bus to the beach of the salt people. The woman at the desk said that in winter on the island no buses ran to the beach, only in the summer, they got on a bus, there was no one on the bus except them. Past green hills and the rocky parts, the sun infusing their bones in a clear low way, they came to a place of salt. He felt he was in a cousin of Death Valley, the salt plain where he had been left for dead, where he died, his obits said. (Had he died? Did he die? He looked for passengers to tell him.) He went to the front. There was no driver! The bus was driving itself in winter here on Ibiza. Obama was on the bus, when Johnny came back to the back. Obama was talking to Stella, asking her about chromo-change. He had on the white shirt and a pair of jeans, like anybody. Johnny was happy in a fresh pang: as if everybody he knew hadn't died.

As if only for a moment he couldn't be lonely, as if you could roll back the years.

The bus stopped.

They had seen the salt sea from the window.

They walked to where the salt surge had frozen, impacted. The edge of the sand contained two-to-three-metre salt waves.

They wandered to the shoreline, a salt line. It was all crystal crunch. It looked like hard snow. Frozen days from where? They took off their shoes and walked out on the salt hard crystals. Their feet were fine. Stella was on his shoulder. Sancho held his hand. Johnny had a feeling that his friend Stan hadn't died, the way Sancho held his hand.

He couldn't see Stan.

A man in espadrilles and pants to his shins and a rolled-up shirt and a straw hat carried a pickaxe. A bunch of men like him were pickaxing the salt. A man with a shovel was shovelling the salt.

They were standing against a wall of salt taller than the tallest of them. The sun was bright. Obama explained that there was a certain confluence of latitudes and longitudes and he picked up a shovel and began to work with the salt men.

They worked in a line. Johnny had a feeling like you do in an emergency when you feel it like work again; like you are needed.

A couple of the men had rolled cigarettes in their mouths as they shovelled. Two men with cigarettes were working a shovel where a second handle had been tied with rope to the first, from the opposite direction. One pushed the salt, a second pulled it.

The men loaded the salt in big baskets, put the baskets on their heads, a line of men with salt burdens on their heads walking out into the salt water.

They dumped the baskets of salt when they got to the shore. Others pickaxed the walls of salt. A work train on a narrow track came tootling along to pick up the salt.

Obama called him over. Obama had made a discovery. He was digging the salt with his shovel when he hit something below, something hard. The other men came over and they shovelled together. Johnny was watching: a large wooden box.

They wiped the salt off, some of it in big crusts. They opened the lid. Johnny sat up. It was him! He didn't die! He'd been preserved in salt. He stepped out of the coffin. He watched himself step out of his pine box.

They all shook his hand.

He said, "I'll do a reading." They sat down on the salt with their picks and shovels. Johnny reached down into the coffin, pulled out an aging yellowing paper clipping. "What demon is this?"

"Can't hear you!" a salt worker shouted from the back.

"I said, 'What demon is this?'" he said, punching the newspaper. "Here. This. Check out this headline, will you? I mean, look to the obits if you want to get a taste of some fake ink." He held up the newspaper to the assembly on the salt. Obama was making a sign with his hand of up-up-up. "Volume," Obama yodelled.

"Can somebody please get the sound system working? What do I have to do, kill myself, to get a decent mic? I'm reading my obit here."

The sun was shining so brightly in that island way that nobody could read the newspaper headline. They had to rely on the reliable source standing aloft in his coffin. "Says here, 'Renowned author Johnny Coma found dead in Death Valley in Presumed Love Triangle.' I mean, okay, people. People people people. What do I have to do around here? Proofread my own death notice? Well, *apparently*. First, the word *author*. I would never have used the word *author*. Anybody got a pen?"

A sun shower began. Little raindrops.

"Ah, perfect," Johnny said, as the first raindrop erased the word *author*. "Okay, fine. So, in your mind substitute the word *writer*. Right? Much better. Great."

In the background, a couple sailboats were tilting into the rain.

"'Renowned writer Johnny Coma found dead.' Do I look dead to you?"

The salt beach audience applauded. Apparently, the free people have their own opinions. "Well, fancy that. But I beg to differ. I was *presumed* dead. My life was one big series of corrections back with the want ads. And: *Love Triangle*."

"Still can't hear you!" the voice shouted.

"Volume!" Obama said, all cool in his white shirt, leaning on his shovel, inhaling in the sunny bleach.

Shouting out, Johnny gurgled, "It wasn't a damn love triangle, it was a damn love rectangle, I'll have you know. Dear Obituary Editor, stick to the living."

"When does the show begin?" one of the salt shovellers said to another. "I understood there was to be entertainment."

"Furthermore, I –"

Boo hiss, hiss boom boo. The audience of ten or fifteen souls booed him out of his obit-correcting coffin.

"Hang on," he said, scrounging in his pockets, the goatskin shroud falling off his shoulders onto the beach. "I might have a little extra something, a kind of a post-logue, a backtro if you will. An *outré* outro." A scrap of paper came out of his pocket, all wrinkled. "Ah," he said, "perhaps, maybe, perchance an opportunity to amuse the masses with something a bit more, ahem."

He read out, back straight, chest out, *tetas arriba*, "Down to where the water does not run to the sea, and the flood waters have no place to go, the rain poured down like a thunder ballad. The man called Johnny Coma was in a low basin, two hundred and eighty feet below sea level. The notes of the sky ballad were filling up the basin. Badwater Basin, Death Valley, twelve years ago. Johnny Coma was impacted in salt; he was a salt mummy."

Small applause from the back. A parasympathetic nerve above poured more rain to go with the reading.

He climbed back into the coffin, standing tall.

"The salt plain was saturated blue, a blue reflecting the rain. There was the twilit sky, in its indigo blueing; there was the salt that looked like a lake; there was a man, bleeding from wounds made by his friend with a knife; and bighorn sheep came down from the high grey desert mountains, looking for water in the drought times. Drought and flood. Heat and cold."

The two sailboats that had been in the bright sunshine had sailed close to the salt, as the rain got whipped by the grey wind. The sailors sat down on the bow for the reading event.

Johnny turned the single torn crumpled page over, and continued reading: "A ladder appeared, a man appeared at a hatch in a flying machine. He lowered the ladder into the basin where the salt mummy's blood made him a mummy in pink saltation. The man climbed down the ladder, took Johnny Coma's body, attached a kind of a sky hook, gave a signal and the man whose books had the name Johnny Coma rose up from below the sea to the medevac –"

"Bravo," one of the salt audience shouted. "Mummies!"

Johnny's phone rang. His phone? Oh, bloody hell. Ignore the battery-dying pest.

" . . . from below the sea up to the medevac plane. The news had *already* declared him dead."

"Yeah, what was *that* all about?" one of the audience chimed in. "Boo to that." They had been boo-hissing him, but now his syllables in the salt sea venue had done a pivot of their hearts. He had enchanted them! The writer's deepest desire: To put a spell on you. To besot you to a kind of wondering, that there might be a future, with some fun inside the unconquerable beauty. That all the raindrops might leave only a fragment of a rune to see, a jotted hieroglyphic of all your life's endeavours. That all the redactions of all the barbarians might pass into dust and there might be some gathering again, in the salt bright of the neighbourhood.

The phone rang again. The phone was in the coffin!

"Buzz off," he said.

The pickaxe and shovel listeners applauded. I mean, seriously, phones were so yesterday. Best used by the very young and the very old.

"To conclude," Johnny said. "Yes, I know. Well, as the story goes, the newsstands declared him dead, missing, presumed dead, dead. As you can imagine, even dead, there were at least one hundred factual errors in my obits. Proofread your obit? Who has the time? Correct the menaces? And so, as I bid you all farewell, perhaps only for the nonce and anon, let me leave you with these updates: My wife's name is spelled V-i-v-i-e-n-n-e, not V-i-v-i-a-n. Her last name is Pink, not Coma. My dead daughter's name was Stella, not Sharon. Although it has to be said that the *Daily Planet* came close, calling her St. Ella."

He bowed. He lay back down in the coffin. The rain was pouring down, yes, just like in the story, as if in your wildest writerly dreams the sky itself were listening, an accompanist to your body tune. He sat up. He leaned over the edge of the coffin. The man known as Johnny Coma whispered (but in that loud stage whisper way), "Psst. I am not really Johnny Coma at all. I am Jon Quixote. Yes, I am on a quest; crazy man is me. I came to find my daughter. I came to find my book, I came in search of words. Who reads today? Nobody. Who wants to know a book? Not a person. Who wants my name? Everybody. But it is not even my name. Nobody but a crazy nut would write a long involved novel. I am that person, people. People I am Salt Quixote. Call me Quixote in a Hurricane. Quixote in the Rain. She died on us, and we were lost. They said if we followed their secular steps religiously, we would be reclaimed. But damn them and all their steps, it is one big fat money-making lie. There are no steps to the grief pool. You cannot get out of the void with a stairway. It is a new tongue, a new dialect."

The salt workers were sitting on Ibiza at the far beach looking out at the water hit by the rain.

"Grief is an island. We went there. Quixote and Vivienne. She does not know, people, that her husband is insane."

He lay back down. He pulled the hook on the inside, closed the coffin.

The audience rose to its feet, applauded him.

The coffin lid opened. "Great, eh," he said. "Whew. Feels good to finally pull off the mask. Been wearing that mask of my name all my life. Feels free to be the freak I am. *Yo soy un freak*. Freakismos. Let's drink."

Everyone agreed. Someone had a goatskin flask. They passed it around. It felt good to be alive, again.

The phone rang, *again*. That poor needy thing. Like a dog who won't let you leave home. Like a pesky relation. Like the loneliest of the lonely and the most persistent of the door-to-door salesmen. Like a snake-oil pest, camped on your doorstep. Ring ring ring. Fine, have it your way, you little surveillance stalker.

The phone spoke: "Robby is calling you."

Johnny was puzzled. It was a head-scratcher. He didn't know any "Robby." Who was Robby. Robby?

The phone said, "Here's Robby."

The salt men and Barack Obama and Stella and Sancho with Johnny gathered round the plastic device, which lit up like a hopeful prayer book.

Robby's voice came out of the plastic rectangle in Johnny's hand.

"No dreams," Robby's voice said. Oh for pity's sake. In a fog, Johnny remembered: Robby was the retrograde crud they shipped in to edit him, when his friend Stan the editor died. Robby spoke, "No dreams; I won't publish a novel with dreams in it. No dreams, no guns, no metaphors on elevators. I hate guns. I never remember my dreams; cut them or you're not coming out in the fall."

They all laughed. Barack Obama took his shovel and beat the hell out of the phone. "Your editor has redialled," the phone assistant said. "No dreams."

They all took shovels to the phone, beat it until it was twisted, bent, broken, in parts.

They didn't know what to do with the plastic parts. The beach was salt, the sea was salt, you wore a white shirt and jeans.

They all walked up the beach and up a berm to a restaurant that was closed for the holidays. The new chalkboard was still up. The sign up top read: BACALAOS. TAPAS. VINOS. CAFÉ y LICORES.

Straight short wooden chairs, square wooden tables. A man appeared. He served them *bacalao* – the salt cod – and potatoes, they drank wine in short glasses, and salad and short strong coffee. They passed around various folios of his obit, remarking on the wide variations in style and fact and fiction. Obama said some droll things and lit up a smoke. The wind was blowing the salt chunks around. It was good to feel alive.

HE'D SLEPT SO long in his REM gut.

He'd been here before. He had been in the Zone of the Salt before. He had lived here once. Lived in town, bused out here to the salt beach. Here was the location of the primary lesion. Ibiza.

He had come in his earliest writing days, when he was pepped up and hepped up and hopeful. All puppy-dog and untechnical. He had seen a beautiful blonde woman with her hair in bangs around Ibiza back then, 1971. One day he took the ferry from Ibiza out to the satellite island of Formentera, and he took a bus on that flat island to the one rocky shore. A lighthouse stood there. Legend had it that Bob Dylan, who won the Nobel Prize for literature two months ago, once upon a youthful sojourn, holed up in that very Formentera lighthouse, there in the Pitiüses. Johnny had always loved that word: *Pitiüses*, used to describe the two islands of Ibiza and Formentera.

And legend has it that Joni Mitchell, living that year of 1971 on Formentera and maybe Ibiza too, wrote the songs of her milestone album, *Blue*.

To Johnny, *Blue* had the secret resistance thread, the subtly defiant river running under it, because when Joni Mitchell wrote the tunes on *Blue*, the Fascists were still in charge in Spain, and the islands of Ibiza and Formentera were part of Catalonia and the Catalan language was still illegal and the islands were sanctuary islands, informally and importantly.

One of the most emotive Christmas songs of all time, Joni's "River," was, as legend has it, written on a Spanish/Catalan/Balearic/Pitüise island of palm trees, rocky shores, Mediterranean sailboats, blue water.

The Catalan question that year was how to write about Canada, longing for a frozen river to skate on, to fly away on, while living in the balmy palm-laden Mediterranean. The light is legend in Ibiza. The magnetism from eight directions is lore passed through generations.

Funny how that works, Johnny thought, opening the balcony doors, looking out to the sailboats, like pencil shavings in triangles against late morning. To write about your home, you have to go away. To write about an icy Canadian river with clarity, you might have to be staring off into Mediterranean space across moving water to continents not your own. You have to make your own sweet barrio of your heart, it's a true thing. He had been looking for an intimate hope for such a long time, a body of water: us. An airport where every departure is listed as DEATH. Though they might call it Barcelona.

The joyful life is one in which you prepare with great fullness for the day of your departure. They handed you your boarding pass the day you arrived, sailing like a mash-up of tissues and wails from your mother's water.

They exile us from ourselves, send us out like reject organs from our great and possible inventions. How to get back to your Mediterranean eyes.

The refugees arriving at Ibiza, say, in the Franco Fascist days were from *inside* Spain, in the days when their own *patria* chased them down.

Hiding back of salt walls, hiding in smoky bars, hiding in full view in that freedom known as the public café terrace. To smoke and drink outside without fear is the daily carry of democracy. By boat, by putt-putt, by dinghy, sailing from the Peninsula of Peril: artists, writers were in exile on Ibiza, bringing laissez-faire, cannabis, style, paint, quiet defiance, photography, craft. Riding no-speed bikes up and down the hills, living in town or farming enclaves. Exile in Catalonia. On Ibiza, Sanctuary Island.

Democracy, I can't quit you, babe . . . you had tombs in your eyes, and still I can't quit you. I was once engaged, I want to be engaged, with the page, again . . .

So, here he was again. The tyrant dies, democracy comes in, what's your excuse now, little writer?

And why primary lesion? Why was Ibiza the location of his primary lesion, the wound that never heals? Because when his daughter died, he was here on Ibiza, in great joy. The writing was going so well. But the place he wanted to be in his work was the great betrayer. You get there, you enter the zone, you shuck off your family, your friends, you go incommunicado and your worst nightmare happens. Your joy becomes a punishment. The joy of finding the words became a wound: the lesion without repair.

Because he was on Ibiza trying to write a book when Stella was in her fatal accident over the ocean, back in T.O. Stella was being rushed down University Avenue to SickKids, a fast-travelling dot inside the dot that is Toronto on the map, on the shore of Lake Ontario. And casting your eyes east on the map, across the Atlantic, across the Iberian Peninsula into the Mediterranean, Johnny Coma was the tinier dot in the dot that was the hotel on Ibiza, where he scribbled in bed, trying to catch the last lucid shreds of dreams to make them into a story.

But even if Johnny had been home that day, home in his hometown, home in his home country, the bicyclist in a hurry would still have ridden with clear intention down the wrong way on a well-marked one-way street in their T.O. neighbourhood. In the rainy dusk with no bike lights and low visibility, he still would have struck Stella on Euclid Avenue.

That he never got to find her, that he the father never got to call 911 about his concussed daughter, that he was never there to accompany the ambulance, there to check her in, to be the responsible instantly-on-site adult, that when they put the many long tubes into her, he wasn't there for the first life support consolation . . . He felt, when he flew in on a compassion flight from Barcelona, his gut in a sick panic, straight down that perilous 401 . . . the ravines, the lake . . . he felt, walking into Sick Kids wheeling his luggage, that he was a visitor to his own life. There was Rhonda, the aunt in full charge, acting like she was Stella's mother. Vivienne had been away working, too. The war in Iraq, *that* lie had set Vivi's photojournalism in motion. The lies of politicians; the lies we tell ourselves. He had been loving the days and the nights in Ibiza, and the writing had been going so well and he had been living La Vida Catalana, oblivious that fate was arranging the furniture on the Good Ship *Abyss* for him and Vivienne.

Arranging the serrated edge to slash down the middle of their marriage.

NOVEMBER 2004

The day Stella got hit was a Tuesday. Johnny left the hotel in Ibiza Town early, took the bus to the salt beach. He sat and sketched and wrote and walked up the berm to the restaurant and ate *bacalao* with potatoes and coffee and wine and salad and smoked a joint and caught a dusk bus back. He stopped at a corner café in town and had a tapa or two and some wine and some coffee and went to another café and had some mint tea and a water pipe. He went back to the hotel and took a nap. He went out to Teatro Pereyra and listened to some great rock starting about one in the morning and switched to *agua con gas*. When he got back to the hotel the night man gave him his key and he went back to sleep.

In the morning when he came down the woman at the front was out getting a coffee at the side bar. Johnny went back to his corner café and wrote a chapter in his Moleskine. He went to the ferry dock and thought about taking a ferry back to that island.

He came back to the hotel, as best he could remember, about eleven, eleven thirty, maybe even noon. There were umpteen voice messages from Vivienne. From the Oberoi Hotel in Mosul; from the Mosul train station; from the Al-Mansour Melia Hotel in Baghdad; one from somewhere – on the road to the Baghdad airport? – definitely the sound of a scud missile; several messages from Vivi from inside the Baghdad airport with weird sounds in the background, shelling or people being shuffled; Paris Charles de Gaulle, more messages, robotic voice in French in the background; a message from her seat in the plane, the old-school handset back-of-seat phones in the air; a message from Pearson after she landed in T.O. Vivienne had made it from Baghdad to Toronto faster than he did from Ibiza to Barcelona. He had never been able to do that math.

Voicemail to his room, and messages Vivi had given to the front desk, too. Those messages written in a chicken scratch – much like his own *pollo cursive* – from the front desk woman in the Hotel Marina.

He phoned home, he spoke to Vivi on the landline.

Stella had been in an accident. Stella was at SickKids. Stella was brain-dead.

Shock takes over. Shock says, I just talked to her last week, she can't be dead. Shock says, How can she be dead? She's my little girl. I can't be here and be hearing this; this is not real. The fiction writer's head fills with the flood of shock: this is not real, this is surreal, tell me this is some kind of sick joke. It *is* a joke. She came to them late in life, when they were least expecting it and that was the gentle joke they often said. "We're expecting, though we hardly expected it." Stella, like some kind of charisma given to them by the gods, and they didn't have to give anything in return except love for the little girl.

She got hit on Tuesday, Vivi had said. ICU, OR, ER. A room number. Your own language is a foreign language, when they die. He didn't understand the numbers or the words. He didn't know what *Tuesday* meant. He asked the reception woman what day it was. She said, *Miércoles*. He could translate that –Wednesday – but he couldn't comprehend it.

They take paradise and put up an ICU.

He had to get off the island to the peninsula. He had to get off the peninsula and across the ocean. He had to fly an ocean to a lake. On the shores of Lake Ontario, he sat in the back of an airport taxi to get to his dying child, already dead.

He had to travel by Air Grief from a hotel to a hospital bed. From the brilliant blue on an island of salt to the grey November of nowhere town.

His nostrils inhaled a chemical medley. The hospital smelled like dread. Stella was hooked up to the automatic gills pushing air into her. The sight of all the plastic tubes, the pale little sweetheart. She used to call him Mister Pitzel. His child called him Mister Little Guy.

THE DAYS BECAME nameless, hospital days.

A man poked his head in the doorway. He walked in, uninvited. He glanced at Stella, embarrassed at her dying. "I, ah, so sorry, well what can you do. A better place and all that. Look, if it wouldn't be too much trouble at all," the stranger in the hospital room said, pulling out a sanitary napkin from his anorak. "I know, right? All I could find, under the circumstances. But if you wouldn't mind, the wife would really appreciate it. She's a big fan. Me, who has the time to read anymore. Don't tell anybody but I pilfered the pad from the supply, ah, cupboard. So look I'm going to get a ticket if you could hurry it up, and no worries, I travel with a pen. Bit of a scribbler myself, you know, but that's for another time, right, Mister Coma, may I call you Johnny? Sign it to Cherie if you don't mind. No, no, not as in French, S-H-E-R-I. Boy, man is that like steno, shorthand? Anybody ever tell you, you have terrible handwriting but hey."

22

THE LIAR INSIDE YOU

JOHNNY HAD COFFEE in the Hotel La Marina at the portside bar. An old TV was showing a black and white film it looked like. A portable twelve-inch TV, the screen jumping with horizontal static. The picture settled. A bloated well-fed face appeared in close-up. A man with a chin raised, the way a mean geezer can raise his chin, mad that he lost the three-legged race at the picnic. Johnny wondered which Fellini this was, maybe Marcello Mastroianni would appear all drollness and style and romance. The camera pulled back a bit. The bloated face . . . it could be he was a prelate in, was it *La Dolce Vita* . . . or could be a Rossellini, *Rome, Open City,* a preposterous character actor, perhaps, one of those sat-in-the-back-room guys who had fixers.

The camera pulled way back. Johnny leaned forward on the bar top. In the TV, a lineup of folk, all dressed to the nines, wind blowing hair around. Overcoats, ties, dresses, the bloated face had a bloated suit, which looked like one of those pricey men's suits that looked cheap anyway, ill-fitting. His tie was flapping. The vibe was like one of those great Japanese films about degenerate businessmen. The sea voyage, the time on Ibiza had cleansed his mind. His own lies were having a shluf inside him.

He had come here to Ibiza to write, yes, time and again in autumn. And the November when the bicyclist hit Stella, hit and *ran*, took off and was never located, he had been here. Feeling the feeling he was feeling right now. The divine gruel of the sweat equity of the mystery and amputation of words.

Grief is muscle memory. Grief calendars the night away.

Wind blowing, rain beginning, the folk on the TV screen held umbrellas up over their tailored duds. Shit, fabulous – there were Barack and Michelle Obama. The bloated man in the bloated suit in the show on TV had his hand on a Bible.

Hang on, oh Lord in his mercy, the Fellini movie on TV was the inauguration of Donald J. Trump, in the role of the new president of the United States.

Johnny missed the Obamas already.

Stella crawled into the bar. She zoomed up to the bottle shelf, and between a Macallan and Lagavulin she began to crawl all over the face of the newbie pres, swearing truth on the Good Book with a stunned look in his eyes, and that chin raised like a sore winner.

"What a punim," Stella said. "A face like that could sink a thousand ships. He shoulda studied with Stanislavski. Worst method actor, ever." She crawled down from Trump's nose on the screen to Johnny. "We sailing soon, Dad?"

"I love it here, Stel. Maybe we'll stay."

"You said we were going to the Atlantic. Oh, typical. 'Sorry, Stella, I have a new assignment.' I died, and you're still too busy for me. Did you attend Stella's funeral? Never mind don't answer, we know."

"Stella, please."

The TV was showing something much more relaxing, a tense battle between FC Barcelona and Real Madrid. Lionel Messi on the scene.

Stella expanded her body, chromo-morphed to a deep blue, almost purple, put four arms around Johnny's neck, said with her beak at his ear, "Don't die on me, Dad, please. Do me a personal favour. You know how, remember how, when Zayde Izzy died down in the alley, how Mommy never was the same again. How Zayde took a heart attack and . . . My mommy wasn't so old when she lost her daddy, was she, Dad?"

"No, she wasn't, honey. But he got to know you, so you were his blessing."

"Did I die before Zayde did?"

"Stella, why so many questions?"

"Just don't lie to me, Poppa."

"Yes, Stella. You did. You died before your grandfather did."

"Was he sad?"

"His heart was broken."

"I didn't break his heart, did I?"

"Stella, you *were* his heart. His only grandchild, are you kidding me?"

"He liked to take me to his office. I used to crawl under his desk and listen to him and all those backroom boys. I liked that. You don't hang around much, do you, Dad?"

"Not much."

"It's a lonely life."

"It's solitary. Writing fiction isn't a group grope activity. It's more like making love."

"You made love to your books, but not to Mommy."

Aw. Oh shit. Man. The kids see everything. Even when they die, even when this is their next life, even when they come back as a cephalopod, they have the goods on you.

"Did Zayde Izzy's heart actually break? Like for real?"

"It distorted, honey. You've got a tip on your heart, a thing they call the apex. Izzy's apex began to balloon. When you died, your grandfather got that, yes, he got broken heart syndrome. Not in pieces, but distorted. Not normal."

"I'm sorry, Dad. Did I kill him?"

"No, darling. But your absence hurt his heart too much."

"What about you, Mister Pitzel, did I kill you too? My grandfather, my father, did I kill everybody?"

"Stella, what I got was what Zayde got, and your mom got it too. All our hearts got distorted and fucked up and got that weird apex ballooning. We all had broken hearts when you were gone."

"Waterworks?"

"We cried until the deserts hurt, then we cried some more."

THEY STAYED A few more days. Stella and Sancho roaming the white-washed hills of the island together, investigating bookstores, fashion shops, cafés, a 2:00 a.m. movie in the cinema near the town square. Johnny wandering the port, sketching the ships, napping, sitting on the tiny balcony looking on a clear day to the coast of North Africa.

They got back on the white ship and sailed away.

Goodbye, Ibiza, bleached as a winter fossil with terraces.

23

THE BIG CANARY

THEY SAILED INTO the narrow waters that lay between southern Spain and Morocco. The wind blew them empty, the wind blew new music into them, human ocarinas. With Granada on their right to the north and Tunis, Algiers, Rabat on their left, the waterway passage got more narrow and became the Strait of Gibraltar. The blue of the Mediterranean became the green of the Atlantic Ocean. The Atlantic at last!

Out into the Atlantic, sailing south of Marrakesh and just west of the Western Sahara, they entered the Canary Basin. The Canary archipelago lay ahead at latitude 28, the Canary Islands on a parallel with South Florida.

Sancho stood on the deck of the ship.

"Ahoy, my liege," Sancho said. "I see La Palma ahead." A speck in the roiling water.

"You mean Las Palmas," Johnny said.

"I beg your leave, I mean La Palma."

"It's plural."

"It's singular."

"Sancho, Las Palmas is a city, the capital of the Big Canary. La Palma is a Canary unto itself."

"*Muchas gracias, Profesor,*" Sancho said, with sidekick sarcasm. "And what of Palma de Mallorca, huh?"

The Big Canary, Gran Canaria, was moving closer to them. The Atlantic

Ocean had its own face, its own rhythm. For starters, the water was so big, the waves wilder, it was not mid-terrain as the Mediterranean had been, it was more a roiling gorgeous void, made of water, a creature onto itself, bewitching and deep.

On a map, their ship was a dot on the curvy edge of a green-grey shape out in the Atlantic. To a passenger on a plane sitting in the window seat landing at Las Palmas airport, they were a toy white ship moving on green water to the harbour's edge of a sparkling city with high-rises, green spaces, forest, rocks, city warrens of ancient alleys of shops, restaurants, bazaars, traders, outdoor terraces, newspaper-and-tobacco kiosks, curving beaches. From a plane looking down you would see, on a lousy grey stormy day, the wild surfers at Las Canteras beach, the surf spot where Vivienne Pink had taken her photographs of the tenement surfers, the soon-to-be-expropriated class who rode the waves.

All three – Johnny, Stella and Sancho – felt a thick crackling energy in the Big Canary air. Sancho in particular felt compelled to tell Stella a story before they docked.

Stella had appeared on deck with two espressos for Sancho and six for herself.

"Sanchy, you're looking like you've got something to tell me." She crawled up to Sancho's neck, rested her executive brain on his chest. "Where did you come from? How come you live on the street?"

Sancho was not at all embarrassed. He and Stella had a certain bond. They shared that scarring, that thing a homeless man might share with a little girl who had been murdered.

There is no right time to tell your story, simply the right listener. Sailed far into weather and love, the waves were high, banging the good ship *Stella Atlantis*'s hull. Sancho spoke from the deck of the ship:

"Amen, I atone in these days for all the substances I put into my poor bodily shell. Alas, I knew him well, Sancho who began as Steve. I was born in the GDR a.k.a. the DDR; I had a sister born in the DRC; you see, my dad was a diplomat. Diplomatic cover: dad was a spook. His father was a Jew from Buenos Aires, my grandfather. My grandmother was originally from Oaxaca in Mexico. Her family moved to California way back when it was Mexican. She met my grandfather in San Francisco. I grew up a Bay boy. I always had a taste for the salt, for the far climes. I fell down, it all tumbled, I woke up. One day I was in Marin, the next day I was in San Francisco on Leavenworth Street. I fell for the crystal meth like it was my new country. It made every day a party; I miss it still. I was the king of my impulses. Every day, you see," he tickled the top of Stella's head, "was an ice cream party." Johnny shuffled closer to Sancho, as the Big Canary seemed to sail toward them, and they held their breath, listening to Sancho's origin story.

He went on, whispering as if in a personal sidebar to Johnny: "With the meth, I always felt sexy. My body was a rocket. I was fireworks; I was attractive. Ha."

Turning back to the Stella-Octo on his chest. "My teeth got yellow, my teeth fell out, take care of your teeth, honey," he said, then his eyes got that rheumy look Johnny knew from the public square back in Barcelona. He horked some phlegm up. "I'm talking to an octopus about teeth. Amen. I went to meetings, didn't help. I was a good talker, I BS'd my sponsor. I said I was clean, and that was a dirty lie. I found it hard to find recovery. I loved the life of the lie too much."

Sancho looked out to the water, a green painters of water ache to find, trying some grey sky with some warm blue Mediterranean and some icy Atlantic ridge.

"I got a job as a counterman at a ratty hotel, I loved the work. It was work. I had to turn up, rain or fog. The Shawmut Hotel, RIP on O'Farrell Street."

Sancho's eyes got that faraway look. "One day, a suit comes in. Had the baseball cap backward, the grey T-shirt, billionaire look of that day. Smirk gave him away. I might've been too sexed up from the crystal meth, my liege, but this yabbo had the air that his one true love was money. He said, 'My good man,' to me. Like he, if I may, wanted to own people. Like a person behind a counter was not a worker in the barrio but his servant. Everybody's got to own somebody. Man alive."

Stella wrapped three more arms round Sancho's neck. Johnny got the feeling that only out on the water did Sancho the old salt feel free enough to speak of the past.

"Guy had a clipboard. Clipboard, iPad, what's the diff? You could see eviction in his smirk. We the people were a major impediment to his PowerPoint presentation. I was afraid for my well-being. I was afraid if I lost my dear daily job at the ratty hotel front, I would go back on the meth.

"And so, amen, I atone again."

The water dared you to your own risk horizon. The risk of openness with each other. The inspirational power of the ocean.

AS THE SHIP tried to set anchor, to tie up at the Canary wharf, the sky turned green. The wind picked up energy. Ropes took on lives of their own. The ship was torn up, and needed repairs, a cleaning. Rudder, refit, slops. The palms were bending and swaying like fronds at prayer.

The three of them swayed, held on to each other, got off the ship, almost got hit, their first minute on the Big Canary, by a flying palm. Many palms flew through the air, a few impaling car windshields. The sky turned dark origin green informed by indigo. Cars began to fly. Cars landed on boats, boats landed on streets. Thank god their hotel was only a few blocks away, a posh affair built with steep stairs from the street to the entrance. It started to shit-pour rain. "It's a hurricane," said the man behind the reception desk, who was sporting a wine blazer and was impeccable as the shambles of the storm unfolded behind him on the other side of the plate glass windows. A man on a bike carrying a surfboard under his arm pedalled through the hurricane rain. The green sky was almost all black.

The man at reception gave them a room on a high floor due to the storm in progress.

They put their stuff in the room, took the elevator to the hotel restaurant, which was on the top floor with a view. The view was of rain coming in sideways. Horizontal hurricane rain. The view was of Atlantic Ocean waves taller than the top floor of the hotel slamming the glass of the upscale eatery, the swells pounding the shit out of the view.

No one else but them in the vast dining room. A buffet laid out for ghosts. White tablecloths, crystal, nice flatware, all set up for swarms of nobody. The three of them ordered food from a genuinely pleasant and totally oblivious waiter, who hustled off to the kitchen with his order pad as the first restaurant window was breached and the water from the ocean below poured into the twenty-fourth floor of the hotel.

The waiter brought them some sand sandwiches on a fancy silver platter, with a side dish of aioli to go with the sand. They had sad coffee.

The elevator back to their room whined and whinged on the ropes.

Their room had flooded! All their stuff was okay, because they'd dumped their bags on the beds, and the water was up only to the bedskirts.

With the logic of the stunned in shock, they checked out of the hotel, began to wander into the old section of the city proper, mistrusting high floors in a hurricane. The front-page headline in the local paper, *El Diario de Canarias,* was "El Centro Esta Collapsado." The Centre Has Collapsed.

In wet stone alleys, the three bedraggled sailors with their backpacks on their backs, stepping over the fallen palm trees, saw an amber light inside a pocket-sized food spot with aromas of grilling meats, spices, dry herbs wafting out to the palm-fallen street.

They entered the tiny restaurant. The proprietor greeted them with towels and hot tea. They were so weary they carried each other across the threshold – an act defying physics but not friendship.

Soon, the old life lesions had been left behind. They were in a disaster, sitting in the elsewhere between continents. Johnny was here, with his daughter at last in the Atlantic. He had a new male pal, not a small gift, seriously.

The restaurant man, who appeared to be the only staff, didn't bring them a menu. He said he would bring them all his best offerings, and he did. They ate lamb and they ate kebabs and they ate things sweet yet salty yet acrid in that tongue-tingling way, and Stella became the brainy mascot of the day. She had charm. Octopuses do.

Charm and higher intelligence. By then, 2017, it was well-known that octopuses were like chimps and dolphins. Those wily smarts. Besides the decentralized clusters of neurons, those brainy ganglia, her eyes had lenses, her eyes had memory. Johnny imagined how she might be, someday, as a photographic assistant to her mother. A war photog, able to leap tall fascists in a single bound while blinding them with ink, snapping a pic of them, whipping their weapons out of their hands, while chokeholding their creepy wattles and rescuing the captured. (While morphing into camouflage and out.)

Smart arms and limbic independence. She had forgiven him, she had been compassionate, she called him Mister Pitzel, she said he was an okay dad. She loved colours. Eight arms to aggravate you, eight arms to hug you after. He had dreamed of a far-flung adventure with his daughter and this was the dream trip.

Cozy inside the eatery, Sancho was stuffing some delicious lamb in his mouth. Stella was enjoying some crab. Johnny was sipping a hot seafood stew.

The owner – large head, short body, full head of grey hair, Johnny made him as maybe sixty – invited Stella to join him in the kitchen out of sight of Johnny and Sancho. She slithered around from the side of the frying pans to the side of the back-burner stew pots to the counter, where she put a couple ends of her arms around a mortar and ground some turmeric and cumin with the stone pestle.

Sancho's hair was wild and wet, a hurricane mayhem. "Milord, I have a matter of some urgent concern to report," he said. "I can speak of my own distress, now." And so Sancho, on the hurricane-ravaged island, told Johnny more of his personal story:

"Once upon a time in flight, I happened to sit in one of those middle sections, nice little girl beside me, child and mom, you know, sweet. Flying from SFO to BCN. Long voyage, my friend, many legs. The mom was some kind of prof at, I believe if my brain cheese is correct, Stanford, data lady of some sort. Short story, the Data Prof was against vaccinating her child, so the child had measles but didn't show yet. I got measles on the plane from the un-vaxed tot. Doc in Barce said an antiviral would help heal the measles scars."

He sipped the short Turkish coffee, like righteous mud jolts. He continued: "Turns out I'm one of the folks who have a real bad reaction to the antiviral Acyclovir. I was taking five tablets a day of a blue pill, which was altering my mental stability. These miracle pills put the virus into retreat. But I got the side effect: You take the antiviral, you feel like your organs emigrated from your body. You believe every fever, every visit from your dead relations in your nightmare nights, that you yourself have joined them, yet you walk to the store for bread and kibble. I wasn't the living dead, I was the dead living, my liege. I was tilting at reality. I got up in the night and started baking. I'd wake up with a molten chocolate cake rising with sprinkles of *The Bat* by Nesbø on top; I ate cake with soupçons of Harry Hole in his worst bender in Bangkok. I came down to the Embarcadero, staring out at Alcatraz Island, asking passersby if they knew what had happened to my dearly departed pancreas. Big Pharma made me a nutcase.

"I made my way from the port of San Francisco to the port of Barcelona, a sailor on the streets. I used to like it when you sat down beside me on the bench in the Pla de Palau, most folks didn't. I liked your vibe, I liked your hair. Well, all three hairs, my dear liege. I liked to watch you read on the bench; you weren't a snoot, you never asked to take a picture of me.

"You thought I was a nutter when you met me. Right?"

"No, well yeah but no, look," Johnny said. "Me? Sancho, I jumped off a cliff to live with words in the void. How could I say anybody was nuts, except me?"

"I longed for my lungs, when the sun went down over the wall of the city," Sancho continued. "I wrote love letters to the small intestine I had so taken for granted. In my night sweats, I pictured the insides of my body living in pretty little boxes in subdivisions under other names. They call it the delusion of negation. The antiviral took reality away from me. I was a walking talking corpse, my friend. I wore a long overcoat in summer; I grew my hair like some old white fright wig. I was a kook in the open. Only you befriended me. You put up with my sense that I was a topcoat without a lung, a heart, an aorta in a corner. I barked on occasion; you kept reading your dog-eared paperbacks. You left me ciggies. A pack or two a week, Canadian smokes, Rothmans, flip-top box. You were kind, year on year. I didn't know you from a knight errant in the nautical dawn.

"One day, the exiled organs began to sail back into my body. The virus lurks forever like guerrilla forces in your neurons, but the delusion of negation was gone. Ha! – I was back in the mess called real life, at last. My prodigal lungs had made their pilgrimage back inside me. I could breathe. Happy days."

The refreshing ocean air informed the narrow old Gran Canaria quarter and mixed with the aromas of the cuisine. The effervescent feast of spicings.

"Ha," Sancho leaned back. Leaned forward, a bit agitated. Took a long sip of the short coffee. Spooned some of the local dessert delicacy of honey and almonds, *bienmesabe*, into his mouth. With sticky melting paste on his lips, he rested.

Stella was moving down the apron of the Turkish restaurant owner who was chuckling with unexpected joy. Stella crawled into a large pitcher of water, the better to refresh her gills.

Johnny finished up the last of his *papas arrugadas*, wrinkled potatoes, while watching Stella morph like an octopus light show inside her own skin inside the water pitcher. She might have been, sure, an octopus, originally, and when she was born from Vivienne's womb, the invertebrate might have been reincarnated as a vertebrate girl. Johnny chuckled, snarfing potatoes. I don't even believe in reincarnation, yet I believe that my human daughter has come back as an octopus. And not only that, but maybe Stella was an octopus to begin with.

Stella turned aquamarine, then stretched, turning her skin an ochre with burnt sienna, then she grabbed Johnny's coffee cup and Sancho's coffee cup and drank their coffees down, her beak the only hard part of her body.

Sancho scratched his head. "And here we be. I emptied my pockets of karma." He put his hand on Johnny's arm. "If I may make so bold, here on the Big Canary with you and Queen Stella, I feel that I am here, right now." He chortled, coughing up phlegm. "I am in the delusion of reality, Jon."

The owner came over with more pastries, this time pistachio and honey, and a plate of parrot fish, *vieja*, grilled with the garlic emanating from the skin, crispy. And rabbit. *Conejo con mojo rojo.* When they force you behind your closed doors, it will be the tender feasts you shared together you will remember. Along with your dead parents, food smells will come back in the fever sweats all night, the smells just out of reach, and you will wake with ludicrous sobs, missing all the seafood by the sea. Giant orange prawns will walk across your brain and that's all right.

Johnny was chuffed that Sancho had spilled so much of his personal story, yet Johnny had held back his own story. He was a good listener, that was the upside of him. The downside was that he absorbed everybody's stories, and kept his own all bottled up, like secret treasure. It made him feel important, to keep his pain to himself. It made him feel safe. It was that perilous a venture. He had a chance, though, for a true friend in Sancho, née Steve.

You can't replace your dead friends, the few, but here was an offering to be close. A man's a mess, trying to cement friendship in the good old male way, which is so reliant on silence. Even the male bluster is a form of not saying what is on your mind. Sancho's heart was open; Johnny's heart was lost inside his own body.

Grief has neurons. Grief is an octopus. Grief has neurons on every part of grief's body. You walk like a human, you talk like a human, but counter-intuitively you are not human when you grieve. You are interspecies, for no human could possibly have so much feeling that does not know what to do with itself and hides it away like a corrupt politician.

In clouds of lichen they did lie down . . .

THE YEAR BEGAN, the air was fresh, the winds strong. The bright eternal spring made promises of mild weather and delivered. Gran Canaria was a great place to set up a routine of word-making. Like Barcelona, in a way, with walled warrens, and an ancient feel; yet, in a way, not, due to the big open water, the Atlantic itself, and the size of the waves. They took an informal lease on a modest apartment deep in the old Las Palmas quarter of shops, narrow streets.

Sancho, breathing more slowly, agreed to try Johnny's recommendation of doing the minimum number of words – five hundred words non-nego-tiable – every day. By the end of February, he had twenty-eight thousand words, about seventy book pages. A handsome offering. By the beginning of April, he was forty-five thousand words into his piece of fiction. About a hundred and ten book pages. He liked being with the big people, the pros, counting words the way a real writer does, talking to Johnny about the fossil ironies and origins of the mysterious semicolon, even the history of the paragraph and the period. He had sailed in his mind so far from ideas and so deeply into the rhythm, the lift, the intent, the music of a sentence that he could laugh at his pretenses of days gone by. Johnny, for his part, was still fiddling with the scribbling in his Stella story, trying to keep from making it too literal or, heaven forfend, doing research. The ocean was his morning wiki; the walks along the Canary promenade his eye library. The world *is* elsewhere and when you get there, the rhythm of the seven elsewhere waves enters you and you take the ocean, your old body part, in like literary osmosis. Grief is out there, playing the xylophone, but that's all right. Stella joined in the writing group. Each on their own, none of them talking about what they were doing. Stella was writing a story about a girl and her dad, and she was looking for some kind of cephalopod solace. In her story, the dad dies in the desert and the young girl is left bereft, her old pal gone.

The tyrannical clock morphed into days of adjudicating the light, interrogating the shadows.

They were, as in bohemian days of old and refugee dark smoldering nights of sharing art work, making their art cabal of three. Mornings were reserved for writing. They exited the stone warrens in the early afternoon, walked the windy oceanic promenade, marvelled at the Atlantic. They kept their heads down; their fealty was to the word.

At night, the night was really night.

ONE NIGHT, IN insomnia, Johnny lay in his bunk, listening to Stella talk to herself in the bunk above his head. "I could come back as a little girl."

Then, a second voice, "I'm not sure it works that way."

Back to Stella-Octo's voice, a pleasant alto. "What if I came back, and I'm somebody else's little girl and you're like walking down the street, 'I know her. That's Stella, why are you calling her Amanda?' Or a – what if I came back as that guy Robby who told you a woman can't have sex with a man in a book unless they get to know each other first? You and Mommy had sex I bet like the first *minute* you met."

The second voice: "What do you know about that?"

"Tell. Spill, Chrome Dome."

He was overhearing the playlets kids do to figure things out. Shit, three hearts to love you, nine brains to slay you, eight arms to hold you, a beak like the street and she might turn out to be a playwright, working out the dialogue at sea in the night in a wood-panelled cabin.

"We waited a while."

"Dad."

"Okay. Forty-five minutes. We waited forty-five minutes."

"That Robby guy – I think we better call him Mister Pencilhead – Mister Pencilhead wouldn't let people have sex after forty-five minutes."

"Nope."

"Why?"

"He admires the delicate feelings of men who have fainting couches in case a woman is lusty."

"Mommy is *lusty*, isn't she?"

"You bet she is."

"What if I came back in my next life as a camera, Dad?"

"A camera?"

"Then I could always be with Mommy."

NOCHE DE LOS *Perros*, Night of the Dogs, as the local paper called the hurricane onslaught. And well, oddly, night dogs do pass.

So time passed on the Atlantic island in a circular way, a non-chronological way, shops had calendars from some year some month, time was a tchotchke, their bodies reset by sun-up and sundown. They say that on the Big Canary you live in eternal spring. Yet the trade winds will have their way, the weird wintertime confluence of warm Gulf currents will cross-hatch with cold Atlantic waters and super bolt lightning will be brewing.

Deep in the Canary winter, Johnny began to speak to Sancho like a brother. They read each other poetry, they spoke of their scarred lives.

One Monday, when they were the only customers at an elevated oceanside café, Johnny opened up about Stella. Slowly, then all at once. How Stella had died on her home street in her hometown of eight generations of her Jewish clan. Rainy day, early dark, wrong-way bike hopped the curb, Stella on the sidewalk, November, 911, ambulance, concussion. Sancho asked him to elaborate.

"Tell me, what was it like? When you came home and . . . your daughter . . . ?"

"I . . . It . . . "

Sancho put his hand closer to Johnny, on the terrace table overlooking the ocean. "Tell me. You and her . . . "

"I was here."

"Go on."

"I wasn't home the day of. I came to go here. Here? Not here. There. Ibiza."

"You were in Ibiza."

"I didn't come home, to home-home. I came home to . . . "

"Yes." Sancho moved his chair a bit closer to Johnny so they both faced the waves. "Home to?"

"'It can't be true.' That was me." He was grasping at his mental hoard.

"You said that." Sancho's matted hair was blowing in the ocean wind.

"That; yes. That: 'It can't be true. She can't be dead. I was on the phone with her two days ago, is this some kind of a joke.'"

"You thought, 'Somebody punked me.'"

"Yes. No." Johnny got up from his chair, walked to the seawall. It would be easy to walk into the waves. Much harder to talk about the muteness inside him. He walked back to the chair, sat. Said, "I went into shock. I put shock in a box, put the box in my body. I was numb. I was an imposter of a human."

They drank wine together. Sancho gestured for a new bottle of red. He put his calloused hand on Johnny's forearm. Big winds. The water was wide open.

Johnny said, "With her death I had no distance. You know what I felt?"

"What?"

"I felt: if I can write, I can live. I did. I wrote."

"And?"

"And it was crap. A-plus crap. A clever dystopian turd."

"And what of the vaunted turd, my friend? Your manuscript."

"I threw it all away. Four hundred pages. Compost."

"It wasn't you."

"It wasn't me; it was me. I wrote like a callow kid. But, Sancho, I'd been through something *harrowing*." He looked out to the Atlantic. "I knew how to sit shiva for the elders. I was an adept in the worst of the AIDs wakes, memorials. I knew the rites. Prayers with the minyan at dusk. Soap the mirrors in the house. No photos of the dead. I knew shivas. But for my little girl? They don't teach you what to do when you have to mourn your eleven-year-old. They don't teach you abnormal heart. They don't, Steve. They don't."

Steve.

"When you came home and found Stella, were you in the house? On the sidewalk? What did you do?" Rubbing Johnny's arm across the windblown table, the napkins, placemats skittering.

Johnny had never lied as an act of commission. But he had forever lied by omission. He did it again. He deflected; he spoke not of what he did but what Vivienne did.

"Vivi had other light. She poured grief like kerosene on her maternal body, went into her darkroom, struck a match, went for days without sleep, printing old war pictures. She got skeletal, worked, didn't eat, committed artistic arson on her organs, after Stella died. She closed herself off from me. Everybody survives in their own fashion. Her *fuck off* was fabulous."

Sancho was patient. "How was it for you?"

"I still needed to be liked by people I had no fucking time for. It curled back on my prose. I guess I thought if I was clever enough, my heart wouldn't hurt so badly. My daughter died; I wrote irony."

Sancho listened with an open heart, his ear *simpático*. Johnny could feel the crap moulting off his body. Stella had forgiven him on the island of Ibiza;

Sancho had listened well on Gran Canaria. He felt heard. Ipseity, the sense that we exist. Identity.

After Stella died, he gave up God. He went back to God. After all, God ran the universe like a comedy club. God was the greatest stand-up who never lived.

He spoke these things in the middle of the Atlantic Ocean to Sancho, his best friend. They had earned the status together. The word *friend* had been debased. It made Johnny's heart tender to know the word still had use.

"There was no future," Johnny said. "For so long in our life, we were forever making plans. The future was always there. I used to write her."

"Stella."

"Stella. Yes. Yeah. I wrote her letters when I was away working on a book. How we were going to do this, going to do that when I got home. Stella and her dad. She died, Sancho, Steve. She died."

Sancho's eyebrows danced a pain dance, in concert with Johnny.

Sancho poured some more congenial *tinto* into their glasses. They sat drinking and drinking until the late afternoon glints sparkled on the big grey waves. On the sand below, dogs ran as dogs run on the sand everywhere, their masters and mistresses indentured in great love to follow them on the shoreline.

"Hard to accept," Johnny said. "I got that far. I could say that. To myself I could say it. I could say, 'It seems surreal.' I could say, 'I can't believe it.' But that was all."

He took Steve's hand. "I was too scared to look at my own grief."

That he had never said this to anybody was evident to Sancho-Steve.

Sancho said. "We're on loan, my brother. We're cells on parole to the universe."

In synch they moved their chairs toward each other. Ordered eats. A seafood platter, fried – you want grease when you're grieving.

We are the current. Soon, we will be the former. We are the *is*. Soon we will be the *was*. Life is what happens between *is* and *was*.

AT THE OCEANSIDE terrace café, Sancho moved his chair all the way around beside Johnny.

"I hate you," Johnny said to Sancho.

"At last," Sancho said. "My song. 'Holding Back the Years,' marvellous voice. 'At Last,' yes, Little Jimmy Scott, we must listen to him soon, if not sooner." He warbled some throat gravel, how his lonely days were gone, at last. "Do you really hate me?"

"A lot."

"How much? As much as I hate you?"

"I hate you more."

"Finally. A slow dance could be in the air, my liege. I hate you so much."

WHILE THERE NEVER are replacement friends, Sancho became a true friend, that winter on Gran Canaria. They woke the next day to a window framing a sky all powdery red particulate. The red sand of the Sahara Desert was blowing west into the Atlantic. All the Canary Islands were getting covered in red dust. Winds at a hundred and thirty kilometres an hour blew the desert out upon the ocean. Crazy rain poured red sheets down on the island.

Sancho had somehow cadged tickets to the big concert going on that night at the Auditorio Alfredo Kraus overlooking the surfers' beach of Las Canteras. The word was that the reclusive conductor Carlos Kleiber, long rumoured to be dead, would magically appear to conduct the Bavarian Radio Symphony Orchestra. The house was sold out. Great excitement mixed with the wind and the rain. Was Maestro Kleiber dead or alive? Until the last minute, nobody knew. Ozone poured like hexes and cures onto the rocks below the hall. The concertgoers were all dressed up, the way it used to be at a grand occasion. Stella produced a blue velvet cape and looked magnificent. Sancho, for the occasion, looked very much like a tidied-up Steve. Johnny shaved his pate. They walked beside the ocean toward Ravel and Mozart.

The acoustics were magnificent. The wind was inside and out. The island breathed in through its nose and out through its mouth. At the interval, elegant staff walked with trays of cigars, Canary cigars, very fine. During the second half, Stella shape-shifted into a merlot ball, in camouflage with her comfy seat.

The notes lingered as they walked back along the open shore to their modest digs in Las Palmas' souk-like warrens, Sancho trying to keep his Canary cigar lit in the rain. They'd walked without umbrellas; they were sodden and content. It's so very fine to make a real goodbye for yourself. *Una despedida en la lluvia.* A goodbye in the rain. The winter in the Atlantic had brought each of them to their own personal elsewhere.

Their sailing ship was almost repaired. Yes, the winter currents on open water were creating super bolts, that supercharged lightning a thousand times more powerful than regular lightning. As they packed their things, looking at the walls of their apartment rental, Johnny thought, Soon someone else will live here, and they won't know anything about us or how we were here or how much it meant to us, this small tender space in that long ago tender winter. The present is so fleeting that it is already past as we leave it.

THE RED SAND kept blowing, creating what they call a *calima,* a haze, the singular event occurring when the Saharan sand blows onto the Canary Islands.

They set sail in great red rain. The white ship sailed like a stain. Meantime, inland, wildfires erupted. Desert, water, fire, floods, Atlantic spring.

And a super bolt did come down from the sky, setting the ship on fire, and the ship listed to one side, and the ship took on water. Johnny and Sancho swam up the stairs to the deck; Stella was up there already. The air was yellow, sulphurous; they were sinking.

The sky lit up with one million joules of lightning power. It was the season: hot and cold currents in early springtime over open ocean. A super bolt collects power, a ship takes a direct hit, the good ship *Stella Atlantis* bursts into flame, the ship sinks. As they went down, the sight of the Canary archipelago, the steep rocks, the green mists, the hidden life underneath in the high seas' coastal reefs was a painting from a smoky age, a dread age, amber, resin, poison, capture. Hell in Atlantis trenches, and down they went to the deeps.

Into the levels of green and blue shades and the miraculously surviving goofy-faced fishes and the schools inside shoals, drifted the written words in blurring ink. Inlaid work was as fast food to the currents. Down below, octopuses and random molluscs wore plastic cups as bucket hat stylizations and suffocated, their gills trapped in plastic Crocs footwear. Fast fashion and slow creature death.

The electrocution of the sky persisted. As the ship went down, a couple in dressy clothes danced on the tilting deck. The barman served the last call of chestnut-shaded malt whisky. Johnny drank, watched the couple on the upper deck turn their backs to his view. The ship had righted itself. The night looked calm. Shock will do that, tell you the panic ship has righted, make you so calm you will hallucinate that I'm all right, Ma, I'm only drowning.

The ship took on water fast.

Johnny saw Vivienne.

There was Vivi, at the doorway. There was Vivi, a storm in a storm. There was Vivienne with her bald head so lovely, her slim body so curvaceous, her smile. That shy bold thing. And there at the door was Stella. The dark braids, the David Bowie T-shirt, all glitter as she walked to them, the freckles, the reddish hair, the Spanish Sephardic bloodline miscegenated with the Ashkenazi bloodline, Spain and Russia – fierce!

They were dancing, hip bones in green water, as the floor tilted south and the floor tilted north, Stella dancing with her mom, the way kids and moms, kids and grandmothers, have always danced at do's, together, holding hands at a distance, swaying. Only they were swimming in the green waters rising, in the bar on the scriptorium ship, sinking.

A second super bolt of lightning hit the ocean. Stella swam with her dad inside green mind. They saw an old man leaning on a piece of rock, his grey-mauve velvet robes on and a ventilator tube down his throat. He handed Stella a card. It read: *My name is Jeremiah. I lament the destruction of Jerusalem.* Intubated Jeremiah.

They swam together through the muddy green, Stella waving all eight of her arms around. The infinite water grew a dark ceiling. They swam inside a second nighttime. Skulls lay on rocks like *vanitas* scruff. A skull smoked a menthol cig once shilled to the ladies.

Johnny did not know how, but they were swimming without air tanks. With the dead you can swim like a fish. You have gills with the dead. Fish pedalled unicycles through the coral reefs. Coral: rest in peace, may your memory be a blessing.

Up ahead, the corpse of a plane. Bleached, moulting steel, paint. One wing broken. Mummified heads with hollow eyes looked out their window seats.

They swam to the cockpit. A stuffed dummy was sitting inside, the pilot. A beatific smile in red stitching on the effigy's face; the stuffing was coming out of it at the mouth. The mummy pilot was dressed in a baggy blue suit with a long red tie, which was draped over the stick in the cockpit, where a red light was still flashing. A Post-it Note sat on the pilot's dashboard. It read: *Carnage.* Once we were heads of state.

Sancho was paddling behind Johnny and Stella, stopping to talk to an errant night crab or three. Beautiful rainbow word-fish swam all around Johnny's head, a consortium of octopuses crawled by, followed by a siege of herring. He felt at one with all the lost parts of himself: It had never been inspiration he had been looking for. It had been the diamond precision of how to access his known tool kit for the emotional narrative job at hand. How to break his own rib cage, to save his own heart.

The fish loved Stella. The molluscs of all descriptions flocked to her, the family connection of squid and cuttlefish and nautiloids, the fossil mish-poche swam on by, swam back to pay their nibbling respects to La Reina Stellita.

The sea floor was filled with shops named for Stella: the Stellerias abounded. A seaweed public square had a statue of her with her curlicue arms, her proud head, her sturdy beak. Johnny heard the music again, the bone music as it once was, in olden days, when Stella was a baby born, the unexpected child.

They swam to a brown chest, with old gold flaking off it, gilt from the day. Stella prised the chest open. "Aha," she called out. "Dad. Mister Pitzel,

Sanchy. I found the stolen ballots. I found the purloined votes, from the Catalan referendum. I think Tweety Bird formed a special alliance across the aisle with Sylvester, and the two of them rats dumped the votes in the ocean."

Stella put the ballots into an old plastic bag she prised from the mouth of a dead corvina, and she swam with the votes on her back.

Fish gotta swim, dead gotta vote.

A giant animatronic spider walked on the sea floor toward them. Tall as buildings, powerful as egg sacs from a mighty woman, the egg sacs hanging down. Stella climbed up on the sacs; the spider in steel paused. It was one of Louise Bourgeois's magnificent spider sculptures called *Maman,* in homage to her mother.

Oceans are a form of speech. Johnny felt the old neurology of words, as if, like Stella, he had his brain in his wrists and fingers. His wounds would never heal, not really. But he might get used to their song.

As in Odysseus days, I swam away to return. I set out from Barcelona, for the great gratitude voyage of the return. If you never leave, you never know what it is to see your homeland skyline sail away. If you never return, you never know the gratitude of seeing the shoreline come back into view with all the people, the sea sparkle, the *terraza* DNA.

24

SOLO PINK

IT WAS GREY and dark, and Vivienne walked along an Amsterdam canal. Northern light, and she pulled the collar of her trench coat up around her neck. She missed Alexi already. Stupid, but there you are. She walked in green lichen mind. She walked easy in the city where tides met time, and everything was shored up. The thing about Amsterdam, besides the thing about space and restraint, is that Amsterdam had been sinking from its birth. A simple old rose beside an exquisite cup, a Zurbarán by gloaming. Low wet light and the lorn music returned.

Lorn: Lady Pink on soul sax. Lorn: the condition of women. Lady Fuchsia on anti-fascist saxophone. Down by water she walked with the objects of her photographic desire and solitary moxie. The idea is to be the tool kit for others, for living through the hard times and for joy in the odd green moments, in your art. It isn't about you. Only the you doing it out in the elsewhere. She'd been conned by love, by good-guy lovers, by little boy men. Why should she believe this guy? A guy who knew her dad, fixed stuff for Izzy. And Vulcan did receive the letter brought by Apollo, which told Vulcan that his wife had been off, trysting with Mars.

Are we all on the rebound?

Gyro-orbits. Gyro-tonics. Toxic gyrations. Look out humans, here comes the plague.

Yet love.

The canal boats drifted the city, the green willow-laden ponds held bike bits and blood and the memories of green mirrors and grey-brown oyster lumens and the silver nacre low country shining.

Low light – well, it thrilled her. The way skies died at sundown. The way, in the low country, the wet painted itself as if from below, as if on invisible brushes from the sea world rising.

She reached into her grey trench coat, pulled out a citron glove, wiped her forehead, wiped her scalp. Yeah, before she noshed her eyes, she needed to nosh her growling belly.

Her feet led her up and down the Overtoom, thinking of the way those old Dutch paintings of the riches of domestic life were, sure, how men of means peed around the edges of their capitalistic turf, but still Vivi found them oddly mesmerizing when she saw them in person.

Because work was valued, and the paintings showed such craft. She had this in common with Johnny, it was the mortar of their marriage: you don't block your own way to your own artistic labours, you get out of your own way with fleet moves, long aged in divine boredom. You put your name on your art, you put it out in the marketplace, you take a chance on strangers. Otherwise, it's just the recirculated applause of family. You jump, no net, into the darker.

The seventeenth-century city was still so seventeenth century, as she walked. The light in the city of Amsterdam mimicked the paintings of the Dutch golden age. The city on a dour day could be like a place without electricity. Or a place where electric lighting was new and still in its pupal amber stage.

In her rust suede boots and her grey trench coat, she passed houses of rust suede under a trench coat sky. She had brick legs; the tall brown willow sky was a scarf insert.

She entered the Rijksmuseum through the welcoming tunnel, like an old hand in the neighbourhood, in a fugue by intention. Back to that same Rembrandt room. Then her eyes were on *The Jewish Bride* again. Behind the bride and groom, Vivi noticed for the first time how the background was the burnt-umber colour of low polder water, outside. As if Rembrandt had himself been some sort of filtration system of love and deep attention, never mind the muscle memory of his brush stroke empathy – and then those rich tones.

Vivienne took her citron gloves out of her pocket. She had the painting to herself, had to act fast, no guards about. A found opportunity. She walked up to *The Jewish Bride*. Held up one citron glove beside it. The citron glove in her hand was like the crazy cousin at the wedding. The bride and the groom were avatars of autumn, fallen leaves, golden low-lit pathways, last chance saloons. The citron glove was the first acid green of springtime.

God, she loved parsing all this. Her mind felt calm. That restful aloneness. She loved light, its material wanton nature. If you don't love your materials, quit and make room for those who do, she thought, and felt buoyed up, in private sass in a museum.

Just then, the bride turned and looked at her. The groom shifted, looked at his bride examining Vivienne. Were there extreme forms of missing someone that can reconfigure all your senses? She pulled on the gloves, slowly, keeping an eye on the betrothed couple. It was only her and them.

They had been beloved by Rembrandt, in his incomparable intimacy and compassion. They had reached out to her, newly married fever phantoms. She had made the introduction to them of herself and her gloves and thus, she felt, of her and Alexi.

By nightfall in the day, she took a late boat tour, simply to float and dream of a reunion with Alexi. She realized she wasn't dreaming of a reunion with her own husband, Johnny. She knew that missing was a proper habit of love, and once you give up your ritual of missing your sweetheart, something else, something dissonant, begins. Then, outside of volition, or so it seems, you crave the dissonance.

BACK TO THE hotel, solo.

She undressed to take a bath, room 46, a rare hotel room that still has a tub. The tub was about two metres long and at least a metre deep. A tub meant for Dutch giants.

She had her robe on when she heard a buzzing. The desk downstairs?

She picked up the bedside phone. Nothing. Buzz-buzz. It wasn't the sound of her mobile. The buzz in the room was old basso. It was in the cupboard. She opened the wooden cupboard door. The buzzing was coming from her backpack. She unzipped it, unzipped her secret pocket. A flip phone was the source of the buzzing. She flipped it open, pressed a tiny side button. *"Habla?"* Again, in stress, automatically talking in her conflict second language.

"Is de Ville there, *por favor*?"

Alexi.

"You put this phone here."

"Of course. What did you think?"

"A flip phone? What year is this? And you – you say you're a – never mind." She didn't, out of caution, want to say.

"It's okay, Miss. You can't track a flip phone."

Vivi went and lay down on the bed. "I bet *you* could."

"Another matter entirely. How are you?"

She didn't want to say, either, how she missed him. She hoped her voice would express that.

"I went back to *The Jewish Bride*," she said.

"And how was the happy couple?" he asked.

"Beautiful," she answered. "Complete."

Vivi could picture the scar by his right eye, how it lifted into the eye crinkles when he smiled, and his voice was smiling now on the airwaves between the city of palm trees and the city of willows. How he had attended to his knee, a tell or a kucked-up surfer knee.

"I'll be back tomorrow. Do you want to come to Barcelona with me?"

This was sudden, but not really. The gyro-rotation goes on without us, like a soft snap of the finger we are moving with the axis of the planet.

"Where are you?"

"I'm coming back tomorrow."

"Your work is done?"

"It's work. Blazers and notes."

"I might have to. Well . . . " She wasn't sure what she was planning to do.

"I said I wanted to get you in the water – the Mediterranean – remember?"

"I do."

They sat in that particular silence that intimates have on phones with each other. Particularly phones used for talking on the phone. Vivi realized that all of Alexi's choices, like the image player, like the phone, were old school and analog. Of course, his goal was safety and security, discretion and privacy. Spies use landlines. Spies meet in person. Even a booth in an eatery could be compromised by the big ears in the next booth. Anything that could track you was out. No wonder he didn't send her images to her up-to-date phone. No wonder he didn't call her on the hotel line to her room. Their room, her mind said. That sneaky mind with its own ideas about the story.

"You didn't say where you were," she said.

"On the Born."

"On the Born; where on the Born?"

"Leaning on a wall outside Bar El Born."

"I know it. On Calders. Cauldron Street. Steam."

He laughed. "You figure?"

"What time is it there?" She had blurred out, forgotten that Amsterdam and Barcelona were in the same time zone. The latitude and the light were so completely different, you could imagine the clock had altered.

"Your time," he said. Vivi could picture the alley, like all the alleys in the Born where graffiti artists, creative and rote, had tagged the pull-down aluminum storefronts, during night crawls, which meant that by day nobody saw their graffiti art, and by night, soon enough, they were displayed only for the pooches and the sots.

"When do I see you tomorrow?" she asked him, the barrio in Barcelona implanted in her head, while at the same time she looked out the window of room 46 down into the night garden. The Amsterdam sky like sleeping sheep, like a golden nubble. Drifting the ovine clouds down.

With the flip phone in one hand, she went into the bathroom, put the plug in the tub, began to run the water.

"What's that I hear?" Alexi said.

"Water," Vivi said. "I'm running a tub."

"We could have breakfast," Alexi said. Pause. "In the tub."

"Call me when you get in."

"The tub?"

"Cute. Call me tomorrow."

"I'll think of you all night in your moss chamber of secrets, Vivienne Pink. Good night. Oh, and when you get a chance, press the blue button on the back of the phone, then throw it in the garbage, okay?"

"As in, 'This conversation never happened'?"

"Something like that," he said. She could hear the scar moving toward his eye, as he smiled at the other end of the line. "I used to do it with Izzy."

"My dad? Do what? You did what with him?"

"Talk on phones that never existed about things that never happened, which the conversation was never about –"

"That never existed."

She got into the tub, water to her neck. There was still room in the tub for Alexi, Rembrandt, Van Gogh and Velázquez, that dreamed-of dinner party reconfigured as tapas in the tub. Form decides content, Vivienne Pink thought.

"Did you talk about me? With my dad?" she asked.

"Always. Inevitably. Usually. Of course. Now . . . good night, Pink."

She sank real deep into the tub, thinking, He really likes me. More – he respects me. He called me by my last name, like a true comrade. The way Johnny used to, in the early love and artwork days, when they called each other Pink and Coma.

IN THE MORNING, Vivienne was restless. She ate in the Owl's breakfast room, enjoying the time alone. In the garden, under heavy skies, the green humidity soothed her eyes.

Then she walked across the bridge to the Leidseplein. Quiet Amsterdam, the land below sea level, at the get. So many bicycle riders solo.

Just beyond the Americain Hotel with the Café Americain in it, she saw a ticket event office. Who knows? she thought. I could see if anything's on, surprise Alexi when he comes back home. Home? Jungian slip?

Ah, there on the list was Joe Lovano. Vivi loved Lovano, the great saxophonist. Lovano and his jazz nonet. She and Johnny had seen him a couple times in T.O.

"Are there tickets for Joe Lovano left?"

"Sure. Good choice. You like jazz?"

"I do."

"He's at the Bimhuis."

"Is that far?"

"Not at all, down by the water, near the Central Station."

"Two for Lovano," she said.

Amsterdam and Barcelona. Like two sides of her personality. You could say that Amsterdam was where you invented things against all odds, kept to yourself, stayed in detailed intimacy with your art and your art brain, and pushed things out, blunt and droll. Close autumn with rusty metallic rain. If Amsterdam was the metal, Barcelona was the fire. The foundry. If Amsterdam was the invention and the commerce, and yes, even the sea, too, even water, then Barcelona had that duende element, that secret spirit, that throwing it all away to walk across the lorn music. Each place in its latitude, its different water, taught Vivienne Pink about light – her elemental material.

By the dark canals or by the prismatic wide sea, her methodology was to love the light with no restraint, so that the light might get a crush on her, too, and they could go out together. Any hour of day or night, and the light begins to move for you, like music. Light runs off the leash and you begin again.

Inside her backpack, inside a pocket more secret than her secret zip pocket out of which she had pulled the homicide vocabulary in Spanish to show Alexi was a vibrating light. The light was a photographic print. A print of the photograph she took when Stella lay dying.

Vivi took the photo out of its padded envelope.

Stella in a hospital bed at SickKids. Stella hooked up to life support. Stella, her daughter, being kept alive by plastic tubing. Stella, her mouth with a breathing device over it, her small nose obscured by the oxygen machinery. Her thin strong arms with tubes attached, further attached to stand-up devices like oxygen and intravenous sentries. When Vivienne lifted up her camera to take photos of her dying daughter, she felt, in concert, her own lungs breathing with the breathing machines. Her own gouged lungs, deeply scarred. When Vivi breathed, normally, she felt herself take each and every breath, due to the scars. She felt scar music when she inhaled a breath. Watching Stella, half-human and half-machine, it seemed to Vivienne, the labouring scars went deeper, went darker, were lung ruts, and her breath was trapped inside her.

Anyone with severe asthma knows: An asthma attack feels from the inside not that you can't catch a breath to inhale, but that all the breath in the world is captured inside you and you can't get out of yourself. You're trapped in an avalanche of air.

Then, Vivi, having taken half a roll of film, eighteen photos of her daughter – brain-dead, the doctors were saying – lay down beside Stella on the hospital bed, and took more photos, of her and her daughter. Blurred, most of them. Appropriately. Vivi stretched her right arm out, got her and Stella's faces together. Got out of the bed after taking eight photos, set up her portable tripod and her timer, and took ten more, two of them with her prone on her stomach, holding Stella in her many long tubes stretching out of her, Vivi with her shirt hiked up.

At the door to the hospital room, Vivi took one last shot, an adieu, a ciao, an adiós, of Stella on life support.

Then Vivi told the doctor that it was time to remove the tubes.

Vivi had never shown Johnny the photos. For years, she worked on making prints of them, working as a solo artist in her darkroom, the red light burning, and then, for a break, she walked the lane named after her father, Izzy Pink Lane, three blocks from the house. Wandered and wondered about the night watchman in the night garage, in his improv foundry, his metal-worker's shop, with his blowtorch and fine car doors being repurposed into sustainable dreaming.

UNTIL PHOTOGRAPHY WAS invented in 1839, no mother had ever had a photograph of her own child to look at if the child died. No photograph of herself with her child to look back on. In the early days of photography, a household might contain only one single photograph, a daguerreotype of a young child in her coffin.

It is not *closure* we seek – closure the panic, closure the outsourcing to businesses that whisk the dead from our eyes, closure like an autocrat, a censor, an eraser, to close us off from our mourning, our water. No. We seek to be *open*. We seek to have the balconies open wide to the dead. "If I die, leave the balcony open," wrote Lorca.

The dead are not tidy. The dead forgot to get a haircut. The dead have frayed ropes around their necks from travails past; the dead are coming for you in the morning, climbing up to greet you on your pigeon balustrades. Please be so kind as to leave the balcony open, if you die.

When I die, Vivienne Pink thought, let me die with my hair on, floating in divestments of pain. If the pain persists, and the pain will persist, then let me lead with my scars, at least. Let my lung lesions sing.

Let my cells make entente with all the sick wards of all the nations. Let me listen to the hard winds. Let me see the refuge waters, let my scars be as x-rays to the sunken escape boats. Okay, let grief eat my face. If I die, please publish my secret photos of my daughter dying. It is not so very long a time from the prehistoric cave drawings done with beetle blood and ash.

Time has come.

We are here on Earth in order to pay our karmic debt. Here we are, all so beautiful and sundry. We who have come with our beggar hands to proffer our karmic IOUs.

VIVIENNE PINK HAD worked in her darkroom to make prints of her daughter, Stella Coma, on life support in the hospital bed. Sweat equity in the void of labour. Shot on 35 mm film. Bathed in red light, Vivi saw Stella in a negative placed under the enlarger as a dark figure with long white hair, dark tubing. Vivi, the mother, chose with fierce delicacy the exposure, the time, the waving of her hands under the enlarger's lens, to vignette, soften the exposure light. She chose the chemicals in the trays, she inhaled the chemicals into her lung lesions as she worked. When Stella was printed on the photographic paper, Vivi bathed her in the chemical wash, hung the prints up on her darkroom clothesline. Sat and wept on the floor, seeing the exquisiteness of time the strangler.

Stella gone. And returned in art. If you're an artist *closure* is somebody else's language. Every new shill will be debunked, in time, but, baby, they can't debunk your heart.

Vivi had kept all the photographic prints of Stella dying hidden. Except for this one, which she kept in her backpack, secure. She thought, Maybe I'm going to show Alexi this pic of my daughter.

She took her book of Lorca poetry, *Poeta en Nueva York,* with the fuchsia cover and the green lettering that looked gold on the brilliantine pink. Vivi opened the book at random. Page 96. There it was – coincidence, or karma? A line jumped out from the Lorca – *"Los muertos diminutos por las riberas."* The small dead by the shorelines.

Vivi had to laugh. What are the chances?

She placed the photo of Stella on life support inside the Lorca book, a bookmark as if on the shoreline, awaiting the return of our beloveds.

ALEXI ARRIVED BACK at the Owl by noon. They hung around together until darkness, went down by taxi to the Bimhuis, a modern concert venue, and decided to stand on the mezzanine. Alexi had his long arms around Vivi's waist from behind. Joe Lovano had a nice bopping and ballad group with him, of the nine players four were on sax – two on tenor, one on alto, one baritone – plus trumpet, trombone, piano, bass and drums. The acoustics were very fine.

They walked back to the Owl along deserted train tracks in the deep dark into the main lit area by the shadow of the Central Station and over the bridge past green water.

Walking in the dark, Vivi said to Alexi, "I miss T.O. right now."

"How so?"

"In Toronto, we could light up some sweet cannabis and walk home getting a buzz on, no problem. All the nabes in T.O., where you need two million to even get a look-in at a two-storey brick semi-detached house for sale, reek of weed. Like picture Vermeer's *Little Street,* with all those nice ladies, sewing and sweeping and toking, all day, in Canada. But in Amsterdam, are you kidding me? It's like Amsterdam is in a time warp about weed. Right now we'd have to go looking for some damn *coffeeshop,* all bourgie and proper."

"It's not done on the street in Amsterdam."

"Only in *coffeeshops.* Never in *cafés.* Crazy."

He put his arm around her. "I'm glad you're here. You're light's avatar, you know."

In the morning dark, they got coffee in the Owl's breakfast room. Quiet, together, beside the glass wall looking out into the garden. Amsterdam, latitude 52. The green lesion. Mokum Aleph.

On a late afternoon flight, Alexi and Vivi flew from Amsterdam to Barcelona.

The child on life support was the secret image in the carry-on bag of her mother, stowed in the overhead.

25

HOLDING BACK THE YEARS

IN BLIND BLACK like a ballad, reincarnated with gills, born again in watery graves, smooth in the waves, Johnny, Stella and Sancho swam through the delicate serifs of the S-shaped Atlantic. On they drifted, fluorescent, spiny.

On they swam, in the green origin water, Mokum Verde, liquid in their belonging, far from purges and *autos-da-fés*.

The Canary archipelago drifted away, the Atlantic sailed away, they swam beneath the waters of the Strait of Gibraltar – Granada on the left, North Africa on the right – into the Mediterranean, up along the coast, passing Valencia in shades of azure and the deeper maxixe, and back into Barcelona harbour.

They skimmed the surface of the water. Johnny, Stella, Sancho, holding hands, splayed out like manta rays. Hello, Barcelona. I'm back. *Bon dia,* how've you been, while I was away at sea? Was time kind? What are you thinking, lately? Don't forget me when I go. When you return, you feel the pang of the next time you'll make your departure.

They splashed up on the beach at Playa de San Sebastián, in Barceloneta. Briny, slimy, they shot out of the water and landed right at the feet of the tables of – yes – the El Petit Far. They were back at the Little Lighthouse Café.

"Well, I'll be," Sancho said, spitting sea water from his mouth. (Also a nice Pandora fish.) "I haven't been to the beach in a dog's year. Marvellous." He turned to look at the Barcelona shoreline, how it curved from this far end in the sea mist all the way up to the massive copper fish of Frank Gehry, the familiar landmark in its singular skeletal maritime shape. Stella, meanwhile, was inside a cortado glass, happy in the cut milk dregs of caffeine, letting the liquid enter her, tasting the coffee with her arms. There was a light drizzle.

"Can you hear the rain, Dad?"

Indeed he could. His ears had sharpened on the island in the ocean. He had prayed for Stella's return and she had come back. But no. He hadn't *prayed*. He had written to her; his prayers, as a writer, were words. His faith as a scribe was in the power of the empty page. She died; she returned. Grief yearns for the prodigal beloveds. Right here, last November, when it was so warm, she had emerged. He had been a numb puppet; he had stuffed that numb avatar in a bottle. The bottle was his own body. Yes, yeah he had sent her a letter in a bottle, he had hoped for the infinite healing power of the surf. He could express his longing for a greater existence but only clandestinely for the page. Grief had incarcerated him in his own skin. He had had no recourse but to write, and to put the writing in the shape of letters to Stella, because he had become desperate. The block had become the daily systole and diastole of his own bloodstream.

Here she was, the model for all our experiments into intelligence. Stella Octopus so oblivious of her father's gratitude. With the dead, you can feel at home, for the story has already been told. And now he was a family with her, a single father perhaps, with a good pal, Sancho, for the Stella-sitting.

They sat at a beachside table by the surf school. Ali, his same café waiter, was there in a Barceloneta minute. A cortado for Johnny, a beer for Sancho, *chocolate con churros* for Stella. They felt like ghosts in that happy way you do when you return from a trip. Ghosts with camera eyes. I used to be here. Nobody knows I went away. Nobody knows I was in a coma, Johnny thought. Nobody knows I have four or five dozen bookmarks, all of them my obituaries. Nobody here on the beach knows that my death in Death Valley was widely reported, the correction that I was still alive – not so much.

Sancho was writing a few lines, looking out on the pale masts of sailing ships in the water, using Johnny's old Moleskine notebook and a grey Palomino Blackwing 602 pencil he had cadged from Johnny back on the Big

Canary, which Sancho had worn to a short stub with a much reduced eraser. The world had edited itself down to the dogs on the beach, the look of coffee in a short curvaceous glass, the limbs of humans who had shed their winter coverings. The wind carried the smell of food to their nostrils.

So, after coffee, they walked up the seaside promenade and through Barceloneta, that separate urban duchy, up Joan de Borbó, the masts of the sailing ships across the way at the Port Vell on their left. Johnny and Sancho wobbled, bowlegged, the stone squares feeling like a ship's deck. Stella rode on Johnny's bald head, saying, "Listen to the rain; when it rains, remember me. Dovecote, seacote, Stelleria."

As they walked back from the beach café, Johnny felt filled with the dead and the living municipality. The sun was long, the streets had such a yen to be inhabited. The people woke slowly, as they do in Barcelona, then all at once, the city was alive with sails and sailors and the conviviality of cafés, bars and restaurants. Grazing all day. When tyranny comes back, it comes back as fear of social closeness. When autocracy makes its way into ousting democracy, it comes in the emotional hysteria of the fear of people in large groups. The pulse of the city requires heartbeat-to-heartbeat, face-to-face, mano-a-mano. He had cocooned as sailors do. The shore life was bright, a revelation to his eyes, his wobbly legs.

He felt alive with time. Everyone was alive; everyone was dead. Cellular matter, physics, dinner. Johnny felt the bone marrow of the dead talking inside his bones. He felt the revving energy of the young, with their shining and soiled futures. He felt ozone. The built city on a curve.

He was layered with the past, the sun shining at his back, long shadows up Joan de Borbó past the Barceloneta Metro stairs, ghosts in coats emerging, the dead from Solentiname the Nicaraguan volcano, ghosts from the murder at the mass in Managua, the ghost of the priest-poet Ernesto Cardenal. The murders of the indigent, the Indigenous on the green perfection lake, the lake of Panajachel, the magnificent water of Lake Atitlán (the hordes of gringos clustered together there, playing at being poor, living cheap with beauty and war all around them, the Third World a moral plaything of the day), his murdered friends in the Guatemalan highlands, they too emerged from the

Metro stairs, they did walk up and down the Rambles. The green and paling dead did bear witness to their own disappearance. Johnny did not have his land legs or his land mind. This was ideal. He was no longer, after a winter on an Atlantic island, concerned with the numerous pointillist dots of the passing rage of each citizen's feverish disinterest. The dead came back, they rode the subways, they rode the *subtes*, they rode the international atoll of death Metros, as the pretty women chain-smoked by the Metro stairs, a thousand dots of stylish scarves passed by on the skeletal frames of the murdered and disenfranchised. Just walking around, as the sea rose. They had been in the deeps, it was fine to return.

Visions of the refugee camps he and Vivi had gone to in the depth of Mexico near the southern border, so rancid, so squalid even the United Nations did not list them, officially. The radical priest from San Cristóbal de las Casas who took them in disguise to see the poorest of the poor, the marginalized even within the margin refugees; the death threats to Vivi when she returned, the babykins voice on the big neo-Nazi woman, who threatened to murder Vivi and Stella; and the dead that day when they came back to Barcelona were, to Johnny, travelling ghosts as if the plane had been delayed forever. That plane is on hold for the afterlife. The dead of all the Nazi rallies, the train and railway systems the ultimate enablers of the murder of his people. The dead stopped in convivial noon groups to chat, as they do in sweet Barcelona, as they gather to meet at the Metro steps to share a skull cigarette. All up the blue avenue the eateries were open, and the dead did eat seafood, which had been proven to not only keep you young, but to keep your children all the more brilliant.

When the plague came, even the dead moulted their carapaces to show their hearts within. And, as if the seas had indeed risen, the ailing were fitted with breathing devices, and we missed our cafés so much, our shores, the wind in our hair, the combs of rust we so took for granted.

26

THE PYTHON CUFF

IN THE TAXI from the airport, the changeover began in her eyes, the willows of Amsterdam replaced by the tall palm trees of Barcelona. Two cities always wet, always humid, but the humidity in Barcelona had a sparkle, like glaze breaking up, like Mediterranean mezzotint all day.

Vivi was in such an agreeable fog, feeling a comfort and familiarity in her return to Barcelona and the precincts of her beloved Catalonia, that she hardly paid attention when Alexi gave the *taxista* directions. Mountain on the left, sea on the right, Montjuïc, *mar*, the road curving at the port, then the straightaway down the palm parade to the little plaza of the neighbourhood. For the first time, she exited the taxi with a man who wasn't her husband.

Exiting, she realized, at the Pla de Palau. Her normal destination. Hang on, she thought, standing by the Irish pub, the Al Passatore pizzeria, seeing the good old newspaper kiosk in the square. What am I . . . How did he . . . What the . . . ?

This was the neighbourhood where she and Johnny had their modest roof studio.

Alexi was walking at a good brisk pace the few steps into the stone warrens, walking casually and with offhand intent. How did this surf medico she had met by chance on a plane from Toronto to Amsterdam know the way in Barcelona to her roof *pied-à-terre* in the Born?

They walked up the stone alley called Dames to the alley where the hidden door to her place lay. The official address was on Esparteria, but it was a short dark stub off Esparteria, actually. The alley had a low stone overhang, an arch at each end, which made you feel enclosed and secret inside a stone box with the sky above.

Alexi stopped partway up the alley in front of an unimpressive piece of splintered wood, which sat against the stone. The wood was layered with old posters, graffiti, mangled advert sheets. Vivi watched him. He pulled a key fob from his leather jacket, waved it at the klutzed-up wood – voila! The wood moved. Alexi held it aside for her, in the ridiculously narrow space between the wooden piece and the actual front door – to *her* building.

They squeezed through the narrow space into the dark vestibule where, up a couple of stone steps, was the miniscule ancient elevator.

Vivi felt feverish, dizzy. Was this a joke? Did this surf doctor have a key to hers and Johnny's place on the roof? She kept quiet, letting the scene unroll.

They got in. An elevator built for two. Her nose was the level of his armpit. He pressed *E*. Vivienne forgot what *E* stood for. So, okay, it wasn't the key to her apartment, because to get to the roof, you used a key in the elevator. If this wasn't a joke or a trick, it was some fierce kind of fate in a wet Barcelona alley.

Up they rode, the elevator buttons in the familiar European style a kind of jumbled poetry, reading: O E 1 P 2 3 keyhole. For a seven-storey building.

He had his arm around her waist. They stopped at *E*; the curtain opened. Alexi pushed open the elevator door.

There was no hallway, only a landing fit to hold two people in an embrace. Off the embraceable landing a couple of doors. Old Europe was all about economies of space. You made a life in the ingenuity of tucking yourself and your goods in and out of designs and niches. The wide world you got to know by going out.

Alexi waved his key fob at the door immediately on their right.

When he opened the door to the apartment E-1, Vivienne was stunned at how much space there was. A large living room, a nice kitchen with a – seriously – full wooden table. A washroom to the left. A door to another room, which must be a bedroom. A balcony at the end of the living area.

She could see in the barrio vernacular a small round café table set out on the balcony, with two spindly chairs. What more did you need?

"I forget what *E* is," she said.

"*E?*" he asked, plopping his bag on the dining table.

"In the elevator. *E*. What floor are we on?"

"*Entresuelo*. In-between floor."

"So, our floor is called the floor in between floors?"

He was out on the balcony, looking down on Esparteria. A misty rain was falling. They stood on the balcony together, bumping against the table and chairs. They were in the same building as Johnny. They were on *Entresuelo*, Johnny was on the *Ático* roof.

Vivi and Alexi stayed in most of the day, in bed. At around ten in the evening, they took a chance on getting in at Bar del Pla on Montcada past the Picasso Museum, the exceedingly narrow eatery much favoured by locals, a superb eats place. From the dark part of the uphill tilt of Montcada almost at Princesa it looked like a pocket bar with a counter and a few tables, but it had a lot of space to cram folks in, and a well-known yet hardly known back room. The guy behind the bar said, yeah, there was a *mesa al fondo,* a table at the back.

A healthy swath of sublime grilled squid, wild potatoes, *coca de sardinas*, Rioja *y café* later, they wandered out to the walled municipal hallways, kissed awhile against the dark public walls. They slipped in to their front door via the innocuous piece of wood on the stone.

Up a couple steps, opened the elevator door, Vivienne looking in the elevator mirror. How in hell had it happened that she was looking at herself in a mirror with this tall sad-eyed guy?

"I used to have different eyes," he said. "I had to have them operated on. While they were in there, they rearranged my face. They suctioned out the bruises under my eyes."

She laughed. She pressed *E*. "It sounds like something from that movie, you know, the one where Sam Jaffe, was it?, plays the doctor who's about to perform plastic surgery on the criminal and Jaffe-the-doc says – I think it was *Out of the Past,* Bogart with the bandages, was that the one? Anyways, the doc says, 'You're my first patient who *talked*.'"

"I don't think it was Sam Jaffe. *Out of the Past* was Mitchum and, oh my, what a crush I had on Jane Greer. She was *bad.* Bogie, I think you're thinking of *Dark Passage.* Loved the book."

"David Goodis. None better. Philly. Do you love him?"

"Love."

So he loved noir, loved Goodis and was saying, blithe as you please, that he'd had plastic surgery. Perp or police? Or citizen afraid?

"I got it done by a top guy in Miami," Alexi said.

"Oh, is that so?" Vivi took a pic of the two of them in the elevator mirror, loving how the infinite images reflected back.

The elevator clanked. He opened the elevator curtain. "Something like that. Miami . . . it could have been Buenos Aires. My chin," he said without further details. He had a nice deep cleft.

"What were you in? Some kind of – bandages on your face? Peepholes?"

"Later," he said. "You have to ask the right question to get the right answer."

Well, well, she thought. Who gets a chin job, an eye job? What kind of man? Witness protection? Double agent? Surf spy? After Stella died, her dad was so bereft – at least as her mom, Roz, told the story – that Izzy called in some favours from some investigators he had known when he was T.O. mayor, asked them to check into whether there was anything Metro's Finest missed when looking into Stella's murder.

Vivi dimly remembered that her mother had said, only in passing, that Izzy had hired a guy who had had his face changed, once upon a time, due to his double, or was it triple, agent status. A guy who didn't need a safe house, because his new face was his safety.

Could it be? That the guy who the guy who knew a guy knew, was – Alexi? Did Izzy Pink, the mayor among mayors, her own dad, hire this man to check out who might have run down his shaina maidel granddaughter, Stella? Alexi had said that he worked, as a young man and then later, as some kind of a fixer for Izzy. Had it gone beyond that? Beyond security at a shiva, beyond fix-its negotiated at Izzy's favourite booth at a restaurant near the house in Koreatown, where Izzy had a regular spot at the back by the kitchen. Beyond late lunch midtown bento boxes and envelopes of cash. Times are tough, Alexi might gig as a chop shop guy, an art welder, a private investigator, while getting you up on a surfboard to confront your skittish heart of fear.

ON THE SECOND day in Barcelona together, the air felt stormy, humid, empty and windy. Alexi said, "Let's get you in the water." He was standing on the balcony, holding his hand out to see how the weather was.

When they got to the beach – the same twelve-minute walk Johnny took every day – Alexi slipped into the dogleg entrance to the Escola de Surf and came out with two boards. Two wetsuits.

"I don't think so," she said. "How 'bout if you go, and I'll get coffee over there and watch you."

She started toward the café right there, El Petit Far. Lord in his mercy, there was Johnny. Johnny gesticulating, Johnny standing up, Johnny sitting down, Johnny biting into a croissant, Johnny holding the croissant like a butter-laden sock puppet, talking to it. It was Johnny, all right.

"Him. It's okay," Alexi said. "Leave him be."

"That's my husband."

"I know. I've met him."

"You've met Johnny?" she said, moving Alexi with a push a few steps down the beach promenade to face away from Johnny. "No you didn't! You met him? Oh, come on. When?"

"Last week."

"Wrong."

"Okay," Alexi said, laughing. "A couple of weeks ago. Probably a month."

"You were here?"

"Sure."

"Doing what?"

"Resting my eyes, doing some side work." He was in his wetsuit, zipping up. "Come on. What are you going to do, stay and watch me with your husband, who thinks you're in Amsterdam?"

Vivienne got in the wetsuit. Johnny wouldn't be looking for her here. Yet, here she was, entering into the therapy of the surf with Alexi the Surf Doctor, her husband a five-second walk away.

Johnny stood up. He held his notebook aloft, he declaimed to the air. The wind carried his words away. Vivienne lifted the edge of her wetsuit hood to hear her husband. Johnny's head was turned toward his own shoulder, speaking, "Oh my grey sponge! Oh my throat cut open! Oh my great river! *¡Oh esponja mía gris . . .* "

Jesus, Vivi thought, I'm watching my husband talk to an imaginary *something,* as he recites García Lorca. "Navidad en el Hudson," "Christmas on the Hudson." 1929, Lorca in New York City. *"¡Oh filo de mi amor!"* Johnny gesticulating about the wounding blade. He sat down, leaning forward, cupping something invisible in his hands. Laughing, he said, "Yes, yes, I agree completely."

Alexi was watching her watch Johnny.

Vivi watching Johnny patting something on his neck. Johnny talking to his coffee cup. The coffee, improbably, splashing seemingly of its own accord at his face. Johnny taking the blue-black liquid from his forehead, writing in his notebook with his finger, all stained the tint of old pictures.

"Here," Alexi said, handing her a bright yellow board. "Come with me." He walked her to the edge of the sand and the sea. Two figures in wetsuits. He zipped hers to the top. "Lie on top of it. Paddle like a seal."

Vivienne was standing there in a mental drop-off.

Alexi said, "Look: I was here. I was right here. Confession time: The day I left you solo in Amsterdam I was at a thing, the thing doesn't matter, it had to do with security, idea theft. I was with a colleague, we came down here from the W hotel to have a coffee at the beach café, this guy comes over, we think he's the waiter, right?"

Vivienne had no idea what he was talking about.

"It was that guy." He gestured with his chin in Johnny's direction. Johnny had a sugar packet in his fingers, he was talking to it. He was gathering the air, putting something invisible on his shoulder, nodding, laughing. "He was quite a riot, he offered us, I think it was a donkey smothered in anchovies. *Burro con espuma* maybe. He held forth about how his wife supports him. He acted like a talky waiter. He said how they thought he was a night-watcher, a guy who roamed the night alleys. Said he wrote a book and they got him mixed up with his *protagonist.* It was his wife who was the nighthawk; he said *she* hung at the all-night Bathurst-Dupont diner. His wife shot the night – he was telling us this – and he used her negatives, her contact sheets. He talked about surfaces, stars, the grain of the ocean. He sat down beside me, he whispered in my ear that his *wife's* father was a big deal guy, there was a lane named after him. Goya, the galaxy, connections. He reminded me of my art history prof. My colleague, she taped his performance."

Vivienne was absorbing this. Her husband who looked like a local kook. And who was the "she" Alexi referred to? A colleague with or without benefits? She was resisting the urge to impose ownership on Alexi. You learn that, after a lot of decades of possession mania.

"Get on your board," he said. "Paddle out with me. Knees. Feet."

They got a fair distance into the grey foam on dirty charcoal water so joyful and bounding in their faces. Vivienne shouted to Alexi, "You taped him?"

Alexi shouted to Vivienne, "My friend did. Our IP buttons were lapel cameras."

This put the unbelieving steam on Vivienne. She paddled hard.

"Okay, crouch. Get up." Alexi was on his board beside her, moving fast. "Knees. Feet!"

The waves were good; they were gentle here.

She was in a crouch, her husband standing up patting his shoulder, gathering his things, walking away, walking up the beachside. Her knees creaked into position. She put her front foot down way too far too fast. She fell off her board.

The water slammed her a wave reprimand right in the kisser.

At least it didn't knock her two-part jaw asunder. Her jaw was still in two parts. Awaiting the bone to grow itself back in the gap in her facial structure.

Alexi swam over to her. "Okay, let's go again."

This beach that she had known for decades felt like a beach from outer space. Barcelona reconfigured. She had been a *voyeuse* with a lens on the black-suited otter-like surfers, paddling out. She had used fast Tri-X film, old school, to shoot them in black and white, otters, sea lions on boards into the grey spume. To feel the energy of water roiling fast and high like fire, taking spit and salt and oxygen and the rotation of the tidal planet. Now, standing in sandy soak, even as a surf-noob, she was part of the picture that she had previously only observed. She was wet with the image she had taken. Between pupa and imago, with a new man.

The sea is dying, the sea will rise again. The kelp, the coral, the anchovy millions. The common ozone. The abyssopelagic tablemounts like wild grain can come again, nurtured by earth shepherds. By shepherds of the sea. Even the water has been gentrified. The whales have been chased out of the old sonar neighbourhoods. We have been amputated on earth. We are already vanished. Why not make beautiful things?

Oh, sweet spongy knees. Surf, anyway. Knobs and knurls ahoy!

Oh, shooting pain, ride it to the event horizon. Unroll the carapace, this mask you have been wearing, and make of your own skin a mask of glinting fierceness.

Out of their wetsuits, back in the home alley, Alexi motioned her to the leather atelier across from their front door. He tapped the display window. "Would you fancy that for your wrist?" In the window, a purse, a belt, a black leather cuff sending off gold glints in bits of sun intruding the window.

"I'd love that." She thought he was bantering. Window-shopping.

"I thought of you," he said. "I went in. It'll be ready tonight."

Inside the atelier at the back on a raised area, a bearded man wearing a leather apron was leaning over a table, doing close work under a lamp. Knives, scissors, glues, chamois cloths, he waved them in. The smell was intoxicating to Vivi. An artisan at work with his tannery materials. The bearded man walked toward Vivi with a cuff. "Let's try it on," he said. She was reminded of the day years ago when the glover fitted her for the citron gloves. Only this guy was maybe fifty with the new old-craft vibe, a very self-contained man with a mission. Make the item of beauty and use, and use will be its beauty, when the plague times come.

The cuff fit. Vivi stroked it. "Python," Alexi said.

"It's from Singapore," the artisan said. "It's legal, don't worry, the python has papers." Like Alexi, he was droll. Attentive, wearing the world and experience lightly. "I need to shine it up. If you want to come back in a half-hour?"

"I could tuck it in my carry-on with my vocabulary," she said to Alexi.

"Try it on again," he said. She did. "It looks great on your wrist."

"Lead with my scars?" she said to the atelier space.

"I do," said the atelier man.

The python cuff joined the story.

27

RIDING IN THE RAIN WITH BILL WITHERS

ALEXI AND VIVI were at Vegetalia, around the corner from the apartment, sitting right beside the bright green wooden ledge at the window. They were looking out at the big public memorial space, built over a cemetery and dedicated to the Catalan martyrs of the War of Spanish Succession at the Siege of Barcelona in 1714. It was five o'clock in the afternoon. Alexi was eating the Vegetalia "brunch": a big plate of fruit, eggs, salad, cheese, nutty strudel and a glass of red. Vivi was having her usual veg paella and a café solo.

Alexi opened his phone screen, tapped it, put the phone on the table so that Vivi could see it. "This," he said.

The screen was dark, covered with old moving rain. She recognized her street over the ocean in T.O. A figure, shot from the back, riding in black, no lights, on a bike. Riding in the rain. Alexi tapped the screen. "Let me rewind," he said.

"What's going on, Alexi?" Vivi asked.

"Here," he said. "Have a look."

She didn't like the expression on his face. Solemn.

He showed her the screen. A figure walking down – yeah – Izzy Pink Lane. The phone had lifted to show the sign: *Izzy Pink Ln.*

The video tracked the figure, who took a bike from the side of a garage, got on, rode slowly in the rain away from the camera, left on Follis, down Euclid. Riding at speed the wrong way, baseball cap, no bike light, rain.

Alexi got up, came to her side of the table, looked over her shoulder, gestured at the phone. "I called the ambulance."

"What no. My bloody sister, Rhonda, did."

"It was me," Alexi said, sitting back down across from her.

"You're saying you . . . ?"

He put his arm across the table to take hers. "I'm so sorry, Vivi. Baby, I saw him hit her."

"You saw my daughter get hit."

His eyes were burning the air. "I did. I called 911."

"Who is that?" she asked, pointing at the phone.

"I think it's Brian." A beat. "Maybe."

"*Brian*? Brian-Brian?"

"He rode away. I was calling 911. I tried to resuscitate her. Your Stella."

"Rhonda's Brian? Four-year-old Nazi-hunter Brian?"

"I'm not sure. I think. He used to lurk around my garage studio at night."

"Rhonda didn't ride in the ambulance?"

"Your sister wasn't there. She came out of the house when the ambulance arrived, got in."

"Have you got evidence of Brian?"

"They haven't found any, definitely."

"They?"

"Us."

"She's gone." Several beats. "It doesn't matter. The hurt never dies."

They finished their food.

THAT NIGHT THEY went to the *Messiah* at Santa Maria del Mar, walked the one minute from the apartment to the basilica. A Catalan chamber group, a modest magnificent gathering of musicians and singers warming the basilica vault, the stained glass windows in winter, the capacity crowd, it pulled the anxious over-worry out of Vivienne's body. Handel had written the *Messiah* three hundred and fifty-seven years after Santa Maria del Mar was built, from stones hauled up from the Mediterranean and from the Barcelona mountain, Montjuïc, the Mount of the Jews. It passes; it all passes. The lies pass, we pass. Her anger at Rhonda would never pass, not really, it would always be a family ghost. But chasing after liars' lies is a full-time job. Joy, like Atlantis, is the dream, the myth, and we have to go there. Even for scraps on the reef, even for scrabbly bits off the dying coral. Vivi, sitting in the basilica pew beside Alexi, chuckled in a mordant droll way – a Jew's joy – to realize, as she felt bathed in the acoustics and the secret sonar of Handel, that the word for chorus in Catalan was *coral*. And so shall the chorus of coral from the deep sea be whole again in oceanic hallelujahs.

VIVI AND ALEXI in Barcelona:

They got a dog, a shepherd. They walked around with baguettes under their arms. A daily paper, *un diario*, folded with the bread, and walking the dog. From private intention and professional morphing, they aimed to live local and look local, too. No new white sneakers. No overly bright colours. Alexi wore an ochre field coat, the blue chore pants; with a baguette and a folded newspaper, no one in passing took him for a potential pocket to pick. Vivi wore a new moss green merino wool scarf from long-time Basque weavers, which she bought from the pocket-sized design and fine goods shop tucked into the stone wall seven steps from their front door. The duende of the scarf was that she bought it after the Vegetalia conversation with Alexi, about Rhonda. It was her moss green merino scarf of resistance.

Barcelona is all about the lonely accessories. The things seemingly extra that add up to the tendermost life. *Nighthawks at the Terraza.*

YES, DEAR READER, Alexi and Vivi did indeed live in the same building as Johnny. They simply avoided his hours. He was the dawn lark, he was the stranger to the night. He was the man who wrote a novel set at night, and to do it he used Vivi's alley, laneway, night street, night watch photos. So, Vivi and Alexi steered themselves to their natural part of the clock. The best way to avoid someone in a city is to go out and about on a different schedule, as if the city was a different city depending on time of day, and it is.

ONE NIGHT THEY decided to go eat at Bormuth, a six-minute walk from their *Entresuelo* digs. As they passed the Creperia on the Born, Bobby the bartender, whom Vivi had known well when she and Johnny were together, was standing in the doorway. He was a cool guy, his eyes flickered when he saw Vivi approaching, a guy who was clearly not Johnny with his arm around her.

Bobby stepped forward. "Milady," he said, kissing Vivi's hand. It was droll yet sincere. "How are you?" He hugged her, kissed her on one cheek, then the other. "Hey, man," he said to Alexi.

"This is Bobby," Vivi said to Alexi. "We go back."

Alexi and Bobby shook hands. Not exactly the polar ice cap, but not exactly the polar ice cap melting, either.

"You're back," Bobby said to Vivi. "That's brilliant." Bobby of the normal open-hearted multilingual millennials. Bobby whom she adored, and it was mutual, that bartender-client mutual admiration society that makes commerce libations and the life and death of cities go round. Momentarily, Alexi her sweetheart was the third wheel.

"You coming in?" Bobby said. "Asparagus and goat cheese crepe, right?" He remembered her order. Vivi hesitated.

Then the clear pour of Bill Withers's voice came out from the bar into the street. Like the truth in a mistral from the place where poetry swims, Withers knew we missed our water when it was gone. Bill Withers, singing "Ain't No Sunshine." Singing from the deformation of the heartache spaces. The moment, in a bar, when every patron is solo. The moment when you knew that Edward Hopper brush-stroked notes of Bill Withers all over the canvas.

"We're going to walk a bit," she said. She gave Bobby another hug. Black jeans, black tee, hair short in the back, long on the top, the familiar bartender look.

She and Alexi walked to Rec, hung a left, walked the long block to Bormuth. Vivi had a craving for their *berenjena*, the miracle eggplant chips in a light batter. They got her favourite table by the window, a nice two-top, looking out on the hill where Sabateret turned into Fusina, with the nailed-down public armchairs. They drank *tinto*, they ordered *pulpo, bravas*.

Even the food she was eating was a culinary bigamy. She had discovered Bormuth with Johnny, they had made it a usual spot. The *berenjena* she had eaten with him she was eating with Alexi. The artist was redrawing her own life picture. *Besame mucho y cuentame más*. Kiss me all over the place and tell me another story. Savour the tapas with me I used to savour with my husband.

Vivi looked out the window while Alexi went to the loo.

Johnny. There he was, sitting in one of the nailed-down chairs. He looked rough. His hair looked wet, greasy. He wore torn pants. His legs were stretched out from a long dark tweed overcoat. He was staring out into the great nowhere. Was this her husband? Her dreamboat from the day?

His left espadrille had a piece of rope hanging from the sole. Since when did he wear pale green espadrilles? When the wife goes away, the husband's garb and hygiene fall away. He took a smoke from his pocket. Ah, only a roach. He lit it. Looked to the Spanish night. He moved his espadrille into the lamplight: green, cotton, soles from the esparto plant.

She popped some crispy eggplant in her mouth.

Alexi returned to the table. Before he sat down across from her, he kissed her cheek. She played with the python cuff on her right wrist. In the slight light, it gave off the shucked skin's gold sparks. She felt that urban thing: nobody knows the stories that apparent strangers have been in with each other.

An apparent bum in a mental daze on a street chair, and just inside those nice glass windows he's facing, a woman in black velvet pants, a red shiny silk shirt, a leopard scarf for a flare, an indigo jean jacket over her shoulders – who would have imagined, that those two were husband and wife? We know so little, we hardly are aware of the clandestine magnetisms of our own places.

She and Johnny had drifted. Two vessels on an ocean without wind.

When the two of them, Alexi and Vivi, walked back home, arms around each other, down the Passeig del Born, passing Creps al Born, Bill Withers was back singing, the music out of the night bar, the night, the *nit*. Bill

Withers like a magnet himself, with his signature long patient waits between the aches of knowing all the known unknowns, the old world had seen a few things. Don't ever be a tourist, babe, to your own soul. With Alexi she felt at home as a freak, she felt cozy being damaged, a babbling mute, all eyes. The idea is to go deeper, let your audience come to you, let them feel what it feels like to be with you on your travel to the pelagic layers even greener, even more onyx, even without light. Art is not a service industry. It is an intimacy industry. A thing like a python cuff made of the shucked skin of planetary creatures. Glints of gold, scales of black.

"Ain't No Sunshine," 1971, still Laos, still Mao, apocalypse in the rear-view mirror revving up to stalk you down, and yes, Mr. Withers, all time is long time with the dead. And with the dead, every avenue is lonely and you're out in the dark in the rain crooning multiples of I know, to nobody.

THEY WERE SOAKING wet. It was January 2017, beside the sea. Rain on the roof, rain on their balcony.

Across the way someone opened their green painted shutters wide. Out of a lit window came Neil Young's "Harvest." Goddamn it, 1971 did know something. A war in its sick end in southeast Asia, a wall still up in Berlin, arms still to ship to Iran, cocaine *caballeros* still growing up, Franco the dictator still alive in España. I know. I know. The body is not a plan, the body is an ecology; the globe is not a line, the map is very round.

"Harvest," "Ain't No Sunshine," "River."

The tyrant redraws the map. You miss the rivers most when the rivers are gone. You miss your baby most when the compass rose has been assassinated.

When I die, fly me to Barcelona, and dress me in stone and sand and night.

ALEXI AND VIVI went to the beach most every day, in the best lousy stormy days with the headline being that they went to surf. But, although Vivi on her first try had acquitted herself admirably as a noob on the board, she just didn't warm to it.

Alexi would instruct her, and she wanted instruction – after all it was his skill set and if she wanted (and she did want) respect for her art skills then she had to give respect to others. It went like this:

Two boards on the sand. Vivi lies down, a bald otter, she lifts her body, kneels – now! Alexi, instructing, kind of stomped forward with his right leg, as if slipping but in control. Vivi followed his moves. She didn't want it enough. She could feel it was fun, but she didn't want it enough to have it be even a fun hobby. She wanted the light behind the surfers. The light was her turf. The energy of the waves, the agon of the surfer, to combat or join forces with the wave, to challenge the universe that way, no. Her agon was in her eyes; she loved to see surfers' forms, their fights.

Like a doodler of doggerel versus a novelist – she didn't have the craving koyach to pursue *that* quest. She was a surf doodler. But the lumen fluidity, oh, now that bewitched her cellular being down to the iris core. She was mesmerized by how the line of the horizon was so pretty and silver when her head was tilted on a board.

After a few weeks, Vivi wondered, was that Alexi's intent? Was surfing the McGuffin? Was he trying to lead her to where she would see light as a new and more emboldening lover? To return her to her homeland, the ions of photographic transference? How the sea knows things, a thing or three about masquerading, water going in drag as silver hypnotism?

If I die, put me on a longboard.

Tow me out to the border of silver. Let me surf a wall of water bent on destroying me. Let me rest for a moment in its curve.

Let me ride the silver horizon and re-enter life in the new spring. Let me enter new silvers, new morning ghost mists. If I become a dream bird, she thought, maybe I can hatch little hatchlings of light. Maybe light will eat out of my hands.

Cupid held up the mirror so that his mother, Venus, could see herself, a beautiful voluptuous smudge in reflection. Venus came out of the water carrying her surfboard. A tall man with long legs greeted her at the shoreline. Nearby was another man, in the silverized air of the beach. A couple on the beach, two lovers, a man and a woman, and her husband in an overcoat babbling poetry and coffee spittle to the magnificent wind.

28

OCTOPUS ON LA RAMBLA

THE NEXT NIGHT, when it was safely dark and the dead were out and about to a movie, Johnny took Stella up to the retro cinema, Cine Maldà on Carrer del Pi. He paused for a mourner's Kaddish at the foot of the Angel's Gate where the former Paris cinema (where he and Vivi had seen *El Lobo*) used to be, and which now was one more H & M fast fashion store. Johnny and Stella entered Cine Maldà with five other people, happy to catch *Inland Empire*, all three hours of it, with an inexplicable intermission, so it was about one forty-five in the morning when they emerged with all the spectres from their respective cine viewing, to thread the Barcelona night out to Cafè de l'Òpera on the Rambles, ease back, watch the night people ramble, the dead with the living and Johnny with sea eyes saw it all like bubbles of climate cyanosis with a half-litre of red.

"Dad, I liked the part in the movie where the donkey was ironing."

"It was great," he said, still in his seabed *cabeza*, drifting with mental coral.

The time in November years ago when they had taxied in the dark up to L'Auditori to see Keith Jarrett who had returned to Barcelona after a twenty-five-year absence. The thrill of the audience bonding with his singular attention to his keys, a key-weaver.

Johnny thinking, If you cut out the cafés, there is no true Barcelona. This moment, here, now. The moment was powerful, being so momentary. And, he thought, there was no Barcelona, there was only *that* Barcelona in *that* year of your life, that warm season. The next season it's way chilly and they're tearing up the street so the view to the sea is all construction nets and street machines in the early morning, and it's a different Barcelona. The café is there; the next year, there is no café. The pharmacy becomes an eyeglasses joint. The other *farmacia* becomes ghost hoardings for years. One bar stays, the other is a shoe shop, suddenly. A man is pushed from a balcony. A man rides a bicycle against traffic; a child is hit and dies.

One year, the public life is on fire, a fever of communality and paldom, and *la vida terraza*. The next year, it is the terror. Or it is the hurricane. Or the madman. And the poor abandoned terraces miss the people so much. The sports arenas wish for their booing fans. The city becomes an empty built place, like a tiny maquette for the next century. The miracle year becomes the *annus horribilis,* slowly, then all at once. The writer who woke up with chairs in his finger and sketched them, before going out to the public square, is quarantined inside and the only café chairs he will experience are in his wrist and his digits.

The busy late night crowd rambles on the Rambles, site of where the Fascists aerial-bombed Barcelona into surrender. Barcelona and the years of municipal *besos*. He loved Barcelona, it was consensual. The rings of the tree of time showed his decades of love letters to the city. Thousands of people out into the dawn.

The Rambles, once the green river of the municipality, then the people became the river, in their stop-start informal chats, solving the world, in footsteps. Johnny's heart was full with the public life, the Theatre of La Rambla, the Theatre of the Urban Cosmo. Density and the dreams. Every half-metre another sidebar theatrical moment. The dead were always the understudies in the old Euro cities.

Johnny sketched a bit on his arm, not having his notebook handy, while Stella messed around with the food and wine at the Cafè de l'Òpera *terraza*. The dead were twitching in his wrists, his forearms, the combatants of resistance, the legendary leftists with their ghostly infighting out-fight-ing self-harming, and every day the ghosts of the resistance walked with their prosthetics and their paramedical tattoos down the cement river, the Rambles, along with the visitors in their thousands and feeling that rare light of a golden amber family, sheltered momentarily by the canopy of plane trees, down the Rambles.

It didn't hurt, Johnny figured, to have had his brain reconfigured, as Stella was suggesting, by David Lynch and *Inland Empire* and the donkeys. Unexplained cinema house intervals and throngs of 2:00 a.m. eaters was a very Barcelona thing. Like well-tailored land bridges from heart to heart, the iota motes of nighttime in the Catalan capital city. Democracy resuscitated and struggling, like a songwriter temporarily bereft of the song.

Johnny could feel the music in between the lines. Finally, after so long, he felt *tomorrow's hands.* Sitting watching the human shadows inhabit the street and it being only about two in the morning, the Rambles was chockablock with people. Johnny knew Stella had been a grown-up girl, even as a tot. As an octo-female she was the best company. He didn't know how he got this moral redo, but he was quietly grateful.

They shared that half bottle of Paternina red, some *pulpo a la plancha* ("ironed octopus," a.k.a. grilled), some *sepia en su tinta.* They watched the late-night buskers, and Johnny reminisced about that guy with the frog marionette who used to work the Rambles near the Boqueria back in the '90s and they observed the few late-night living statues in paint and feathers change poses.

Buzz-buzz, Johnny's rear pocket. Oh man, the phone. He put it on the night café tabletop. Stella crawled over to look at it with him.

Election Alert!!! STELLA DAY results are Final!!!! The people have voted NO WAY!!! Stella Coma never existed. It was a baby actor. Rhonda would like to thank all the Deniers and all the Affirmers who participated. Winner of our Comatone Colour Chart was Doctor Mickle from Palmerston Ave. Latkes gratis courtesy Rhonda. Don't miss Brian's show at the JCC – "I Captured Eichmann in Hamburg." See you at next year's Stella Day!!! Confirm or Deny: everybody has an opinion!!!!

Stella squirted a goodly load of ink on the phone screen. "Feh on that," she said.

Johnny put the phone back in his ass pocket. "Honestly, Rhonda," he said to the air.

"Hang on, Dad. Look," Stella said. She'd caught sight of a woman temporarily blinding another woman who was walking alone on the Rambles. Attacking her body, by first hurling goopy yogurt into her eyes, on her jacket, and then putting her hands on the surprised woman. Then, a man who was the female attacker's accomplice began to paw the woman walking, pinching her rear end, grabbing her breasts, hunting for pockets.

Stella shot out of her seat, landed on the face of the pickypocky lady, squirted octopus ink in her eyes, grabbed the yogurt tub, scooped up the blueberry yogurt, smeared it on the lady aggressor's ponytail. Then Stella landed on the crotch of the man who was trying to unzip the walking woman's front security pocket, and squirted an undiluted mass of octo-ink on his crotch. Then on his cheek, which would be permanent or close to it. The pants of the pickypocky perp were 100 per cent pure *pulpo* stain.

With a couple of her other hands, she picked back the pockets of the pickypocky people, acting momentarily as the outlaw octopus, taking back the pilfered lucre from the semi-skilled crook duo.

Your daughter can pick one pocket at a time? Ha. My daughter can pick three pockets, while setting up a three-card monte table, and waving to her two ringers in the crowd. Yeah. Pick a petty pocket perusing patsies, saps, gulls, geeks, marks while picking apart your argument, picking a little nit, and all the while she makes fine ink to record her octo-feats with.

My girl. Like a phylum of one turning criminals into canvases, Stella jumped from head to head, staining the clothing, the cheeks, the eyelids of the petty crooks, then shot back to Johnny at the table. Father and daughter sat, content under the eternal limelights of late-night dining in Europe, in the brief openings of freedom, as the ghosts of the resistance rambled down the old green river ditches.

Johnny sipped some red, said, "Did you know, Stel, that Luis Buñuel and Salvador Dalí and García Lorca used to sit and hang out right here? Talk and write and make movies and collaborate. They wrote each other letters."

"You miss having friends, don't you, Mister Pitzel?"

"I do."

"You miss Stan, don't you? He was your best friend. Did he tell you he was going to, you know? With the rope. How do you do that? I don't get it, Dad. With a doorknob."

"I can't answer that, Stella. Please. No. No, I didn't know. I knew he was depressed, that's all. Don't ask me."

"Dad, I liked it on the Big Canary. I was writing my memoir, wasn't I?"

"Chances are."

"I might make it a story, like true or not true. I could make a novel, like you. You could be my editor. We don't have to tell anybody."

The 2:00 a.m. crowd on the Rambles thinned slightly. Johnny the morning lark didn't care, the clock was a psycho like everything else these days in the fog machine of life. His bones felt more at home with themselves since he had become saturated with the sea and the ocean. His hands felt there was a future out there.

Johnny said to Stella, "You know, on my deathbed, you know what I'm going to say?"

But Stella had jumped into the lees of the wine in the glass, and she was snoring midst a second red, a quite lovely petite bottle of Faustino I Gran Reserva, snoring pulpo REMs midst oak and umami tannins. Johnny said it anyway.

"On my deathbed, I'm going to say, 'I am so glad I spent the time to go to the Canaries with you, Stellita.' I'm going to say, 'Going to Ibiza with you was a lifesaver.'"

She stirred as if she'd heard, but who can say? The octopus wants what the octopus wants. Her arms, with their thousands of sensory neurons, uncurled. Curled back into a cozy cephalopodic ball. Stella the octopus snored some serious trombone in her glass of Rioja.

And so it was: A two-armed dad and his eight-armed daughter on the Rambles in the wee hours after a three-hour David Lynch. The quarters are small, the rooms are tiny, the city is your living room in the city. The people still like to be out among the people. We'll miss our sidewalks when they're gone.

EVERYONE'S IN PUBLIC; everyone feels invisible. Metropolis invisible, metropolis seen. Metro like a ballad, metro like an opera, by times all soap. Metro indivisible, incorrigible, dirty, untamed, tamed, prim, prudish, licentious, one big Venn diaphragm. Johnny had always loved the Cafè de l'Òpera, situated not just where the river once ran, but where the walls of the city once sat. Here sat an eatery from at least the eighteenth century, morphing in and out from tavern, inn, a fancy restaurant owned by a Mallorcan, always popular, three hundred and sixty-five days a year, eighteen hours a day, including during Spanish Civil War *horas*. It had never closed, even for war, for three hundred years. It comforted Johnny to know that though he had been coming to the Cafè de l'Òpera for over forty years, he was a drop in the customer bucket. The pointillist starlight of the dead, the swaths of abstract inner moonlight, the skulls that had fed the Spanish wine into their maws, in gabbing rambling jocularity.

"Let's go home," Stella said, popping up out of the Rioja. "I've got a – excuse my French – a *memoir* to write." She whispered in his ear as they made that left turn up Ferran. "No worries, Pappa, I won't go all schmaltzy and emo on you. Zayde Izzy told me I should be a writer like you, or a photographer like Mommy. I told Zayde I wanted to be a painter."

Going up in the elevator, the key in the slot for the roof, Johnny said to her, "You still can be. Memoirist, painter. You could be a Patti Smith kind of art-octo."

"How 'bout Joni Mitchell? She's the whole package, Dad. Paints, writes, sings . . . Mister Pitzel, I could live in a box of paints!"

The elevator groaned, clanked, like a lumbago-laden complaining alter kacker.

Johnny by this point in his life – twelve books in – was a word-warts-and-all writer. Take me as I am, I have made love on the page for you. Soon, as the seas rise to engulf us, we'll snorkel the streets for coffee. As we drown we age, and our inner water goes away. Grant me blue water at the end. Grant my mind the blue moisture. For one brief moment, let my hands be made of the sea. Ha. The marriage erodes, and with the dead you can float.

The dead are dead, but it is only the dead who really get the joke.

The dead are not looking for understanding; the dead have been amputated.

Stella holed up in the bathroom with her notebook and pen and a mug of mint tea with honey and her miniature Neruda and four free arms to feel the universe in a humid tiled space.

Johnny lay down on the couch near the table. He wasn't used to being so revved up in the night. He gave a rictus giggle. He'd written a bestseller called *Night Street* but he knew bubkes from night. It was Vivi who knew Toronto-at-night like a lover. (He did have fun going along with interviewers, who wanted to know what was on his mind as he wandered the nighttime of the built metropolis. He just made it up, imagining himself into answers, as he'd imagined the night streets.)

AND WHAT, YOU ask, what of Sancho? What of the man wearing Johnny Coma's blue striped pyjamas and windbreaker? The man who had switched clothes with Johnny on the sea voyage?

Well, Sancho had calmed down considerably. As April arrived, he had no memory of his mania of last November, when he was lured by the lunatic notion he might write a novel in a month. The manic episode was gone, like a blackout. And guess what? He had read the book *Quixote* on Gran Canaria, writing in the morning, taking the big hardcover tome with him to one of the windswept terraces on the Atlantic, having a lunch for one, with the First Part of *The Ingenious Gentleman Don Quixote of La Mancha,* the heft of the book so pleasing. Four hundred and forty-nine pages for the party of the First Part. Another five hundred plus for the Second Part. A time in winter.

Johnny had brought the book in his luggage. And one day, Sancho carried the big book with him to the terrace by the waves. He was surprised at the way his posture got more upright just by walking with a book in public. As he had seen the younger folks doing more and more. Stepping back from digital devices that made you bend over and get an old-person posture, instead finding a freshness in the physicality, rips and tears, signatures and hardbacks and how sexy you could look with a real live book held against your body. As if the hilarity, wit, willingness to do *anything*, say *anything*, try *anything* of the writer Cervantes seeped through the fine paper.

The great thing about coming to the greats later in life is you realize that all the people who kept telling you to read them, hocking you day and night, did not hock you *enough*. Sancho was in a pleasure dome, reading *Quixote*. How could he have ever thought he would write the big novel, when he had never read *the* big novel of all time?

He came quickly to page fifty-seven in *Don Quixote*, in the exquisitely fine translation by Edith Grossman, on the first day of his reading, alone, facing the Atlantic. Okay. Quixote *thought* the windmill was a giant. Okay, Sancho mused. Good one. Okay. Don Quixote, a guy with glaucoma, a guy who needed distance lenses.

Sancho was agitated. Got up, paid the bill, walked from the wide terrace and the crazy wind back into the stone warrens all agitated. Agitated, because how come nobody had ever told him that the reason Don Quixote flipped out was because *he read too much!*

The deal with Quixote wasn't windmills, it was books! Books had made Quixote quixotic. Don Quixote had set out to live inside those chivalric romances.

The thing about Cervantes was his hero wasn't a nutcase with "windmill delusion"; his hero was a bookworm. Don Quixote was a geek for the ages. And Sancho saw that it was Johnny who was the crazy one of the two of them. Crazy on a quest, the definition of an art worker. Working to make something out of nothing, which nobody wants, and you do it anyway. You make hats for the headless – that's art.

No wonder he'd never been able to settle down and make his invisible air-typing into a real book. He thought somebody wanted to hear from him. Johnny had been right: Sancho had been planning the wedding dress he would wear before he had even dated.

He was enchanted by how well he felt, how he felt in a different kind of recovery, reading.

The damage done, the years gone by, wanted something. Here it was. The intimacy of reading thrilled him with its secret knowledge, even if the world knew all about it. He might have to keep the secret of how good you felt reading an actual book to himself, lest the knobs got in on it. He didn't feel that loneliness you feel when every day is jet lag, though you haven't been on a jet in ages. The ink on the page, the loopy shenanigans of Quixote and Sancho and Co. calmed him. He got lost. The way you can in love or packing for a trip with the emotion that you are packing to die.

Meth, crystal meth, the devil that had entered his body and possessed him in the old stateside days with grand schemes, grand quests never equipped or enacted, meth-bragging, meth-imaginary ladders, meth the ladder-climber's pal . . . Fame in his head had been his Dulcinea, his imaginary perfect mate. On the Big Canary, all that calmed into the permission to love life, if it included the blooming fact of fiction. Johnny had been kind, Sancho could see that now. He had not mocked him for his delusion of writing the big novel. But reading Quixote, by example, Miguel de Cervantes did.

"You fucker," Sancho said, sitting in the Turk's tiny eatery. "You left everything on the page. Fuck you, Cervantes. You held nothing back for the better day." The muscular sweat of fun only the one with the chops can get done, the skill set, the tool kit in hand, to blow a solo, Cervantes like Sonny Rollins on "Doxy."

Sancho was embarrassed – but only a tad – to feel his chest tighten. To feel hot tears. How he loved to lie so much he became addicted to meth in order to live lies like a second language. Then, what happens is you don't do it to get high, you do it to not feel you're going to die. You feel so well, then you're sick every day. Your everyday soul carry is your sick. Who knew a book could be good medicine, especially if the guy who wrote it had the use of only one arm; had been a POW; had been a Navy man – just like him!; had been arrested – check; had met pirates – you know it, man, check; had seen war – Cambodia, check.

The world was mean, and the mean looked down on the kind.

But Sancho could see now, you don't get to kind from further degrees of mean.

And the bonus: It was still only the First Part of Quixote he'd read. There were two parts! Who knew? Like a movie seven and half hours long, with a quick windmill scene in the first ten minutes, there was the Second Part to look forward to. The best!

SPRING WAS BRIGHT on the Mediterranean. Sancho had worked his muscles over the winter, so that now, back in Barcelona – with Johnny's experienced approval – he could up his scribbling game to one thousand words a day. Two and a half book pages. He slept on the fold-out couch in the front room of the attic studio, a wall separating him from Johnny's bedroom. He got up, before the earliest shreds of pale dawn, out of respect for Johnny who woke as the morning lark with the first pooch howls from the rooftops, long before the first Santa Maria del Mar bells. He wrote long-hand, following Johnny's example.

Back in winter days, Johnny had told Sancho that a beginner tends to get his advice from the least reliable source – his own brain. It was Johnny who told him that you have to teach your body the way to tell the story before you can outsource your muscles to a machine. Sancho liked a wider notebook than the ones Johnny used and that was fine.

He sat, as in years past, on the Pla de Palau bench. Only now, Sancho the air-typist was a real writer with a real notebook and a real pen. Though true, Johnny preferred his Palomino Blackwing 602s. Sancho looked the same. Well, he did have on Johnny's pyjamas, since Johnny wore Sancho's old tweed wool coat.

After his morning writing on the public bench, Sancho liked to take a walk to a café with the Second Part of *Don Quixote*. There was so much going on in the book he had never heard about. Quixote's entire sojourn in Barcelona! It was hysterical, a fair quixotic riot. Quixote and Sancho rambled from this very neighbourhood up through the Barri Gòtic to the Jewish Quarter to the print shop. Oh, how Sancho loved the part where Quixote experiences his very first print shop. Sancho got that feeling you get sometimes, that the author is speaking across the bones of the ages directly to you. And Sancho sussed that maybe in Barcelona, Cervantes's own heart softened. You could tell how much he loved the port city, so bustling with ambition and modesty and beauty on the shorelines back then in the 1600s.

In *Quixote,* Cervantes wrote of Barcelona with deep tenderness, calling it the "archives of courtesy," and "the hospital of the poor," and "beauty, unique." Late in life, Miguel de Cervantes got a serious crush on Barcelona. Why was everyone obsessed with the frigging windmills? Because, they never entered the book to feel the love, the magic, the possibilities of how *the words* are elsewhere. How Cervantes loved to explore Barcelona. How he'd set up Quixote to have a duel on horseback at the surfer beach. How it must have hurt him to make Quixote lose. Yet Sancho could feel how much Cervantes liked to go to the beach at Barceloneta, just like Johnny Coma did, to write about a guy besotted with books. How the duel on horseback between Don Quixote and the Knight of the White Moon on the beach in Barceloneta was a keystone scene in all of world literature, and it was not marked anywhere on the beach. How you lose, you love, you're a freak and broken-hearted, you still adore the place of your greatest defeat.

As Sancho began to feel closer and closer to Cervantes, he felt closer to Johnny, how you do when you realize friendship has so much to do with tolerance of the other. He'd been a tatterdemalion, wearing ragged linen espadrilles in pale rose. He'd been a sailor ex of the Navy ex of the war ex of the drug addiction, a piece of hopeful flotsam washed ashore in Catalonia by the sea, and Johnny had loved him, as a man, a guy, a pal. No judgment. Sancho had been blessed, granted offerings by the karmic void and he had not even recognized the stuff when it was in his lap. In the mute colloquy of men.

Around page two hundred of the Second Part of *Don Quixote,* which is to say almost at page seven hundred of the entire tome, Sancho started to panic. At nine hundred pages and serious change, the book was way too short. What would he do when the book was over? Oh man. He had never had this feeling before. Was this how his dad felt when his mother died, after their forty-five-year marriage? The life together so long, the life together so short.

He tried to slow down his reading pace.

He couldn't do it.

He tried to be kind to the book, to not rush it, to let it take its own time to get there. What if after finishing the book, the old haunt of the old sick came back? The spring sunshine that sucks the calcium from your bones and brings that feeling of being in love with spring fever, all dizzy – he felt this *in excelsis.*

He organized his days to write, to walk, to read only before bedtime. Doling out the pleasure. Getting dopamine hits from the anticipation.

Giggling at the parts where the brigantine's captain, captured, stands on the deck of the ship with a noose around his neck and then he turns out to be a she, masquerading as a man so as to man a ship, womanly in disguise. And her father, a macher, turns up at the last minute to assist her, and the woman who the ship's captain had been romancing turns out to be a man. Nobody ever talked about cross-dressing and gender code-switching in *Don Quixote.* They all abandoned reading the book at page fifty-eight and fifty-nine, at the *windmill amuse-bouche!*

Sancho had heard that reading kept you young and that coffee kept you young and so did wine and going to museums and taking on impossible quests.

And yeah, the more Sancho read *Quixote,* the more urgent became his quest to beat that dead fucker. No wonder Jon was grumpy. Everything had already been written. They were walking on the bones of the dead and the dead were laughing.

He could never beat Cervantes; it couldn't be done. But maybe, just maybe, he could beat Johnny Coma.

Sancho wanted to kill his best friend, Johnny Coma. Now we're talking. Now we're talking about the real art life. Paranoid and obsessed with the placement of commas. Seeing the mordant invasion of the ruination of your self in every serif.

Exit, pursued by a notebook.

29

WILL AND MIGUEL DIED TODAY

IT WAS BOOKS and Roses Day in Barcelona.

It was April 23, 2017, and the yellow roses of resistance were blooming. Sant Jordi Day, St. George the patron saint of Catalonia, and the day, beautifully coincidentally, that both Shakespeare and Cervantes died. And of course, never forget that the day Shakespeare and Cervantes died was also Stella Coma's birthday.

Every year on April 23, hundreds of thousands of Catalans filled the streets of Barcelona to enact the ritual of buying books and buying roses. There was no separation between *amor* and *libros* – they were celebrated on the same day. Typically, on that one day, about a million and a half books were sold in Barcelona, at the outdoor kiosks. One and a half million books, and seven million roses.

Red roses, traditional signal of love, sold in their millions; in recent years, yellow roses, signal of the Catalan independence, sold in their six hundred thousands. Everyone understood the meaning of the yellow roses, as well as the yellow ribbons people wore out and about in the crowds that day, so law enforcement was keeping an eye out for yellow roses, and yellow scarves, and little yellow ribbons.

Scuttling through the stone warrens of their lower barrio up into the wide open air of Rambla de Catalunya and Passeig de Gràcia, laden with bookstalls and the mob scene of book lovers, came Johnny Coma and Stella Coma. The whole city had come out for her birthday!

They pushed through the crowds, happy to do so. Stella rode shotgun on Johnny's bald head.

Well up the avenue into the Eixample, Stella perched on a pile of yellow and black books, the classic noir series in Catalan. Her eight arms curled back into her body; she made herself small; she disappeared into a David Goodis. Only a bit of her grey flesh showed from the inside pages of *El Anochecer. Nightfall* in English.

She made a sound, followed by a spit of ink. Her arms hidden, she moved from the Goodis to crawl into *La Gran Dormida* by Raymond Chandler. She peeked her head out of *The Big Sleep* and said, "Dad, I don't feel well. Can we get ice cream?"

"Is it the crowds?"

"I feel nauseous."

"Could we get you a book? You might feel better." He picked up *El Carter Sempre Truca Dues Vegades*, loving the way the Catalan felt pleasingly from another planet, making the James M. Cain postman ringing twice, always, feel strange in a good way. He held up the Cain to her. "We could get you this."

Stella crawled back in to the elongated shlufy. Ink spurted out, soaking the spine. "I feel bad. Can we leave?"

"Are you sure you don't want a book? Your choice."

She crawled out, propulsed onto his shirt, into his shirt pocket, said, "Dad, stop trying to fix me. Don't tinker. I don't feel well. Can we get ice cream at Farggi?"

Stella was pale, and her chromo-chameleon self did not change to a brighter more rosy hue. They headed down Rambla de Catalunya.

Stella's arms were circling, curlicuing over and over again, like a human who was scratching skin off compulsively. Johnny felt a panic sweat. Stella was up on his shoulders, their habit now, but she was crawling in and out of his shirt with a compulsive curling of all her eight arms down his neck and back. They went into Farggi, in sight of the book crowd. A man came in selling yellow roses and miniature books. Johnny bought Stella a yellow rose. She picked out a miniature book of poems by Otto René Castillo, the Guatemalan poet. Stella did not look well at all.

She picked up the tiny book, *Vamos Patria a Caminar,* a few centimetres each way in size; she whispered the famous poem about the apolitical intellectuals, about how one day the poor people will ask them what they did when their community was extinguished like a fire, *pequeño y solitario.* How no one will care about their passing fashions or the meaning of life or even the recessions or myths. As Otto René wrote in the 1960s, the poor who made the apolitical intellectuals' lives possible will ask, "What did you do when the poor suffered, when tenderness and life burned out in them?"

The Guatemalan military captured the thirty-three-year-old Otto René Castillo in 1967, and in that "summer of love," they set the poet on fire and burned him alive. Stella was reading the part of Castillo's poem where he wrote that the apolitical intellectuals will stand, mute with shame.

Stella knew that her mother, Vivienne, had gone to language school in the exact highland city in Guatemala, Quetzaltenango, the place of the quetzals, where Otto René was born and raised. Vivi talked to Johnny about that time in her life, a kind of a linguistic lesion on her heart and tongue-brain. Stella used to sit in the kitchen, when her parents were happy, it seemed, at least talking to each other in the same physical space, contented and talking close, chair to chair, after dinner. Stella the big-eared kiddo, and Vivi would talk about the Guatemalan school, the helicopters all day long from the American forces there, keeping an eye on their coup. And Vivi would talk about Otto René and wonder if any of her language teachers were still alive. Her first teacher, Alva from Totonicapán, Alva from "Toto," who taught her the death words.

Vivienne used to talk about *the first and the second lesions.* Stella didn't know what that meant. It seemed to mean something about when her mother got weird and did her best work and stayed in her darkroom until all hours making pictures of things she had photographed, too raw for new, or too raw for now, or maybe secrets her mother had about her camera and poetry. It meant her mom slept in her darkroom with the toxic vats of chemicals.

And so Stella laid her body down on the poem. She squirted ink on it, staining the inert intellectuals.

Then Stella, revved in a fever, shot from the poetry to the ice cream counter glass. She banged her head, her beak against it; she shot back to the table, began banging her head over and over.

She bit off the end of one arm.

The amputated limb crawled across the floor, up the ice cream glass to the other side, went inside the dulce de leche, began scooping it up with the multiple arm suckers. In octopus anatomy, an amputated limb can live on its own. And the severed limb can regrow on the body.

But Stella was up at Johnny's ear.

"Dad, I got pregnant. I'm going to have a hundred babies."

"Honey."

"I'm pregnant."

"Stel, I didn't know."

She came around, put her beak on his nostril opening. "I'm telling you now."

"When?"

"When you weren't looking."

"Have something to eat. We could go up to Txapela, get you some tapas." He tried to serve her some ice cream with a little spoon. She pushed it away.

"I'm pregnant."

"Have something to eat," he said. "Tell me what you want to do." He felt helpless. He wanted his wife to be here to tell him how he felt. He wanted Vivi to handle his heart, direct it, be his clock, his guide.

"I lost my appetite," she said. "I heard it happens. Dad, we don't have long together anymore. You're quite the writer, you know. Stella Atlantis did love the letters sent from her father. She kept them in a bundle in a pirate's green glass bottle. Dad. Mister Coma is all right. We have only a short while left."

Johnny felt like a shipwreck in a chair. *Un náufrago.*

A shipwreck with vertigo, underwater in an ice cream parlour. What do women know, and when do they know it?

Stella got up on Johnny's head, began to bang her body, to swirl and curl her arms like snakes, like he was Daddy Medusa.

"Let's get you home."

"When I die, Dad, don't forget me."

As they walked, she spoke frantic words, kept shooting off into store windows all the way down Angel's Gate past Joe Oriole Square across Laietana, down the Argentería hill, round the steps of Santa Maria del Mar, into their petit alley, up to the roof. He laid Stella down on the roof patio in the waning sunshine, her little Otto René Castillo tucked under one arm.

THE NEXT MORNING, Stella wasn't in the studio.

A smudged note was on the kitchen counter with a cup of coffee, a saucer set on top to keep it hot, the note on top of the plate. Written in octopus ink, more a sketch than a note, a self-portrait of sorts: Stella had smudgily sketched herself on top of some hasty waves. She was in the realm of nausea and moons. Gone to ground, underwater, to be private. He missed her.

Johnny wandered out into the plain stone world of the lower part of the city he'd adored a lifetime. Across the Passeig del Born, along Montcada, across Princesa to the other side, in and out of the high walls, the local laundry like a wet painting, the vertical windows set by the slim balconies. He lost his way in the dark; shining at a dead end was a full-wall painting of a white skeleton head.

A white and black skull with the word *LOVE* in red. On the ground in a puddle left for days in the declivities never-ending of stone alleys in cities was a furry dog's head. Left from some puzzle, some fiesta, some party time. Johnny put it on. This is me, he said to himself. A damp dog whose daughter left home, this time alive. Missing her so, the missing brought back the death, and the death brought back the imminent death of his marriage.

Yet, there was something clean about being at the end of your rope.

But where had Stella gone?

DOWN ALONG THE shoreline of the many beaches of Barceloneta, Stella-Octo had returned to the sea, gone down to brood her hundreds of eggs, after they had emerged from her body into the water. She was pale as her dad had noticed on Book Day. She was, however, a toughie, tougher than some octopuses; she was hanging on. Her chromo-chameleon self was using a much more restrained palette, the way an artist in waning life might see the essence of seaweed starlight, of the granular in the stone walkways. Then, one afternoon, she took a chance to travel from the beach back to the roof studio, hitching a ride in the elevator with a random man eating a Manchego and jamón de Canaria sandwich on a fresh ciabatta pequeña. The man got off at *Entresuelo*; tall, he offered her a bite of the sandwich, he had a droll smile.

Stella was back. She crawled onto the bed near Johnny. As he was napping, she slept on the pillow beside him. When he woke up he said, "I must be dreaming. Who goes there? Is that the ghost of my daughter?" And he fell asleep and when he woke for real, he told her that he dreamed that she had died in Toronto, and he was wheeling her along Christie in a Dutch cargo bike with plastic on top. It was raining, and he was smothering her unintentionally in the cargo hold under the wet coverage.

"Dad, it's just a James Rosenquist we saw in New York at the Guggenheim," she said. "The one of the little girl whose face was covered in Cellophane like a doll. So, Dad, I can't stay long. My eggs will become baby octopuses any day now. Dad, I'm going to have two thousand children!"

Inside his relief that she hadn't disappeared. "She doesn't look at all well," Johnny said to Sancho that night. She looked way too white. She was listless, then she was manic. Sancho had come by at the hour of the tapas to fetch Johnny and had been thrilled that his *reina* had returned from giving birth and brooding and the sea. When she saw Sancho, she came close, her arms coiling and uncoiling like a pulp Medusa. Then she shot around the studio hitting herself over and over on the glass sliding doors. She pushed the door to the patio open, began to bang herself on the hard terracotta tiles. Again, as she had that other time on Book Day, she knocked an arm off. That arm got a glass of water, sipped it while she tried to dismember herself, all her arms, self-harm.

"Dad, it's just the way it is. After my eggs hatch, I will die. It's just the way of the octopus. Don't cry, Dad. You might have a hundred and fifty octopus grandkids. You might live as long as Noah. Meet you on the ark, Mister Pitzel. I might be an elephant! I could come back as a slat of wood, on the parquet floor for forty days and forty nights."

Johnny felt ill. What punishment was this? He felt ill in a kind of joy.

Stella said, "Did I ever tell you how I fertilize my eggs? It's kinda cool. That guy-octopus, well, he rips off his arm for me. He's got all his sperm on his arm, don't ask. So he amputates his arm, gives it to me like a totally actually weird sex-ed class, right? So, I have the guy's arm, I stow it in my mantle. Dad, I had sperm right up against my oxygen gills, my heart, I had the guy's sperm on hold. Then, when I decide to hatch my eggs, I get to kind of do a sea-weaving and when I've got them all together, then I take that guy-octopus's arm out of storage and I rub that guy's amputated sex-arm all spermy all over my eggs. Stella gets to be in charge of the sperm! Now you're talking."

"You can't go, Stel. Stellita, you only came back."

He knew he meant Stella; he also knew he meant himself.

"They say I could brood those eggs for days, I could brood those eggs for weeks. I might even hang on and brood those eggs for a year."

"That would be nice," he said. He hated the word *nice*. He was pale at how short a time a year was. When a death sentence is a given, time is a psychopath.

Here she was: species.

To you we pledge loyalty, queen of the sea. If in democratic times, we erred, forgive us, Queen Stella, for our over-plasticity, our ignorance, our love of the man-made things. Forgive us, Queen Stella, for leaving so little on the floor.

Here Stella was: semelparous. Here he was: iteroparous. She, in her species, reproduced once, then died. He, in his species – via his Vivi – reproduced multiple times. Potentially. Yet, it had happened only once. Late in their marriage, their only child. Gone, returned, reincarnated to die again.

Inner moonlight explodes your carapace. The octopus eggs hatch like galaxies into the water. An octopus community to come, a small town of cephalopods all at once, and all of them will be the children of Queen Stella.

On the roof in the deep walled shoreline, as the paired pigeons cooed, buff and grey, and the roof dogs barked away the day midst ancient TV antennae, it was August in Barcelona. Stella was in last preparations before she was due to die, again.

Johnny was stricken. She looked awful. "Dad, I don't have long. Can we go up the Rambles, one more time, you and me? To the Cafè de l'Òpera? We had so much fun after the movie with the donkeys and how I repicked the pickypocky pocket of the pickypocky lady. Can we, please?"

She had returned from the grave for a while in late autumn, and then into the early exceptionally mild part of winter, then in through winter in the Mediterranean waters on Ibiza, and on the sailing ship and she had returned to him to sail out into the very Atlantic, to survive hurricanes, to spend the winter writing and walking and all the months of wind and water, and he had regained his blue mind in multiples. He had blue gratitude. He had been soothed and solaced, and maybe partially cured, by being beside water. His daughter was a water creature, all brine and bolshie with "Da-ad" comments. They had sailed with cleaner minds like cleaner fish that clean the hadal levels of the sea, how dreams are meant to be night cleaners, too. She had been on loan, always. Then, when she returned from the water mysteries, she had been on loan for six more months, as that winter became spring, and now it was late summer. It was mid-August. August 17, 2017.

A man in a van was driving to the Plaza Catalunya in Barcelona, to prepare his terrorist attack that day.

30

DARK DAY IN BARCELONA

FIVE IN THE afternoon.

At five in the afternoon, the terror man in a rental van prepared to drive his vehicle down La Rambla, the pedestrian boulevard in the centre of Barcelona, the legendary tree-lined public space long known for its dozens of outside cafés, its newspaper kiosks, flower market, La Boqueria – the legendary food market, the epic Joan Miró mosaic built into the boulevard, the sense of humanity on the move. The soothing, exciting, calming air of the people in a performance and the people watching the people in a performance. The urban life in Barcelona-by-the-sea, crowded with tourists. That August day, the man in the van planned to plow down La Rambla and kill as many people as possible. His weapon was his rented vehicle.

It jumped the curb at the top of the boulevard.

Down in the medieval quarter, Stella and Johnny and Sancho set out on foot for La Rambla, to have a bite at Cafè de l'Òpera, for Stella's last visit before death.

The van revved its engine, a vehicle on La Rambla where none were permitted.

Stella, Johnny and Sancho walked out of their building, up Argenteria, across Laietana, up Llibreteria, through Plaza Sant Jaume, along Ferran to the lower Rambla. Crowded, hot summer, the people like to be where the people are.

A one-minute walk up to the Cafè de l'Òpera. Uh-oh, all the tables were occupied, legs stretched out. Sun bright. Here on La Rambla, a key site in the Spanish Civil War, when the forces of Franco Fascism aerial-bombed the citizens' boulevard, and citizens conducted war on each other, and within their factions. Here, where the war ghosts and the war veterans mingled with food and wine.

The van at the top of La Rambla began to spew exhaust. Further down the way, the trio went to Plan B.

"Let's go get some food to take home so we can have something to eat after we eat," Stella said, and they all agreed this was a splendid idea.

"Let's go to the Boqueria," Johnny said. "It's a three-minute walk, max."

The van was speeding down La Rambla knocking ramblers down.

On the way to the Boqueria food market, they paused to pay their respects to the Miró Mosaic. They stood on the red, blue, yellow tiles. Sancho held forth, "*Mi reina*, note the black outline, note the bold hues, shades, so you can see the mosaic from anywhere. Note the footprints, the shoe prints, the dust of humanity. Walking on art. Now *that's* living."

They entered the food market. Or tried to. They got elbows in their eyes, their clavicles, their pancreatic environs. Tourists were madly snapping grab shots of the counters and stalls, like film festival paparazzi ambushing comestibles. Lust for the image of chorizo. Cravings for a pic of cheese. Perhaps a pin-up of a tiny ciabatta to carry in a wallet. None of the tourists in the food market seemed interested in *eating*. Across Johnny's mind briefly flitted the word *anhedonia* – the loss of the desire for pleasure.

The new eating was taking pictures of food.

Well-meaning invaders, in slow-moving clots or single-file like children with a leader with a flag at the front, in a category error, gawping at the food stalls as if the Boqueria was a red-light district of come-hither noshes. Blocking the actual customers, snubbing the actual vendors trying to make a living, disrupting local life for the sake of a photo of a comely stalk of asparagus.

The van sped down La Rambla, crushing bone, rising over spines, knocking down tourist and local alike, riding at humanity with hate for humanity, with hate a fire under steel.

Stella, Johnny, Sancho pushed to get out of the Boqueria, unable to buy anything, so clotted up was the market with the tourists who were pushing through, simultaneously invasive and listless. Agog at items in their natural habitat.

"Dad, I'm having trouble breathing," Stella said. "My third heart isn't getting oxygen. I'm hurting in my blue rivers. Can we get out of here?"

Sancho grabbed Stella, pushed through the crowd. Johnny could see them at the market exit, out on La Rambla now. They walked down La Rambla a short distance to look more closely at the Miro Mosaic.

La Rambla was full of blood. It was five in the afternoon. The van sped down, massacring human after human.

In the frame of the market doorway, Johnny saw the fast-moving van. He saw Sancho and Stella get hit. He thought he saw them in the doorway. He was catapulting forward and backward on a wheel of time in shock. The shock paralyzed him. The old shock of her first death came out of hiding in his body and hit the present shock and his body and mind did not know what the sequence of events was.

He was howling in the Boqueria.

He was out on La Rambla. He saw Stella get hit, go flying. He saw her on the mosaic. La Rambla was turning in circles in a bright terror mandala, swimming in jagged angles, a murder carousel. The injured and dying were wailing. The magnificent walkway, the legendary boulevard with filtered light through the plane trees was spinning, the civic axis was being murdered. Café patrons, bicyclists, walkers, families. Old, young.

Johnny was running in a frenzy. He was made crazy by hate on the move. The van hopped the curb; it drove in a rampage at high speed, murdering the summer pedestrians, until the van took control of the driver down La Rambla at the Miró Mosaic. The van braked on the mosaic. Johnny was howling on La Rambla across from the old umbrella store. He was frantic to find Stella. The van was empty, the driver's door open. Sitting on the Miró Mosaic of red and blue and yellow. Maybe, in a way you do not want to question too much, the mosaic made the terror stop. Maybe Miró saved lives, that August 17, 2017, day.

Sancho was wearing Johnny's pyjamas, windbreaker. Sancho was breathing. He crawled to the side of La Rambla and in between the legs of a café table upturned. Johnny saw Sancho crawl away but he couldn't put it in order, he was falling off the planet. He didn't know what he did or where he went. His mind in memory was in shock blackout.

People came to the city in August because they had holidays then, because kids were out of school then, because of every reason and every alibi. Barcelona in summer was fine but not *his* Barcelona. He liked Barcelona in autumn, and he liked Barcelona in spring, and he loved Barcelona when the winter was shy and beginning, when he could reminisce about how he loved her in autumn, best of all. First in the orange mid-light of the changing plane trees in late September, then the perfect October shelter of the La Rambla plane tree chuppah under which he and Vivienne had walked, falling in love with each other as they fell in love with Barcelona: that ménage à trois you can have, as a couple, with a city.

WHERE LIVING STATUES busked, where locals mingled with tourists, the former river of green was made into chaos by the agency of hate. Where Sancho's dad, before he became a diplomat, had been an American brigadista in the Spanish Civil War. La Rambla, site of so many battles, inside the resistance, inside the Republic, from outside freedom, by foot, by rifle, by air, here where bombs fell, here where they first came to the pre-renovation more scrubby Café Zurich by the Catalunya Metro stop stairs, where so many young people gathered, beautiful and young and hopeful and smoking cigarettes dusk till dawn into the after-parties. Here under the too-bright sunshine of the long days on the Mediterranean, that August of 2017, Johnny was inside the story, his brain swirling, only later did he hear that the terror van had hopped the upper Rambla curb and rode with intent to kill as many humans as possible, until his van braked. The killer rabbited out of the van. He disappeared into the chaos he had created. The van sat on the Miró Mosaic. Stella was under one of the tires.

You look back, you think: the terror van was rushing down La Rambla like an emergency vehicle rushing to the scene of a crime. As it came speeding down the crowded boulevard on a killing spree, Sancho was standing with Stella on the famous Miró Mosaic built into the pedestrian boulevard. Five in the afternoon. They had exited the Boqueria market and walked to the mosaic. They had their heads bowed, examining the colours of tile Miró used, commenting on them. Sancho had been saying to Stella that many a visitor walked right on top of the famous mosaic without even seeing it, even though it was as wide as a street and as long as a house front. The large cerulean blue circle of tiles rimmed by black. The wider white rim with abstract squiggles, and a red circle, and a black circle, and a yellow cone.

The injured lay on the Rambles, the injured had been catapulted into the cement, into iron chairs, into storefronts. As in history gone by, there was blood on the Rambles.

As the terror van at highway speed zoomed through pedestrians, it hit Sancho and Stella as they stood in great joy at the art of Miró, and his well-worn mosaic.

When the killing van braked, it hit Stella.

GREEN WORLD, WHAT are these terrors you keep enacting upon us, as if to punish our very guilt? We who love light so much, and then you rotate us, whoever you are, you do rotate us to the far side of the moon.

SANCHO LAY ON the mosaic of Miró, gravely wounded, crawling away, saying, "The knife is low, my liege. The knife is slow. They have put blood on the lush and the reefs are no longer coral. Yet, my friend, I dream of better days between us."

Johnny remembered how he howled in the Boqueria, how he came running, pushing through the tourists naturally huddled in the food market. How his heart was already a wailing cantor, how his heart – partly healed from the water, the Atlantic, the redoubt of life on an ocean island – had begun to recover from its octopus-pot heartbroken shape back into its normal systole and diastole blood-and-oxygen shape, how he could literally feel it distorting again as he ran in shock out of the Boqueria looking for Stella. The Kaddish had begun without him. In mourning already, his body told him a story to comprehend that the Earth had fallen from the sky.

Hineni. I am ready. Only the ready are really ready, and the ready prepare for death all their lives.

Take me, but don't take my daughter. For that is truly a distortion, to mourn your children.

He had punched the tourists, who, before they heard the news that people were dying outside the food market, had been gathered with untamed lust and kind of horny self-benediction to pose with food.

The terror van sat empty.

The terror driver, the premeditated murderer had escaped.

The van sat like a white corpse, emptied of meaning.

A terror day is a day without continuity. A terror event is pure atom collider.

There was Sancho, mangled. Sancho in the windbreaker and striped blue pyjamas, bloody. Sancho, crawling in Johnny's clothes, with Johnny's old OHIP health card with Johnny's photo in his PJ pocket and wearing Johnny's shade of espadrille, the eau de Nil. Bald Johnny in a long tweed overcoat in summer. And Stella was yonder.

Her arms flailing, three torn off. Her head concussed, as it had been concussed, that year she first died, in Toronto. Johnny was in an emergency fog of focus. In front of him, the dying octopus was turning into a little girl, long dark braids, black jeans, David Bowie glitter T-shirt, pink-purple high-tops. Stella as ever was, once upon a time in Toronto, before a bike rider hit her, biking south on a one-way-north street. The first death.

Before a terrorist ran her over, once upon a time in Barcelona. The second death.

In the first death, she had been making chalk drawings on the pavement; in the second death, she had been learning to love a Miró Mosaic embedded in a boulevard.

He had howled in the Boqueria. He was howling in the Boqueria. He was pushing people, he was howling the world in public. He was mourning his daughter, the octopus. She had called him Mister Pitzel. Why had they gone to sea? you might ask. They had gone to sea so that when Stella was killed by the terror van on the Rambles that August day, Johnny would have the sea adventure for blue solace.

Because if you can't torment yourself with memories that are sweet, what can you do when the dead die all over again? Stella was due to die, naturally, of her species' normal evolution, then Stella died a death most unnatural, as she had the first time she died on the other side of the ocean.

Johnny was bent double on La Rambla, where Stella had morphed in his eyes into the little girl on Euclid Avenue. And morphed back again. Stella-Octo. The octopus mother of hundreds. La Rambla again a rising river, the bones of the combatants from wars past built into the promenades, thirteen dead, one hundred and thirty injured. Johnny carried the octopus away. He carried her down a side street, running, yes running down Ferran with all the people running down Ferran, carrying Stella, her neurology fading.

He ran under an iron arch into an alcove-like stub of an alley, he sat down on a chair, he saw the people running away, though the terror van had stopped. The man had gotten away. He could be running after people, he could have a knife.

Through the glass at the end of the alley, Johnny saw a café. He went in. Cozy, informal, a bit bohemian. He told the people what had happened; some of them were reading about it on their phones. The café man locked the door. Johnny put Stella on a table. Out the café window, police in snorkel uniforms floated by, followed by the dead in the cortège on rising water. Stella crawled toward him.

She changed from pink to blue, from blue to pink. She said to her father, "Down in the secret chamber, where the moss secrets live, when you and me, we go to sleep under the ground, the little secrets will come out to play. They will fly around like fireflies and it won't be so bad, after all. I liked the part in the story where they had the secret hideout on the plane. Nobody knows you're there, except when they bring around the special snacks. Papa, they told the world you were dead in Death Valley and they lied. It was only a coma in the salt below the sea. Now I have to say goodbye. Remember, Dad, I love you."

He drank two coffees, then he drank a third. He had cake. Beautiful homemade cheesecake with blackberries. He'd lost track of Sancho. He'd left his pal behind in the chaos escape. He realized he was sitting in the Miró alley. He had found shelter running away from mortal danger the same way Dulce had with her New Year's brute. He had run down Ferran from the Rambles and deked into the alley where Miró was born.

The municipal map loves us.

He paid the man at the counter, who, as he rang in the bill, spoke to Johnny in a low rapid accent that Johnny recognized as that Italian-sounding lilt of Spanish from Buenos Aires. The proprietor said, handing Johnny his change, that this day reminded him of B.A. in the 1980s. Meaning: under the military.

Johnny carried Stella home. He wrapped her in his soft coffee sock, wrapped her in the delicate personal chorreador cloth still gritty with grounds. The simplicity was mandatory.

IN THE MORNING, he went early to the sea. Down the promenade, he saw a tall man in black adjusting the long white dress of his beloved. It must be a bride and groom, he thought, so he sketched it that way. He could see in the dusky light the tender caress the man gave to his bride's collar and that drew him toward the marital couple.

Perfect! It wasn't a bride and groom, it was a surfer in a black wetsuit, making an adjustment, tenderly, to his white surfboard, stood on end.

He walked up those stairs at the end of the seaside promenade, where the Little Lighthouse Café used to be, the wide stairs, that's right, up behind the W Hotel onto an elevated promenade overlooking the sea. On a wide overlook with the Mediterranean stretched out below you.

Johnny Coma walked on the elevated promenade as if in infinity above the naked sea. At a railing with sharp rocks below, the sea meeting the grey rocks, he threw the body of his daughter, Stella the octopus, in her shroud over the railing into the water.

Goodbye, little one. Safe journey.

Your Papa loved you.

HE THOUGHT, WHAT if the dead forget *us?*

What if we die and our beloveds are there to meet and greet us, and they act like they never saw us before in their lives?

The walruses will be buried in the long pine box along with the ice, and we will look at the old photos of our planet, so beautiful it once was, so fresh and lively, so green. And the green chemical planet will bubble and fade. We can hope for ions as our last grace. We will look at photos of the busy city now so empty with disease, and we will mourn our own company. We used to like it so much, on the terraces, just being stupid with drinks and friends.

Sail on, world shiva, sail on. In brucha and pelagic sail on. The hired mourners will soon arrive. The moirologists will arrive with plainsong and in minyans. Be kind. Say a Kaddish for your loved ones. Say a Mourner's Kaddish for the city.

Goodbye, Stella.

A dot on a wave.

31

WABI-SABI DAYS

A YEAR LATER, the loud sound of helicopters over the city of Barcelona. December 21, 2018, the borders to the city were closed. A bunch of bigwigs in government were having a big meet, and scared of the demonstrators amassing to march at the meeting building, the authorities closed down the port city. In a great coincidence the building was the La Llotja, formerly the legendary art school, at the far end of the Pla de Palau, the public square where Johnny and Sancho met to sit on their bench and natter and confab and become pals, over time. But that day, the people were banned from the square and the big avenues and stone warrens surrounding it. By nine in the morning, the warning said, be elsewhere, or be in your place, sheltered.

Johnny Coma looked down from his rooftop patio, leaning over the stone ledge to the narrow alleys below.

Three policemen wearing lime-green fluorescent vests were stretching a gate across Dames Street. Clusters of early demonstrators were hoofing it with purpose along the alley leading to the square. Word was that by eleven you better be away from the confrontations due to happen. Word in the Spanish and Catalan papers was that between fifteen hundred and nine thousand police would be in the Born neighbourhood to guard the meeting politicians. Word was that if you did go out into the barrio, you would be asked to show ID even if you were steps from your own home or business.

Ay yay yay, Johnny thought. Better to go out early, before all the security gates had the locals hemmed in. So fearful was the government of its own people. He'd eyeballed the international press: no mention that Barcelona was on lockdown, four days before Christmas. Helicopter noise above his roof patio, already. Twenty-eight roads into Barcelona closed. Tourists stranded all over Spain, on holiday breaks, planning to come into the city. Who knew that Johnny and Sancho's sojourn bench in the Pla de Palau would be a locale non grata, because it was too close to where the government guys would be meeting. The threat to public safety of benches in a small public square. The ragged-trousered folk who might be upstarts. Johnny was in no mood to be stopped and asked to show his papers because he strolled to the beach for a coffee.

That year, 2018, it was warmer than usual in December. Eight or nine degrees when Johnny got up and drew some simple chairs, ten degrees by the time the sun rose at eight twenty in the morning, twelve degrees by the time the police were swarming into the narrow barrio alley below. By the time the shouts of the demonstrators began to echo off the alley's stone wall, it was a humid sixteen degrees on a December 21 day.

Before he had to be inside or face interrogation, Johnny went for a walk in the dawn hours to the Ciutadella Park on Picasso Street. Even from half a block away, as he came up Princesa, he could see the iron fence of the huge park festooned with the yellow ribbons of the Catalan independence movement.

The park had been closed down. You never knew what the people would get up to in green spaces.

He walked along Passeig de Pujades, the footpath alongside the park. The park was trapped in, enclosed, gates shut, yet he could peek inside to the green and forever moisture, and see that, somehow, the independence yellow ribbons had been tied to benches and to trees inside the gates. All up the side of the iron fencing thousands of ribbons, tied militantly, discreetly.

He crossed Picasso to the other side. For some years now, the homeless had been sleeping on the sidewalk on either side of the new modern boutique hotel inserted into the arcade. Johnny could see an early rising traveller sitting on a loveseat in the lobby, working on his laptop, a man in a thin hoodie, eyes on a lit screen. The homeless had moved a few metres down Picasso closer to Princesa, under the arcade's overhang.

The city had that eerie feeling you get if you know the natural hum of an urban congeries. Disarray at dawn yet it felt *too* quiet. Silence and the planes strafe.

In the cardboard homeless mini-barrio under the overhang shelter of the old shopping arcade, folks sitting up, sleeping, having a smoke, the light drift of cannabis. A couple walked past, each of them wearing a Catalan flag in yellow and red as a cape, probably hustling to where, nearby, the police were ready to face off with the demonstrators. Chants of "Libertad!" came from down the hill and from rooftops. Another couple exited the shmancy hotel built into the colonnade. They looked puzzled and irritated.

Johnny paused at the corner of Picasso and Princesa. Oy gevalt, he saw – was it Dulce? Her hair bigger, her clothes as mismatched as before, she rose from a golden sleeping bag. "Well, I'll be," she said, coughing. The cough of a lifetime of smokes and bad living on cement, on sidewalks, even in shelters. "Him. You. Come on, sleep with me."

Did she recognize him?

High-end hotel steps from distressed humanity, the pillow-top people mixing with the bruised, as helicopters moved in to the city once bombed into surrender.

Johnny went closer to the woman. It was Dulce.

She lifted her dress, to show him the bruises on her left thigh, and on her chest. She was black and blue from her left knee to her left armpit. Her right breast was yellow, a bruise healing. She looked about ten years older than when he had seen her last, two years ago.

"Come home with me," he said.

"Lie down with me, here. I don't want a thing to do with the police, no way. They're saying –" she pointed back into the homeless village – "saying the police are in Barce in their thousands. He coulda been police. Came and found me. Found me –" she hacked that cough again – "New Year's Eve, the laugh of the century." She laughed a rictus laugh. Her pain was lucid and Johnny felt rising in himself that bile he felt for how socially distancing his own world of writing books had become, with its naive opining and its circumscribed pride of the low bars.

He and Dulce sat down on the sidewalk on Passeig de Picasso. She said, "He came to hunt me down. How dare I escape? It's a riot, don't you see? He couldn't choreograph his way out of a cardboard box, so you tell me, why all the ladies came to him to have tea, and gossip. What world are they *in?*

"He came to me with anchovies. See, he knew I hated them. See, he knew I'd never have them. See, he knew if he broke into my place – that old studio, remember, right across the roof from you – knew if he picked the lock, snuck up the stairs, knew if he left a frying pan on my bed with fried anchovies on it, I could read the code. I did. I left everything and came here. Guy found me, anyway. Anything's okay, except independence, right? He came in the night, he dragged me out of my REMs, I drank a lot the night before the night he came for me, I was all groggy, he dragged me across the street – right there – he rammed my head.

"Repeatedly.

"Repeatedly he rammed my head against that iron fence across the street. Yeah, he took me to the park and beat me with the fence. He dragged me up the side, it was dark, in the shadow up the street he beat my head until my nose broke. Then he raped me. It was New Year's Eve, again."

Johnny eased Dulce to her feet.

They started walking down the Princesa hill, past Círculo del Arte where he had bought Saura's *Vanished Spain.* And now the gallery bookstore had vanished too. The city and its dark developments. More helicopters in the sky.

Up on the roof of the attic apartment, Dulce came in the door with Johnny. She was restless, she went out to the roof patio. She lay down on the red terracotta tiles. The echoes of demonstrators threading through the narrow alleys bounced off the high stone walls of the barrio. The old roof dogs barked. The familiar bells of Santa Maria del Mar basilica rang one chime for a quarter after some hour. Johnny lay down on the winter red tiles with Dulce.

His eyes hurt. He got up, went inside the apartment, located a piece of handmade paper from that fine paper store on Montcada that closed in 2016, a lovely lime green, a green Vivi had always been partial to, and using his stalwart loyal Palomino Blackwing 602 with *Half the Pressure, Twice the Speed* stamped in gold on one of the ridges, he wrote:

Dear Stella,

Things are rough, they are exquisite, they are over before we get started.
It's wabi-sabi days.

Ash between our fingers. I have come to my imperfections to bow to them. I am here with the air. We never love enough. We are brought to earth to abandon ourselves.

He cupped his hand around the rag paper to hide his words, the way he had in years gone by, on planes or in communal cafés, when he felt private in public. He felt that way in his own bedroom. That somebody might see the words he meant to publish.

The paper from the paper store that closed, a couple doors down from the bakery that had new ownership and turned the counter a different way, next door to the newspaper stand that had closed down too, the paper on which Johnny Coma wrote was the municipal representative of all that had gone missing. His words were beautiful transients.

His books were on remainder. Sail on, sailors, sail on.

His novels had been mulched. Sail away, dear papyrus, darling parchment, sail in the wind to the windmills deep in the oil derrick country.

Sail away, printers' hats of urgent news of the day. Sail in urban puddles, in urban storms, in backcountry flooding, sail in boats on top of houses, dear pooches in their water rescues. Sail outside your lanes. Ports of call, sail on.

Apostates and alleys, sail on, Stella, *Stella Atlantis*.

HE WENT OUTSIDE to the roof. Dulce was up on the patio's stone ledge, seven storeys above the alley below. Oh no, Johnny thought.

She smiled. She had her tap shoes on.

"Watch me go," she said, and she began to tap dance the bejesus out of that balustrade, slamming the stone with fervent metal foot percussion, doing a buck and a wing – whoa – arms down and out and hunched and rhythmic, yeah! A buck and a wing on a wing and a prayer into a softer shoe as the basilica rang three bells for a quarter to something.

Dulce reached into a pocket of her skirt, pulled out a rope.

What was she planning? "Dulcinea, don't do it," Johnny said.

He reached out his arms to her. She tied the rope in a circle, threw it over his head. She kept tapping hard, time steps, then leaning arms out, tightening the rope around his neck, laughing. Singing, "Gyro-tonic, gyro-change, gyro-changes, you ready, you coming with me?"

Her snarly hair was all over the place; she was freedom in gnarly motion. Her scars were in charge. Her feet remembered their original musical lesions. She got her feet into a thing Johnny marvelled at, closing his eyes, hearing her fine-tuned metal on stone. Dulce was doing a thing with her heels as they conversed with her toes and feet balls, where the beat came before the beat and syncopation was the name of the saint. The basilica chimed once. The hours seemed circular.

Shouts from below, the *manifestation*. Dulce gave a final tap on the balustrade, sat down, looking at the mass of people, the police, the barriers set up within the barrio to keep the people in their apartments. She motioned to Johnny to join her. They watched the movement of people below in the narrow space between the stone walls. Horizontal thinking.

"I liked the look of you that first time, you don't remember, do you?"

"Sure," he said. He wasn't totally all that sure, actually. "And this was, remind me."

"Back years, oh. We could be talking two, three. No wait, I'm thinking four years."

Dulce was speaking more lucidly. Or, at least, less foggily. The precious in and out privileges we have to our own brains.

She played with the rope. She had messed-up fingers, bitten nails. There was a metal anchor at the end of the rope, like a mountain climber might use. She ran it along her arm, making a scratch.

"Remember couple years ago, when I first laid eyes on you. I was on the Passeig del Born, you were on a bench. I was running away from the monster, friend of mine throws me down a rope to climb up. I did a tap dance for you. I was trying to catch the rhythm, after he came after me again and it was the dead hours of morning. There's you, all goofy and you sure were in love with that book you were writing in. I liked the stripes on your pyjamas."

The memory came back to him from its hiding place in his cerebellum.

"You, writing in some notebook or thingamabob or other. Me, I'm singing, 'Gyro-tonic, gyro-whoosie.'"

Sure, of course. The morning that felt long ago when he had drifted down to the empty street all jet lagged. The woman climbing a rope up the side of a building in the pre-dawn, when he had just bought a coffee from Mister We Have No Hours, in the days before a sweet hip guy took over the space, made it a bakery where Johnny never went, a place with éclairs and posted hours.

"He tried to strangle me. He found me. He said, 'Let's talk. Come.' He said, 'Let's be friends.' He said, 'Let's not fight, okay.'"

She turned her body on the balustrade to face the patio. She and Johnny were face to face.

"The thing with we women is: we want to make a better story. You wake up one day, you can't believe you're in the story you're in." She leaned forward, took Johnny's hands. "So, you, that morning on the Passeig del Born. There you were sitting on that stone bench in your blue striped pyjamas. Sharpening a pencil. I liked the look of your story."

She eased down from the stone ledge. Johnny twisted around, eased down too. They put arms around each other, kissed. She pulled a set of keys from her pocket.

"These keys?" she said. "They're for there." Pointing to the other roof studio, Ático 1. Johnny lived in Ático 2.

"Dulce, querida. You were living on the street on Picasso in the homeless enclave."

"I was. For safety. He knew where I lived. Or, where the good Samaritan gave me the keys to."

"Oh yeah. That guy. The Samaritan. You ever see him again?"

"Nope. Hear he surfs around Barceloneta."

"Who's been living in your attic, then?" Johnny asked. "I haven't seen anybody there in dogs' years."

"Nobody," she answered. "It was too dangerous. I couldn't risk it."

"And now?"

"I can risk it. Maybe. We could live on the roof."

"Like two pigeons?"

"Maybe," she said. "Maybe a dovecote."

And then Dulce did some hard knocks with her taps on the terracotta pat-pat-patio, up onto the wood-slatted chair side and a knock on the table leg. Clap went her hands in hard short melismas in dictation from other soul places of Spanish duende. Clapping her hands to make her hands as potent as her metal tapping feet, she tapped her way to the door of Ático 1, inserted her key, waved a wave to Johnny from the open door, passed inside.

32

VULCAN'S FORGE

THE NEXT YEAR, November 2019, as in years gone by, it was dark and the sun never shone but only low on the horizon. Daytime in November in Amsterdam and the bicyclists would not stop pedalling in the hegemony of two wheels in the seventeenth-century city.

Vivi walked the dark curves by the water to the Rijksmuseum, approached the magnificence of the stone structure, entered the stone tunnel, down the stairs into the brightly lit main floor, her pupils dilating, then upstairs into the temporary exhibit of *Rembrandt-Velázquez*. On for a few months, only until late January 2020. She was excited to see the pairings of paintings, the duets these guys would play on the walls.

The moment she saw *Vulcan's Forge* by Diego Velázquez, 1630, was a moment like an event, a swerve in her bloodstream. Five men in a workshop. Vivienne Pink began weeping. Her body inhaling the painting before her mind could intervene.

In the unmediated moments . . .

Five men, in balance, the composition, etc., etc., but what was the mystery beyond artistry? (What did Velázquez know and when did he know it?)

What is the purpose, she thought, weeping in front of the painting, Vivi Pink unembarrassed, like a traveller stranded in emotion between concourses in a phantom airport where it announces itself – there is no happy ending, and why did Velázquez do it?

Because they hired him. Because he had to. Because he *had* to. Because greatness is not skill – skill is the silverware, the cutlery. Because greatness is conversation. You are not alone – but more. Here were men. Bodies like yours. Here, we loved mystery, but anything we made we made of the flesh of humans. In Catholic Spain, Velázquez's art seems transgressively secular. Gods are men.

Like oxygen in brush strokes. Here was work. Labour and illumination, a burlap cloth, metal being worked, guys in rust folds, backbones, prominent clavicles, the guy with a grey headscarf and a goatee and moustache, the huge size of the figures in paint, the elegant respect to the tools, an angel as if a guy in orange leaves and bright rain just dropped in to give the dawn workers a message.

Time collapsed, Velázquez's intense passion for the reality of these men made every ochre a time machine. Her retina in the Rijksmuseum became a space oddity. The way the painting from five hundred years ago was so modern had captured her lungs, it had forced the waterworks from her eyes. The feeling on the canvas was "So, I mean like shit, man, I totally like walk into this place, the guy's garage where he – No guff and then three other guys are there and a guy – with blue shoes on! And I mean, was I high or what? It was amazing."

Four guys at work, a fifth in the background, and the sixth, an arrived angel like a more delicate bodied courier. All of the humans and the angel had feet on the ground. No wings in evidence. No sky, only the autumn tones of the forge mornings.

Vivi walked back and forth, unembarrassed to be on fire with the foundry boys, fuelled further by knowing that this exhibit was in passing, a limited time in the big picture. She stepped close, she walked back to the doorway, walked out, re-entered, to have the virgin thrill again. The thrill repeated. She wanted *Vulcan's Forge* on a turntable, on vinyl, just you, just me, and play the grey, brown, charcoal all day.

Six guys in an autobody shop. One guy like a guy on a hot day only in shorts, shirtless, working on a silver fender. Three other guys with hammers, forges, the heat. An angelic lad walks in . . . An angel walks into a forgery

. . . Vivi's tears were hot, rolling down her cheeks, jet lag joined in the fracas of her psyche. The main guy, shirtless, moustache, goatee, he turned from the orange-clad angel, and he looked at her and she knew it had to be jet lag – she and Alexi had flown in from Toronto last night – but it didn't matter what she *knew*. Here was Velázquez . . . he must be behind the painting, he must be motes with a brush still, he must be looking at her through secret peepholes in the brush strokes.

Her body was a nomad and nobody knew her in true. That was okay, the paint told her, go ahead and be all left brain in November in Amsterdam. The noise of jabbering modernity was cancelled, and the signal of work, attention, the mysterious crime of deep time conversation, paint linguistics, pain, the man, the Spaniard Velázquez pushing past achievement into chord structures of his hidden human palette.

If she had only ever seen just this painting, and had died, she would have died content.

Dark in the galleries, amber, mahogany, Velázquez like John Coltrane. You can't parse your way out of the masters.

She remembered her father. Izzy. The painting triggered an emotion of Izzy, in the – of course! – night alley by their house in Toronto. Izzy in the alley, his heart attack outside the night workshop of Alexi's dad. Izzy on the two-hundred-and-seventy-five-step-long alley, chancing to die with the work lights of a garage casting a background when he fell down among vines and scarlet. The stone, the wood, the scrawls on the garage doors, the miniscule passageways from the alleys to the backyards of houses, off-zone structures in cinder blocks, and Izzy went down. She could hear far away tinny sirens, the ambulance arriving, and it arrived on the outskirts of the painting she was absorbing. Velázquez had, somehow, painted a scene of Vulcan and Apollo and the posse, which knew that she, like Johnny, had found many tactics and many strategies for not grieving the ones she had most loved. She had created entire inner metropolises of absent shapes. Velázquez like a poet-priest who chose paint as his métier of conversation with your being,

Dress your dead like workers in a foundry. Dress your beloved like bad news and love, dress like tough times and you'll never be wrong. Dress like a wake and lie on your bed and refuse takeout from logic. Charcoal brown, russet, black, green olive, amber of silkworm's labour, dust. Brush the commentaries with quick respect, brush the humans with long regard, dress them like a dull day in February. Dress the protagonists like the end of autumn.

She couldn't wait to come back tomorrow. Your need is your need and nobody's need but yours.

Inside her grey trench coat pocket she felt the soft leather of her good luck citron gloves. She put the gloves on, continued through the dark galleries, lit in the way of the seventeenth century. How they saw their paintings, by lamplight. Lovers in discrete swarms gone to sienna, gone to mud, gone to umber, as the paintings looked out at their new suitors. Sunday in Amsterdam with Vivienne Pink.

Vivi walked down the back way from the Rijksmuseum, along the side street, Hobbemastraat, to the Vondelpark stairs and into the Vondelpark, carrying the yellow citron gloves in her trench coat.

In the darkened light of the city, she walked through the DNA of lamplight, as if all of Amsterdam in November was actually inside. Lit kindly. Low light, low-lit, fallen light, war light, lost light, light MIA.

Late morning, she laid one citron glove on a bench by a pond laden with willow strands. A crow landed to examine it. Pigeons waddled by the scrollwork on the poolside benches, looking like models for the scroll of bird images. A couple, young, watched the water. A young guy alone came, sat down on the next bench. The reflections were epic in a local way of greens and their gentle watery cotillions on a Sunday in the park with Vivi. She carried the glove from its posing on the bench to a hidden graffiti enclave but decided to walk to the Blue Teahouse, the better to pose the citron glove against the wet blue tables of the café.

Everything wet, everything droplets. In ten years, what will be in your hands to show?

The blue outdoor tables at the Vondelpark Blue Teahouse that Sunday were post-sodden. Nobody sat outside. Okay, yeah, one woman, coat open in the dank chill, a welcoming spectre, looking at Vivi as she approached with the lust of a gorgeous lesbian. And then gone. In the mist up from trams, tracks, the terror vans appear, poof gone, riders in the vicious rain. In wet pelts of furry metal grief rides a bike. Fury on four wheels pursues grief on two wheels. Grief is the fur that never stops whispering the name of the dead to you.

The chlorophyll would not stop producing, in mystery, without sunlight. As persistent as an artist in pain, the grass grew like LSD, the willows in the park hung anodynes into the water. Dolorous, the days. She walked up the Vondelpark stone steps, down an incline, onto the one-block-long Roemer Visscherstraat, the street named after a poet, and down the steps into the Owl Hotel, and up in the elevator to room 46.

Alexi was waiting for her on the bed. "C'mere," she said.

"You come here," he said. The vibe was low-lit joy. The city outside the windows was painting itself in puddles and charcoal and ambition by the sea routes. They embraced. "How were your pals?" he asked. She knew he was referring to Velázquez and Rembrandt, her need to see the exhibit first, alone, to commune with the eyes of the dead men with her own deadeye retinal fever in the dim rooms.

"Come with me, come back with me, tomorrow? Let's walk through it, together."

"You bet," he said.

This, already, was their ritual: their third anniversary of when they met, their third year of this hotel, this room, this bed. Nothing had changed, the world was still chaotic on its axis. Petite cruelty and grand hope coexisted.

THE NEXT DAY, early, before the crowds, they left the Owl and walked beside the canal the eight-minute walk to the Rijksmuseum. They entered at the opening hour of 9:00 a.m. The slim window of the early art birds. Through the portal, they could see *Vulcan's Forge*, the Velázquez painting, now and again, with him, with Alexi. The noob wants one of everything, the pro wants the same thing, in forensic repetition. She whispered in Alexi's ear, "That's you, my sweetie, there you are." He started to weep, but softly, and hid it, but she could tell.

The day before, the emotion induced was a memory of her dad in the alley. Today, on a second viewing, it was, with Alexi, how he had been in the picture all along.

The slim, almost skinny-ribbed man in the painting, with the beard, the grey rag on his head, a startle rippling through his torso, leaning ever so slightly back, had the posture that Alexi had had in the Izzy Pink alley workshop, when she walked past that dark night, three years ago. In the mythology, angelic Apollo delivers to Vulcan the bad news that Vulcan's wife, Venus, has gone off to make love with Mars. Yes, the god of fire finds out that the goddess of beauty is having an affair with the god of war. (And war and beauty created Cupid.) In the foundry workshop of Vulcan's forge, the Dear Vulcan letter had been delivered.

In the night smithies, these melting lorn messages.

Can a modern-day man get the bad news of love betrayed and love tossed under the bus in much the same fashion as it had been told in a seventeenth-century painting? What did the year 1630 in Spain know, and when did it know it? What was Velázquez's *Vulcan's Forge*, except the dark autumn futurology of love betrayed, and always?

It is sung in word and myth that Vulcan, born, was so ugly his momma tossed him from a mountaintop, and he landed at the bottom of the sea. Vulcan was raised in an underwater grotto. Vulcan created fire in an underwater grotto down below the land mountains and he created lightning bolts, and fire and green jealous jewellery came from the green deep elsewhere. (Even mad Quixote wore addlepated armour and Vulcan invented armour in his smithy.) Velázquez's art was to make Vulcan a man and his worker buddies men, and yet the bad news of betrayal came in a message in the shades of amber, ochre, sienna, charcoal, silver and humanity.

So, can a modern man get a Get Lost letter as in Vulcan? You bet he can. It happened. It happened to Alexi three years back in his metalworking garage in Toronto, on Izzy Pink Lane, and by coincidence, Vivi Pink had been walking past his workshop on her night watch walks and shot the scene. She shot, by chance or by kismet, the moment when her future sweetheart's heart was rent asunder, and the thunder was silent but she felt it. Fate, kismet, serendipity, bashert.

Even a man who holds lightning in his hands can get the bad news, someday.

Further along in the exhibit in the Rijksmuseum, they came to two self-portraits side by side. Velázquez and Rembrandt. Rembrandt and Velázquez, brothers from another palette. One man Dutch from a Protestant horizontal democracy, the other man Spanish from a Catholic royal vertical hierarchy. Yet, their palettes were so similar.

Alexi put his arm around Vivi's waist. "Your two policemen," he said.

"It's amazing," she said. It did amaze her. The seas are rife with the dismembered bodies, the decapitated artists, the migrant souls, art may be a therapy for a while, a respite, a way to look and stay young, live longer to fight the fucking bastards. Vivienne Pink's eyes were filled with the face of Diego Velázquez, the intense "try me" eyes. "I swear, the policeman in the Café Americain *was* Velázquez, I swear. Or Velázquez's double."

"A Spanish cop on the job, maybe?"

"Could have been. But I saw him – them, them both – in the Vondelpark. They could have been investigators. A lot of these terrorist guys move from the Netherlands to Spain and back, you know."

"Don't I know it." He went up close to the Rembrandt self-portrait, pointed back and forth between the two men. "Softer, as you say. Rembrandt blurred his face; Velázquez made his hard-edged."

They stood back a bit from the paintings, to see the two works in perspective. Vivi said, "Rembrandt is like Dr. Watson, an older kindly Watson, a wise Watson."

"And your pal Velázquez, then?"

"Velázquez could be Sherlock, sure. But he looks like a – an – I don't know." She laughed. "Like a punk Sherlock." She stroked Alexi's cheek. "He looks like you."

"I can't look like Vulcan *and* the guy who painted Vulcan, baby."

"Why not?"

THEY WENT INTO the room in the temporary exhibit where, for now, Rembrandt's *The Jewish Bride* sat on the wall. They sat on the couch opposite, taking in the tenderness of the painting, the tenderness that rotated with the planet, stayed the same, was always different. Visiting *The Jewish Bride* was a ritual too, every year now. You could say they met in the Toronto airport, eyeing each other, or hours before that in her home alley named after her dad. Or on the plane, same row, or when he got down her luggage for her and started talking surfing on the Big Canary, or when they chanced to be in the same Amsterdam hotel on a particular November day.

Or you could say that they met at a painting. Rembrandt's *The Jewish Bride*, 1665.

That day, out of the past, when Alexi was in the museum, looked in from the portal, and saw how Vivienne looked at the bride and groom.

They walked together up to the bride and groom, looked at their hands, how they looked into the unknown together, how they looked into the future, how Rembrandt had built into his paint both hope and tenderness and the deep lack of knowing what lay ahead for the couple.

But the hope was built into a future. And the future was outside the frame. The bride and the groom had been gazing together into the unknown for three hundred years and counting.

When the tyrants take over, they long for the past, and they erase the future. The populace, in distress, does not plan; the future feels abducted, stolen, how you feel grief in grief, when there is no tomorrow. Only the Never-ending.

What tyrants do is create the Big Shiva.

A HALF-HOUR LATER, in the Rijksmuseum café-restaurant upstairs, Alexi reached into his leather jacket and slid a large photo book across the table to her. Her new book, just out, *The Book of Hands*. On the cover, a black and white photo with gloves in citron yellow, like a colour shock.

A black and white photo of a pair of gloves on top of a pillow, under a wall photo of a woman smoking on the street, the tone lonely with an aura of defiance, quiet, with a slash of yellow across the gloves. Your eyes go to the gloves, to the intention of the citron slash, to the long ago pic of a lanky stylish woman in the photo in the room, an unmade bed, then your eye catches a pair of shoes at the edge of the bed, a man you guess. Who owns the gloves? A woman? Where is she? What went on in the room, or what will go on? And how private and what story does the photographer want us to know? A book sits on an end table: Federico García Lorca, *Poeta en Nueva York*. From a series called: *Los Ineludibles*. The Unavoidables.

The photo is about a moment. Only a pair of gloves, gloves on a pillow, a pair of shoes at the bedside, a photo inside the photo, a book of poetry, a small room. The dead make you do it.

In the Rijksmuseum eatery, with the book sitting on their table, Vivi glanced across the aisle to the table where two men sat, chatting, looking over the railing at the people below, in the atrium. Wait – it was the cops! The two who she had seen in the Vondelpark that day, years back, when the man in the white rental van crept alongside her. The two cops – or so she had surmised – in the Café Americain the day that stranger with the silver suitcase mistook her for some photog named Fanny de Ville. She and Alexi had just been looking at the self-portraits, and here the painters were, they had jumped off the Rijksmuseum wall to get a nosh.

One looked like Velázquez; the other looked like Rembrandt. They sat, eating roast beef sandwiches with mustard, drinking beer. One was a dead ringer for Alexi, the other had softer features. Had she been kept safe by the cops who resembled painters?

They nodded to her like they knew her. Like they were from the old neighbourhood.

Vivi and Alexi left the Rijksmuseum, went back to the Owl, sat on the bed in the room, looking again at the book's cover, with the photograph of the room they were in.

"Pompa?" he said. "Lamb tacos?"

"Sure," she said. "Or we could go to the Café Americain. We haven't been there in ages."

"We went last year."

"That first time, I was Fanny, you were Johnny."

"You wore my ribbon ring on top of your wedding ring."

She twisted the ring on her finger. It wasn't the same silver wedding ring she had been wearing when they first met, her wedding ring with Johnny. The new ring was gold.

"Your hair looks good," Alexi said, stroking the light curls.

"Who knew it would grow back? Against all prediction." She ran her hands through her short hair, which had grown back extra red and extra wiry. Her eyebrows too. They grew back in their old black shade, though thinner. Her right wrist sported the python cuff.

The amateur has the luxury of being the perfect parent to their efforts, keeping the efforts close, tidying them up, working to perfect the little darlings they keep hidden from the light. It's nice.

The professional, on the other hand, is obliged to a heartache of abandonment. Sweet abandonment. To put their darlings out the door, long before they are ready. Or at least that's how it is to parent. To let them be independent of you, never finished, never done. In that, even an artist from the West experiences the Eastern philosophy of impermanence, of humility, minor chords, beauty, a moment you learn to burnish like an event.

The art is in the walking away. The art is in the quarantine, the cocoon and then the public life. *Quarantina*, forty days and forty nights.

And in the Passover Seder, we tell the story of the plagues, ten plagues in ten weeks, a plague a week. Blood. Frogs. Lice. Wild Beasts. Cattle Plague. Hail. Locusts. Darkness. The death of the first-born. Dam. Tzefarde'a. Kinim . . .

After we have a Seder, eat in the order of things, dress me in luciferins, dress me in bioluminescent shoes, let me swim with the beasts to our watery graves.

THE LITTLE LIGHTHOUSE Café? El Petit Far? Well, they dismantled it one day when Johnny Coma wasn't looking. Like a stage set, a real café in his life was loaded onto trucks and wheeled away. Nothing but sand where he had taken morning coffee, every day. Nobody knew the story of him and Stella and the Moleskine notebook and the days of sea air. Before you die, they take away your café.

And Sancho got a book contract and moved into the building, into the other apartment on Floor Between Floors, next door to Vivi and Alexi.

Five souls in a medieval building in the old fishermen's quarter of Barcelona, as intertwined as a textile unrolling. As layered on each other as paper. Johnny, Dulce, Vivi, Alexi, Sancho.

A little wine, a little weed, a little compassion, resistance in the hinterland until it's safe to bring it to the street. And even then, to bring it.

In the palladium of dusk, the hearse goes riding.

33

ONE ARM TO HOLD YOU

APRIL 23, 2020

Barcelona – Renowned Canadian author Johnny Coma, 68, best known for his 2004 novel *Night Street,* a surprise international hit, has died in Barcelona, Spain. His ex-wife, photographer Vivienne Pink, said in a statement this morning that Coma died of a heart attack from complications of the novel coronavirus COVID-19.

Pink said Coma had had an underlying heart condition, angina, for many years, and had had triple bypass surgery in 1993. What with the restrictions on movement in the city of Barcelona, she and her husband, Alexi Green, a metal sculptor and security consultant, had been staying in their apartment, as had Coma, who lived upstairs from them. Pink and Green went to the roof last night so that she could take photographs as part of a project she had begun, aerial shots of the streets during the current plague confinement. There they found Johnny Coma dead, his body lying on the roof tiles. Inside the apartment Pink found the manuscript of a new novel, *Blue Mind.*

Johnny Coma had been dead, the coroner reported, at least three days, by the dispiriting condition of his body, due partly to the spring rains. Under his body was a notebook of the type, Pink said, he always used, and a pencil in his hand, apparently half-chewed by a rodent. She said Coma had apparently been writing a letter to their daughter, Stella, who predeceased him in 2004, when a bicyclist riding the wrong way near their home in Toronto hit the eleven-year-old child. Coma was also predeceased by his parents, Murray and Shirley Comasky. Other than his ex-wife, Vivienne Pink, he leaves no immediate family.

It is unclear at the moment how the body will be transported over the Atlantic. Most international flights have been cancelled and Spain's borders have been closed since March, due to the pandemic. Pink said in her statement that in normal times Coma would be buried within twenty-four hours, in the Jewish tradition. She added that, in normal days, there would be a memorial service for Johnny Coma, with hundreds of people gathered together. She expects to make arrangements in the next few days to fly to Toronto with her husband, and her ex-husband's body.

LIVOR MORTIS; ALGOR mortis; rigor mortis. First, discolouration as the body's blood drains from the extremities. Then, the chill, as the body temperature drops. Then, the body stiffens.

THE DOOR TO the roof patio was open. An octopus arm crawled out to the tabletop. A misty spring rain was falling. There was a leftover piece of handmade paper sitting on the tabletop, a pale blue, made of rag, absorbent. The octopus arm, amputated along life's voyage, began to squirt ink on the handmade paper.

And so the octopus wrote a story. Of her little poppa, who she used to call Chrome Dome and Mister Pitzel, and who she used to love so much but she rarely told him.

The dead were lonely, so the octopus arm, so pulpy and so independent, made some special sentences to cheer them up. The living could not come close to the dead; the dead were in quarantine, the dead were missing their old requiems, which the living used to sing to them so nicely. The arm wrote about how the barrio was lonely for itself, how the city was like a lonely corpse, lonely for its municipal organs, which were the people and their fun and their commerce. The arm wrote:

Dear Dad, remember the days when the cities were so full of people, and we used go around? The Little Poppa and Stella. Remember The Gates that time you took me to New York, and the two of us walked up under the saffron flags of Christo and Jeanne-Claude in the dusk past the sticks of trees, and into the snow time? Little Poppa, we skated on the rink. We sang that Joni Mitchell song about the river and we tap danced on the path in Central Park and you took me to that Café Europa and we looked out the windows at all the people passing by, and you told me how Mommy says everybody walks a different way, some fast, some slow and we walked around with all the people. Poppa, you said The Gates were just for a while, so we went back into the park one more time under those orange banners, and then they took The Gates away. You said it was like winter music. You said we'd always have The Gates and February. I'm just an arm now, in Barcelona, and I miss my little poppa so and the –

The octopus arm began to crack up with feeling embedded in her arm, her arm had a mind of its own, there was so much neurology in those arms, with neurons to smell you, to taste you, and the arm wrote on: *I liked to josh you and now you're gone.*

Truth is, at the word *poppa*, the arm curled back in on herself so it looked like a small grey spiral. Then the arm of Stella forged on: *You know, Dad, you were always kinda posthumous from the start.*

The arm folded the letter, crawled over to the body on the roof, her father. His lungs had failed. The virus was vicious as a coup. She was about to put the letter into his ragged pyjama shirt pocket, but she heard a noise. She curled up in a ball again, hid at the base of one of the table legs, watched her mother and the new guy discover the body of Johnny Coma, novelist, RIP, may his memory be a blessing.

THE OCTOPUS ARM crawled down the stone wall from the roof to the barrio Born, made her way up past the empty precincts. Quiet. Spectral. A municipal stage set for living. As in days medieval, the people stood on their balconies, but there were no parades, no entries on horseback, no pedestrians crowding the alleys for comestibles and clothing. Up empty Argenteria, across Laietana with no cars. The arm went up Bookstore Street so silent; across the vacant Sant Jaume square, city hall and the provincial building facing each other minus the governments; up into the old Call, the Jewish quarter of centuries gone by. Into the Call Major and the Call Menor the octo arm voyaged by land, past the ghost of Quixote's print shop on Carrer del Call, and in the plague days the arm turned left into a damp alley, smaller than small, darker than dark, Baixada de Santa Eulàlia. Parts of the stone wall had been left dissolving, exposed to the original stone from a millennium ago and more. Here, Jews, forbidden to pray overtly, wrote down prayers and slipped them into the stone walls. Making an ark of the city. A Talmudic intimacy, perhaps.

Crawling up the blocks of stone, the arm took the letter to her dad, slipped it in one of the cracks. A postal system for the secret forevers.

The octopus arm decided to keep the letter company. She made herself very small, coiled up real tight and tiny, flattened herself out. Then the arm of Stella slid herself into a narrow crevice between two ancient stones.

It was joyful to return. The dark damp alley got darker. It began to rain.

ACKNOWLEDGEMENTS

THE TEAM AT Wolsak and Wynn – Noelle Allen, Paul Vermeersch, Ashley Hisson, Jennifer Rawlinson – thank you. Added to your usual burden of acquisitions, editing, deadlines, sales, publicity was the viral pandemic of COVID-19. You handled the reshuffling with grace, and with dedication to books and publishing. How lucky I am to have such a solid work foundation in hard times.

My hands-on editor, Paul Vermeersch, *el maestro*. From the inspirational power of the desert in my previous novel, *Death Valley*, to the healing power of water – blue mind – in *Stella Atlantis*, Paul has been a wonderful eye and ear, as we hiked and sailed the manuscripts into being.

Facts. In *Stella Atlantis*, the fictional characters move in and out of real public events. Assassinations, terror attacks, anti-government demonstrations. I have kept the actual dates of these events, except for one: The October 2017 referendum for Catalan independence. In the book it takes place a year earlier, in 2016, to fit the rhythm of the story.

In chapter 3, the phrase "waste and softness" is a direct quote from Robert Rauschenberg about making art using materials at hand.

Tadoussac. The Quebec fishing village, home to whales. Where the Saguenay River joins the St. Lawrence. From 1985 on, the Glassco family – first Bill, then later Rufus and Dinora and their children – welcomed my husband, Dennis, and me to their summer home; it's where Dennis asked me to marry him. Without their friendship and hospitality, and the years of long dinners and conversation, parts of *Stella Atlantis* would not exist.

Queridísimo D. My husband of thirty-five years, Dennis. My best friend. Sweetheart, without you . . . you inhabit the music, you know the duende, you are the soul of the man who hears the wrist singing, who lives in the line. While the noise goes on all around us, you are the signal.

To the readers. I acknowledge you with great thanks. I write for you.

And to the dead. May your memory be a blessing. With the dead we can float.